THE BUTTERFLY STONE

THE BUTTERFLY STONE

WYVERN'S PEAK PUBLISHING
An imprint of The McGannon Group, Ltd. Co.

The Butterfly Stone

The Stones of Power, Book 1

Written by Laurie Bell – www.solothefirst.wordpress.com

Copyright © 2018 Laurie Bell

Published by Wyvern's Peak Publishing. 2018
An imprint of The McGannon Group, Ltd. Co.

Cover design by www.FlirtationDesigns.com

The Butterfly Stone / by Laurie Bell – 1st Ed.

Summary: Working at her uncle's detective agency for magical types, a mysterious case about a missing necklace known as the Butterfly Stone turns a girl's life inside-out as secrets from her past are revealed and a shadow threatens everything and everyone she loves.

1 2 3 4 5 6 7 8 9

ISBN-13: 978-0-9990212-2-4

www.WyvernsPeak.com

The Butterfly Stone is dedicated to Nana and Poppa Bell. You taught me the joy of reading, took me to the library, inspired me, read to me, read next to me, and showed me just how important books could be. Look, I wrote one!

To Taylah, Skye, Mark, Bree and baby on the way, Chloe and Bryce, Elsa, Emily and Hannah, Cody and Corey: You are why I do this. Be brave, be strong. Always help where you can and read to whoever will listen. (And to those who don't, read to them anyway.) Magic is inside you if you believe it is.

Believe.

-Laurie Bell

"Five spirited Mages,
Five stones of power ..."

1

Bored out of her mind, Tracey Masters spent her day online, flicking between the Internet and the Mage-Net, or M-Net, as her friend Tony called it. There wasn't much to do, but it was a cushy summer job as summer jobs go, if only it was a little more exciting. Uncle Donny wasn't a particularly good detective, nor was he a very powerful Mage. His office was hidden away in a crumbling and disused shopping strip on the outskirts of town, where a shoe store once occupied, but now the filthy sign on the front window read:

DONALD JAMES: *Private Investigator—Magical Guidance.*

I should probably clean the window. Tracey didn't move off her chair. Clicking on the latest edition of the M-Net gossip blog, *GossENews,* she quickly lost herself in the excitement of the latest trailer release for *Trap Michaels, Pirate Lord.*

The door rattled.

Tracey's head shot up. A tall, blonde stepped inside as if she was walking on live spiders—giant hairy ones. Her foundation was two shades too dark for her face and didn't do a thing to hide the bags under her eyes. She twitched when she spied Tracey and didn't maintain eye contact. Her gaze darted around the tiny office.

Gathering her magic, Tracey focused hard, picturing a glowing ball behind the imaginary door in her chest. Cracking open the little door, she unleashed her magic and let a wide sensory scan settle over the room like an invisible blanket. She couldn't feel a Mage-kind buzz in the air. All she got was an empty void. She sat up straighter.

What's a Norm doing in a Mage-kind detective agency?

Glancing at the closed door of her uncle's private office, Tracey bet a whole chocolate bar her uncle was playing solitaire, or maybe he was asleep. He got a lot of sleep working as a detective. She slid the latest past due notice under her tablet as Madam Blonde jolted forward. When the door to the small office slammed shut behind her, the woman's head snapped back to check over her shoulder.

Tracey interlaced her fingers and rested them on the top of her desk. "May I help you?" *Please be a client.* She was dying to assist her uncle on a real live case. That was if Uncle Donny remembered his promise. Her palms started to sweat. She fervently hoped the woman would not hold out her hand to shake.

Madam Blonde's eyebrows drew together, and she looked Tracey up and down. Lipstick stained teeth nibbled on her blood-red lower lip.

"May I help you?" Tracey asked again.

"Is this the office of Donald James?" The woman's voice was deep, like a man's, and kind of husky.

"Yes, Ma'am," Tracey replied. *Be a client, be a client.*

Madam Blonde glanced around again and then swallowed. "And, he's a Mage-kind detective?"

Tracey nearly pointed to the window sign. Instead she buried the urge and smiled brightly trying to put the woman at ease. "Yes Ma'am."

The woman stepped cautiously forward in her high crimson pumps — the same color as her trembling lips. "Does … does he charge as highly for non-magic cases?

He'd take anything that paid. The way Madam Blonde was acting put Tracey on edge. If this woman *was* a client, she wasn't going to be an easy one. Now a little worried for her uncle, she waited for the woman to make her intentions clear.

"Is Mr. James available?"

"May I tell him what this is about?"

"It is a private matter."

Well, that was no help. "I'm afraid Mr. James is booked this afternoon." *Liar.* "Perhaps I can squeeze you in if you'd give me some more information?"

The woman's face scrunched, reminding Tracey of her cat's face when

Mom tried to feed it day old meat. "Very well. An important necklace has been stolen and I need Mr. James to get it back for me."

Tracey almost cheered aloud. *Yes! A real client.* Some excitement at last. "And your name, Ma'am?"

After another glance over her shoulder she said in a hushed whisper, "It's Tearning. Miss Catherine Tearning."

Tracey gestured to the faded red sofa her uncle considered the waiting area. "I'll be right back. You can sit down if you like." She forced a big smile when the woman remained standing. Knocking once, Tracey slipped into her uncle's private office. She didn't speak until she was sure the door was closed. "Hey Boss."

Uncle Donny's eyes poked up from behind his computer screen. "What's up, kiddo? You want to leave early?" He was slouched in his office chair, tapping lazily on the computer mouse. *Ha! Solitaire it is.* Her eyes moved to the Mage-kind identifier around his wrist, which had a thin green line running through the center. It was similar to the band her brother Peter received when he passed his final Mage exam last week. Some adults, like her dad, wore their band as a watch, some wore a bracelet. Her mom did. Fewer still wore it like her Uncle Donny, as a wrist sweatband. *Ask him.*

She leaned over the desk to find he *was* playing solitaire, just as she'd thought. "You have to straighten up," she said, gesturing to his shirt open at the top two buttons. "Is that ketchup?"

He glanced at his rounded belly and at the red stain on the cream material. "Let me guess, someone's outside?"

"Yes."

He froze. "Not a lawyer? I … ah … I haven't responded to that last—"

"I don't think so. Her name is Catherine Tearning. She says her necklace was stolen."

"Oh good, a paying client."

Hopefully. Tracey grabbed his jacket from the hanger behind the door, thinking he could use it to hide the stain and waved it around. He rose and tucked his wrinkled shirt into his pants, the buttons straining to keep his belly covered. She helped him into his jacket. The cuff button on his right wrist was missing. She bit back a sigh.

"Did you sense anything from her?" he asked.

"She's a Norm. That's about it," she told him and sniffed loudly. No bad smells lingered in the room. He must have eaten lunch out of the office today. Tracey rubbed her sweaty palms against her trousers. *Now is the perfect time to ask him.*

"A Norm? What's she doing here then? Barty Johnstone up the street could—"

"Shhhh." Tracey waved at the door. "Paying client."

His eyes widened. "Of course, send her in."

"Hair."

Donald James flattened his hands over greying curls and tugged them into a slightly less tousled look. There wasn't anything he could do about the stubble on his face, but Tracey assured him it made him look dangerous and not slobbish, so he stopped fussing. She stepped back and examined the whole package carefully. Holding in a smile, this one genuine, she brushed her hands over his shoulders and stared up into his honey-brown eyes, the same color as her own. "Ready?"

He sat down and activated the screensaver on his laptop. "Okay, ready."

Before she opened the door she looked up at him through her eyelashes. "Uncle Donny. Is this the one?"

"What one?"

"You said I could help on your next case." She bounced a little on her toes as she waited for his answer.

His gaze darted away. "Ah, honey. We'll see."

Tracey's enthusiasm popped like a balloon. "You promised."

He pointed to the door.

She grit her teeth and tugged the handle hard. The door flew open. "Mr. James can see you now."

Miss Tearning edged past Tracey and stepped into Uncle Donny's office. As soon as the door shut, Tracey ducked down and pressed her ear to the wood. She couldn't make out more than the mumble of voices beyond. *Rats!* She'd use a listening spell if she thought she could get away with it, but Uncle Donny had protections in place to stop eavesdropping. Slinking away, she returned to her desk. *See, this is what you get from watching all of those crime shows Mum loves.* Tapping her fingers against the corner of her desk, she wondered about the stolen necklace. It was so frustrating. Of course Uncle Donny would get a case now. Tomorrow was the first day of the new school year, meaning she'd now only be available after school and on weekends. *He'll let me help. He promised.*

Uncle Donny's office door was still closed when Tracey left for the night. Disappointed, she sent him a text message to let him know she was going home so he wouldn't worry. For the whole bus trip, she couldn't get Miss Tearning out of her mind. She rubbed at her chest — imagining the little door rattling with each stroke — and willed her magic to settle. Her whirring mind seemed to make it more active than usual. Why would a Norm come to a Mage-kind detective? What made the necklace so important?

Later that night, perched in her preferred spot on the sofa binge-watching the latest season of her favorite show, Tracey found she was still thinking about the case and not even the insane action on screen could hold her attention. She paused the program and flipped the remote back onto the coffee table. Her throw was terrible and it bounced off, hitting the carpet with a dull thud. The conversation with Miss Tearning kept replaying in Tracey's head. *Is it a family heirloom or a key to a hidden treasure? Maybe it's proof of long lost royalty?*

Voices rose from the kitchen where her nearly seventeen-year-old twin brothers noisily recounted their latest football game to her parents. An instant later the thump, thump of heavy bass drowned out the chatter. Her sister Sarah protesting the vocal sports report, no doubt.

Just another night in the Masters household.

Tracey stretched for the flat screen remote. With an electrical crackle and a spark of light it twitched and flew into her hand. She really wanted to finish her show, but her thoughts kept drifting back to Miss Tearning and Uncle Donny. A stolen necklace. *It doesn't sound too dangerous. Surely Uncle Donny will let me help this time.* She could contact all the local pawn shops or even pay them a visit and ask about the necklace. The market was on next weekend, and she could look around for it there too. Picturing the conversation with her uncle, she imagined he'd look surprised by her great ideas and grin proudly. "Of course, honey. I couldn't do it without you."

Giving up the television for a lost cause, Tracey wandered outside and found her oldest brother, Peter, with his head beneath the hood of his car.

He caught her eye and shot her a manic look. "Heya Trace, want to go for a spin?" Peter only received his licenses a few weeks ago—his driver's license and his Mage-kind license. He was still looking for any excuse to drive, even if it involved chauffeuring his fifteen-year-old sister around.

"Um, what's wrong with the car?"

"Oh, nothing." His response came a little too quickly.

"Then why were you looking under the hood?"

"Just admiring her beauty."

She rolled her eyes. *Boys are so weird.*

Climbing in, she tugged her coat closer around her neck. It was unseasonably cold outside, but somehow even colder inside Peter's car. "Isn't it supposed to be summer? Gah, would you turn the heating up?"

"Doesn't work." He glanced at her from the corner of his eye. "You know the spell for that, why don't you use it? You're not going to be like Aunt Gemma, are you?"

No way. Tracey liked her magic, thank you very much. Aunt Gemma was so weird. She didn't like magic. She said it was too easy and that it made people fat and lazy. Mom called her a born again Norm after she'd joined one of those revival groups that said magic was the work of the devil.

It wasn't easy being Mage-kind. People still gave Tracey the cold shoulder when they spied her bracelet. She thought of Miss Tearning's behavior and cringed—some people didn't hide their fear very well. As far as Tracey was concerned her magical studies were twice as hard as her regular math or English classes. Control was so important, which was why it was so darned hard to achieve. Tracey's chest tightened as thoughts of Nana popped into her mind. She shook off her dark thoughts. Tracey couldn't wait to fully master her abilities. Magic was awesome. Who wouldn't want to use it?

Okay, a heating spell ... but which heating spell? One to fix the heater, or one to create a bubble of warmer air inside the car? Maybe she should cast an inside spell. After all, they were *inside* the car, and then they could both be warm. *Magic is so complicated!*

"So Mom told me you have Mrs. Arctalie for History Studies this year."

Tracey let out a sigh and scrunched down in her seat, "Yeah."

"I think you have to do the 1820 Mage-kind Rebellion this year, don't you?"

"Didn't Mrs. Arctalie fail you?"

"Sure did." Tracey could see his grin in the darkness. "It wasn't a rebellion. It was a coming out party."

Tracey gaped at him. "Peter, lots of people died! That's why registration started, before women could even vote! There has to be rules about using magic."

"Look, Trace, most of the books you'll study were written by Norm historians. They don't tell our side of the story."

Our side? Tracey stared out through the window. "I asked Mom once," she mumbled. "When I was little. About the bracelet and why we have to wear it."

"What'd she say?"

"She ... she didn't. It was when Nana ..."

"Oh, yeah. Mom was pretty distracted back then. You should ask Grandma next time she visits."

Tracey's phone vibrated.

`Hey kid, stakeout at Jessie Park. Need a bathroom break. If Pete or your mom can bring you down, you can help me out, yeah?`

A grin split Tracey's face in half. *Finally!*

Peter craned his neck to see, always the nosy one. "Who's that from? A boy?"

"No!" her voice shrieked—like her sister when the boys used up all the hot water. She cleared her throat. "Uncle Donny needs my help. Can you swing by the park?"

When she'd accepted the job working for her detective uncle during the school break, she'd thought she'd spend most of her time chasing goons and acting as the derring-do assistant to a brilliant detective while investigating the dark underworld of magical crime. Instead, she made coffee and typed invoices. But now, finally, she was going to see some action. Uncle Donny wanted *her* help. At last, she could prove to him she was real assistant material.

As her brother turned toward the park, Tracey imagined the sign on Uncle Donny's window changing to read: *Donald James and Tracey Masters — Private Investigators.*

"Spelled to hold, will and wish,
Binding soul to life, forever …"

2

So what's Uncle Donny doing in Jessie Park?"

Good question. Tracey peered through the car window and tried to figure out where they were. As they passed under a street light she recognized the road they were on. They weren't far from the park. In the distance, she could see the film studio still lit up like a Christmas tree even though it was nearly 10 p.m.

"Good work on the spell," Peter said. "I didn't see your lips move."

"What spell?"

"You can't feel that?" He peered through the fog gathering on the inside of the windows and flipped on the de-mister.

It *was* warmer in the car. The skin on the back of her neck tingled. "Your heater must have started working." Either that, or Peter had done the spell silently and was winding her up.

"Just like that?"

"Well, I didn't cast anything." Even though she got away with little spells all the time, she knew she wasn't supposed to use magic outside of home or Camp Mindflower — the closest camp for Mage-kind students in her area — until she came of age. Her student license, carried in the form of an unbreakable bracelet, hung around her left wrist and gave off a faint humming sound every time she moved her hand. Now glowing green, the bracelet was supposed to flash red if she used her abilities outside the designated safe areas. Mild magic use didn't set it off because her parents had raised the threshold on her bracelet when she'd started working for Uncle Donny; sort of a *just-in-case* measure, which Peter knew all about. She certainly hadn't used it now. Her brother had to have cast the spell and was having fun at her expense.

Peter turned the car into Jessie Park's southern lot and parked beside Uncle Donny's compact. Their uncle sprang out of the car as soon as they pulled up beside him. He jumped into Peter's backseat and waved his hands. Peter looked at him like the older man had gone mad.

"Face forward," Tracey said, hitting her brother in the arm.

"Ow, fine. What's up, Uncle Donny?" Peter asked, turning his head to face the front of the car. He drummed his fingers against the steering wheel.

Tracey wanted to know that answer, too, but she didn't look back.

Their uncle wriggled around until he was extended like a snake over the central column. "See that red car?" His finger poked up for a second, then disappeared. In the distance was a sporty vehicle. Tracey couldn't tell the color in the dark.

"Yes."

"I'm surveilling it, but I gotta pee. Peter, you're going to drive me to the closest gas station and Tracey, you're going to take over the watch."

"I am?" Her excitement faded as she peered around. The park was dark and creepy. She didn't want to be out here alone any longer than she had to. "It's not going to do anything, right?" It occurred to her that this wasn't the sort of attitude a derring-do private investigator should have and if she wanted to convince her uncle she was old enough to assist on his case she needed to start acting like it. Pumping energy into her voice she said, "Okay, great."

"Just watch the car."

"Does it have anything to do with Miss Tearning? Who does the car belong to? Why are you watching it?" Questions shot out of her like the pops made when squashing bubble wrapping.

"This car was seen the night the necklace disappeared."

"Disappeared? Miss Tearning told me it was stolen." Tracey's skin tingled. "You mean the necklace thief owns this car?" It was a pretty fancy looking car. The thief must be good at his job.

"The client thinks so."

"Okay so why—"

"Tracey." Uncle Donny huffed out a breath. "Just watch the car. We'll be back before you know it."

She licked her lips, "Sure," and scurried over to her uncle's car. The door opened with a quick flick of her hand—an easy spell—and hunkered down in the driver's seat as her brother drove her uncle away.

It was warm inside his car. Tracey pulled off her coat and stared through the window, but it was too dark to see anything clearly. Shadows danced as the wind moved tree branches outside. Restless, she tugged her cell phone from her jeans, pulled her earphones from a different pocket, and started her favorite playlist.

Figuring a short text message wouldn't cause her to miss anything important, she unlocked her phone. Scrolling through her messages she found the latest sent by her friend, Tony, and typed quickly, `Are you awake?`

Glancing up, she confirmed the car hadn't moved, turned into an elephant, or done anything else unusual, and looked back down as her phone buzzed in her lap.

`Yeah, but what you still doing up?`

`Surveillance for Boss.`

`Seriously? He's letting you work a case?`

Her phone buzzed again.

`Where are you?`

Her thumbs flew over the phone's touch keyboard as she replied, `Jessie Park. Are you excited about tomorrow?`

`Well no, 'cause it's school. But at least I won't be the only Mage-kind there.`

`Mostly they just ignore me.`

She glanced up again—the car was still a car. *How boring.* Uncle Donny never mentioned surveillance could be so dull. Scrolling through her phone she searched for a game to play while she waited for Tony's next message. A clicking sound outside pulled her head up sharply. Heart thumping, she peered through the window, but couldn't make out a thing in the darkness. Imagining her magical senses again, she mentally pictured throwing them out of her chest. Given her heightened nerves, her magic sprang through the car's frame like it was invisible and floated out over the park. When everything remained still, she let her body relax back into the seat and nearly jumped out of her skin when her phone buzzed again.

Nervously, she giggled. *I'm scaring myself!* Tony's message said he was going to bed. Tracey dropped her phone into her lap and glanced at the dash clock. The time was 10:07. She tugged open the glove compartment searching for a notepad. *Jump online and search for the car. Get a make and model.* Her neck tingled, a bug-like crawling over her skin. *Use your phone, dummy.* She glanced through the window and then bolted upright.

The car—the possible thief's car—was gone. Tracey snatched up her coat and was out of her uncle's vehicle in a flash. It was there only a moment ago. Maybe she just couldn't see it because she was tired, or had fallen asleep, or, or … *Oh God, Uncle Donny's going to kill me!*

She spun around, eyes hunting every shadow. Nothing.

Her cell phone was still in her hand, she directed its flashlight beam over the road. No clues, no footprints, no tracks, nothing to tell her where the car had gone. She was totally screwed.

Time to try something a little more magical.

Sitting on the pavement, she closed her eyes and focused on the search spell she and Tony had practiced to death together last year.

Focus! Lack of concentration could kill her spell and a failed spell might give off a discharge, which could blow off a finger—or worse. The disappointed look on her uncle's face kept popping into her head. *Oh God, he'll never let me help again.*

Placing both hands onto the road surface, she pictured the missing car from the tires to the style of windows. She should have taken a photo of it with her phone earlier. Her ID bracelet slipped down her arm, clicking loudly against the asphalt. It buzzed at the use of her magic, but the light remained green.

The air around her thickened. Sounds slowed and became louder. "Find," she whispered, picturing the car again in her mind.

Camp Mindflower taught Tracey to imagine her magic as a power that flowed from her core. She cracked open the imaginary door that sealed her magic inside her chest and let her power flow out and down her arms. It rose up to tickle her nose. She slapped at it, annoyed. *Focus!* Wrestling her magic back down, she pictured the car again and placed her palms against the crumbly asphalt. Her bracelet hummed, still glowing a safe emerald.

The warmth lining the road rose at her Touch. When she opened her eyes, the warmth had taken on a deep orange glow and hovered above the ground like a long cord that disappeared into the darkness. Tracey scrambled to her feet. The conjured path would fade soon—as soon as the warmth disappeared from the road. She didn't have long.

Tracey ran along the fenced border of Jessie Park, then up Stock Street following the magical line for a block before turning down Acton Drive. It wasn't long before a stitch was burning in her side. *See, this is why you don't exercise. It hurts!*

The wisp of magic cord disappeared with a pop.

She spun in a circle. *Where did it go?*

Dropping to her knees she Touched the road. Stone cold. She swore, a soft sound that puffed out of her as her as she deflated. *What am I going to tell Uncle Donny?*

Biting her bottom lip, she walked slowly back to Acton Street. In her head, she tried to compose a text message that wouldn't get her shouted at, but it was no use. Nothing sounded reasonable. She'd lost focus and the suspect had disappeared on her watch. Uncle Donny would *never* let her help an investigation again. She rubbed at the sudden ache in her chest. *Useless!*

Something moved at the corner of her eye. Her footsteps slowed. An icy gust blew her hair back and stole its way under her clothing. Unsettled, she squinted into the darkness.

A shadow darker than night stood in the middle of the road. The top of the shadow twisted and tilted as though … searching for something.

What the heck is that?

It straightened suddenly, its head snapping in her direction. Tracey felt a spot of cold blossom against her face.

Whatever it was—it wasn't good. She slapped at her arm finding only skin. No emergency band. *Oh fruit tingles, that's right. I stopped wearing it ages ago.* Tension filled her. For a moment no one moved. The shadowy figure sprang toward her. Tracey spun on a heel and ran. Somehow, she knew she had to reach the nearest streetlight before the Shadowman caught her. There was no time to think of a light spell, no time to concentrate on her magic — all she could do was run and not look back. Freezing tongues of air licked at her spine. The Shadowman was getting closer. She could feel it reaching for her, imagining shadowy fingers brushing against her coat. Her chest hurt. Breath ghosted from her mouth as she panted.

Just ahead, a streetlight cast a cone of warm yellow light on the ground. Should she stop under the light or just keep running?

The air grew thicker, making it harder to breathe. As soon as her foot crossed the threshold of the light she collapsed, hitting the asphalt hard. Blood welled on her palms. Her head shot up, scanning the night for movement. *Where is it?*

Under the streetlight, everything beyond the bright circle was even darker.

The ice on her skin grew so thick she was afraid it would encase her body and freeze her solid. She tried to stand, but couldn't move. And then … it disappeared. The Shadowman, the cold, everything.

Tracey blinked. *Did a shadow in the shape of a man seriously just chase me down the street?* She shivered at the phantom feeling of cold pressing against her body. The back of her neck still tingled. She pulled her cell phone from her pocket. Three new texts and two missed calls from her uncle. She dialed him back.

"Where are you?" he demanded.

She couldn't see a street sign but was pretty sure she'd run back to Stock Street. "Off Stock, near the turn off to the first lane. I'm not sure how far down I am, but you can't miss me. I'm under a streetlight."

"Wait right there."

She wasn't planning to go anywhere. Wriggling around to get comfortable, she crossed her legs and sent a ball of magic out to scan the darkness. Usually, she could sense people pretty clearly. The air felt thicker around Tony and her family, like their magic was a bubble gently pressing against her own. Right now, she couldn't Feel or See a thing outside her cone of protection. *Why did it come after me? Something to do with the missing car? Oh heck, I bet the Shadowman is connected to the necklace thief.* It was some heavy

26

duty magic if that was the case. Her skin still felt chilled and kinda sticky.

What if the necklace thief was Mage-kind? Would he go after Tracey's uncle because he was investigating this case? Then a really scary thought occurred to her. What if the Shadowman had nothing to do with the necklace at all? It had come after her. Why? Her stomach flip-flopped hard enough to hurt. She clenched her fingers so tightly around her phone the case crackled.

A male voice spoke out of the darkness. "Are you okay there, miss?"

"Who's there?" Tracey squeaked, jumping to her feet. Her magic buzzed like angry wasps inside her chest. She threw out another scanning ball and it settled over the area, highlighting a corridor of blankness.

The Norm stepped into the light. The sight of his uniform didn't ease Tracey's flight response. "Officer Rick Jameson. Miss, can you show me your wrist, please?"

Tracey quickly pulled up her sleeve to expose her Mage-kind identification bracelet.

The Norm straightened, becoming more alert. "Can you tell me your name, miss?"

"Tracey Masters, sir."

She could hear her mom's voice inside her head telling her to be careful.

The officer's eyes narrowed. "May I ask what you are doing out on this street tonight?"

What could she tell him that wouldn't make her sound totally crazy? "I'm waiting for my uncle. He's only a few streets away. I was a little scared, so I thought I would wait under the streetlight for him."

He watched her silently, then said, "I'll remain here until they arrive."

"Um, okay," she blurted. The Norm remained on the other side of the streetlight. He looked about her brother's height and a bit beefier. *Probably muscle. Definitely muscle. Muscle is good. Shut up. Stop rambling!*

The silence was making her itch. She shifted her weight from her left foot to the right, freezing in place when the officer tensed. "You're a bit young to be a police officer, aren't you?" she asked, and then clapped a hand over her mouth. *Oh God, shut up Tracey.* She sounded like Princess

Leia from one of those old Star Wars movies — she'd watched them with Tony when the new movies came out. Her face felt like it was on fire.

He looked away. "First year out, but I'm not *that* young. What are you, like sixteen?"

"Fifteen."

Tracey tried to keep her expression steady, but knew she'd failed when he straightened and stepped forward. His radio squawked loudly, shattering the silence.

"Yes, sir. I read you." He stepped back. There was an incomprehensible reply. "No, sir. I will remain here until the Mage-kind is picked up."

Again the voice said something garbled. Tracey tilted her head and sent a spark of magic up her chest to her ear but even her magically assisted hearing couldn't make out what was being said. "Yes, sir. Corner of Park and Stock."

The loud thrum of Peter's car as it approached could be heard all the way down the street. "That's him," she said, nodding in that direction.

The officer didn't look particularly happy. She assumed that being a police officer he probably was trained to look that way. "You take care then, miss. I don't want to see you out alone again this late after dark." His stare was making her squirm.

"Thank you, Officer Jameson," she said in a soft voice.

Peter parked on the opposite side of the street. "You're welcome, Miss Masters." He gave a little wave toward the car, and then disappeared back into the night.

"It might seem scary, honey,
but it is meant to be."

3

Get in the car, hurry!" Uncle Donny called through the open window. Tracey dove into the back seat.

"Was that a cop?" Peter asked.

"Where did the car go?" Uncle Donny said, speaking over her brother.

Tracey answered them both. "Yes, cop. Car? I don't know. I lost it. I'm so sorry Uncle Donny." She buckled her belt and slumped back, her stomach whirring. Peter pulled away from the curb. The tension knotting Tracey's neck into a solid mass hardened into concrete as her uncle remained silent.

After a moment, he peered back at her. "Did you see who drove it away?"

"No. It was there and then suddenly it wasn't."

Uncle Donny turned his face forward. He hummed and then said, "Luckily, I put a tracer on the car. Magical, of course. I'll know where it is in moments."

"I should take Trace home, Uncle Donny," Peter said.

Betrayed by her own brother, Tracey couldn't hold back her whine. Peter sounded so determined.

He glanced into the rear-view mirror catching Tracey's eye and raised an eyebrow. When she frowned at him and shook her head, he raised his other eyebrow. She sighed dramatically and turned to the grown up beside him. "Uncle Donny, please. The car was here. It came through here. If you take me all the way home and then come back, the trail will be colder than freezing."

Uncle Donny stayed silent, mulling over her point.

Come on, come on.

"Ten minutes," he said at last.

Yes! Maybe she could still salvage her part in this mess. Magical energy gathered around Uncle Donny as he focused on the road. Tracey's skin crawled at the sensation. Uncle Donny's power always felt like it seeped from his skin like oil. She cracked open the little door in her chest and drew her power out to join with his. The air inside the car hummed. Uncle Donny's spell would work a lot faster if he had help. She punched Peter in the arm and felt his power join them.

Being family, their magic intertwined like a thick coil of rope, twisting and strengthening until it was unbreakable. Tracey grabbed hold of her uncle's tracking spell when she felt his magic sputter. Her chest tightened. Magic came in different strengths and depended on the skill and innate ability of the individual wielding it. *Poor Uncle Donny.* As his focus floundered she quickly piggy-backed his magic and took control of the tracking spell. It manifested as a glowing yellow balloon bobbing in front of the car, plain as day.

"Find," Tracey whispered beneath her breath. The buzz of magic grew thicker, tickling her inner ear. Their rope of power latched onto the balloon and all three were jerked forward in their seats as it tugged them forward. *Gotcha!*

Peter directed the car to follow the tugs and drove them to Main Street. The yellow balloon pulled the power rope behind it like a kite caught on a gust of air. It halted suddenly and bobbed in place. Peter stopped the car outside of the Central Grand Hotel.

"Cool spell, Uncle Donny. The balloon visual is awesome," Tracey said, unbuckling her belt.

"Yeah." Peter shot her a long look. She shrugged back at him.

"Wow, yes that was a good spell … balloon?" Uncle Donny's voice was faint. He twisted his head around.

Peter and Tracey exchanged looks. "So here you go," Peter said. "Central Grand Hotel. I should take Trace home now."

"No wait, we can't go yet. What if the suspect leaves? We still need to identify the driver." The words tripped out of Tracey's mouth.

Uncle Donny hesitated.

Please don't send me home.

Finally, and with what appeared to be a great deal of reluctance, he turned to Tracey. "If I let you stay here to keep watch, I want you to go inside the hotel. Do not leave! Peter will take me straight to my car, and then he will take you home."

Tracey's body became a live wire. "Thank you, I—"

"Do not go anywhere. Sit near that window and watch the entrance. If one of the attendants fetches the car, take note of the driver. Do not approach him. Do you understand?"

Tracey nodded so rapidly her neck hurt at the whiplash. *I didn't ruin everything.* Tears prickled in the corners of her eyes. She would not let him down again. "Yes, Uncle Donny."

"What about school tomorrow?" Peter was ever the voice of reason, and a voice she didn't want to hear.

She willed Uncle Donny to listen to her and not her brother, blurting out, "Ten minutes. Will ten minutes really make that much difference? I'll sit inside and watch the parking guy."

"Valet," her brother said.

"What?"

"Valet. That's what the parking guy is called."

She narrowed her eyes. "Whatever. I'll watch the valet guys from inside the hotel. If I see the red car I'll send you a message. I won't leave. I'll stay right there." She pointed to one of several empty armchairs in the hotel's lobby.

"Turbo Jetfire," Peter said, shooting her a grin.

"What?" she didn't take her eyes off her uncle. Their eyeball tug of war was reaching epic battle status. *Come on!* He knew how desperately she wanted this.

"The red car is a Turbo Jetfire."

Tracey threw her head back. "Peter! Oh my God, who cares?"

"Details, sis—you work in a detail specific job, you should pay more attention."

Feeling heat flood her face again, she glared at him.

"All right." Uncle Donny's voice snapped her gaze back to his face.

She shot out of the car before he could change his mind. At the hotel's large entrance, she held her thumbs up as Peter drove them away.

Trying to project the image of someone used to hanging around hotels, she straightened her shoulders and kept her head still.

She must have failed miserably. A voice shouted, "Hey."

Fruit tingles! Spinning on a heel she pictured her sister's perpetually haughty expression and stared down her nose, snapping, "Excuse me?"

"Can I help you, miss?" The man speaking looked official in his perfectly fitted suit and red vest. His cheeks and forehead were awash with red pimples. *Poor thing.* They looked like they hurt. Tracey noted the lack of a wristband.

"Oh, no, I'm good. Just waiting for someone." The hotel's automatic doors slid open as she approached. *Ask him about the car. Or is that too obvious? Oh, screw it.* "Actually …" She peeked at his name tag. "Sam. Did you park all of the cars here tonight? I think my friend arrived earlier." She smiled brightly and widened her eyes. Tony called it her *dumb-blonde* look. Apparently, it was very successful at making people want to help her.

After a few seconds of this face, Sam caved. "What kind of car was your friend driving?"

Yes! "A red Turbo Jetfire."

"Yeah, sweet ride." His eyes darted to hers as his jaw dropped. "Wait, you're a friend of his? Really?"

Tracey nodded and said, "Absolutely." She awkwardly touched Sam's arm. "I didn't realize you knew him, too." *Who is the driver? He sounds important.*

Sam shrugged, his neck turning pink. "Well, sort of … I mean, he lets me park his car." He gestured to the hotel's lobby. "He got back about thirty minutes ago."

"Oh great, thank you." Tracey made her way to the hotel's revolving doors. Sam's shout stopped her before she traveled more than two steps.

"It must be cool knowing a prince." He sounded awed.

Tracey sputtered. *Prince?* "Oh, yeah."

Sam laughed loudly and checked his phone.

She stumbled as the word sunk in. *What's Uncle Donny gotten himself into now?* There was a chair near the window with a good view of the street outside. Plonking herself down in it she blew out a breath, her mind unable to stop replaying what Sam the Valet had said. *A prince?*

It was too quiet in the lobby. Even her breathing sounded loud. Feeling eyes on the back of her neck, she peered over her shoulder. The concierge was staring at her. Not many teenagers must loiter in his lobby at nearly midnight. He probably thought she was a troublemaker.

She inched lower in the chair hoping that if she was out of sight, she'd be out of mind. A tingle brushed the back of her neck. Through the window she watched the reflection of six men stalk past her chair. Five of the men were dressed in black suits, looking very much like they were protecting the man in the middle. *The prince?* She shuffled the armchair around and peeked, but couldn't see the man's face.

Low-level power emanated from their direction and gave away that at least one of the men was Mage-kind. To make sure they didn't sense her, she scooted lower and held her hand over her heart picturing a shutter that she dragged down over her magic door. Her senses shrank until she could barely feel them. The air around her grew dull, colors faded, and she felt a little cold. Hopefully she wouldn't need to stay closed off for long.

The group walked toward the reception desk. Straightening his vest, the concierge smiled broadly showing a lot of teeth. He held out a small box. The man in the middle of the huddle took it from him and spoke quietly. The concierge nodded, mouthing *"Three-oh-one."* The men headed for the elevator, leaving the lobby suddenly empty.

Whispering to another man at the desk, the concierge squinted toward a slouching Tracey. She turned her gaze back to the window—no sign of Peter or her uncle. Was the man she'd just seen the owner of the car she had trailed? If he was, she didn't want to lose him again. But Uncle Donny had ordered her not to leave. Twisting around, her heart beating a loud pulse in her ears, she peered back at the front desk. The concierge disappeared into the back office.

The moment he was out of sight, she sucked in a breath and ran to the elevators. When the doors sprang open she punched the button for the third floor. Technically, she wasn't leaving the hotel. The doors closed just as the concierge returned to the desk. She ducked to one side so she was hidden behind the closing door and seconds later stepped out onto the third floor. A heavy silence seemed to eat up the very sound of her footsteps as she walked down the corridor. Her hands twitched. *What on earth am I doing?* She should have waited for Uncle Donny. Any second now someone was going to open a door and find her standing alone in the corridor. Tracey checked the number of the closest door. 311.

She turned around. 309, 307, 305. As she closed in on the room her chest grew tighter. 303. The next door was located at the end of the corridor and was wide open. Tiptoeing closer, Tracey listened for any sound coming from within the suite, but there was nothing. Raising the shutter, she loosened the imaginary door inside her chest and drew on her power. She couldn't See or Feel anyone.

Inhaling sharply, she stepped inside.

"She said change was coming.
But good change or bad change?"

4

Room 301 looked like every other hotel room Tracey had ever seen, only much bigger. *Much* bigger. Okay, maybe the room was a lot fancier than what she was used to. Wide-eyed and taken by all the space and the humongous gift basket filled with fruit, chocolates, and bottles of fancy water on the kitchen bar, Tracey pinched herself. *Focus.*

She stood in the entry hall. To her right, the room opened out into a living space that easily fit the ten-seater sofa. Shaped like an L, it was in front of an unlit fireplace. Beyond the living area was a kitchen with a long dining table. Every fixture she could see was shiny, silver and clean. Looking over her shoulder, she spied a short hallway which hosted several doors, all closed—probably bedrooms, though she assumed one had to be a bathroom.

She forced her feet into the main living area. *What am I doing? Breaking and Entering? This is super illegal.* There were no papers, books or envelopes to identify who was staying here. A thump drew her attention to one of the closed doors. *Fruit tingles!* She ran for the suite's front door, stepping outside just as one of the doors popped open. A man emerged dressed in grey sweatpants and a deep maroon polo shirt. His feet were bare and he was scrubbing a towel over his head. When he looked up and caught sight of her, he stumbled back a step.

"I'm so sorry," she stammered. Her face flared supernova hot—she was afraid she was going to combust. "I … I … The door was open."

The man pointed at her, fabric still in hand. It was the man from downstairs. *Busted!* She dropped her stare to the floor, wanting to back up and run down the corridor to the elevator. His face flashed into her mind and recognition suddenly dawned. *Oh MY GOD!* Prince Henry, the fifth son of King Edvard and Princess Margaret of that European place … oh … she couldn't remember the name of the country! It was tiny though. Prince Henry, the actor Prince.

"How did you get in here?"

"I'm so sorry, it was an accident." She'd been caught in a stranger's hotel room. *He'll call the cops on me!* She backed up nervously waving her hands around. *But the necklace? Does he have it?* Her hands clenched into fists. *Omg, omg! I need an excuse to go back in.* She could practically feel the flames burning her cheeks. "I am so so sorry for bothering you," she said glancing at him with Shy Look #4. Tony had them all numbered. "But I was hoping—uh—could I get an autograph?" She giggled loudly to sound like a fangirl. *Giggling! What am I, thirteen?*

He let out a sigh worthy of an award show nomination for best actor. "Paper?" She shrugged awkwardly. "Come on—if you don't have any paper, I'll grab you a glossy. Wait here." The man disappeared into one of the corridor rooms. She heard his voice call out. "I don't want to see your phone. No selfies, okay?"

Her hand slapped at her pocket with a mind of its own. "No problem," she croaked. Any second now this man's bodyguards were going to appear and chuck her out. Her cell phone vibrated in her pocket. She wasn't about to pull it out to check if it was Uncle Donny. The prince might think she was going to take his picture after all.

"Aha," he cried, appearing and brandishing a glossy card. Tracey inched forward, digging her nails into the top cushions of the sofa as she chewed at her lips. He handed her the picture with a flourish.

It was a photo of him grinning wildly, dressed in an outfit from the eighteen hundreds, all fluffy and high-necked. She clutched the photo tight in her hand.

"Oh, hey, don't crease it!"

"Sorry, sorry," she said, and handed him back the photo.

He uncapped a pen and sat down on the sofa. "So, what's your name?"

"Tracey Masters."

"Well, Miss Masters, I'm Hank."

A giggle popped out before she could stop it. "Hank? Shouldn't I call

40

you Your Highness, or something? Tony will never believe this."

No one in the world was going to believe this story. Tracey barely believed it, and she was standing next to the man's sofa.

Shaking his head, he said, "Who's Tony?"

Oh fruit tingles, I said that aloud. "My friend. I wish I could call him. Oh god!" Prince Henry's eyes twinkled—no way could she think of him as Hank. She looked into his face and realized he was laughing at her, not with her. She sucked in a quick breath as fire burned through her once again—this time in anger. The emotion was a good thing—she didn't feel faint anymore. "So, could I get a picture for him too?" Prince Henry's earlier annoyed look returned as he stood up again.

There was a reason she was here after all. She should be using her sudden alone time to search the room. Instead, she sat there staring at the glossy photo on the table. By the time her thoughts cleared enough to think properly about moving, the door opened and he returned with another glossy photo and a bottle of water.

"Hi," she muttered, mashing her lips together. Why couldn't she think of something smarter to say? *Idiot! You had an opportunity to look for the necklace and you blew it.* Uncle Donny would not be impressed.

"What are you doing wandering around a hotel at this time of night?"

Can I tell him? She didn't know him—certainly not well enough to tell him the truth. What excuse could she use that would make any sense at this point? Then again, there was that jewelry box she'd seen him take from the concierge. And it *had* been his car Uncle Donny was surveilling. She bit her lip and bounced from foot to foot.

"What? Oh—" He was a prince, she ought to be able to trust him, right? "This is going to sound really odd, but do you have a multi-colored inlaid gold necklace shaped like a butterfly?"

He froze with the water bottle halfway to his lips and stared at her over the plastic rim. "How do you know about that?"

Confirmation. She should ask to see it, but whatever she said, she couldn't mention Uncle Donny's client believed he'd stolen it. That would probably not go down well.

"How do you know about the necklace?" he asked again, his voice suddenly sharper.

Her power was still banked behind the little door in her chest, but she cracked it open enough to feel his shock give way to something determined. Her bracelet buzzed a warning but did not change color. She stumbled back.

He didn't move from the center of the kitchen. Lowering the bottle, he asked, "Well?"

Get out, get out. "It's a long story."

Not going for it, he pointed to the sofa. "Sit."

"Uh, no." she stepped back again.

"Then I think you should leave." He hadn't moved, but somehow he seemed suddenly bigger.

"I probably should," she agreed. His eyes followed her all the way to the door. When she tugged it open two of the men who escorted him through the lobby stared at her blankly. One held a key.

Prince Henry appeared behind her. "It's okay boys, Tracey was just leaving."

She didn't look back as she scooted past the glaring bodyguards. Heart thundering, she shot a quick glance over her shoulder. The prince was watching her, his face expressionless. At the ding of the elevator, Tracey swiftly stepped inside, shaking. Her palms were sweaty. She looked down at her hands. *Oh damn. I left the photos behind.* Tony was definitely never going to believe her now.

"To contain or conceal,

Enslave or ensnare …?"

5

By the time she reached the hotel lobby, her heart still pounding like she'd run a marathon, Peter was waiting for her. He let her know Uncle Donny had parked further down the street where he could spy on the valet without being seen and insisted he take her home. Tracey didn't tell Peter of her run in with Prince Henry — she didn't even text Tony. She'd spill all the details to him at school anyway. She did text her uncle — only to tell him she hadn't seen the owner of the car leave. She held back on telling him it belonged to Prince Henry. Besides, why would a prince need to steal a necklace? He couldn't be the thief.

Thinking back on last night, otherwise known as four hours ago, Tracey realized what a crazy thing it had been going into that hotel suite alone.

In a few minutes, her alarm would start screaming and she'd have to get up. Her head ached from lack of sleep. *I met Prince Henry — talked to Prince Henry — me!* And he possibly had something to do with Uncle Donny's new client and her missing necklace. She rolled over and let out a huge yawn. Her sleep, what little she'd had of it, had been filled with dreams of her uncle discovering she'd kept Prince Henry a secret and of him alternatively shouting at her, or firing her. When she wasn't facing her uncle's wrath, she'd jolted awake with visions of her nana screaming. It was an old nightmare — one she'd had for a long time. Somehow it was more comforting than the new one, of being chased by a living shadow. *I need to talk to Uncle Donny.* This meant she had to get out of bed, survive the school day and get to the office to tell him the truth. She eyed the clock. 6:58. Sighing sadly, she let her thoughts drift back to last night.

Officer Jameson saved her from that Shadowman — she was certain of that. His timing was near perfect. An image of the Shadowman reared up in her mind. Her breath caught in her throat and her coughing fit only stopped when she fell out of bed and her alarm went off.

Slamming her hand against the button to cut off the noise, she stood and shook her pajama legs down from where they had tangled around her knees. A fist pounded on her bedroom door. Tracey's sister Sarah cracked it open. Her dark chocolate colored hair was sleep tousled and looked rather evil witch-like. "I'm going in the bathroom first!"

"Sarah!" Tracey shouted, but her sister had already shut the door. Chasing after her, Tracey banged against the locked bathroom door. "Sarah!"

She could hear her sister cackling inside. This was the biggest problem with having such a large family — there were never enough bathrooms. Heaving a sigh worthy enough for an Olympic gold medal, Tracey dragged her sleep deprived body back to her room to collect her robe. Guess she was eating breakfast first today.

Mom and all three of her brothers were in the kitchen when she walked in. Technically, Mom and Simon were at the table. Peter stood at the bench with half a square of toast hanging from his mouth, his eyes fixed to his phone. Charlie hovered anxiously in front of the coffee machine as if his stare could somehow make it drip faster. Simon and Charlie hardly looked like twins this morning. Simon's sun-streaked, honey colored hair stuck up all over the place, and Charlie's face was covered in spots. The void around Simon bothered Tracey this morning. It itched at her mind like a mosquito bite. No one could explain why the Mage-kind gene triggered in some people and not others, but Tracey's twin brothers really were special. Charlie being Mage-kind, and Simon, a Norm.

"Should you even be having coffee?" Tracey grumbled, pushing Charlie aside to pull her cereal box from the cupboard. Charlie swore energetically for someone who looked like he hadn't had any more sleep than she had. She wondered what his excuse was. Online gaming probably.

"Mom!" Tracey complained, but as usual her mother was head down in her own mug of coffee. Her delicate hands clasped the coffee mug like the liquid inside would give her life. Her bracelet — a thin bangle with a green center light, tapped against the mug's side every time she raised it. She ignored everyone.

It looked like they were a family of grumps today.

Drumming her fingers restlessly against the table top as she mindlessly scooped cereal into her mouth, Tracey thought about school and Tony. Immediately she slapped at her dressing gown pockets. "Damn it!" She shot her mom a worried look, but her mother was still staring at her mug. "I mean, darn it." Her phone was still upstairs with all her school stuff. Social media free at the table meant she finished her breakfast in record time. Peter gave a half-hearted wave as she dragged her tired body back upstairs. Her departure didn't get a response from either of the twins. Mom's voice stopped her at the base of the stairs.

"Where were you last night?"

Oh, look at that. First coffee consumed and Mom was finally speaking like a human. Tracey pointed at Peter and simply said, "Uncle Donny."

Her mom's sigh followed her all the way up the stairs. She heard grumbling and then her mom yelled, "I'm going to have words with Donald."

Me too, Tracey thought, though she wouldn't be able to do that until after school. She bashed against the bathroom door as she passed it. The door opened, expelling a cloud of steam. From it emerged her almost thirteen-year-old sister—dressed like a sixteen-year-old. "You'd better not let Mom catch you wearing that," Tracey told her.

"Psh," Sarah flung up a hand and flounced past. While Tracey really wanted to listen to the coming explosion, she needed a shower first. A little while later she stared at her damp reflection and poked at the dark circles under her eyes. Foundation wasn't going to cover them, but it was worth a try. Combing her shoulder-length, boring brown hair into a ponytail, she wondered how she must have looked to Prince Henry last night. As she watched, her face turned an awful shade of red. Oh, she must have looked like such a tomato! No wonder the prince laughed at her.

Tracey's hair and eyes were hardly memorable; her nose was too big for her face and her chin far too pointy. She poked at the circles under her eyes again and swore. Catching her gaze in the mirror, she told herself to suck it up. "You are awesome."

Problem was she didn't really believe it. Returning to her room she found her phone vibrating softly on her bed.

It was Tony. "You're panicking?" she asked.

His nasally voice laughed back at her. "Nope, I just need to know where to meet you."

Tracey had promised Tony a quick tour of the school and to show him the best places to go to avoid the demons their school possessed. David Stanley and Dave Betts, otherwise known as Dave One and Dave Two were big-shouldered, thick-necked football players who loved to make every student's life a misery—especially new kids. Tracey refused to let Tony get dragged under on his first day.

"Side gate off Elm—most of the nerds use it," she told him. It was perfectly fine to use the term *nerd,* she was one herself. Safety in numbers and all that. She promised Tony she'd introduce her Norm friends at the gate and hung up. Jonny and Tony would hit it off instantly, she was sure. Not in a *together* kind of way, though that was a funny thought. Jonny was straighter than a ruler, and Tracey loved how he accepted everyone. He didn't care that Tracey was Mage-kind or that she was a giant comic book loving science fiction fan. He loved video games, and so did Tony. Between discussions over their favorite roleplaying games and sci-fi films, Tracey guessed her other, less nerdy friend Laura might finally chuck in her friendship.

Tracey hunted out her new superhero shirt, threw a green button-down sleeveless shirt over it and dragged on her jeans. Pausing in the doorway she looked back at her bed. Her emergency band—the one Mom and Dad gave her as a little kid—hung over the bed post. She'd stopped wearing it years ago after getting her first cell phone. Her thoughts flew back to the Shadowman. Should she take it with her? *Don't be silly. You were probably imagining it. Alone, in the dark—it's just in your head.* Grabbing her jacket, she shot a last look of longing at her bed and headed out.

Tony's nervous expression disappeared and he gave her a giant grin when she got to the gate. "Ah, stop it—I'll lose all vision staring at those pearly whites," she cried, flinging a hand dramatically over her eyes. The braces had come off last year, leaving Tony with the cutest smile. He looked very nice in his black jacket, green shirt, and black jeans. His student bracelet hung loosely on his right wrist, reminding Tracey he was left-handed. *Weirdo!*

"'Bout time you showed," he complained, punching her in the shoulder. At the touch of his hand, they both shivered, their magic reconnecting after the week break from camp. It was like coming home, a similar feeling to the connection she had with her brothers—all warm and glowy.

"What's that?" he asked stepping back to focus on the growling sound growing louder behind them. Tracey turned. "That, my friend, is Jonny." A modified bicycle with a motor attached came roaring around the corner. Jonny was sitting astride it and made straight for them.

The motor cut out as he coasted to stop right at Tony's boots. "Hey," he said, pulling off his helmet.

"Hey." Tracey pointed, "Is that a motorbike helmet?"

"Yup, cool right?" The handsome black boy shot her a crooked smile and pushed his glasses back up his nose. He looked Tony up and down curiously. "This the new guy?"

"Jonny, meet Tony. Tony, this is Jonny." The boys shook hands like it was some right-of-passage thing. It was weird to see them acting all grown up. "Tony goes to my summer camp," she reminded Jonny.

"Cool," he said and clapped a dark-skinned hand over Tony's shoulder. "Welcome to hell."

Tracey groaned. "Cut that out, Jonny. I've spent six weeks trying to convince him this school's okay."

Within moments, the two guys were talking the latest super hero flick and RPG avatars with the occasional school subject thrown into the mix. Tracey watched them with a strange feeling. She was glad her two friends had clicked so quickly but was surprised at how left out she suddenly felt.

The feeling didn't leave her until Laura bumped her shoulder. Tracey spun around and gave her friend a quick hug. Laura's perfume danced up

Tracey's nose making her sneeze.

"Hey there. Bummer to be back, huh?"

Sometimes Tracey wondered why Laura was her best friend. Laura was everything Tracey was not. Laura was all class and sophistication, beauty and fashion with perfectly styled dark tresses that fell in waves around her shoulders. Light silver eyeshadow highlighted her blue eyes, and her pink lips always looked recently glossed. It was like she'd just stepped out of a fashion magazine, leaving Tracey feeling completely dull and uninteresting in comparison. "Hey. Yeah, it sucks. Did you enjoy your holiday?"

"Beach was great." Laura's eyes darted up and down Tracey's outfit. "New shirt?"

"You know it." Tracey was super aware of just how much she frustrated Laura — she couldn't remember how many times Laura had tried to talk her into wearing lip gloss, heeled boots or even a skirt! *Ha — never gonna happen!* Today, Laura wore a little black skirt and skin-tight red top. Tracey could never pull that outfit off in a million years, and would never want to.

Laura was a Norm, but to Tracey, she always seemed a little bit magical.

The two girls walked arm in arm toward the rear of Hall B. Tracey didn't hear Tony and Jonny following along behind them and turned to find her Mage-kind friend staring at Laura, his mouth open wide. Laura smiled, offered Tony a little wave of her fingers, then grabbed Tracey's arm. "Did you hear about the new guy?"

Tracey shook her hand away. "Uh, *yeah*," she pointed to Tony. "New guy. Laura, this is Tony, my friend from summer camp. Remember, I told you he was coming here this year."

Laura shook her head. "I'm talking about the *other* new guy."

"*Other* new guy?"

"Yes," Laura practically purred. She gestured with her nose toward the rear of Hall B. Some students were gathered there on the patchy grass in a large circle. "He's currently surrounded by the Evil Queens and the Dummy D's."

Tracey hazarded a glance at the group in question, but all she could see was Dave One and Dave Two's broad backs. "I can't see," she started to say, but then the crowd parted, and it was like a beam of light shone down from the sky onto the boy in front of them. *Divine!* All pouty lips and dark hair, the new guy wore a well-worn leather jacket and exuded cool. Tracey's heart skipped a beat. She pressed a hand to her chest. "Yum."

Laura's eyes twinkled. "Right?"

Behind Tracey, Tony's speech cut off mid-sentence. After a moment, he sighed, "My heart's all a flutter."

Tracey looked back at him and winked. "Wow." She grabbed Laura's arm and demanded, "Tell me everything."

Tony leaned hard into Tracey's shoulder as Laura filled them in on what little she already knew. The new guy's family had moved into town a few days ago. He was assigned to Homeroom 2. *Damn!* Laura and Tracey were in Homeroom 3, and Tony and Jonny were Homeroom 1. The new guy's name was Damian Carter and he played football. *What a shame.*

She knew Tony would be thinking the same thing and glanced his way. They eyeballed each other and giggled. Tracey's stomach swirled as she peeked back at the new guy. *Who am I kidding? He'll never notice me. Not in a million years.* With a last heartfelt sigh, she looked back at Laura who was still talking.

"He's got a little sister at the junior school and his dad's in the military, which is why he's here. I haven't spoken to him."

Tracey could hear the word "yet" in her friend's voice and smiled. Laura would find a way to talk to Damian Carter, and part of Tracey growled at the thought. *Am I jealous?* She was so shocked she nearly missed Laura's next statement.

"He's what?"

Laura looked at her with a knowing smirk. "I said he's single, as far as I know. I heard Carla tell Meena about it in the bathroom, but hey, that could totally be wrong."

Tracey shook her head. She'd learned back in third grade never to trust anything Meena and Carla said. Fortunately for Tracey and her friends, Meena and Carla—the Evil Queens—mostly ignored them. It was better that way. They could be quite nasty if crossed.

"So that's it, that's all I know."

Tony's eyes focused and he shot Tracey a wry glance. "Do you think any of those girls will talk about *me* like this? Or the boys? I'm new, too."

That set Tracey off laughing hysterically. Her stomach ached by the time she'd managed to calm down. "I have news," she said a little breathlessly. Everyone stopped walking and looked back at her. She raised an eyebrow, "What? I can have news."

Jonny said what they were all thinking. "Since when?"

She scowled and turned her back on him. Eyeballing Tony, she told him about last night's adventure at the hotel. Her voice raced as she couldn't hide her excitement.

"Shut up!" Tony gasped. His hand clutched at his shirt. She grinned at his over-the-top reaction.

Feeling giddy inside, she nodded. "It's true."

"His room?" Laura whispered. "Pictures, I want pictures. Where are the pictures?"

Fruit tingles, I knew I'd need evidence. "Well, I don't—"

Jonny cut in. "Prince Henry? Naw … you're seriously saying you met Prince Henry?"

Tracey widened her eyes and nodded even more slowly. Her friends stared at her in silence until the bell rang.

Laura held up her hands. Her eyes wide as she stated, "I am officially speechless. Trace, you have outdone yourself. I am honest-to-God speechless that you DID NOT CALL ME!"

Tracey giggled and followed her friends toward Hall B's south entrance, not noticing the bag strap on the ground until one of her shoes got caught in it. She tripped and fell against something warm and firm. Roaring laughter exploded all around her.

Her face heated with embarrassment as two large hands grabbed her shoulders. "Whoops," she said, and looked up into the most beautiful brown eyes she'd ever seen.

"Bewitch or betray,

Deceive or repay …?"

6

This is not happening! She slammed her eyes shut and prayed that when she opened them again she'd be back in bed and very late for school. Cracking open one eye, she quickly closed it again. Her stomach landed on the ground at her feet. *Fruit tingles!*

A low chuckle emanated from the chest she was pressed against. "Are you okay?"

Better get it over with. She pushed away gently. "I am so unbelievably sorry." The schoolyard around them fell silent, waiting for an explosion. It wasn't a good sign that Damian Carter had been talking with the Double D's and the Evil Queens until just before Tracey tripped into him.

She sensed Tony and Jonny stepping closer to her back—just in case—and watched Damian's gorgeous brown eyes flick over them before focusing back on her. They'd all been marked now. Tracey usually didn't rate high enough on the Double D's radar to be bothered with, but that could change depending on what happened in the next few minutes. Meena and Carla glared in her direction. Tracey swallowed hard and checked to make sure her magic was sealed tightly inside. Now was not the time to panic and have her magic burst free to try and save her.

Then Damian Carter did something totally unexpected. He apologized. "I wasn't watching where I was going. You'll forgive me, right? I'm Damian. You must be the Mage-kind I keep hearing about. Tracey?"

Her eyes widened and her pulse accelerated. She stared at his mouth, the mouth that was talking to her before she glanced around at the students surrounding them. Yep. That mouth. It was his, and he was using it to talk to her. *He apologized?*

When he waved a hand in front of her face she realized she hadn't

answered. He must think she was a total loser. "Yes, that's me, Tracey."
Cracking open the door in her chest she drew on her power and reached
out to him. Maybe he'd asked about her magic because he was Mage-kind
too. She felt nothing. Now more confused than ever she wondered why
he was even talking to her. "You're not Mage-kind?"

He ducked his head and rubbed the back of his suddenly pink neck.
"No. I heard this was a mixed school but I hadn't seen any Mage-kind yet."

"Yeah, well we look like everyone else," Tracey answered, feeling
stupid. Students hovered, scuffing the grass as they waited to witness a
scandal they could spread. Tracey's existence as Mage-kind had never been
raised at school before. At best she was ignored, or given a wide berth.
This was probably the first public confrontation the school had ever had,
and of course she was right in the thick of it.

The air around them grew tense. The sun seemed hotter. She could
feel eyes darting from her to Damian and back again, and her skin crawled
with the sensation of being judged. Her fingertips tingled as her bracelet
buzzed a warning.

She stepped back, suddenly afraid of why Damian was talking to her.
It was forbidden for Mage-kind to use their powers at a Norm school. She
didn't want to get mad and explode if he said something nasty. Her brothers had told her some awful stories about what other students could say.

Damian, noticing the move, held up his hands. "No, no it's cool."
He looked at the students gathered around them and snapped, "Don't
you all have places to be?" He held the stare until the Evil Queens raised
their noses and flounced away. As soon as they left, chatter resumed and
the rest of the students disappeared. Damian's face splotched red in the
morning light. Tracey felt a little sorry for him. She hated being the center
of attention too. It made her feel squinchy in the stomach.

"I'm so sorry about that," he said and lowered his voice. "My sister
is Mage-kind — over at the junior school. I just wanted to say I think
it's cool that we can go to the same school now. I didn't realize it would
cause such a ... *thing*."

Tracey let out a huge sigh of relief, but her friends still hovered
protectively. "No probs. We'd better get to class, though." She waved a

hand toward the building redundantly. *You idiot—he knows where the school building is.*

Laura raised a delicate eyebrow, but Tracey's shooing gesture covered her, too. Tracey trailed after her friends, unable to stop from peeking back over her shoulder. Damian was watching. Her face heated as she raced to catch up with Tony.

"Good or bad?" he whispered.

"I don't know yet," she muttered back.

Once she sat down she checked her phone under the table, staying careful to hide it from her English teacher, Mr. Michaels. A dozen messages popped up from Laura, Tony, and Jonny, all wanting to talk about Damian. Her head spun. Laura demanded they get together after school to discuss him further. She glanced up. Mr. Michaels had his back to the class as he wrote questions on the tablet attached to the electric whiteboard. It looked like his bald spot had widened over the break. Rough break.

Biting her lip, she risked sending out one group message writing they could meet her at Uncle Donny's office after school, then she opened the class book on her tablet and proceeded not to pay any attention to Mr. Michaels whatsoever. All she could think about was heat, muscles, and really nice brown eyes. Damian smelled so sweet, like sugar and hot donuts, and his whole body had vibrated when he laughed.

"Miss Masters?"

Her head shot up, "Sir?" It was possibly not the first time Mr. Michaels had called her name given the thunderous expression on his face. Her bracelet vibrated softly, buzzing against her heated skin.

She mashed her lips together and sunk lower in her chair, wishing her magic was powerful enough to make her disappear as he proceeded to lecture her on the importance of paying attention.

The first day back at school always felt as though it lasted a hundred. The only excitement came when Dave One and Dave Two smashed a science window with a loose basketball during the lunch break. Tracey's adventurous night had caught up with her by early afternoon, and she was feeling zombie-like by the time she arrived at Uncle Donny's office. Yawning loudly, she entered with the mail from the box outside. Uncle Donny's private door was closed, so she dumped the mail on her desk and switched on her computer. The clock on her cell told her she had about twenty minutes before her friends arrived. Enough time to do her usual office chores.

A strange smell lingered in the room. She sniffed loudly but couldn't pinpoint the scent. When her computer beeped she logged in and sent a message to Uncle Donny letting him know she was there and opened the mail. If he didn't have a client, he'd pop his head out and beg for coffee. When the door remained closed, she finished sorting the mail and flipped the pile of past due notices into her in-tray, scanning slower through the enquiry emails searching for potential clients. Nothing struck her as interesting.

Grabbing the trash to take outside, she sniffed again. The strange smell wasn't coming from the trash. She'd just flicked the switch on the coffee machine when Uncle Donny's door rattled and swung wide. She opened her mouth to greet him but stopped when she realized he was not alone. Miss Tearning stood just inside talking to him. Oh, that was the smell. Tracey dropped the trash bag under her desk and sat down, hoping to catch the last of their conversation. She craned her head in the open door's direction and stared at her computer screen as if reading something. Out of the corner of her eye, she peeked back at Uncle Donny's office. Today, Miss Tearning wore a perfectly tailored navy pantsuit. Her hair was tied at the nape of her neck, and her painted fingernails matched her grey shoes. She looked up and caught sight of Tracey, turning her gaze back to Uncle Donny almost immediately. Tracey hunched her shoulders and wished she'd taken the time to brush her hair before starting work. She was glaringly aware of the trash beneath her desk.

"I'm positive I'll have a lead shortly. Last night was very promising. There's a few more things to look into before I can give you a full report." Uncle Donny's face was shiny, leading Tracey to assume he'd forgotten to open the window in his office again.

"Of course, Mr. James. Please keep me informed of your progress."

Uncle Donny assured Miss Tearning he would and escorted her to the door. As soon as it closed behind her, Tracey waved. "How's it going?"

"Hey there, kiddo." He moved straight to the coffee machine. Sighing loudly, he pressed his face into the machine. Tracey could hear the *drip, drip* of coffee landing in his cup. "She wants progress—I have nothing for her."

Tracey cringed. "About that ..."

He spun around so fast his foot came clear out of his shoe. She stifled a giggle as he tried to get the shoe back onto his foot. When he finally succeeded, he stared at her demanding, "What do you know?" He pointed to his private office. She followed him in but left the door wide open.

It was like a sauna inside. "See this hole in the wall, Boss? It's called a window," she tugged on the frame until it snapped open. "When is that air conditioner you promised me coming?"

"When we get paid." He slumped down into his chair and pointed a finger at her, waving it around.

Unable to stall any longer, she dropped into the seat in front of his desk. Cold air flooded over her through the open window, and she sighed at the relief it brought to the stuffy room. Uncle Donny slurped at his coffee. "Last night, you said to watch the valet from the window of the hotel, but while I was waiting I saw something weird ... so I sort of ... investigated."

He straightened in his chair. "Go on."

She told him about the six guards and of the man in the middle taking possession of the mysterious jewelry box.

"Prince Henry?" Uncle Donny eyebrows rose so high on his forehead they buried themselves in his hair.

"It was a jewelry box, I'm certain of it. You spelled the red car and it brought us straight to his hotel. That means he has the necklace, right?"

Her uncle nodded. "I used a basic search spell. Yes, I'd say he's definitely got it."

The question she'd been pondering since the night before popped into her mouth. "Uncle Donny, why would a prince need to steal a necklace?

It doesn't make any sense. And how does Miss Tearning know him?"

"I have a bigger question for you," he said, dropping his head into his hands. All she could see was his messy curls—no bald spot yet. His voice sounded muffled under his palms. "How do I get it back?"

They sat in silence, thinking about the answer.

Her uncle leaned back and tapped his chin. "I know—I need a spell."

Fruit tingles! "What kind of spell?" It was her job to rein him in when he got like this. At least, according to her mother it was. Uncle Donny's spells didn't always work as he wanted them to. His magic was a little too weak for his will. "Hank took it into his suite."

"Hank?"

She imagined her face bursting into flames. "I meant Prince Henry. Uncle Donny, there were bodyguards everywhere."

"What about a disguise spell?"

She stared at him, opening her eyes wide and raising her eyebrows. "A disguise spell won't work."

"Why not?"

Leaning forward she put her elbows onto his desk. "Disguise yourself as who, the concierge?"

"No, no, no …" Uncle Donny tucked his hands behind his head. "I use the disguise spell to become the prince."

"You *what?*" He was deluded. His magic was not strong enough to hold a disguise spell that intricate for more than a few minutes. She was going to have to strengthen it. Disguise spells were illegal, for obvious reasons. "So what, you just walk in and ask for the key to his room because you lost it? It's a high-class hotel. They'll have decent anti-magic protections in place." That was the part about his crazy plan that worried her the most. These days, businesses with any smarts and money used comprehensive protection spells to guard their stock. Usually, they were out of date, which gave you a little leeway if you came up with a variation to a current hacking spell, but Tracey's uncle had almost been caught because of up-to-date magical security systems before. She'd been forced to listen to him over the phone tap dance his way through a really hard-to-believe excuse and get the heck out of the client's ex-employer's office—without the copies of the phony pay slips he'd gone in to retrieve. She had no idea what she would have done in that situation. It was one of the few times she'd been glad she was left behind. "I think if you're going to do this, it should be without magic. You could sneak in? You've done it before. Remember when you broke into the penthouse as a room service guy?"

Her uncle nodded. "I could, but this will be better because I'll be disguised as a traveler who has already checked in. No, this is the perfect plan."

"But what if the prince is in his suite, or his bodyguards are there?" There were too many variables for Tracey's liking.

"That's why I need you to come with me."

Wait— What? She hadn't exactly told him the whole story about last night. "I can't."

"I thought you wanted to help me?"

He had her there. "What if they see me?"

"Disguise spell," he sang at her.

She stared at the floor. Sucking in a deep breath, she counted to five.

With a flurry of movement, Uncle Donny jumped to his feet. "I'm going to pop down to the hotel and get a sample."

"Wait, wait. Stop." Tracey stood in front of the door. "You're not going to just walk in there and get a DNA sample from Prince Henry. He's famous. You won't even get close to him. Besides, people must try that all the time." She heard the bell go at the front door and peeked out to see who was there. She waved her uncle back into his seat. "It's just Laura and the guys," she said. Stepping out of his office, she hoped he would take some time to rethink his plan. Before she could even draw a breath to greet her friends, Uncle Donny breezed past her with his jacket in his hands.

"I'll be back soon," he called, and raced out the door.

"He was real, wasn't he?
Someone can't just disappear,
can they?"

1

He was gone before she could stop him. Her face must have shown her worry because Laura immediately asked what happened. Tracey shook her head in response, not entirely sure how she should be feeling. She'd wanted to assist Uncle Donny on a case for so long, but now that the chance was finally here she was feeling all wobbly inside. Excitement was supposed to feel good, so why did it feel bad at the same time? Was that normal?

If Uncle Donny was going to get himself into trouble, there was nothing she could do about it. He wanted her involved and his plan called for a disguise spell. She'd never done one before. If she got caught her mom would totally ground her. Heck, she'd ban Tracey from ever working for Uncle Donny again. And that was just Mom. Imagine if the police caught her—and involved the Mage-kind special police, M-Force. *Oh God!* She might be forbidden from using her magic at all. Suddenly, the risks were too real. Her breathing grew labored as she pictured a prison cell full of tattooed woman in orange jumpsuits. Then she imagined her mom's face, and all breathing stopped. She couldn't get air into her lungs, her mouth gaped open.

"Tracey, what's wrong?" Laura asked.

She swallowed back her fear. She couldn't tell Laura and Jonny about the disguise spell—as Norms they would be expected to turn her in, but they were her friends and she knew they wouldn't do that. She didn't want them to have to make that choice. Best to keep quiet for now. "Nothing," she said and smiled. It felt weird.

Tony shot her a knowing look. He had probably felt her panic. Her mental shields were a little wonky given how little sleep she'd had.

Resolving to worry about it later, she flopped down onto the sofa next to Laura. Her friend sat daintily, properly, not a single hair out of place while Tracey felt like a giant mess of stray hairs and food stains. Jonny stood at the coffee machine. As usual, he pulled several hot chocolate packets out of the cupboard and proceeded to play barista.

Tony walked around the room with a fascinated expression on his face. "So, this is the great detective agency?" he asked.

She had forgotten Tony just moved into town. Tracey took him on a quick tour, trying to see her uncle's office as if she was looking at it for the first time. "This is the main reception area," she announced. "My desk, phone, and computer, blah, blah, blah. And there's the kitchen with client coffee machine," she added, waving her hands at Jonny.

"*Our* machine," Jonny countered.

Tracey rolled her eyes at him, but he wasn't wrong.

"Is that a trash bag under your desk?" Laura asked, sounding horrified.

"Whoops." Tracey grabbed the bag and raced through the little door beside the coffee machine that opened out into the alley behind the office. "Stinky alley," she proclaimed, gesturing behind her as she walked back in. She washed her hands in the little kitchen sink along the wall and took her mug from Jonny's outstretched hand.

She was stalling and they totally knew it.

Laura's tiny nose twitched, her eyes widened and her lips curled up. "Enough of this," she blurted at last.

Tracey slumped down onto the sofa. "He's so dreamy," she said, thinking of her hands pressed up against Damian's firm chest. "You can tell he plays football because he's all muscles ..."

"Ahem," Laura coughed dramatically and poked at Tracey's arm. "I meant Prince Henry."

She flushed again. "Whoops." They laughed even harder when she told them about last night's adventure.

"Wait," Jonny interrupted. His fingers drummed against the side of his mug, the yellow one with a smiling emoji face on the side. "So what's the deal with the necklace?"

Tracey pointed at him and said, "Exactly."

"Why would a prince steal a necklace? Who is Miss Tearning?" he continued.

She paused as Jonny's question registered. Straightening her back Tracey scooted forward on the sofa cushion. "Good question. What if Prince Henry didn't take it? What if Miss Tearning is planning to steal it from *him*, and she's trying to con Uncle Donny into doing it for her?"

"Seriously?" Laura stood, putting her hands on her hips. She probably thought it made her look intimidating, but Tracey couldn't help imagining her friend as a superhero. "You always come up with the craziest theories, Trace. Miss Tearning was probably dating the prince — he's an actor right? He's good-looking, young, and rich. He's not the heir to the throne, so he plays around, knowing he can get away with it. Miss Tearning is just upset he broke up with her. She probably wishes she'd kept the present she threw back at him when he broke it off."

Tracey stared at Laura in surprise. "And you say *my* theories are elaborate?"

"Internet!" Jonny shouted, racing to Tracey's desk. Tony's head dropped, his phone appearing in his hand, blue light casting a flickering glare across his eyes. He swiped at the screen and for a few seconds, and all they could hear was tapping.

Laura nudged Tracey's knee, "Damian *is* pretty cute, huh?"

"Oh, yeah," she said and glanced at the boys to make sure they were distracted.

Jonny stopped their gossiping a moment later with loud cry. Tracey and Laura jumped up to crowd around to the desk and examine the three windows Jonny had open on the screen. One was of the M-Net film blog, one was *GossENews*, and the last was a photo sharing site. "Miss Catherine Tearning did date Prince Henry for about three months," he said.

"Sounds like it was a bad breakup," Tony added, scrolling through Miss Tearning's social feeds on his phone. "She says he cheated."

"*He* says otherwise," Jonny insisted.

"Are there any photos of her wearing the necklace?" Laura asked.

Jonny expanded the publicity photographs he found of Catherine Tearning and Prince Henry. One was from his latest film premiere, two were from an award show after party, and one was taken of them leaving a fancy restaurant. Miss Tearning was wearing the necklace in every shot.

"I can see why she wants it back," Laura said.

Tracey agreed. The pendant was made of crystal in the shape of a butterfly. You couldn't tell from the media photos, but she knew from the insurer's photo in her uncle's file that the green and red gems set into the wings were emeralds and rubies.

"Did she say the necklace was lost, missing, or stolen?" Laura asked.

"She said stolen — oh, maybe she doesn't know Hank was involved?" Tracey wondered, leaning over Jonny to expand another photo.

The room fell silent.

She looked up to find them staring at her. "What?"

"*Hank?*" Laura asked.

Tracey's face flamed when she couldn't come up with a quick excuse for using such a casual name for the European Prince and fifth in line to the throne.

"Oh. My. *God!* What else happened last night?" Tony swatted at Tracey's arm as if that would make her tell him any faster. She pushed him away and quick-paced to the kitchenette. Her chest buzzed with emotional magic. She gulped and mentally fanned herself.

"Prince Henry told me to call him that."

Three open mouths greeted that statement.

"Look, I'm worried about what Uncle Donny is planning to do tonight," she said, getting back to the matter at hand. The distraction worked, though the expression on Laura's face told Tracey to expect a long-winded phone call later.

That night, Tracey wished she *had* dragged one of her pain-in-the-butt friends along with her. Even though there was no way they could be allowed to know what she was actually doing, which was freezing to death standing alone in front of the Central Grand Hotel, it would have been nice to have someone to talk to while she watched the door. Her mission was to keep a look out for the real Prince Henry and his entourage. Catching sight of long pale arms and elegant fingers in the window's reflection, she realized she was still freaking out. Somehow, God help him, her uncle had gotten his hands on Miss Tearning's hair. Tracey was now the spitting image of their client, thanks to her uncle's "lookalike" spell.

She was surprised the spell had worked. *Not surprised, amazed.* Teetering on a pair of ridiculously high pumps, she wondered how on earth she was ever going to be able to convince anyone she was Miss Tearning. Looking at her reflection in the window, she frowned, or tried to. Her forehead didn't move. She scrunched her eyes and twitched her nose but nothing happened. It was too freaky for words. And then there was the dress she wore. It looked like it had come from Grandma's closet. There was no way the real Miss Tearning would ever be caught dead wearing this floral nightmare.

Uncle Donny was due to make his grand entrance any minute now and anticipation buzzed low in her belly like she'd swallowed a swarm of bees. Curiously, she wondered why excitement and terror usually felt the same.

Her phone trilled with a text message from her uncle. She quickly messaged back that she hadn't seen the prince at all. *This is going to be such a disaster.* The famous man might be upstairs or could appear in the lobby at any moment. It was Tracey's job to distract him if he did. Well, she would certainly achieve that when she tripped on these stupid pumps and fell flat on her face. Uncle Donny texted again to tell her he was close enough for her to activate the listening spell.

She closed her eyes and touched her ear. "Focus," she muttered and drew her power from her chest to push a spark of magic into her earring. When it buzzed, she said, "Contact Boss."

A click, a sharp squeal, and then Uncle Donny was puffing into her ear like a steam train. "What's going on, why do you sound like you're running?" she demanded.

"I might have activated the disguise spell a little too early," came his breathless reply.

She pictured him running down the street being chased by half a dozen screaming fangirls and stifled a laugh. "You weren't supposed to draw attention to yourself," she said. She caught sight of her disguised self in the mirror again and grinned.

"Two minutes."

Standing straighter, Tracey glanced over everyone standing in the lobby. It was reasonably late so there were not too many people around.

Right on the dot, her uncle entered the lobby. She had no idea how he'd managed to steal a sample of Prince Henry's hair, but the spell was as effective as the one he'd cast on her. He looked exactly like the prince.

The hotel's staff came to life the instant they saw him. Two uniformed men behind the check-in counter stopped talking. Instead of the man from last night, a woman with the concierge badge strode forward and smiled broadly, exposing crooked teeth. How was that for luck? He might actually pull this off.

Staying in her dark corner, she watched Uncle Donny recreate the prince's behavior perfectly. He slumped a little too much, but the arrogant look on his face was spot on. Speaking quickly to the concierge he explained how he'd lost his room key.

The concierge brushed blunt-nailed fingers against her hair, ensuring not a strand was out of place and moved quickly to the desk. "Of course, Your Highness. I'll reprogram a card for you immediately."

"Excellent work," Tracey whispered. Her uncle didn't answer. He tapped his fingers in a rapid *one, two, three* against the desk and turned around. When he saw Tracey, his face cycled through three separate expressions: surprise, joy, and then suspicion. The buzzing in Tracey's stomach leapt into her chest and closed her throat.

Uncle Donny's voice gasped in her ear. "Sorry, was on mute—don't know how that happened. What's a good job?"

Oh, no!

Prince Henry—the *real* Prince Henry—walked straight toward Tracey. She searched desperately for somewhere to hide, but it was too late. "Uncle Donny, you're not in the lobby, are you?"

"No, not yet. Why, aren't you—" The earring crackled. "He's there, isn't he?"

She couldn't answer. Prince Henry stopped right in front of her. His eyes trailed up and down her body, taking in the dress and strappy pumps.

"You look … nice," he said when his eyes met hers.

She thought about the woman she'd met only briefly and searched for an appropriate response. Her mind went blank.

A shadow pulled away from the darkness,
taking on the shape of a man.

8

I didn't think you'd be here," she said lowering her voice to sound huskier. She hoped he wouldn't hear the difference and work out something was wrong. Her mouth was dry and her hands were shaking. *Don't notice!* Who was she kidding? Of course he was going to notice. She was going to get found out and arrested. *Oh God!* She didn't want to go to prison.

"I left something upstairs." He stood well within her personal space, and she fought her instinctive need to stammer and step back.

Uncle Donny was just outside—if the real prince saw him, they'd be done for. Her mind raced. She had to convince the prince to leave. If she got him out of the way quickly enough, maybe her uncle's plan would still work. *What a joke!* She'd be lucky to get out of here in one piece.

His fingers caressed her fake arms. Maybe her second biggest fear.

"Ah ..." *Great response, Tracey.* "I shouldn't have come here."

Prince Henry smiled. Unlike last night, this smile didn't reach his eyes. "No, you shouldn't have." His hand tightened on her arm. "But since you *are* here, we should talk."

Tracey tugged, but he wouldn't let her go.

Uncle Donny whispered, "Take him to the bar, I need ten minutes. Get me ten minutes."

I'm going to kill Uncle Donny. Tracey escaped the prince's grasp and hissed, "Not here. Please Hank, not here. The bar, perhaps?"

He nodded, "Always thinking of my reputation, darling? That's why we work so well together." He gestured toward the elevators. "Let's go upstairs."

That was the complete opposite of where she wanted him to go. "No," she said as firmly as she could. She pictured her mom talking to her uncle and firmed her stance. "Let's go to the bar."

"I won't keep you long, my dear."

Fruit tingles! She turned her head and mumbled a warning to her uncle. When Prince Henry put his hand on her back, she flinched.

"Darling?"

"It's nothing," she said quickly.

"Your Highness!" Tracey welcomed the high-pitched voice of the concierge. The woman's brisk footsteps followed. She held out a small box. Prince Henry took it and directed Tracey toward the elevators. *Help!*

When the doors closed sealing them inside he pressed a hand to her back and leaned close whispering. "Darling, you said the next time you saw me it would be freezing in hell. Why did you come back?"

She opened her mouth, but no sound emerged.

"Well, this is a first. I've never seen you stunned silent before. I think I like it."

The instant the elevator stopped, Tracey squeezed through the opening doors. In her ear, Uncle Donny panted, but managed to say, "Keep him busy."

Yeah, she didn't think keeping the prince busy was going to be the problem. She paced outside room 301, wobbling unsteadily in her unfamiliar pumps. As the prince made his way toward her, each footstep thudded in her stomach like the Emperor's March. His eyes narrowed as he stared at her. With a tilt of his head, he smiled and unlocked the door.

Tracey ended up right where she stood last night. Prince Henry tossed the box the concierge gave him lightly from one hand to the other. She wanted a look inside. Maybe it was the necklace her uncle was looking for. Prince Henry seemed to have a lot of jewelry delivered. He couldn't be a thief — *what's really going on here?* Thinking about the case took her mind off her precarious situation for a moment. The moment ended too quickly.

"I'm surprised," he said.

"Why?"

"You haven't started shouting at me yet."

Tracey shuffled sideways until the sofa was between them. "Oh, yes, well, you don't want me to start now, do you?" She held up a hand as if that would stop him from approaching.

"Good point." He turned instead toward the fridge. "Drink?"

Her eyes dropped to the jewelry box he placed on the table. She had one shot at this. "Something complicated."

He laughed at that. "Now you sound like yourself. One complicated drink, coming up."

The second he turned away to pull a fancy looking bottle off the shelf, she snuck up to the jewelry box and flipped open the lid. *A pair of earrings?*

A hand touched her wrist.

"Oh!" She jumped, knocking her hand against the delicate looking glass he held.

"What the—?" He yanked the glass away from his body as drips of pink liquid slid down his arm.

"Oh, sorry," she muttered.

"Why are you acting so strangely?"

Why, indeed. "Well, we've broken up and … and it wasn't very nice. I'm a little bit jumpy." She took the glass from his hand rather than leave him holding it. "Thanks."

"Well, you've spoiled it anyway," he said slumping down onto the sofa. His gaze fell to the plush carpet as his forehead wrinkled. He scrubbed a hand over his face and looked up at her from beneath long, dark lashes. Tracey reached out to pat his arm. She stopped her hand just above his shirt sleeve.

"Spoiled what?"

"The earrings. They're for you. I've been searching for the perfect pair all week to win you back, but now you've spoiled the surprise." In a flat voice he added, "Surprise."

Tracey sipped at her glass. The liquid was strong, bitter, and a little bit sweet. She coughed at the burn.

Jumping to his feet, he patted her back hard. "And now I've ruined your favorite drink, it appears. I ruin everything." He dropped his head and plonked back down onto the sofa cushions.

"No, don't think that." This whole plan was becoming a complete disaster. Prince Henry didn't have the necklace and Tracey couldn't stay here trying to make him feel better. She reminded herself she wasn't really his girlfriend — *ex*-girlfriend? "I shouldn't be here."

He chased her to the door, "Wait, Cath. Wait." Pressing the door closed with one hand, he asked, "Why did you come back?"

This time she was the one to drop her head. In her ear, Uncle Donny told her to ask for the necklace. Looking up into Prince Henry's pained eyes, she found she couldn't do it. Ignoring her uncle's order, she said, "I'm so sorry, Hank. I really do like you. But I just can't …" she let her voice trail away. This was a trick she'd seen her mom use on her dad. She'd start to say something, then stop and let him fill in the blanks. Her mom learned a lot of secrets that way.

To her delight, Prince Henry nodded slowly. "The acting. I know, I *know*, but I love it."

Tracey turned back, hoping to keep him talking. "The time …"

"It's only eight weeks. London's not that far away, and …"

She could use this. "I know, but I just can't …"

Again, he answered for her, "Long distance. I'm so sorry, honey, but it's my job."

"I know." She allowed him to pull her into an embrace. As he ran his hand down her back, it shocked her to realize that in this body she was nearly his height. Her head rested on the curve of his neck. In the mirror beside the door, it looked as though Miss Tearning was embracing the prince. *Remember, it's only a role.* But it was all too easy to get swept up in the romance of the moment. He smelled so nice, like fresh cut wood. She turned her head so she couldn't see them in the mirror anymore and tightened her arms. He radiated heat. "And you have to do it. I love that you do it, it's just …" she mumbled into his neck.

He lifted her head with a finger against her chin. She looked into his sad eyes. "What is it?" he asked.

"The necklace, remember!" Uncle Donny shouted in her ear.

Tracey fought her flinch. "It's silly."

"What is?"

She hesitated. "When we were fighting …" *What did Laura say?* Hoping her friend was right, she said, "I threw it back at you. I really wish I hadn't."

"The necklace?" he looked surprised.

Holy crap! Go Laura. "I told you it was silly."

He laughed. "You want it back?"

"It reminds me of you … of when you gave it to me." *I am an awful, awful person.*

Prince Henry tugged her away from the door. "Let me get it for you."

"Oh don't, it's silly," she said, ignoring her uncle's frantic shouting. She'd seen her mom do this, too. Pretend something didn't matter when it clearly did.

The prince disappeared into the back room and returned before she could say anything else. In his hands, he held a chain that sparkled against the light. Hanging from it was a butterfly. Instead of handing her the chain he nudged her shoulder. She turned at his urging. His hands touched her neck, and then the butterfly appeared over her head to lay heavy against her chest

"It's so pretty," she gasped.

She felt his warm breath against the sensitive skin of her neck. "That's not what you said the first time I gave it to you." Hot lips pressed gentle kisses at the base of her neck. Tracey's eyes drifted closed. For a moment she let herself pretend Prince Henry was in love with her, and not with the woman she was pretending to be.

A loud knock snapped her head up. Prince Henry sighed softly behind her.

"Your Highness? You are expected at the premiere shortly. We must leave."

"Ah." He dropped his head to the middle of her back. "Always with the bad timing."

"It's okay. I should go." *Yes, go! Come on Trace.*

Opening the door, Prince Henry muttered to his bodyguard that he needed five more minutes. Before he could close the door, the bodyguard's pocket began to scream. The mountain of muscle with tense eyebrows removed a little box from his jacket. Flashing rapidly on top was an orange light. "Sir! There is an active spell in this room, we need to get you out of here!" He spied Tracey and waved the device in her direction. The screaming alarm grew louder. *Fruit tingles! Busted.*

Tracey pushed into the startled man, knocking him into the wall and ran.

"Dealers of death,

Absorbing magic through dreams …"

9

Pressing the elevator button frantically, Tracey bit back a scream when nothing happened. She couldn't wait for it—the bodyguard would catch up to her in seconds. A few steps away, she spied a door with a sign that read *STAIRS*.

Assuming the guards would think she'd gone downstairs, she ran up instead. Before she could hear anyone behind her, she pushed open the door one floor above. "They're after me, Boss," she whispered.

In her ear, Uncle Donny told her, "Go up. No, go down. No, wait, the elevator is coming." *No help there.* Tracey ran along the corridor. A door was cracked open just ahead. This had to be the oddest hotel she'd ever been in—no one ever seemed to close their doors.

She ducked inside, ran to the adjoining bedroom and dove into the closet. The door clicked shut with a gust of air and a magical shimmer.

Fruit tingles. Tracey pressed hard against the door. Locked.

She was trapped.

What a fantastic end to a sucky day!

It was too dark to see much of anything, but by running her fingers across the paneling she could feel the outline of the door—what she couldn't feel was a handle. *Here I am, Mage-kind, wearing an illegal disguise spell and stuck in a closet.* She wasn't a pessimist, oh no, but more often than not, she ended up in crazy situations like this one. For a moment she wished she'd never agreed to work for her uncle.

Puffing her hair out of her eyes, she realized she needed help. It was time to bring out the big guns. Keeping her hands pressed to the door, she closed her eyes and drew on her power.

Magic swelled around her body, lighting her skin and the dark room with a faint orange glow. Her bracelet began to vibrate.

In her mind, Tracey imagined every grain of wood, the lacquer covering the door and each metal hinge. She could feel the spell that was set into the frame. It was not a particularly intricate spell, but sometimes the plain spells were the strongest. She picked at the spell's weave. If she could pull one thread, she might be able to unravel the whole thing.

Flicking at the little orange thread, she felt a tingle start under her toe. Her eyes sprang open as her legs began to shake, a sign that her uncle's disguise spell was wearing off. She squeezed her eyes shut. *Oh no!*

The tingles reached her neck. Her eyes popped, her lips blew up like sausages and her hair stood on end. She wanted to scream, but her vocal cords were changing, so all she could do was gasp.

Everything stretched like an elastic hairband. It stretched and stretched and then—her body shattered apart at the seams. Gulping in air, Tracey clutched her knees and curled in on herself, sobbing quietly.

How long she sat there she didn't know. Eventually she sniffed and wiped a hand over her eyes. Enough tears, she was not a child. *Get up.*

Think about Prince Henry. He wasn't a thief. So why did Miss Tearning want the necklace back so badly, and why hadn't she just asked for it? The butterfly was cold against her flushed skin. Her fingers danced across its wings. It didn't make any sense. Raising her trembling hands to the door, she refocused on that magical orange thread. Before she could catch it, the door was pulled open beneath her hands. Tracey tumbled out, landing at the slippered feet of the woman standing in front of her.

"Who the hell are you?" The woman screeched. Her hair was plastered to her head and dripped as though she'd just stepped out of the shower. Mascara trailed down her face and her clothes were soaked through.

Tracey stammered, "Hi—hello. Sorry."

"You're not *her!*" the woman shrieked higher, her eyes wide and crazy looking.

"No, I'm not her," Tracey said climbing to her feet.

"That cupboard was supposed to catch my sniveling coward of a husband's floozy, but you're just a kid. Who are you?"

Tracey held up a hand, clutching at the dress she wore with the other.

It now engulfed her like a mother's nighty on a five-year-old. "Um, I'm hiding. That's probably why the closet caught me." She shuffled forward, her shoes too big for her feet. She kicked them off and picked them up with her free hand. "From my dad …" Tracey sniffed hard, willing her eyes to tear up. It didn't take long; they were still wet from the pain of the disguise spell breakdown. "I'm sorry. I'm so sorry about hiding in here," she sobbed. *Sorry, dad!* The spelled earring must have fallen from her ear when she changed back into her own body because she couldn't hear Uncle Donny anymore. She could only hope he was waiting for her downstairs.

"Oh, you poor thing." The woman cooed, leading Tracey to the bed. "Sit here. I might have something for you to wear." Minutes later, Tracey raced through the lobby in a pair of fluorescent pink parachute pants and a green tank top. Tucked under the tank top was the butterfly necklace.

"Have you got it?"

Tracey lost her breath as she was yanked into a darkened doorway inches from the lobby exit. Her uncle was her uncle again. Curly hair clung damply to his face, and his eyes were red and puffy.

"Yes," she hissed. "But not here, we need to go." Outside their little alcove, she could hear people running past.

Uncle Donny threw a furtive glance over his shoulder. "They're looking for Miss Tearning, not me," she reminded him.

His shoulders dropped and he looked at her hopefully. "They didn't see you change?"

"No. And even if they suspected a disguise spell, they'll be looking for one person, not two. Let's go." She grabbed his arm and together they strolled right out through the hotel's main door and into bucketing rain that forced them to bolt for Uncle Donny's car. Safely ensconced inside, Tracey examined the necklace. The butterfly was the length of a lipstick tube and glittered brightly. "So, this is it? Case closed?"

Uncle Donny stared at the crystal and gems that made up the wings of the butterfly. Water dripped into his eyes.

"Well?" she snapped when he didn't answer.

"Yes, yes. Case closed. I'll call Miss Tearning in the morning to collect it. Great work, kiddo." The drive was short and it felt like only moments before he pulled into his parking spot behind his office.

Tracey looked at her phone. It had to be wrong. "Three A.M.!" she cried, "Uncle Donny! I have to be at school in six hours!"

"Oh, sorry sweetheart." He held out his hand, "Let me lock it away ..."

Every part of her body ached. "Just take me home."

"There's something about it, isn't there? The pendant, I mean. Look at it." His voice drifted. Tracey didn't think there was anything special about it. Impatiently, she followed him into the darkened office and watched him lock the butterfly necklace away in the safe under his desk. Case closed.

"Strength growing, unknown proportions …"

10

Tracey's head was heavy with exhaustion the next morning. She kept drifting back to last night but it was as though her thoughts were swimming through honey. Everything was overly bright and too loud. After her third yawn in as many minutes, Tony leaned over to whisper, "Did you really use a disguise spell?"

The dark shadows under her eyes from yesterday had shadows of their own today. She knew she looked totally washed out and red-eyed.

"Miss Masters?"

Tracey snapped upright at the sound of her name. Mr. Michaels was staring at her. "Sir?"

"The reading from yesterday …? *And when I told Terry, I said—*' What do you think Marcus was intending to say before he was cut off?"

She must have looked like a startled rabbit, wide-eyed and twitchy. She had no idea what the answer was. "I don't know, sir." Her face flamed. She couldn't explain why she hadn't read the chapter and doubted "I was helping my uncle break into a prince's hotel room" would go down too well.

Sinking lower in her chair, she fervently prayed for a reason to run out of class. Maybe someone would start a fire in chemistry. Behind her, she could hear Meena snickering. Tracey wished for the earth to open up beneath the evil girl's chair. The blaring of an alarm startled them all into looking up.

"Fire drill?" Mr. Michaels pulled the sourest face Tracey had ever seen. "Right, everyone up. Now!"

She ended up sitting on the grass outside the library reading the chapter she was supposed to have read last night. Jonny plopped down next to her, "Great timing, huh?"

"What?" She was at the point in the novel where Marcus was questioning Terry—the exact question Mr. Michaels wanted her to answer, so of course Jonny had to interrupt her now.

"The alarm. I thought you were going to melt into a puddle on the floor when Mr. Michaels glared at you. Then the alarm went off. Be honest with me, did you do that?"

"What?" She shot him a look of surprise. "Jonny, I would never."

"Hey, it's not bad thing. I think it's great."

"It wasn't me," she said vehemently. It was crazy timing though. A cold breeze brushed over her body raising the hairs on her arms. She shivered as she pondered the alarm. *Crazy.*

"Their end will reveal,
The mistakes they've made ..."

11

Uncle Donny wasn't at the office when Tracey arrived that afternoon. Miss Tearning's case file waited for her on her desk, so he'd definitely been in at some point. She had a sudden shock of thought. *Do I need to write a report too?* The cover sheet said Miss Tearning had not collected her property yet. Odd, considering how anxious she'd been to get the necklace back.

Tracey checked the calendar to see where Uncle Donny could be but found no appointments scheduled. Before she could wonder where he was, the phone rang.

"Hey kiddo, has Miss Tearning called?" Uncle Donny sounded out of breath.

"No — why?"

"Strange. I haven't been able to reach her. Can you try calling? Her number's in the file."

"Sure, Boss," she said, but he'd already hung up.

She called every number in the file, but couldn't locate Miss Tearning. The woman wasn't at home or at work, and her cell phone went straight to voicemail.

Trying to ignore a gnawing worry in her stomach, Tracey popped into her uncle's private office to see if he'd left any notes with a new number. Zip. The bell over the outer office door rang bringing Tracey to her feet. She stepped out of Uncle Donny's office and froze.

A large shadow reared up into the shape of a man and lunged for her. Tracey screamed and stumbled back slamming to a stop when she hit the wall.

"It's only a kid. We can handle this. You are not needed." A voice hissed from behind the monster. Tracey couldn't tear her eyes away from the undulating smoke. A wide mouth gaped open, growing closer and stretching to fill her vision. Another scream caught in her throat. The Shadowman swirled into a tornado of black and red before it swept out through the door. Two men wearing black masks stood in front of Tracey's desk and one was holding a gun. Tracey's hands flew up before the men could shout at her.

"Donny James?"

She shook her head, afraid to speak. *Oh God, oh God!* With a wave of his gun, the dark clad figure ordered her out of her uncle's private office. Tracey fell to her knees in front of her desk. The man holding the gun gestured for her to lie down. She buried her face into the floor, her body trembling. She couldn't think, couldn't breathe. Her bracelet began to buzz. Gasping she slapped a hand over it and forced her magic back, running her fingers down her arm to find her emergency band. *Oh God!* She decided not to wear it. *Idiot!* If she got out of this alive, finding it and putting it on would be the first thing she did.

The other man, taller with broader shoulders and a deeper voice demanded, "Where's the necklace, kid?"

With a shaking hand, she pointed to her uncle's private office. Scrunching her eyes shut, she pushed a little of her overflowing magic at the men. They gave no response to her probe — the blank feeling around them a clear sign they weren't Mage-kind. She flinched at the bang of the filing cabinet hitting the floor and clasped her hands over her ears to block the sounds of the men ransacking the office. *Where's Uncle Donny?*

Fearing he would walk right into the robbery worked to get her own fright under control. She had a choice to make, escape now or the try for the phone. They'd hear the bell above the door. No, she couldn't take that risk. If they came after her, they might kill her. If she could just push the second speed dial button on the phone, the police would be connected immediately.

Knowing she couldn't stand up to reach for the phone, she turned to her magic. The phone was a familiar object she used every day, which would make this spell possible. Recreating the phone exactly in her mind, she imagined the feel of the plastic under her fingertips. For a moment nothing happened. Her heart was pounding too fast, she couldn't focus. She glanced over her shoulder at the men in her uncle's office. Any moment now Uncle Donny would come back and ... what would Mom do when she found out? Did the crooks know Tracey was Mage-kind? Her fears raced uncontrolled. Gasping silently, she tried to find enough oxygen to fill her lungs. *Slow down, you have to slow down.* She tried again, drawing on her power to spark the spell. As soon as she felt pressure against her hand she moved her fingers on the floor, sketching out the shape of the phone. The image rose up from the carpet, a perfect three-dimensional replica.

She pressed the speaker button.

Above her head, she heard a click as the speaker button depressed. Quickly she activated the microphone and pressed the second speed dial button.

The sound of the police dispatcher's voice rose up from her desk. "Miltern Falls Police Department. What is your emergency?"

Her plan worked. But how could she tell the police what was happening from the floor?

"Hello? Are you in distress? Do you need help?" The voice grew louder.

"What's that?" The man with the gun stepped out of Uncle Donny's office and looked at Tracey. "Did you say something?"

"Please," she begged loudly. "Please don't shoot me. I'll be good, I promise." Her voice cracked as her pitch increased. *I want my mom!*

"Shut up!" the gunman yelled, kicking at Tracey's leg before returning to Uncle Donny's office. Tears sprang into her eyes at the sudden throbbing pain.

"It's not here," the unarmed man said. His croaky voice rose above the sound of furniture being upended.

"It has to be. Keep looking!"

The handset on Tracey's desk squeaked again, but neither man appeared to hear it.

"Where's the necklace?" the skinny goon demanded. All Tracey could see of the man's face above the scarf covering his mouth were his eyes.

They were small and seemed cold.

Biting back a scream, she said, "In-in the safe?" He'd put it there, hadn't he?

"It's not!" The goon's voice rose high enough to betray his growing panic.

"Look at the phone," Goon Two called suddenly.

Laying with her head pressed to the floor she spied a shirt button near the desk leg. The idea came to her in an instant. Before she had time to think through the dangers she called the button to her hand, spelled it with a spark of magic and sent the object into Goon Two's rolled up trouser cuff. *Please don't feel it.* He didn't look down.

"Where is the detective?" Goon One demanded, standing over Tracey.

"The phone, Mikey!" Goon Two reminded, grabbing his partner's arm.

"Christ, go!" They ran for the door and it slammed shut behind them with enough force to rattle the window. Tracey dropped her head to the floor and released the tears she was holding inside.

The ticking of the wall clock in the sudden silence was loud. Each move of the hand like a drum beat — sounding too slow compared to the rapid thudding of her heart. She tried to count the beats but lost track. When the door opened she peeked up through her fingers, afraid the goons had returned. Two police officers stood in the doorway, and one of them was Officer Jameson.

Both men had drawn their weapons and clasped them tightly. "Stay here," Officer Jameson hissed at her. He and his older, grey-haired partner moved quickly through the small office to clear it.

"They're both gone," Tracey said, but she wasn't sure they heard her — her voice seemed to be as frightened as she was.

Shiny boots appeared at her side. "Are you hurt?"

"No." She took the proffered hand and climbed to her feet, wobbling a little from the spacey feeling in her head.

Officer Jameson led her to the sofa. "You might be in shock. Can I call someone to come and get you?"

She searched her mind through the fog and finally landed on, "My uncle." Her whole body trembled. A blanket wrapped around her shoulders.

Clutching it, she looked up into Officer Jameson's kind face.

"My partner is calling your uncle, Miss Masters. Can you tell me if anything was taken?"

"No, they couldn't find it." Her voice sounded funny, all soft and shaky. She didn't know what was wrong with her. In her head, she kept hearing the goon with the gun shouting at her. Why had she ever thought she was ready to work as an actual detective? Her stomach hurt. She clasped her hands to her belly and hunched over. Thoughts of the necklace slithered into her mind and wrapped around her fears, smothering them. Questions began to surface in her mind. What was so important about the necklace that everyone wanted it so badly?

Officer Jameson sat down. "We have to stop meeting like this," he said. She could hear the smile in his voice.

"What, me terrified and running away from something?"

"You do seem to be a magnet for trouble."

He wasn't wrong. The exact same feeling she had when the Shadowman came after her stole into her body, sending shivers through her small frame. The goons had come for the necklace and brought the Shadowman with them. They were connected. She and her uncle had clearly stumbled onto something darker and more dangerous than they'd ever imagined. It was time to let the experts handle it. For a brief moment, Tracey thought about telling the nice officer about their case. She quickly slammed down on that urge. He was a Norm. He couldn't handle a Mage-kind monster. The tiny voice of reason that sounded a lot like her mom insisted Miss Tearning was a Norm too, therefore, it was a Norm case. But that Shadowman ...

The front door opened, and every head snapped toward the sound. Uncle Donny ran straight in falling to his knees in front of Tracey. He grabbed her hands and fussed over her. "Are you okay? Your mom's going to kill me."

She tried to tell him she was fine but he talked over her, insisting he would buy her anything she wanted to make her feel better. She didn't stop him. Behind her uncle, Officer Jameson's lips twitched.

Assured she was okay, Uncle Donny asked the officers about the break in. Tracey sat quietly until something they said focused her attention. She peered up as Uncle Donny said, "I was meeting a client, but she didn't show." Her uncle was pacing around the small office. Every now and then he paused and fiddled with something on his desk. Officer Jameson stood statue still in the doorway. His measured stare was locked onto her constantly moving uncle.

"Do you have any enemies that might want to hurt you?"

"I have no idea." Uncle Donny smiled, looking a little crazy around the eyes. He was making his *I'm perfectly innocent* face. Tracey hoped the officers wouldn't find it suspicious. She did, and immediately wondered what he was hiding.

Uncle Donny eyed Tracey over Officer Jameson's shoulder. He knew the gunmen had been looking for the necklace but he didn't seem to want the police to know about it. *Why?* "I should take Tracey home."

It wasn't until she was in her uncle's car and they were nearly to her block that he asked, "Are you going to tell your mom?"

She squinted. "Like I can hide it from her. She'll know."

"They were after the necklace, weren't they?"

"I thought you put it in the safe."

He shook his head. "I was meeting with Miss Tearning today to return it."

"So it's gone?" Relief flooded through her at the thought, warming her chilled body. Her hands were still shaking. She clasped them tightly together and looked up at her uncle's silence. She didn't like the expression on his face. "What?"

"Like I said, Miss Tearning didn't show up. I waited for over an hour," he said.

"So where is the necklace?"

He tapped his jacket pocket.

"Boss, one of those jerks had a gun. They wanted the necklace. You have to take it to the police and let them handle it."

"Can't do that, kiddo, but you're right about one thing—it's not safe in the office." He pulled the chain out of his pocket. The butterfly's wings caught the light of the setting sun, reflecting bright colors around the inside of the car. "Take it home with you and hide it in your room."

"*What?*" she all but screamed. "What part of armed and dangerous don't you get?"

As a reply he tossed the necklace onto her lap — it really was very pretty. She looked at it curiously. Opening her magic closet, she poked at the piece of jewelry. There was no response. Nothing tingled or sparked against her touch. It was nothing but a necklace. "This is such a bad idea."

"Just until I find Miss Tearning, then I'll call you and we can give it back to her — case closed."

Tracey closed her eyes and dropped her head to her chest. A creeping cold stole over her body telling her it was not going to be that simple.

"When I use my powers …
have you ever noticed anything strange?"

12

She hid the necklace behind the mirror on her desk where she found her emergency band immediately forcing it over her wrist. It magically stretched and then settled back into its bracelet shape. Bright pink cartoon faces smiled happily all over it. Mom and Dad gave all her siblings one when they were little. Tracey fingered the cold rubber band. It vibrated like her cell phone. The old spell was still active then.

Uncle Donny said he was trying to locate Catherine Tearning, but it was like she'd disappeared off the face of the planet. Or at least out of Miltern Falls. Tracey tried to explain the situation to Jonny and Tony at lunch, but even as she spoke she knew it made little sense.

"Why would she leave?"

"I don't know, Jonny." She couldn't stop her eyes from drifting up to Jonny's bowler hat. On anyone else, it would have looked silly, but Jonny pulled it off. Teamed with a blazer and jeans, he looked nice today.

Tony, on the other hand, couldn't have looked more like a geek if he'd tried. He wore his *I'm With Genius* shirt—the arrow pointed at his face—and torn tracksuit pants. Since she was working tonight, Tracey had picked a logo free shirt and skirt. It was a nice day, not too cold, not too hot. *If only the lunchroom didn't smell like burnt cheese and gym socks*, she thought, it might actually be nice just sitting here. You could pretend you were anywhere else than at school.

Her gaze drifted over the seated students eating as though they hadn't seen food for days. She didn't realize what she was searching for until she spied an artfully tousled head. Damian was turned away from her, talking to a table full of football jocks. He had their rapt attention. She wished he'd turn around so she could see his dreamy face. Feeling heat swell under her collar, she tore her gaze away and back to Tony.

"Any word on the goons?" Tony asked.

"Nope." Tracey popped the "p" sound and took a giant bite out of her apple. As she chewed she said, "The cops haven't called Uncle Donny either."

"Oh, that's disgusting," Jonny complained, covering his eyes. Tracey grinned, displaying the apple between her teeth, knowing it grossed him out. They were waiting for Laura. Her last class before lunch was music and it was located in a small building on the far side of the school grounds, meaning anyone with that class before lunch was always late.

"It's a shame no one knows about those goons. Isn't there a chance they might have gone after Miss Tearning?"

Tracey stared into space thinking about it. Yes, it was possible — if they thought Uncle Donny had already given the necklace back. She recalled the spell she'd put on one of the goons via that shirt button. She could track them to their hideout — but should she?

Jonny snapped his fingers under her nose to bring her attention back to the table. "What are you thinking?" he asked.

"It's nothing." She glanced around the lunch hall. Dave One sat at a table in the far corner. He caught Tracey staring. Even from this distance, she could see his eyes narrow. She turned her head quickly to look at Tony. *Do I admit I used magic?*

He stared back, his eyes focused. She felt a buzz against her skin as he reached out with his power. Little flickers, like pulses of pressure, brushed her arms. She threw up a shield to hide her guilty feelings but it was too late. His eyes widened. "What did you do?"

"Nothing."

"You're giving off the same jittery feeling as when you ate all of my chocolate stash. What did you do?" he asked.

Now discovered, she leaned her head closer. She couldn't meet Tony's eyes. "I might have put a tracking spell on one of the goons."

"What?" He pushed back from the table, his chair screeching loudly across the floor. Tracey could feel every eye in the lunch room swing around to stare at them. "You can't do that," he hissed.

"Sit down!" she said, waving him back to the table. "I did and I can't undo it now."

Jonny laughed and straightened his glasses. "That's brilliant. Now you can tell the cops!"

"She can't," Tony said.

At the same time Tracey said, "Jonny, I can't."

"But why not?"

It felt like her throat had closed up. She coughed trying to clear it. At last, she was able to speak. "If we tell the police, we'll have to tell them about the tracking spell, which means admitting I used magic outside of camp. They'll call in M-Force. They'll have to report the unauthorized use."

Jonny raised an eyebrow. "M-Force?"

"The Mage-kind police," she explained. Jonny's eyes appeared to pop out of his head. "There's Mage-kind police?"

"Don't you watch TV?" she asked, incredulous.

"Not really. Gamer, remember."

The swirling in her stomach was growing faster. She wanted to stop talking about this. *I shouldn't have done it.*

"Illegal magic use has to get reported," Tony confirmed.

"You guys use magic all the time, though," Jonny said, still confused.

Tracey tapped her bracelet. "Of course we do, only little stuff, but we're not supposed to get caught using it outside of home. I don't get my license until I'm eighteen."

"Oh yeah," Jonny said. "Bummer. What about telling the cops you tagged the goons with something your uncle spelled?"

Wouldn't work. "It's a fine line," she muttered.

"What do you mean?"

Tracey buried her face in her hands, her elbows pressed into the table. Through her fingers she admitted, "I created an object of power."

"Oh God," Tony moaned.

"A what? What's that?" Jonny asked.

"I put a spell—magic—onto an everyday object. A button in this case."

"What if —"

"What are you guys whispering about?" Laura's voice punctured their quiet bubble. "Are you talking about Damian?"

"Shhhhh," Tracey hissed as her face flamed, "Oh my God, Laura! Don't say that so loud!" She glanced at Damian again, but he still had his back to her. She'd be mortified if he thought they were talking about him. Her shoulders hiked higher around her ears as she tried to hide.

Laura giggled pulling her chair out. "Shove over, I need to eat. If I see Dave Two right now I'm going to punch him in the nose."

"What did he do?" Jonny asked. He angled his chair up on two legs to balance between the wall and the table.

"He said he hadn't done the reading because it was chapter thirteen, and apparently he has a phobia about the number thirteen."

"Seriously?" Tracey covered her mouth with a hand.

Tony snorted juice from his nose, making them all laugh.

"We spent the whole class reading chapter thirteen from our music theory textbook out loud to him." Laura picked several cheese pieces out of her salad. "So, what were you guys whispering about?"

"Tracey can track the goons who attacked her at Donny's."

"What, really?" Laura raised an eyebrow at Tracey.

Tracey's gaze dropped to the table. Even her ears felt hot now. It had been an impulse to spell the button, but the way they were looking at her—so impressed—just added to her embarrassment. "It doesn't matter because I can't do anything about it."

"You could tell your uncle and let him deal with it," Laura said before stuffing a fork full of lettuce into her mouth.

It was a good point—maybe she should talk to her uncle.

"Orrrr ..." Jonny drew out the word until they were all looking at him. He leaned over the table. "You activate the spell, we find out where the goons are hiding, and then we call the cops with an anonymous tip."

No freaking way. "My magic, Jonny. The cops could match the magical signature to me. They'd know Uncle Donny didn't spell it. My whole family could get in trouble." Her heart thumped hard in her chest. She couldn't take that risk, and said so. Jonny's face fell.

"Yeah, but—"

"I know you think it's a good idea Jonny, but you don't know what will happen," she told him. It was one thing to excitedly help Uncle Donny with a Norm case, it was another when magic was involved and she knew she couldn't get caught using it so flagrantly. Mom would have a fit. Tracey didn't want to think about how disappointed Dad would be. And what if M-Force *was* called in? Both Mom and Dad had scared her and her siblings silly with stories about M-Force. She didn't want to find out if the stories were true.

Tony waved his hand between himself and Tracey. "We have to be careful, Jonny."

"Well you shouldn't have to," Jonny sulked. "The goons are the bad guys, not you. If they don't have the button you can't get into any trouble. These bad guys need to be brought down, Trace. They broke into your uncle's office — they could have hurt you!"

"I'm okay, Jonny," she mumbled. His concern made her love him all the more. She really had the best friends.

"It's just not right," he continued to grumble. "You should be able to protect yourself."

She was still thinking about Jonny's comment later that night. It brought a smile to her face every time. He didn't think there was anything wrong with the use of magic — he even thought it was cool. But he was special and his attitude was rare. Still, his idea could work. On one hand, if they found the goons hideout they could anonymously notify her uncle. They might even be able to identify the masked men. On the other hand, if they were caught, she and her friends would be in serious danger.

It wasn't fair. She wanted to be a detective, like her uncle, but the limitations on magic use were stopping her from having the bad guys arrested.

Her magic. She alone could track them. She could catch the bad guys and potentially solve Uncle Donny's case. Uncle Donny, her parents … they'd all then have to admit she could be her uncle's assistant. She could show them all.

"What is wrong with you?"

"What?" Tracey rolled over on her bed to stare at the doorway, Sarah gaped at her room. Tracey looked around, wondering what her sister was looking at. "Oh."

Tracey's room was a mess. Three jackets and half a dozen different shoes lay in the middle of her room. Her school bag hung off her bed and school books were scattered all over the floor. Her laundry basket contained none of her dirty clothing and there were empty glasses on every available surface. It looked like Simon and Charlie's room, not hers.

"What happened in here? Did something explode?"

"I've been busy."

"You've been staring at the wall. I've stood here for ages, and you haven't moved."

"Why were you watching me?" Disturbed that she hadn't noticed her sister, Tracey quickly explained. "I was just thinking." She sounded guilty. She didn't mean to, it's just that she didn't want Sarah asking what she was thinking about. Sarah's magic was still young and uncontrolled—her focus, as with all young kids, was not all that strong. She'd pick up on Tracey's emotions and figure out she was up to something. If Sarah told mom and dad, Tracey would be grounded quicker than you could say *privacy*. Tracey quickly redirected her thoughts by imagining a football jersey.

"Thinking about a boy?" Sarah grinned. It was the sort of grin that said Sarah was storing the information away to use against Tracey later. "Is it Tony?"

Tracey reared back. "Of course not. He's gay, Sarah."

"So he says."

"Hey!" Having heard enough, Tracey lurched to her feet, and advanced on Sarah. The younger girl actually looked startled at Tracey's anger and backed up quickly. "That's mean, Sarah. I don't want to hear you say that ever again!"

Sarah looked away and shuffled her feet. When she looked up again, her face took on a nasty smirk. "Then who were you thinking about? It was a boy, wasn't it?"

"Either come in or go away," she snapped. *Go away!*

"I'm going." Sarah rolled her eyes. "I just came up here to tell you about the phone."

"What about it?"

"It rang — stop yelling at me."

"So, who was it?"

"Uncle Donny."

Tracey shoved past her sister and raced down the hall to the stairs. Sarah mumbled behind her, "Better not let Mom see your room like that."

"You're not going out, Tracey," Mom said when she reached the living room. Her parents sat on the sofa watching a legal drama.

Tracey waved a hand and snatched up Mom's cell phone. "Hey, Boss."

"Hey, kiddo — listen, I'm not opening the office tomorrow. I've tracked down Miss Tearning, so I'm off to talk to her. Good news for you — you get the afternoon off."

"Oh, cool. Thanks," she said. This made her decision whether or not to tell him about her tracking spell even harder. Shooting a look over her shoulder she could see her parents were listening, no way could she do it now. Jonny's frustrated voice played in her mind. He was right. She should be able to use her magic. In that instant she made a decision. "Okay, see you Friday. Good luck."

When Tracey spun around Mom asked, "So Donald won't be around tomorrow?"

She thought quickly. "Yeah, he's going out of town, but called to ask if I could go into the office to finish the files. He said to keep all the closed signs up." *Liar, liar, pants on fire.*

"I don't like the idea of you working in that office alone," Dad said leaning forward as if he was going to stand up.

"Especially after what happened." Tracey's mom had her angry face on. They sat next to each other on the sofa. Dad put his hand on Mom's arm and it seemed to settle her a little.

Tracey stared at her feet. "I know, Mom." Her heart thumped steadily in her chest. *Come on, don't stop me from going, please?* She willed her mom not to scan her.

Her parents looked at each other. "Tom, I don't think she should be working there at all. She's too young. It's obviously more dangerous working for Donald than we thought."

"Mom. It's fine, please," Tracey whined. "Dad?" *They won't stop me from working with Uncle Donny. They won't, will they?*

"Honey, your mom is right. That man had a gun."

"Dad!" This was not good. Her stomach clenched. She had no idea how to convince her parents that her uncle's office was safe, especially because she wasn't planning to stay there for long. "It was scary, but I'm okay. Those men haven't been back, and Uncle Donny installed a new security system. All the bells and whistles, he said. He even redid the spells on the office." She saw disbelief cross their faces. *Need more.* "I helped."

Mom heaved a sigh of relief and shot her husband a look. He nodded slowly. Tracey did her best to breath evenly.

"Officer Jameson said he'd drive past Uncle Donny's office more often too, so I can't imagine being safer anywhere in the world. Please, it's only for two hours after school. If I call home to tell you I'm okay —" She was such a big fat liar. Her mom was going to work it out and ground Tracey so hard! Or worse, ban Tracey from watching the TV or, or … *oh,* what if Mom took away her WiFi access? She held her dad's gaze fighting very hard not to look away.

"Okay, okay," he yielded, laughing. "I guess that sounds pretty secure."

"Honey, be careful, and yes — call home every half hour when you're there — and wear your emergency band."

Tracey pushed her sleeve up. "Already done. Do I still have to call every thirty minutes?"

"Yes."

"Mom!" Every thirty minutes seemed extreme.

"Your choice."

"Sure, that's fine." She dropped into the closest armchair doing her best to appear dejected when in reality her heart was thumping wildly with excitement as her mom unmuted the television. Her parents returned to Detective Manning chasing this week's bad guy along a dark street.

She *was* going to track those goons down after school tomorrow night, steal the button back and call the cops. And she was going to ask her friends to go with her.

He's my friend.

I thought he was my friend.

"You knew?"

13

I t was dark.

If Tracey squinted, she could almost see the red car. Night around her was so deep she couldn't tell where she was. Her skin turned icy cold; her breath appeared out of her mouth like a cloud of smoky ice. Tingles broke out across the back of her neck as something moved just out of her vision.

She ran. The world disappeared. *This must be a dream—it has to be.* Or a nightmare. As soon as the thought crossed her mind, the world shimmered and changed. Tracey stood in the center of a spotlight. The darkness around the circle of light was all encompassing—black hole black. The scent of dirty soil and rotting leaves filled her nose. Her heart thudded painfully in her throat like it was trying to escape through her mouth. She swallowed it back down, but it became stuck as her throat tightened. She choked and gasped, searching for air, but none could be found.

The darkness laughed. The sound crashed against her skin like waves. The steady beat surrounded her until it was all she could hear. A shadow pulled away from the darkness, taking on the shape of a man. Long, ghostly red fingers shot toward her. Tracey screamed. The laugh grew louder until it echoed in her ears, jolting the base of her spine.

"What do you want?" she cried, unable to hear her own voice. The laughter stopped, and there was only silence.

The Shadowman stepped to the light's edge. He wavered back and forth but did not cross the threshold.

When he spoke, Tracey woke up gasping for air, one word thundered through her mind. "*You.*"

"The one who leads,
Who dreamed of more,
Lost her mind in the fire,
Her charge now her curse ..."

14

The following afternoon, Tracey and her friends gathered inside her uncle's office. The outer door was locked and the *CLOSED* sign was up in the window. Tracey had an old map of Miltern Falls unfolded in front of her as she prepared to cast her search spell. Tony was acting as her anchor, as well as to provide a power boost if she needed it. Hopefully, the goons hadn't left town or the spell was going to be a real fizzle. Guilt niggled at the base of her skull. She scratched at her skin trying to move it away. Every time she closed her eyes, a vision of her mom appeared shaking her head. *Gah, go away!* Rubbing sweaty hands against her trousers, she swirled her tongue behind her lips to moisten her dry mouth.

"So, we've got everything you need now?" Jonny asked for the fifth time. He looked exasperated, his hands waved in the air dramatically.

Tracey had called home twice, finished the files, and cleaned the office. It was time to admit, she *was* stalling. All of her determination from the night before fled from her nightmares. Right now, she was worried she might *actually* find the bad guys. She had to push her worries and fear into a ball and lock them away in her mind. If her heightened emotions affected the spell, it could end up pointing them anywhere. Fear was a powerful negative force. Too much could make spells go wonky, or even reverse them. Fear always got in the way, and right now, Tracey was scared spit-less. "I could do with a glass of water," she whispered.

"Oh, for crying out loud. What are you, four?" Jonny groaned. Laura jumped to her feet and fetched Tracey a cold bottle of water from the mini-fridge.

Tony pointed a finger at Tracey. His power prickled against her shoulder. "Get on with it."

Her stalling was apparently getting on everyone's nerves. Tracey rubbed her shoulder and huffed, "Okay, fine." She reminded herself why she'd been so determined to do this, to prove herself capable.

Closing her eyes, she took a deep breath and released it slowly, letting her thoughts go blank. On her tenth breath, she picked up a small cup of sugar and sprinkled it over the map, pulling on her power. It swelled beneath her rib cage. Still breathing steadily, she reached for Tony in her mind. The touch of his magic filled the gaps in hers and smothered her remaining fear. She was not alone. She was in control. Breathing deep, she tugged a wisp of his energy out to add to her own, letting it swirl inside her chest until it became an orange ball of light. She pushed the ball up her chest and down her right arm. When it gathered in her hand she pushed it out of her body and over the map, picturing the shirt button in detail, from the color and size right down to the little chip on the edge. She blew on the map and said, "Find," while in her head chanting a mix of sounds that formed the song of her spell.

Laura's gasp was like the crack of a twig breaking underfoot. Tracey opened her eyes to watch the sugar on the map swirl up into a mini-tornado of white snow. Rising almost as high as her head, it spun rapidly and then collapsed. A line of sugar crossed the map from the box shape of her uncle's office to the summit of Mount Hawthy. "Huh?" She said staring at the grainy path.

Jonny's mouth was wide open. "I've never seen anything like that."

"That was beautiful." Laura's eyes glittered in the residue light of the spell still filling the room.

Tracey felt her face flame. "I didn't really think that would work," she admitted.

Tony grinned. "Duh!"

"Come on," Jonny said, picking up his backpack.

The hairs on Tracey's arms and neck still tingled with excess energy. She focused inward and imagined sucking her magic back into her chest.

"I know the bus that lets out at the summit. We still have time. Let's go before it gets dark."

She grinned. "In and out. We get the button and call the cops," she said. Her friends all grinned and nodded. "Let's do it!" Jonny fist-pumped the air, making them all laugh.

The bus ride was twenty-five long minutes of bumpy road. The sugar trail ended at a place called Journey Court. Rocketing around the tree-lined corners heading toward the summit, Tracey could only see forest for miles around. The long trip gave her plenty of time to think. *Is this a bad idea?* "Where are all the roads?" she asked.

Her friends ignored her. Laura listened to a new release on her phone and the boys threw paper at one another from the seats behind her. Tracey held on tightly as the bus swerved sharply around another bend. Civilization disappeared through the window. She didn't understand why she was suddenly so afraid. This was what she'd always wanted—danger, adventure, and a chance to use her magic. Her hands were trembling. Goosebumps covered both arms like a rash and she felt queasy—of course, that last one might have been from the bus ride. She slammed into the window as they hurtled around the next bend.

"Last stop, kids." The driver called sooner than she wanted.

They were the only ones left on the bus. "When does the next bus come past?" she asked, hovering in the open doorway.

"Every thirty minutes."

Fruit tingles.

The first thing she did when they got off the bus was call home. After mollifying her mom, she stretched out with her power to get a sense of the area. Beside her, she felt Tony do the same. He flinched and backed up quickly. There was something here—a strange oily energy emanating from somewhere nearby.

She opened her eyes on a dark overgrown area of dense woodland. "You feel that?"

"Feel what?" Jonny asked. He stood on the dirt path that led in the opposite direction. The scent of mulch and dirt filled the air. There was a thickness that muffled sound.

"Kind of a fuzzy wobble," Tony answered.

"What?" Laura eyed Tracey oddly.

She confirmed the feeling with a nod. "It's hard to explain, Laura. It's just a feeling and an image. Like the air is not quite right."

"Not right?" Laura echoed.

"So it's telling you to go this way, right?" Jonny said pointing up the well-trodden path. The look on his face was hopeful but he seemed to know they were not going to say yes. Tony gestured in the direction of the overgrown woods and Jonny's shoulders dropped.

"Come on then." Tracey hitched her backpack higher and led the way toward the bad feeling. The closer they drew to the darkness, the quieter the four friends became. Shadows danced as a light breeze ruffled the tree branches. A *click-clack* sound of wood against wood caused them to twitch and spin in all directions. Tracey held up her hand. "Stop." Closing her eyes, she searched the wood. "Just ahead."

They broke through a wall of trees and emerged onto a silent, cobble-stoned street. "What is this place?" Laura asked in a soft voice.

Tracey couldn't believe what she was looking at. There were eight cottages, four to either side of the street. Fancy lights lined a paved footpath.

In the middle of nowhere, surrounded by a dark wood, was the perfect suburban dream out of another time. There were no signs of life. Nothing. No movement, no sound at all. Tracey waved her hands around as if pushing at the very air itself. Her head felt thick and her nose blocked up. She shook her head and snorted but couldn't clear it. Pinning her nose closed, she sniffed hard.

"It's like a film set waiting for the cast and crew to appear," Jonny muttered.

Tracey had been to the film studio at the base of Mount Hawthy last year, but from what she remembered it had been filled with noise and movement. This was so unlike that memory it was like a comparing chocolate to a cauliflower. Maybe it was an old set built once for a movie and then left abandoned.

"It's like a horror film. Where is everyone?" Laura asked.

Tracey crept forward. Her friends walked so close behind her they

120

practically stepped on her heels. The feeling of dark energy grew until it surrounded them. The air crackled against Tracey's skin. Hairs rose as if electrified. Her fingers tingled.

The dark energy spiked.

Tracey froze.

"Stay away from the shadow.
Don't let it touch you ..."

15

She glanced at Tony. He looked like a spooked horse; all eyes, flared nostrils, and teeth. Moving quickly to his side she put an arm around his shoulders. "Tony, close your eyes." She had to repeat it a few times before he heard her. When he clenched his eyes shut, she pressed her hands against his shoulders and pushed a bubble of magic out to surround him. The instant he was encased, he sighed and sagged into her arms. She collapsed with him to keep his head from smacking the ground.

"What's wrong?" Laura gasped.

Jonny leaned over them. "Is he okay?"

Tracey nodded. "Just give him a minute. There's a dark energy around us that's a little overwhelming."

Laura gave her an odd look but stayed silent. Tracey couldn't explain why she wasn't as affected by the feeling—it should have flattened her, too. Her skin itched like bugs were crawling all over her body. She could feel it scratching at her mind, but forced it back by imaging spaceship shields like those used in her favorite sci-fi movies.

Tony clasped her hand with trembling fingers. They were so cold. She pushed more golden magic at him, pressing over his skin like a blanket. Color seeped back into his cheeks and he began to breathe easier.

"Feel better?" she asked. His expression grew determined as he focused on creating his own shield. At his nod, she withdrew her shield bubble. After a moment, he climbed back to his feet, wobbling only once. Jonny moved up beside him and threw an arm around his shoulder.

Laura inched to Tracey's side. "Is it really bad?"

She thought about the empty stillness that pressed upon her, searching for any crack in her armor. "It's not good."

"Should we leave?" Laura nervously eyed the dark trees behind them.

Tracey clutched Laura's hand. "We're already here. Tony seems to be okay now." Her voice wobbled. She glanced nervously over her shoulder. They'd have to wait for the bus anyway. As a group, they stepped onto the creepy, empty street. "I think it would be faster if we split up."

At the same time, Jonny said, "We should stick together."

Tracey snorted. "Okay, how about one Mage-kind and one Norm. I'll go with Jonny. Tony, you go with Laura. If you see anything or sense anything, whistle."

"I don't like this," Laura muttered. "It's like every horror movie I've ever seen. You don't split up, ever."

"Wait." Tony pulled two small stones from his pocket and held them up.

"Oh, good idea," Tracey said, happily taking one of them. They had been part of a project he'd worked on for camp — to make the stones locate each other when separated. Only Tony's spell hadn't quite worked the way he'd wanted.

If he tapped one stone, the other vibrated. They'd used them to send coded messages to each other instead. Well they did until their camp counselor caught on and confiscated them. Tony must have spelled more. They were the ideal secret communication devices. Who would suspect a stone?

"Two taps if you need help," he said.

Tracey nodded. Turning to Jonny, she pointed to the first house. "Come on."

Laura and Tony disappeared in the opposite direction while Tracey and Jonny crept along the wooden fence that bordered the first house. The fence travelled the entire length of all four yards. As they moved along the fence line, they discovered a small alley ran between house two and house three. Just wider than Jonny's shoulders the alley ran all the way down between the houses and opened up on the street. *Shortcut?* She closed her eyes and reached out with her mind to search for any sign of life. All was quiet.

They crept down the pebbled path. The crunch of their footsteps was enough to send a shiver down her spine.

The stone in her hand buzzed twice. She stared at it in surprise.

Her skin broke out in goose pimples. For a split second, she wanted to run. She smothered the thought. A true detective wouldn't run from danger. She waved frantically at Jonny. He stopped. She held up the stone and pointed across the street.

If the wannabe burglars were hiding in one of the houses, Tracey and Jonny would be seen crossing the road. She tapped on the stone to let Tony know they were coming and waved Jonny to retreat back up the alley.

As they reached the end Jonny cried out and collapsed. *Jonny!* A man dressed in black appeared where Jonny had been standing. He wore a mask over the lower half of his face like a bandit out of an old western film. Tracey gasped and backed up. The man in black stepped over Jonny's body and walked toward Tracey. She turned to run but skidded to a stop. Another man was right in front of her. *Oh God, oh God!* Sweat broke out over her skin. A quick glance over her shoulder showed the first man hadn't moved. He was waiting for her. Her mind went blank.

"Move," the second man said. His magical void was familiar. It was the goon who'd broken into Uncle Donny's office. She twitched her hand toward her emergency band. "Keep your hands where I can see them." Thrusting her hands into the air she led the way back down the tight alley, passing a motionless Jonny. This was all her fault. She tried to pull magic from her chest but nothing happened. *Run!* Her body twisted wanting to follow the direction of her mind. A hard poke in the center of her back stopped her cold. Fear twisted inside her, darkening her vision. She couldn't stop herself from looking back. Jonny lay sprawled on the ground. The sight of his chest moving sent waves of relief through her. *He's alive!* She tried her magic again, but couldn't touch it. She couldn't focus.

When the masked man prodded her again, Tracey fell into the fence, slamming into something cold. *A hinge?* She hadn't seen that earlier. The man made her open the gate in the fence around the second house. She mentally hit herself over the head — she should have known to check for settled spell vibrations. Spells in place for a long time became dormant, activating only when something triggered it. Trembling, she imagined her parents' faces when they were told she was missing. It was a mistake to have come up here. Despair sucked at her stomach as horrors filled her head. *Where are they taking me?*

The two men ushered her through a side door into the house. Her heart beat frantically as she was prodded into a bright kitchen. Her friends sat at the table, their hands tied to the chairs. When she entered, their hopeful expressions fell. Tears glistened in Laura's eyes.

Tracey was pushed into a chair at the head of the table. Laura mouthed Jonny's name. "He's okay," Tracey said quickly, willing it to be true.

One of the masked men tied Tracey's hands to the arms of the chair. The plastic of the tie dug into her skin when she tried to move. She stretched her fingers but couldn't reach her emergency band. Her gaze flew to Tony. His face was red on one side of his cheek like he'd been hit by something. Scared of what was going to happen next, Tracey's mind darted in all directions but she couldn't think of an escape. She couldn't think of anything at all. Tears prickled in her eyes, smearing her vision.

A third man entered the room. He wore black clothing like the others, but his mask was red. The power emanating from him hit Tracey like a punch to the stomach. Wave upon wave of it crashed over her body, tugging at her mind like an ocean tide. She could feel Tony's terror by the way his magic burst open in an uncontrollable spray over the table. It seemed to shake her magic loose. She felt it throw itself against the door in her chest, desperate to get out. As much as she'd wanted to feel her magic before, she was suddenly scared to let it out. She clung onto the door as it rattled. Her instincts screamed at her to keep her magic secret.

The masked man's eyes were nothing more than dark brown orbs as he stared at each of the captives. No one said a word. The quiet scared Tracey more than the shouting of the two goons when they'd broken into her uncle's office. This was something worse. Her heart thundered so loudly in her ears it blocked all other sound.

A curling red smoke seeped from the man's hands. Tracey gulped back a scream as the ghost fingers reached for Laura. No Mage-kind armband or watch was wrapped around his wrist—nothing to indicate he was a registered user. When the smoke fingers came to rest on Laura's shoulders, her face twisted into a silent scream.

Tracey's stomach climbed into her throat. She was going to be sick.

After an endless moment, the masked man released Laura and stepped toward Tony.

"*No!* Stop it!" Tracey cried, tugging frantically at the ties binding her hands, twisting to try and reach her emergency band. She couldn't bend her wrist far enough to touch it. She could do nothing to help her friends. Her mind blanked as a hole in her chest gaped wide. *My fault, it's all my fault.*

The masked man pressed his smoky hands to Tony's shoulders and sighed.

Tony's eyes sprang wide and he gurgled softly. His student bracelet, pinned to the side of the chair, flared red and began to flash.

The masked man straightened as the smoke fingers rose up off Tony's shoulders. "Not you."

Tracey stilled. The man looked at her from across the table, his eyes glittered in anticipation. "What about you?"

"Well, hello there.
I was not expecting you."

16

The window behind Laura shattered as something the size of a baseball sailed through. It landed on the floor between the two goons and burst apart. White smoke spewed from the top quickly filling the kitchen. It stung Tracey's nose and throat, forcing tears from her eyes. The men doubled over, coughing harshly.

"Get back, get back," one shouted.

The man in the red mask swept from the room in a swirl of red smoke. The two goons raced after him.

When they were gone, the kitchen door cracked open.

Jonny poked his head in. "Hey." Tracey deflated as adrenaline left her body. *Jonny's okay.* Her body felt like she'd been boxing for hours. Every part of her ached, especially her chest. But seeing Jonny acted like an energy drink. She breathed deeply and grinned at him. Within seconds he had them untied. Coughing hard and with tears still streaming from their eyes, Tracey and her friends ran outside before the bad guys realized they were gone.

They were halfway down the empty street when Tracey heard a shout behind them. Her head whipped around. The masked men were after them.

"Over there!"

"Go, go!" Tracey shouted, leading her friends straight for the woods. She twisted her hands together and whispered, "Hide, hide, never find," under her breath. It was a spell she'd used against her brothers when she was little playing hide and seek. It should disguise their path through the woods. For it to be really effective though, they would have to actually hide.

She ran up to Jonny, her chanting breaking off as she coughed from whatever it was he had put in the stink bomb. "We need to get undercover," she gasped.

He shot her a crazy look, but she was adamant. Hiding was their only option. The crashes and shouts behind them were growing louder, spurring them into action.

"Over here!" Tony cried, pointing to a scraggy bush. Tracey ran toward it.

"Are you kidding?" Laura skidded to a stop beside them.

Tony pushed the branches away to expose a deep hole. It would be a tight squeeze, but they forced themselves inside. Tracey ended up with Jonny's elbow jammed into her side. Tony's face was smooshed against the trunk while Laura was bent almost double. When they let go, the branches sprang back over them, hiding them from view. A twig dug into Tracey's shoulder. Pollen and crushed leaves saturated the air. Tracey's nose blocked up again. She sneezed.

"Shhhh." Laura gasped, shoving a hand over her own mouth to quiet her rapid breathing. Tracey sucked in a shallow breath and sketched the spell pattern with her hands again. She lowered her voice to barely whisper the spell words, but something was wrong. She couldn't feel any magic at all.

"You're still shielding," Tony hissed.

Oh, she'd forgotten. Peering through one eye, Tracey opened the little door in her chest. If she let her magic out all at once the man in the red mask would sense the sudden release and know where they were hiding. Thinking of Uncle Donny, she let her magic seep into her hands. The sigils she sketched began to glow. When she felt a buzz snap around them, she stopped.

They waited.

Laura dug her nails into Tracey's arm as slow, measured footsteps approached, stopping too close, next to their hiding place. Tracey held her breath, pretending to be a statue, waiting for the inevitable moment when they'd be discovered.

The feet shuffled as though turning in a wide circle, and then a voice spoke. "Interesting." The man chuckled before walking away.

Tracey made them wait another ten long minutes before she pushed them all out of the bush. Her friends were covered in twigs, green leaf fragments, and scratches.

"Do you think they've gone?" Laura asked.

Tracey wasn't sure. She grabbed onto Jonny's arm, her words exploding out of her, "Three questions: Are you okay? What did you do? And *how* did you make a smoke bomb?"

Jonny held up a hand. "Let's get out of here first, then I'll tell you everything."

It wasn't until they were back on the bus that Tracey felt she could finally breathe easy. Her shirt stuck to her back and her skin felt clammy. She called home. It was harder than she'd thought to keep fear from altering her voice. Mom questioned her at length as if she suspected they weren't at Uncle Donny's. When Tracey hung up she felt mentally drained.

Jonny threw himself along the back seat of the bus. Tony, Laura, and Tracey sat a row in front and leaned over the back of their seats to stare at him.

"You just keep the makings of a smoke bomb in your pocket?" Laura asked. Her voice was pitched higher than normal, her words firing out faster.

Jonny stared at her. "Don't you?"

"Cool," Tony said and offered his fist for Jonny to bump.

"Well, I'm sure glad you did today," Tracey told him. "Jonny—are you okay? When that man shot you, I thought you were dead."

Laura and Tony both shouted. "Shot?"

"He pointed that thing at me and then I woke up alone in the middle of who knows where. It must have been a Taser or something. I have a ripping headache."

"You should get checked out, Jonny," Laura told him.

"Naw, it's all good," he said, though he was squinting and his right eye twitched.

"And what about you, Tony?" Tracey asked.

The red mark on Tony's cheek had started to darken into a nasty bruise. "I'm okay," he mumbled. He avoided Tracey's stare. Only the two of them had been able to feel the true power of the masked man and Tony had been physically touched. Tracey's stomach lurched. She clutched her belly with both hands and swallowed, breathing shallowly to stop from throwing up.

"Did we get the button? Who were those goons?" Jonny asked, rubbing at his temples.

"They were definitely the ones who broke into Uncle Donny's office," Tracey told them. It was their voices, she was sure of it. Even covered in masks, their body shapes and movements had sparked a feeling of déjà vu. "We can't call the cops — I didn't get the button back."

"Something is going on up there, that's for sure. Why would they have been wearing masks if they thought no one was around?" Laura asked. "And what's the point of a street full of empty houses in the middle of nowhere? Who would build that?"

No one seemed to have an answer.

"That man in the red mask is so powerful," Tony whispered. Even though they could barely hear him, his words snapped their attention his way. He stared out the window and wouldn't turn around.

Tracey shuddered. The look in the masked man's eyes had scared her silly. "My tracking spell led us up there. We know they're after the necklace. It all comes back to the necklace. Why does everyone want it?"

"We should tell Donny," Laura said. Tracey didn't agree. Her uncle was no match for the man in red. If they told him what happened, he'd want to go up to Mount Hawthy to check it out, putting himself in serious danger.

After a few minutes, Laura spoke again. "It was awful."

"What was?" Tracey examined her friend. Laura was pale and her hands trembled where they lay in her lap.

"When he touched me. It was so cold, like ice pricking at my skin."

"He was *Searching*," Tony whispered, sliding further down on his seat. The bruise on his face was growing darker by the second.

"Searching?" Laura asked.

"Magical *Searching*," Tracey confirmed.

136

"What did it feel like to you, Tony?" Laura asked, leaning forward. Jonny sat up.

For a moment the freaked-out boy didn't answer. He swallowed and finally turned around staring directly at Tracey. "It was cold, like fingers sliding into my brain. He was looking for something. I could feel his disappointment when he didn't find it."

Tracey was glad the man in the red mask hadn't touched her. There was no way she could have blocked an attack like that. *What was he searching for?* The question stayed with her all the way back down the mountain.

When she got home mom was setting the last plate down on the dining table. "Good timing, Tracey," she said. She did a double-take as she really looked at her daughter. "What on earth have you been doing?"

Glancing down at her dirty clothes, Tracey said, "Oh, you know me, clumsy as always. I tripped and fell into a bush." She shrugged, hoping her mom would buy the excuse.

Mom stared for a long time. Tracey felt her mom's magic swell out and swing toward her. She closed herself down and waited. The older woman narrowed her eyes and muttered under her breath before she waved Tracey toward the door. "Go and get changed." She threw up a hand. "Oh, and can you do me a favor? Tomorrow after school, can you pick up some candles and a box of matches for Sarah's birthday?"

Tracey's eyes widened. She'd totally forgotten about Sarah's birthday, hadn't even got a present yet. "You need them tomorrow? Her birthday's next week."

"Yes, and you know we'll forget them." That was true. They forgot candles every birthday. It was almost a tradition at this stage not to have candles on their birthday cakes.

The distraction worked to take her mind off her recent trauma. Tracey raced up the stairs to her bedroom while the sound of a stampede below told her Dad and her siblings were moving into the kitchen. If she didn't hurry there would be no food left for her.

She changed, washed her hands and returned to the table just as Mom placed a bowl of mashed potatoes into the center of the table. Tracey reached for the jug of raspberry soda. In the red liquid she saw ghostly fingers reach toward her. She jerked backward nearly tipping the jug over.

"Tracey?"

The family was all staring at her. "What?" she snapped, squeezing in between Sarah and Charlie.

"What have you been up to?" Charlie asked around a mouthful of food.

"I was at Laura's," she said and piled her plate high. She was starving! Mom shot her another odd look. *Fruit tingles!* She was supposed to be at Uncle Donny's, wasn't she? "I mean, I went there after work." Mom didn't mention Tracey's slip, but her gaze stayed suspicious. All was quiet while the family ate. The spread of food disappeared quickly. Inside her head, Tracey heard a wicked laugh and felt what she imagined as fingers of red stroke her arms.

Sarah leaned over. "Wanna come to the mall with me this weekend?"

Tracey couldn't focus on what her sister was saying, couldn't stop thinking about the man in the red mask. "Yeah, okay. Whatever."

Sarah wriggled in her seat and grinned. "Honey, I had a call from Gemma today," Mom announced, staring at her husband.

Tracey's dad didn't hide the exaggerated roll of his eyes. It made Tracey giggle. It came out like a cackle — too loud — crazy even. Every eye turned her way before returning to Dad as he said, "Oh, yes, and what did she call to complain about today?"

"Tom!" Mom snapped. Then, more gently added, "She's coming to stay for a few days."

"Oh." Dad put down his fork carefully. "Did you forget my mother is coming to stay this week?"

Mom stopped eating. "Oh, dear."

Charlie tried to hide his smile behind a glass of orange juice. Simon sputtered into his potatoes and Peter dropped his head into his hands. Sarah just looked confused. "What's wrong with that? Grandma comes over all the time."

The boys started to laugh. Tracey leaned over to whisper, "Aunt Gemma and Grandma don't get on." Her sister wore an unfamiliar perfume. The scent — strawberry and flowers — tickled Tracey's nose. She pulled back from Sarah and scrubbed at the sneeze locked in her nostrils.

"Really?" Sarah asked, still looking confused.

"Aunt Gemma is an Anti-Mage," Tracey told her, twitching and rubbing the skin of her face.

"Honey, she's not as bad as that," their mom interrupted.

Dad pointed his fork at Sarah and said, "No, she's worse."

That night, Tracey's sleep was disrupted by dreams of creepy trees, and fingers of smoke and ice. Her old nightmare about Nana also made an appearance, but it wasn't as scary as it used to be. It must have been triggered by Grandma's looming visit. Dad's mom was like chocolate to mom's mom being like an egg. They were just so different. It was weird that Tracey's brain had connected the two. She couldn't stop yawning the next morning as she told Tony about the impending visitors. They walked slowly toward their first class, not anxious to get there any sooner than they had to.

"When do they arrive?" he asked.

"This afternoon," she told him. "I won't be there for the initial explosion, though. I'm going straight to Uncle Donny's after school. I wanna know what happened with Miss Tearning."

"Text me if you hear anything interesting," he said leading the way into English class.

Tracey hoped they'd get a chance to do some creative writing today—her bad dreams were inspiring her to write something creepy. The two Daves were huddled together at the back of the room. Tracey wondered who their target would be today. Mr. Michaels connected his tablet to the electronic whiteboard and started typing questions.

A damp projectile hit Tracey in the ear. She glared at the Daves. Dave One wore a black and green football jersey—nowhere to hide a straw. Dave Two fiddled with his baseball hat, and there, hidden in his hand—a broken pen. *Ewwwww, Spitball!*

Mr. Michaels didn't look up. Tracey leaned close to Tony and whispered, "The two Daves are being asshats."

"Yeah, I know. Breathe and ignore them, right?"

"Right."

Another wad of wet paper landed on the table between them. They eyed it and laughed. "Terrible aim," Tony said.

"Hey," a hushed voice behind them snapped. Tracey glanced over her shoulder and saw Damian glaring at the Daves. To her surprise, they raised their hands in surrender. Damian turned around and smiled at Tracey before focusing his attention back on his workbook.

"Oh my God," Tony whispered, leaning into Tracey's side.

All thoughts of the man in the red mask or Miss Tearning's necklace vanished. Tracey's face heated and the smile that blossomed didn't leave her face for the rest of the day.

"What do you want?"

"You."

17

When she got to work that afternoon Uncle Donny was nowhere to be seen. Her skin crawled when she realized she was alone. "Grrrrr!" Shaking her body, she told herself to buck up. She was safe here. If she let her fears control her brain she might as well stay home. Only the brave were private detectives and she still wanted to be one. So the fear had to go—well, be controlled at least.

She got to work sorting out the trash, vacuumed, and then listened to the answering machine. There were two messages, and one could possibly be a new case. The man sounded elderly and spoke with a British accent. He said he had to speak to Donald James about a matter of some urgency and left a number for her uncle to call. The second message was a sales call about a new Internet provider, which she promptly deleted.

The files on her uncle's desk contained a number of new notes. Miss Tearning's case file was in her collect tray. Uncle Donny only put files there if he wanted her to type something.

While she waited for her computer to load, she opened the Tearning file. It looked like Uncle Donny had gone into the city following her trail. With one finger she tapped the page of hand-written notes and wondered why Miss Tearning was on the run. What was so special about the butterfly necklace that made so many people desperate to find it?

She located the insurer's photo and examined it carefully. The pendant was exactly as she remembered, shining with an internal light even in print. The description beside the image detailed its weight and size. The wings were crystal with rubies and emerald chips. A gold chain was attached to the head with a small clasp.

She opened her browser. As Jonny always said—when in doubt,

search the internet. Uncle Donny investigated Miss Tearning and Prince Henry, but had he looked into the necklace itself?

It took some digging, but one site, *A History of Ancient Jewelry*, displayed a drawing of a necklace called the Butterfly Stone. It looked like the same butterfly. *Huh.* How old was Miss Tearning's necklace? The origin of the stone was attached to the image as a long article. She printed it out and collapsed onto the sofa with a cookie and a mug of hot chocolate to read it. After going over it a second time she opened her video messenger on her phone and video-called Tony.

"Hey." The bruise on his face still looked painful.

"Hi, listen I've found something interesting."

"What about?"

"The necklace. What levels are your family?"

"Mostly Intermediate … why?" He looked surprised by her question, which was a normal reaction; it was rude to ask a person's magic level.

"Have they ever mentioned a story called 'The Stones of Power?'"

He shook his head. "Never heard of it. Why, what is it?"

"That's just the thing. Apparently it's an old Mage-kind story, but I've never heard of it. I did a search and the story is everywhere, but unless you know what to look for you can't find it."

"Sounds like a secret keeper spell."

"That's what I thought, too." Tracey felt strangely uneasy talking about the story, which was odd–*A story is just a story, right?*

"So, what's it about?" he asked.

"Five Mage-kind used spelled stones to store their power. They made them into jewelry so they could wear them to augment their natural power."

"So, it's a fairytale?"

"I don't know … but the story says the Five possessed a never-before recorded rating. They named themselves, Maestro."

"That's ridiculous," Tony scoffed. "Come on! *Maestro?* That's a myth. There's only Modest, Intermediate, and Significant. Plus, you can't store magic — it wears off. Objects have to be respelled constantly, everyone knows that. It's just a kid's story that's been blown up to be taken seriously by a bunch of nutjobs."

144

"Yeah, you're probably right, *but … ?*"

"You actually think the necklace is one of these stones?"

Tracey scratched at the back of her neck, but couldn't get at the itch beneath her skin. "I don't know. The necklace looks different, but why would a simple butterfly necklace be stolen twice?"

"What do you mean *stolen twice?*"

"I found two reports in the M-Force database —"

"How does Donny have access to that?" Tony asked.

Tracey grinned. "I've never asked. Anyway, the reports say a necklace matching Miss Tearning's description was stolen in 1951 and again in 1976. And then there's this." Tracey sent him a new picture. It was a drawing of five stones. The center stone had a butterfly painted on it that looked *exactly* like Miss Tearning's necklace.

"That's a drawing," he pointed out.

"I know, but it's the same butterfly."

"Yeah but one's a picture on a stone and the other is an actual butterfly shape."

"Tony, it's the same butterfly; the colors, shape, size. They're identical."

"I think they're two different necklaces."

Ignoring him she continued. "I couldn't find any other pictures of the necklace. The story of the Butterfly Stone is old. The earliest reference I found was from 1820."

"If the story is true."

Why had she'd bothered calling him. He was being so negative. "I want to know —"

"How Prince Henry got it?"

She glared at the camera. "Well, yeah, that too. Look, it can't be a coincidence the butterfly on Miss Tearning's necklace and the butterfly drawn on the stone are identical. Don't you think —"

"You think whoever is after the necklace is actually after the stone?"

"I know it sounds ridiculous," she said, holding his gaze. "The man in the red mask is super powerful, Tony. It makes sense he would be after a magic-infused stone more than a silly necklace." There was something in this. She was sure she was right. It had to be the same necklace.

"It does, but ..." Tony looked away.

Tracey wondered what he was thinking. When he didn't continue, she prompted. "But?"

He looked her right in the eye. "But if the butterfly necklace *is* this stone, then why did Prince Henry give it to Miss Tearning? It must be insanely expensive. And how'd he even get his hands on it in the first place?"

"I don't think *her* necklace *is* the stone," she said.

"What makes you say that?"

"Because, I have it." His eyes sprang wide. Before he could ask how she got it she said, "I don't sense anything magical."

"Okay, yeah that is weird."

"I want to track the necklace back from when Prince Henry gave it to Miss Tearning and see if I can find out where he bought it. I think whoever designed it must have seen the original stone in order to get the image so exact. Can you help? I'm stuck at work."

Tony rolled his eyes. "Sure, I'll have a look."

"Thanks, Tone." The front door jingled and her uncle walked in, carrying several plastic shopping bags. She waved to him. "I have to go, the boss just got back."

She hung up and minimized the video screen. "Did you find Miss Tearning?"

Uncle Donny mumbled around a number of envelopes hanging out of his mouth. She raced over to pull them out, freeing him to speak. "Thanks, kid."

Taking one of the bags she followed him into his private office. He piled the bags onto his desk and slumped down onto his chair sighing loudly, blowing his wavy fringe up off his forehead. His t-shirt had sweat stains under the arms and a splotch of what she hoped was ketchup in the center.

"You look exhausted," she said.

"Yes, it's been a long day and an even longer night. I haven't slept yet." He looked it too. His hair stood up in all directions and there were dark bags under his eyes.

"What happened? Did you find Miss Tearning?"

"No." He slumped further down into his chair and scrubbed a hand over his head, making his hair unrulier. "It was a wash, but I have another lead, hence the shopping." He pointed to the closest bag.

She glanced into it. "New suit?"

"Meet Mr. Duncan, public relations candidate for the new film, *Saving Time*."

"The movie starring Prince Henry?" Tracey shook her head. *This is going to end so badly.* "Why?"

"I want to ask Prince Henry where Miss Tearning would go when she wants to get away. His people won't let me near him."

She debated telling him what she'd uncovered with her research. She also wondered whether she should tell him about the tracking spell and the goons' scary lair up the mountain. In the end, she said nothing. That man in the red mask was too powerful, and her uncle was no match for him. As for her research, that would do no good either. For all she knew, the story of "The Stones of Power" was just a myth. Besides, Grandma was arriving today. If the story was an old one, maybe Grandma had heard of it.

When she got home, she walked right into a screaming match. Aunt Gemma was wagging her finger at Grandma, and it looked like Tracey's mom had just leapt from her chair to get between them. Sarah's mouth hung open and her body was poised to jump off the sofa.

"Um." Everyone turned at Tracey's entrance. *Go for the distraction.* "Hi, all," she said, plastering a giant grin on her face. "Hi, Grandma." She walked right into the middle of the argument, kissed her grandma on the cheek, breathing in a whiff of flour and fresh bread and then turned to her aunt. "Hi, Auntie."

Aunt Gemma was a younger version of Tracey's mom. Her eyes were grey where her mom's were brown, but other than that they looked, well, like sisters.

Tracey's mom used the break to usher her mother-in-law away from her sister and into the kitchen, loudly stating she was making a cup of tea. She shot Tracey a thankful glance over her shoulder and a pointed glare at Aunt Gemma.

Aunt Gemma shrugged it off and pulled Tracey into a hug. "Thanks for saving me from the old dragon," she whispered.

Tracey pressed a finger to her lips and shushed. Everyone knew Grandma had amazing hearing. She looked her aunt up and down. Her pilgrimage to Ireland must have been enjoyable. "How did you get a tan in Ireland?"

"I didn't. I popped over to Haymen Island for a week before I came home," she said with a laugh.

"Of course you did." Tracey didn't know how her aunt could afford it. "And you cut your hair." The new cut gave her a pixie-like appearance that suited her. Tracey wished she could look that good. Last time she cut her hair it went all curly — she'd ended up looking like Simon and Charlie. Aunt Gemma was twelve years older than Tracey, and tiny. Today she wore shorts and a tank top. They hung off her slim body, displaying how much weight she'd lost. Tracey felt cold just looking at her.

Aunt Gemma shrugged. "*So,*" she said with a mischievous glint in her eyes. "What's going on with you? Met any boys lately?"

"Hey!" Tracey knew her eyes had bugged out of her head. She pushed at her aunt playfully and collapsed onto the sofa. "Stop it! Now what were you saying to Grandma that made her so angry?"

"Nothing important." Aunt Gemma roared with laughter and spun on one foot. "I have to unpack."

Tracey shook her head as her aunt disappeared upstairs. It was so typical. Aunt Gemma could never stay still for long. Tracey's head was spinning from the speed at which her aunt moved.

Mom and Grandma walked in, cradling steaming tea cups. Tracey shuffled over on the sofa so they could sit down next to her. Grandma's magic reached out and connected with Tracey. It felt like being wrapped in a giant mental hug.

"Pink?"

The old woman's short curly hair had been dyed hot pink. Last year it was blue, and purple the year before that.

"Yes, do you like it?"

"How could I not?" Tracey loved everything about her grandma. She only wished she would visit more often. The story of the stones popped into her mind. *Should I ask?* A funny feeling in her tummy warned her not to.

"Honey, what is it?" Grandma asked, peering over her glasses. She raised her eyebrows.

Crap. With everything going on, she'd forgotten about Grandma's ability to see straight through her. "Um," she hesitated, not sure where to start.

"Just speak. I can feel something boiling away inside your brain. What can I help you with?"

Significants. They always knew more than you wanted them to. Now she had to ask — her grandma would get it out of her one way or another.

"Grandma, have you ever heard of a story called 'The Stones of Power?'"

"Another in love,
Betrayed by fear …"

18

Grandma turned as white as the living room walls.

Reaching out to touch her shoulder, Tracey's mom asked, "Adele, are you okay?"

Grandma shuddered. She pinned Tracey with a sharp stare. "How did you find out about that?"

"So it *is* a true story?" Tracey's stomach flip-flopped again. *I knew it!*

"No, honey. It's just a legend."

"Will you tell it to me?"

"How did you hear about it?"

Is she stalling? "Oh, online somewhere. I just wondered what it was about, that's all." She felt Grandma's magical feelers stretch out in her direction and quickly blocked her.

Raising her bushy grey eyebrows, Grandma narrowed her eyes, "When do you get rated?"

"In three years. Don't change the subject. Tell me about the story."

Just as Grandma opened her mouth, Tracey's phone rang with the Jaws ring tone she'd programmed in for her uncle. The back of her neck twitched. "Sorry Grandma, I probably need to take this." Strangely, Grandma looked relieved.

Reminding herself to ask about the story again, Tracey answered the call. Her mom mouthed the word "kitchen." Tracey nodded, already heading in that direction. "Boss?"

"They've found Miss Tearning's body," he said, sounding way too excited to be reporting such morbid news. Tracey's body turned cold.

She pulled the cell phone from her ear to stare at it blankly. Raising it again, she asked, "What happened?"

Uncle Donny paused. She heard muffled voices, as if he'd put his hand over the phone. After a moment, his voice became clear again. "Trace, I need you to bring my emergency bag to Miltern Central Hospital."

"Boss, what's going on? Are you okay?"

"Quickly, kiddo," he said, and hung up on her.

Not wanting to worry her mom or grandma, Tracey told them Uncle Donny needed her help at the office and ran outside to find Peter. Twenty minutes later her brother dropped her in front of the hospital. Her feet glued themselves to the footpath. She stared up at the twelve-story white block building and wondered what she was going to find inside. Her fingers tightened around the strap of her uncle's emergency bag. It contained his extra clothes, a mini magic case full of herbs, and other spelled items he might need in a pinch. She tried not to think about why he wanted them. Heaving a heartfelt sigh, she forced her feet to move.

Sneaking past the duty nurse, she located a stairwell and ran up to the third floor. When she found Uncle Donny he was soaking wet, hiding in a janitor's closet.

"What happened to you?" she gasped, handing over the bag.

"Not what, but where," he replied mysteriously. She spun around to let him dress and mulled over his strange answer.

"You said they'd … found Miss Tearning … her body?"

He shuffled through the bag. "Oh good, it's here."

"What is?" Glancing over her shoulder when he didn't respond she was shocked to find him buttoning a pair of grey coveralls. He looked like a janitor. *Oh no!* "Weren't you supposed to be interviewing for a job on the film set? How did you find Miss Tearning's body?"

"I got the job. They were giving me a tour of the various sets when one of the set builders raced up with a pair of red pumps. He said they'd found a body by the river."

Suddenly, Tracey didn't want to know how her uncle had gotten wet. She swallowed, her mouth dry. "What happened to her?"

"I couldn't tell. Once we got her body onto the riverbank the Assistant Producer called the police. The body was brought directly here and the area cordoned off. I couldn't get close to the scene after that."

It was terribly sad to hear that about Miss Tearning. True, Tracey hadn't really liked her, but she hadn't really spoken to her either. No one should end up like that.

Following her uncle out of the janitor's closet, she trailed after him to the elevators. "Where are you going now?" she asked. His enthusiasm had her terrified of his answer. With every step, her pulse ratcheted higher.

"I'm going to sneak into the morgue, and I need you to keep watch."

She halted midstep. "What?" There was no way she was going anywhere near a dead body. It was creepy enough just being in a hospital where there were so many sick people. Hospitals were not her favorite place to visit — not since Nana .... Memories of the elderly woman's constant hospital visits before the dementia diagnosis played in Tracey's mind. Uncle Donny seemed to realize she wasn't following and backtracked to take her arm and tug her forward.

Reluctantly, she followed him into the elevator. "How am I supposed to stop anyone from heading down —?" She cut herself off when she realized they weren't alone. The two nurses nodded politely when they saw her staring at them. Her uncle's strange luck held. The nurses stepped off at the first floor. Tracey and her uncle stayed on board.

When he stepped out on the basement floor, Tracey didn't move.

Aware now of her hesitancy he turned and gestured for her to get out of the elevator. She glanced at the inner buttons, willing the doors to close and save her. "Okay, stay here and hold the doors open. I'll be back in a sec."

Tracey shook her head. Bile rose up in the back of her throat knowing she was even this close to the morgue. She hovered in the open doorway of the elevator finally forced to step outside when it began beeping at her. Uncle Donny disappeared. There was no one in sight along either end of the corridor. Hoping for a distraction, she swiped her phone to check her social media accounts. In moments, she was laughing at Jonny's recent post. His brother, mouth wide open, was sound asleep on the kitchen table — he must have had a big night. Tracey became thoroughly engrossed in the images, so when the elevator bell dinged to announce its arrival she was caught off guard.

Officer Jameson's eyes widened when he saw her. "What are you doing here?"

Tracey scrubbed her free hand over the back of her neck. "Hi, Officer Jameson."

"What are you doing here?" he repeated, his eyes narrowing. He looked up and down the corridor, but there was no one in sight.

Not buying the innocent act, huh? She dropped her head. "Officer Jameson, I'm—"

"Your uncle reported the body, didn't he? You're here because he is." *Maybe the truth would work after all.*

"Officer Jameson—"

He surprised her by winking. "He asked you to keep watch, didn't he?"

She couldn't maintain eye contact, instead stared down at her feet. "I'm really sorry."

"I shouldn't encourage you, but since you're only standing here playing with your phone, all I can really lecture you on is that you shouldn't be in a restricted area."

"Yup, you are so right. I should absolutely go upstairs right now." She shoved her phone into her pocket and backed toward the elevator.

Uncle Donny's voice preceded him down the corridor. "Kid? You'll never believe what I ... Oh, uh, hello officer."

The policeman turned as her uncle skidded to a halt behind him.

"Mr. James?"

With a red face, her uncle held up both hands, palms out. "Officer, I can explain."

Officer Jameson pointed back up the corridor. "What did you find down there?"

"Find? I'm not sure I understand—"

"You said you found something. If you don't want me to arrest you for trespassing *and* disturbing the remains of a homicide victim, then I suggest you tell me what you've found."

Tracey gulped and stepped back, sensing her chance to escape. Officer Jameson pointed at her. "Don't go anywhere, miss."

Fruit tingles. She glared at her uncle. He was obviously running excuses through his head, and by the look in his eyes, he hadn't found one. Finally, he shrugged, "Follow me."

Officer Jameson grabbed her shoulder as he passed. "You too," he ordered.

She did *not* want to go with them but found herself dragged into the cold room despite her unwillingness. She squinted, prepared to run the instant she saw a body, but found the room empty, and incredibly clean. Overhead florescent light reflected off every stainless-steel surface. She glanced only once at the tray of tools beside one of the trolleys before turning away, feeling faint.

Uncle Donny stood near a plastic bag full of clothes, offering a pair of gloves to the policeman identical to the ones he still wore. Tracey stopped paying attention to them as a flicker of darkness skittered across her senses. It was similar to that cold, prickling feeling she'd felt up the mountain. *Where is that coming from?*

Drawing on her power, she reached out and tracked the flicker to its source—the bag of clothing her uncle was searching. She wiped a hand over her eyes. Blinking once, she opened her power-infused eyes and glanced around the room again. A red thread stretched from the bag to one of the little doors stuck in the wall—probably where the dead bodies were stored. *Oh, gross.*

She swallowed and focused on what her uncle was saying. He pointed to a brown object wrapped inside a plastic evidence bag.

"—not at all wet. If she'd drowned, her items would've been damaged by the water, but her belongings show no sign of being submerged. The paper inside is completely dry." Tracey blinked her power away and her vision returned to normal.

Officer Jameson leaned close to examine the handbag. "This will change the direction of the investigation. I'll advise my partner to concentrate the search on the riverbank where she was found rather than the bridge further upstream."

"Can we get out of here now?" Tracey whined. She kept imagining drawers opening and dead bodies climbing out to chase her, howling and gnashing their teeth. She shook her head to dispel the images. *Enough of that!*

Officer Jameson peered at her over his shoulder.

"What?" she asked, not liking the odd expression on his face.

"You're Mage-kind, aren't you?"

She nodded slowly. "Yes. So is my uncle."

Uncle Donny's head snapped up at her comment. "Good thinking, kid." He held his hands out over the bag and closed his eyes. Tracey felt his power seep from his palms. Tentatively, the pulses of power stretched out to touch the bag. Sweat beaded around his hairline; his eyes clenched tightly shut as he concentrated. She sent a little power his way to bolster his energy. His eyes flew open. "I feel … Oh wow, what is that?"

She knew he'd found the darkness she sensed earlier.

"There," Uncle Donny said, pointing to the drawer she'd already pinpointed. "That's where she is. Dark power, such dark power. Her death was no accident, Officer. Catherine Tearning is surrounded by tainted magic. Someone very powerful killed her."

Officer Jameson wrote rapidly into his notebook. "Mage-kind. Damn. We'll have to involve M-Force." Uncle Donny didn't answer.

Tracey drew on a little more power and pushed it toward her uncle.

"I see the river," he said suddenly. Tracey's gaze snapped to her uncle. His eyes were closed. Uncle Donny moved zombie-like around the morgue taking slow measured steps, raising his leg occasionally as if stepping over something only he could see.

Was he having a true *Vision?* Or was he just projecting what he already knew about the location where Miss Tearning's body had been found? She pushed the door in her chest open wider and sent him more. She'd never sent him this much power before and was a little worried about his storage capacity. She often sent little bursts his way if he needed a boost, but if he was having a real Vision then she needed to provide the grounding required to enable him to see everything.

"What else do you See?" Officer Jameson lowered his voice and spoke slowly, almost hypnotically, moving to stand right behind her uncle. Tracey had seen the move before on the television serials her mom watched — how the police encouraged and directed Visions from their Mage-kind witnesses. It was strange to see it occurring right in front of her. She'd always thought it was scripted that way to increase the level of drama.

Officer Jameson waved a hand to get her attention and gestured for her to touch her uncle. He mouthed, "Can you boost his magic?"

Oh God, he knows. Gulping, she stared at the officer blankly until she realized he didn't know she'd done it several times already. He was asking the other magically-powered person in the room to assist with the Vision.

Swallowing away her tension, Tracey tentatively touched her uncle's arm and closed her eyes.

"Trapped, bitter, and frozen;

Vision lost …"

19

When she opened them again she was somewhere else. The morgue with its clean white lines and stainless steel tables had disappeared, replaced by a dark forest. Tracey stood staring at a slow moving, muddy river. Sickly green grass grew along the edge of the riverbank. In the distance, she could make out a grown-over footpath leading from the river up a steep embankment to a road. Her uncle was talking, but it was like listening to him through jelly. She couldn't see him anywhere.

An odd hum surrounded her. Other than that, and the faint sound of Uncle Donny's voice, there was no sound. No smells either. A few steps would take her right up to the water's edge. Her heart leapt into her throat at the thought of seeing Miss Tearning's body floating in the river. Fortunately for Tracey, there was nothing in the water other than forest debris and mud. A hazy filter hovered over everything she looked at. In one part of Tracey's mind, she could feel her uncle's arm beneath her hands and knew she was still standing in the morgue, but her mind—or her *Sight*—was somewhere else. *This is crazy.*

A car stopped at the road's edge. Tracey watched the driver climb from the vehicle and was startled to realize his face was blurry. It was like looking at an out-of-focus photograph. A woman got out of the passenger side of the car and to Tracey's surprise, her face was clear. *Miss Tearning is alive!*

The perfectly coiffed woman spoke to the driver as he led her toward the river. Tracey couldn't hear what they were saying, but Miss Tearning smiled and her body language appeared relaxed. As they drew closer Tracey backed away, worried they would see her. When they looked right through her, that fear evaporated.

The faceless driver led Miss Tearning to the edge of the riverbank.

Even though Tracey stood right beside them, she couldn't make out what they were saying. She did witness the moment Miss Tearning knew something was wrong—the tall woman's eyes widened as her mouth dropped open. The faceless man dissolved in a puff of crimson smoke. Tracey screamed but there was no sound. *Run, run!* Her feet were stuck fast. "Miss Tearning, run!" she tried to shout. She wasn't heard. The smoke engulfed Miss Tearning's horrified form in a tsunami of blood-colored gas. When it dissipated, the woman collapsed, her face frozen mid-scream.

The smoke gathered and rose back up into the shape of a man. Tracey might not have been able to see his face, but she recognized him all the same. The same dark static she'd felt surrounding the man in the red mask poured off the figure in front of her. With a wave of his hand, he sent the body into the river.

Tracey snapped her eyes open. Her hand clenched the grey cotton sleeve covering her uncle's arm. His voice, familiar and safe, filled her ears. She blinked slowly, feeling disoriented and a little nauseous. Uncle Donny was telling Officer Jameson about the car that his Vision showed him. As she listened, she realized he hadn't seen Miss Tearning's murder at all.

Had she imagined it? She'd never heard of anyone piggybacking off another's magic to witness a murder before. Her legs trembled. "I'm going outside," she said, interrupting the hushed conversation.

"Are you okay, Trace?" Lines formed between her uncle's eyes.

Officer Jameson addressed Uncle Donny. "We should take your niece out of here, Mr. James. I would like a detailed statement about the Vision you experienced. Perhaps we can do that upstairs?"

Her uncle hedged and mumbled about how he'd only seen the car from a distance, and that he didn't recall any specific details. Tracey sensed he didn't want to hang around now that he had a clue to investigate.

Moments later they walked through the waiting room on the hospital's ground floor.

Tracey collapsed into the closest plastic chair and gripped the arms tightly as another wave of dizziness crashed into her. Her stomach twitched and sweat popped up all over her skin. "I'm going to wait here," she said.

Uncle Donny patted her head and led the officer away. Tracey breathed shallowly until her stomach settled. A flurry of movement and raised voices caught her attention. She looked up in surprise as several black-clad men swept out of the elevator. Her heart jumped into her throat thinking the bad guys were attacking. Anxiously, she looked around for the man in the red mask. Instead Prince Henry walked in, flanked by even more men. *What is he doing here?* Oh, right—the deceased Miss Tearning was his girlfriend. Her heart rate slowed as her fear turned to sadness. Poor Prince Henry. He must have been asked to formally identify the body.

She ducked lower in her chair, hoping he wouldn't notice her. He probably didn't remember their first encounter—it was the only time she'd looked like herself in his presence—but it would be just her luck if he *did* remember and think she was following him. She watched his reflection in the window stalk through the waiting area. Distraught and stressed family members turned as they realized someone famous walked among them. The bodyguards ushered him toward the elevators, and in moments the prince was gone.

Uncle Donny reappeared and suggested it was time to leave. Tracey couldn't agree more.

The whole way home, he talked about how he'd *Seen* the murderer's car and speculated there must have been an item in the bag containing enough dark energy for him to tap into its power. As usual, he had no idea she'd given him a boost. He said nothing about seeing Miss Tearning's murder. She couldn't ask him about it without giving away what she knew. If he hadn't seen it, she wondered why she had.

A glance at the dashboard clock caused her to groan.

"What?" Uncle Donny's shoulders immediately hunched as if expecting an attack.

"I had a math assignment to do."

"I can write you a note if you need it."

She dropped her head back against the seat rest. "It's okay." It wasn't, though. If she failed any more assignments, her mom and dad would stop her working for Uncle Donny until she got her grades back up. It wasn't fair. No one told her how stupidly busy being a private investigator really was—or how exhausting.

Aunt Gemma was in the kitchen knitting something pink when Tracey arrived home. She caught Tracey with a glare. "What have you been up to? It's late."

Tracey tugged open the refrigerator, grabbed a bottle of water and headed straight to the toaster to drop two slices of bread inside. "Oh, you know, homework and work, nothing unusual." *If only she knew!*

"So you're still working for Donald?"

"Yep. It's good money, and he lets me do my homework if it's a slow day."

"Are you still helping with his magic?"

Tracey froze. Sweat sprang out on her lower back at the tone in her aunt's voice. She spun around. Aunt Gemma was staring at the clacking needles in her hands, "Why are you asking?"

"Sweetie, all of the family knows you help him. Did Beth and Tom alter your bracelet?" She looked up from her knitting at last. There was a smile on her lips but her eyes were angry.

"I don't know what you—"

"*Tracey*. Donald is hopeless, and you shouldn't be helping him. It was wrong of Beth to enable you." The toaster popped. Tracey grabbed her dinner and slathered it quickly with raspberry jelly, wanting to escape to her room.

"Aunt Gemma, it's only the occasional boost of power," she said, edging toward the door. *Go, go. Get out before she—*

Her aunt placed her knitting down on the table and rose. "I don't think you should be doing that. You don't even understand your own abilities."

"Aunt Gemma … I know you don't like to use magic, but I do."

Snatching her needles up from the table, Gemma rolled the excess wool around them tightly and snapped, "It's not that I don't like it. It can be dangerous."

"Of *course* it can, I know that. And if I don't practice, I could lose control. Wouldn't that be worse?"

"Stop bothering her, Gemma," Grandma warned, appearing in the kitchen doorway. Tracey hadn't even heard her footsteps. The look in Grandma's eyes as she stared at Tracey's aunt was scary. Magic swirled around the old woman. Tracey could feel it and knew it was time to leave. Aunt Gemma, actively blocking her own abilities, would have no idea just how mad Grandma Masters truly was.

"Stay out of it, Adele," Aunt Gemma said, her face flaring red.

Tracey's grandma narrowed her eyes and sniffed loudly.

"It's okay Grandma, we were just talking." Hopefully, Tracey could keep their fight to a minimum. She shoved the last of her toast into her mouth and hovered as Grandma put the kettle under the tap to refill it. Tracey didn't know if her presence was exacerbating the tension or keeping it at bay.

"Tracey is a special young lady," Grandma continued. "I won't have you trying to influence her."

Movement drew Tracey's attention to the doorway. Sarah stood on the threshold. She looked from Tracey to their grandma and back before she shot Tracey an angry look, spun on a heel, and raced back upstairs. *God, what's her problem?*

Breathing as though she'd been exercising, Aunt Gemma stepped toward the sink. "I can talk to my niece if I want, Adele."

"Gemma, your views are your own. If you don't want to use the gifts you have been given, that is your choice, but stop forcing your misguided beliefs on my grandchildren."

Shooting another glare at the old woman, Aunt Gemma stormed from the room.

"It really is okay, Grandma. I don't think the same way Aunt Gemma does. But she can talk to me if she wants, she is my aunt."

"Sweetheart, at this stage of your development you should be surrounded only by positive influences."

Tracey hoped her extended family would find their way back to their own homes soon. She could feel Grandma's magic press up against the edges of her mind. "Stop it, Grandma. I know what you're doing."

Grandma's brown eyes twinkled. "Good."

Tony's name flashed on Tracey's cell phone for the third time, but she couldn't pick up. She wasn't allowed to answer the phone at the dinner table, and if she left now she'd miss all the drama.

Aunt Gemma continued to shoot dirty looks at Tracey's grandma every time she turned away. Peter's only reaction was to roll his eyes, likely wishing he was out joyriding. Their dad ignored everyone while Mom kept trying to be the mediator, foolishly getting in between Aunt Gemma and Grandma. Sarah seemed distracted, eating like a robot with her eyes out of focus. Grandma must have dished up dinner because Charlie had chunks of pumpkin, which he hated, so he kept sneakily swapping them for Simon's carrots every time she turned her head.

"Tracey!" Mom finally snapped when her phone vibrated again.

"Sorry," she said switching it to silent.

Her face flushed as Mom warned, "You'd better not answer that."

"I'm not, I'm not," she said, shoving her phone into her pocket. The family finished dinner in an uncomfortable silence, afraid of sparking their mom's anger, and as soon as they could, Tracey and her siblings disappeared from the table.

Closing her bedroom door quietly, she grabbed her phone and scrolled through all of Tony's messages.

Hey can you call me?

Tracey are you there?

Text me when you're free?

I have info.

Tracey?

Helloooooo?

She messaged him back and her phone vibrated barely a second later.

"Where have you been?" he demanded, sounding stressed.

Flopping onto her bed she spoke in a hushed voice. "Family dinner. What's so important?" She nervously eyed the closed door, afraid her mom would hear her talking and barge in to confiscate her phone.

"I just found a bunch of stories about other jewelry robberies."

Tracey sat up. "What?"

"Yeah. Check your email, I sent them to you. Three homes and two

168

second-hand stores were broken into last week. And get this — the photos of the stolen jewelry are replicas of the butterfly necklace. I think you're right. Those masked goons have been searching for it for a long time. When Miss Tearning came to town with Prince Henry, they must have decided hers was the one they were after."

Tracey's heart ached. "Tony ..."

"So, I think that —"

"Tony."

"What?"

"Miss Tearning is dead."

In his answering silence, she switched on her laptop to read the reports for herself. Tony was a lot quieter when he spoke again. "How do you know?"

She just said, "Uncle Donny," and rubbed her belly fearing dinner would make a sudden reappearance. She swallowed and breathed slowly through her nose.

"How'd she die?"

"Drowned, they think. But I'm sure the man in the red mask was behind it." She lay back on her pillow and stared blankly at the circle spinning on her laptop.

"How do you know *that*?"

"I just do," she said, not wanting to admit to her Vision. Even though the practice was common on TV, normal Mage-kind just didn't do that sort of thing. She didn't want him to think she was a freak.

He was silent for a minute and then asked, "Do they know about him? Have the police connected the man in the red mask back to Miss Tearning?"

"Tony, Officer Jameson is not Mage-kind. The man in red is *way* too strong for him. Besides, Uncle Donny told him about sensing dark magic on her bag. I think Jameson is going to call in M-Force." Remembering the creepy feeling, she rubbed at her chest again and opened her email. "So, what connected you to these robberies?"

"I was doing a search on the necklace, like you asked. I figured your uncle probably just checked local pawn shops because he's not much of a computer guy, right? So I scanned the image and ran it through a wider range of online junk shops looking for anything similar. I figured if there were two necklaces with the same butterfly on it, maybe there are more. That's when all the matches came up."

"So the man in the red mask is looking for the necklace, and Miss Tearning was just an accident," she said.

"Looks like."

"Good work, Tone." Tracey flicked through the different reports he'd emailed. They definitely looked like the same butterfly.

"Well, we know they haven't found it yet. The last robbery was two days ago."

She didn't remind him that Miss Tearning's necklace was currently hidden behind her dresser. "Can you run a search to see if there are any more replicas in town?"

Tony paused before he asked, "You think there will be another hit?" He sounded distracted. She could hear the clicking of his keyboard.

"Maybe."

"I'll keep looking."

She reached down over her bed to grab her school bag and pulled out her pencil case.

"Hey, Trace ... be careful, okay? What happened to Miss Tearning sounds really freaky."

"I will be. M-Force will probably take over the case and kick Uncle Donny off it."

"That's a good thing."

"I know, Tony. I wanted an exciting adventure and now Miss Tearning is dead." She fell silent. "Maybe being a detective is not what I want to do anymore."

She ended the call and wirelessly printed the reports to the living room where the family printer was located. Running out, she collected them and raced back to her room before Mom could demand to know what she was doing. There was no reported sign of a break-in at any of the locations listed, and nothing else had been taken except for the jewelry. Even the tablets and laptops had been left alone. Tracey tapped on the page with her capped highlighter.

Why did the man in the red mask want the butterfly necklace so badly? And, more worrying, what would happen if he found it?

"You said there were more memories?"

20

Tracey didn't get to catch up with Tony at all the next morning. The overnight storm knocked out the electricity on her block, resetting all of the family's alarms. Her mom woke Tracey in a panic and she only just made it to school before the bell rang.

Last night's nightmare had been worse than all the others—she'd woken several times covered in a cold sweat, her heart racing and her mind screaming. The Shadowman had gotten so close she could practically taste the hunger on its breath. Her memory kept replaying its smoky voice in her head, whispering that Tracey would hurt everyone she loved.

Her day went from bad to worse when every one of her teachers seemed to be in a bad mood. It was only as Mr. Michaels called for their book reports to be forwarded to his desk that she realized her bad day had become a total disaster.

"No assignment, Miss Masters?" Mr. Michaels did not look surprised. It had to have been a full moon last night. She cursed, slumping further down into her chair. A note would be sent to her parents this time. Her assignment was sitting on her desk at home, forgotten in this morning's rush to get to school. Hopefully her mom would accept her excuse as reasonable and not ground her or stop her from working for Uncle Donny—her standard threat when Tracey's grades slipped.

Distracted, she nearly walked right past Damian in the hall on her way to her next class. Skidding to a halt she waved and squeaked out, "Hi."

He didn't look at her.

"Um, hi Damian."

He grunted and walked away from her.

She stared after him as he disappeared into the moving wave of students.

What was that about? He just walked away. *Rude!* Her eyes continued to follow him as a shiver made its way down her spine. Running to her next class, she barely made it before the second bell, meaning she couldn't complain to Laura about Damian's weird behavior or even use her phone.

Mr. Rachette gave them a pop quiz. After a moment of complaining, the whole class fell silent. They sat head's bent, writing rapidly.

Glancing at the wall above Mr. Rachette's head, Tracey's thoughts drifted from Damian to the dream-like vision she'd experienced at the morgue. Had it been *her* Vision that she'd witnessed, or her uncle's? She was positive the butterfly the man in the red mask wanted was the one from the story, but she doubted the necklace she'd stolen from Prince Henry was the one it referred to. A stone full of magic would surely give off some kind of a magical aura.

She eyed the clock and focused back on the quiz paper beneath her hands, finishing it quickly. Her mark was not going to be pretty. She decided to use the remainder of the class time to practice her magic controls. Mr. Rachette wasn't Mage-kind and neither were any of the students in this particular class, so they'd be none the wiser. Her intention was to replay the Vision from the morgue to see if she could make out what Miss Tearning said to the faceless driver. She'd never done a proper meditation before — that class was held in the final year of camp — but everyone was taught the basic steps as a calming technique.

Closing her eyes, she breathed out slowly and stayed like that, in frozen silence, until she needed to breathe in again. Holding the next breath for as long as she could, she repeated the process.

Her mind drifted as she dropped into a light meditation. After a while she directed her thoughts into a line and drew some power out of her chest. Thinking back to the morgue, she tried to recapture the emotions she'd felt there.

Thus, it came as a complete surprise to feel the tendrils of a fledgling talent reach out to touch hers. Tracey's eyes flew open. She stared at Mr. Rachette. Nothing. Stretching out with her mind she tugged on the orange colored thread. As weak as it was, she expected the thread to trail out of the room. Instead, it led straight to … *Dave Two?*

Tracey's head snapped around to stare at him.

He caught her looking and narrowed his eyes. She tugged on the orange strand again. It was weak, but it was definitely coming from him. Dave Two didn't react to her tug at all. It slowly dawned on her that he didn't know he was Mage-kind at all.

Mage-kind abilities usually manifested by a child's sixth birthday. Tracey had never heard of anyone coming into their powers at fifteen. Upon closer inspection, she found there was no focus in the thread. It drifted around the room aimlessly.

"What are you looking at?" Dave snarled. Heads rose across the room to see what was going on.

Tracey spun back around as Mr. Rachette called Dave's name in warning. *Should I tell him?* She didn't even know if Mage-kind ran in his family. Surely someone else would notice his emerging talent and tell him. Hopefully, when he discovered what he was, he wouldn't be so awful to her and Tony anymore. Then again, the knowledge could possibly make him worse.

The clock above their heads struck the end of class. "Get out of here," Mr. Rachette growled.

Gathering her books, Tracey followed the rest of her classmates toward the door. Dave pushed her out of the way so he could leave the room first. "Freak," he muttered. Tracey hid her grimace and smiled sweetly. If only he knew she wasn't the only freak in this room today.

Four minutes after the final bell rang, Tracey sat with Tony on the stone fence that bordered the exit gate out of school. They were waiting for Jonny and Laura. Tracey didn't share Dave's secret with Tony, deciding it wasn't hers to tell. Finding out he was Mage-kind would be the biggest shock of Dave's life. Discovering his new abilities could trigger an avalanche of emotional stress resulting in an explosion of power. She figured her mother would know what to do. Her mom probably had a list of people to call who would be happy to help Dave Two learn to control his new powers.

Jonny and Laura appeared at the same time, dropping their bags to the ground with loud thumps.

"Hey," Tracey said.

"So, I found something interesting last night," Tony said before reaching out to tap Jonny's fist. Jonny hopped up onto the fence next to Tony.

"What were you looking for?" Jonny asked, twirling a twig.

"A story called 'The Stones of Power.'"

Tracey fidgeted when Tony paused, finally prodding when she couldn't stay quiet anymore. "And?"

He grinned. Tony knew something and was pleased that he knew it before she did. "I found a website on the M-Net that has a bunch of ancient spells on it. I was reading them when you messaged me last night. As soon as you started talking about the butterfly necklace, an Easter egg opened up with a link to a secret site. It was like it heard you or something."

"You mean the website was spelled? How can you spell a website? And why didn't you say something about it last night?" Tracey demanded. How weird was that? A spelled website connected to the necklace. It had to mean something.

"I didn't know it was possible to even spell a website. You asked me to look into the jewelry heists. I only found the second site open when I closed my other browser. It took half the night to make sense of it." Tony pulled the site up on his phone, flicking through it while he talked. He showed them how to unlock the link to the secret site. "So once the Easter egg unlocked the link, I backtracked the hidden IP's of —"

"Don't bore us with all that, Tony," Laura interrupted. Tracey was glad she did. Tony could talk for ages about the technical side of things, and when he got going it was hard to stop him. He flushed but did change the subject.

"If you click on the area of the website your eye naturally avoids, you find a bunch of other links."

"Huh?" Jonny's face twisted up in confusion.

"The website is spelled to make you avoid looking at where the links are hidden?" Tracey asked, her skin prickling at the thought. A lot of work had gone into making sure the site stayed hidden. *But why?*

"Something like that," Tony said. "So I started investigating the creator of the site, Doctor Steven Chan. Turns out, he lives right here in Miltern Falls and works as a historian at the University. I think we need to go see him. His whole website is dedicated to the story of the stones."

Coincidence? "Good work, Tony."

A large meaty hand reached down and snatched Tony's phone from his fingers. Dave One waved the phone around. Dave Two stood a few feet behind him, grinning broadly. "Whatcha looking at? Magic porn?"

"Hey, give that back!" Tracey snapped, her chest tightening as her fists clenched. Her magic closet rattled ominously.

"Are you doing homework in your spare time, freak?" Dave One threw the phone to the ground. There was the crack of breaking glass. Tony groaned. "Magic homework? Naughty, naughty. No magic allowed at school." Both Daves laughed loudly. Tracey wanted to yell at Dave Two and demand he stand up for her and Tony now that he had more in common with them than he ever would with Dave One, but she bit her tongue. She couldn't use her knowledge against him. The door in her chest rattled again. She put her hand over her heart and pushed it closed.

Dave One shoved Jonny back a few steps and taunted, "Why are you hanging around with these losers, Jonny? You could be cool." Laughing, he strode away, Dave Two close on his heels.

"Jerks," Laura mumbled.

"I wish I could just—"

"Jonny, no." Tracey grabbed his arm. "Just forget it."

"But they're such jerks about magic—it's not like you and Tony can help being what you are. I don't get why they don't think it's cool. I think it's cool," he told her.

She grinned, her body relaxing as the threat of danger lifted. "Not everyone thinks that way, Jonny. That's what makes you and Laura so great."

"So, when are we going to go visit this Doctor Chan?" Tony asked, reverting back to their earlier discussion. He picked up his phone and sighed. His shoulders dropped.

"I'm sorry about your cell, Tony," Tracey told him softly.

"It still works," he muttered, touching the screen. "So — Doctor Chan?"

"How about tomorrow? I have the afternoon off from work. We should catch the train to the university."

"I can't do it tomorrow," Jonny complained. "We're visiting my Gran — she's in the hospital for a hip operation."

"Well, that's more important, Jonny," Laura told him. Her eyes softened. "You have to go see her."

"We'll tell you all about it afterward," Tracey promised.

The thirty-minute train ride was a quiet affair in Jonny's absence. Laura read her book and Tony tapped his phone while Tracey watched life rush past the window.

She loved the university. It was a sprawling campus filled with two-hundred-year old buildings and giant trees. The same peaceful feeling fell over her as it had the two times she'd come with school visits. The grounds bustled with students of every age and ethnicity. It took them ten minutes to walk from the entrance to the History Hall. Colorfully dressed students lingered over large volumes and dusty tomes, clutching mugs of coffee like it would save their lives. Tracey's fingers itched to touch the books, even imagining she could smell the paper. Entering the third-floor study hall, she stopped next to a pretty girl with short pink hair. "Excuse me, can you tell me where to find Doctor Steven Chan?"

"Down the hall to the left, second door." She gave Tracey and her friends a strange blank-eyed stare. Tracey thanked her and led the way.

A short Asian man with greying hair and a thin mustache opened the door at their knock. His eyes were hidden behind emerald-tinted spectacles, but his smile was warm. "Can I help you?"

"May we come in, Doctor Chan?" Laura asked politely.

The doctor's eyes widened as he caught sight of Tracey. "You," he whispered. His face lit up. He smiled, exposing stained teeth and ushered them all into his office with an excited hand gesture. He closed the door behind them and raced back to his desk to rifle through a teetering pile of files, all the while muttering, "Amazing, such a resemblance," over and over. Tracey's stomach twirled in warning.

"Doctor Chan?" she asked, leaning forward to catch his eye.

The man seemed to find what he was looking for and sat back, smiling. "Of course, of course. What can I help you with?"

Tony approached the edge of the desk. "Do you host a website called *The History of Mage-kind—Genealogy and Bloodlines?*"

"I do."

"I was reading your site and—"

"You are Mage-kind?"

Tracey's flip-flopping stomach stopped mid-flop, like someone had hit pause on a remote.

Tony stepped back. "Why does that matter?"

The doctor's eyes fell to Tony's covered wrist. Tracey had a sudden fear the man was going to do something to hurt Tony and prepared to raise her shield bubble between them. "Only a Mage-kind can access my website. It's a precaution I take to ensure Norms cannot take advantage of the information contained within."

Tracey jumped in, hoping to lower the tension between them. "Yes sir, Tony is Mage-kind—I am, too." She raised her sleeve to expose her bracelet. Tony sat down and shot her a concerned look. Talking to Doctor Chan didn't feel like such a good idea now.

"I'm not," Laura said. Doctor Chan ignored her.

Cracking open her chest closet, Tracey stretched out with her senses. She couldn't feel any magic around the doctor at all. If he was masking his power, he was very good at it.

He stared straight at her. Cold air brushed over her exposed skin. She clasped her hands together and squeezed so she didn't move. "I have an old drawing here I'd like to show you." He pulled a green file from his desk and removed a plastic sleeve, holding it out to her.

Tracey stared at the image and her mouth dropped open. It was a picture of her.

"Yes, but the time is not right for you to see them."

21

S he couldn't believe it.

Inside the plastic sleeve was a black and white drawing. Her friends leaned forward to examine it. "Wow, that really does look like you," Laura said, her gaze darting from Tracey to the picture and back again.

The picture was of three men and two women. Tracey examined the two men standing behind the three seated figures. Their stern faces gave her the creeps. The woman seated on the left looked exactly like Tracey. She wore a long dress with short sleeves and her dark hair was swept up in an elaborate bun. The other woman had lighter hair and a similar dress. The three men shared dark hair and long coats. *Wait*—five people in the image.

"'The Stones of Power?'" she whispered. Certainty swelled in her chest.

Doctor Chan looked startled. "You know the story?"

Tracey glanced again at the picture. "Not really. We found the name of the story and once we knew what to look for we were able to find other references to it. Can you tell us about it?"

Doctor Chan nodded. "As you are already looking for it, it would be more dangerous for me not to tell you."

"Dangerous?" Laura asked. "How can a story be dangerous?"

"Let me explain. Two hundred years ago, the best and brightest youths of all the Mage-kind clans joined together to dedicate themselves to understanding and strengthening their abilities. Believing Mage-kind to be above Norms both in talent and intelligence, they searched in secret for a way to increase their powers."

Mage-kind clans? What the heck is he talking about? The second part of his statement stuck in her mind. "What do you mean, 'increase their powers?' A level is a level. You can't make yourself more powerful." She glanced at Tony. His shoulders rose as he shook his head. Laura leaned forward in her chair, listening avidly.

"So we believed. The Five were students of the craft. Their skills in metallurgy and chemistry were unsurpassed for their time. Even more interesting, two of the group were Dreamers."

"Dreamers?" Tracey tilted her head. She'd never heard the term before.

Doctor Chan removed his glasses and cleaned them with a wipe. He stared at Tracey through squinted eyes. "There is very little data or historical documentation on the subject, and no medical study has ever been conducted to be sure. However, it is my belief that Dreamers are students of magic who possess an unheard-of level of power. Whose very thoughts can manipulate the building blocks of life." Doctor Chan pointed at Tracey. "Their identities have been lost to time, but their work lives on in forbidden texts — journals of Mage-kind science and manuals of casting." He paused, his eyes bore into Tracey. She wanted to tear her gaze away but she couldn't. "It would be my guess, young lady, that you are the descendant of the young woman in that picture."

Tracey's stomach clenched as her throat closed.

He held out his hand. "May I scan you?"

"You're Mage-kind?" Laura asked, her eyes wide.

Tracey didn't believe it. She'd checked. There was no hint of magic.

"I do not advertise my talents. I'm sure you can understand why."

Both Tony and Tracey nodded. The world was run by Norms. Magical abilities were so regulated and monitored that Mage-kind rarely made it into positions of authority. To be a teacher at a respected university was kind of a big deal. It must be difficult for a man like Doctor Chan to maintain any sense of authority over his Norm students. She wondered if there was a connection between the distrust of Mage-kind and the story of the stones. Could this story be the reason Mage-kind were treated so poorly?

Reluctantly, Tracey held out her hand. Doctor Chan covered it with his own. She felt his magic prickle against her skin before it became a wave that smashed against her body trying to get inside. Her mind shut down against him. The door in her chest slammed shut unintentionally. She tried to push it open but her fear kept it shut. When he leaned back a moment later, his expression was disappointed.

"What happened to the Five? Were they arrested?" she asked, her voice trembling. She cleared it with a grunt. Doctor Chan tapped on the image of the woman who looked exactly like Tracey.

"Madness. Inherited, or perhaps the result of too much power gathered too quickly—it's impossible to know, really. The story implies this woman became unstable, infecting the others. The Five were able to keep their mental disintegration at bay for a time by funneling their excess power into five vessels known as The Stones. Eventually, the madness became too hard to control."

Tracey stared at the image of the woman with her face as a chill crept down her spine. She felt Laura and Tony's shocked gaze and wondered if they feared she had this madness too. She thought of her nana—her crazy nana—and her chest jerked as her heart skipped a beat. *Why does this woman look like me?*

Tony asked, "Doctor, can you tell us what happened to the stones?"

The older teacher shook his head. "I cannot. There is a book I have recently discovered, a journal that may have belonged to one of the Five—it is my hope it will explain what happened to the Five before they disappeared."

"Disappeared?" Tracey looked up at the Doctor in surprise.

"Yes. The journal is in transit from the estate of a collector, but I'm afraid it is not due for several days. Until then, I know nothing more of this tale than what I have shared with you today."

She heard Tony ask for the name of the collector, as well as the names and dates of the lost journal, but her head was spinning. They thanked the doctor for his time and assured him they would return the following week if he would let them view the journal.

As they left, Doctor Chan touched Tracey's arm and gestured for her to remain behind. "Be careful," he hissed. "The magic of the stones is dangerous. If you are indeed related to one of the Five, you must be cautious. Such power would be a magnet for evil. Finding even one of these stones may destroy the one who keeps it."

She pulled away, frightened by his intensity.

"Be careful," he urged as she raced out through the door.

Tracey couldn't get the story of the stones out of her mind. She had to be related to the woman in the picture, but how could she find out for sure? Would her possible ancestor's fate one day become hers? There was only one person she could ask.

She snuck out of the house after dinner with her mind buzzing. The walk to Tavel House was not a long one and she figured she'd be back before her disappearance was discovered. Tavel House, the institution where her nana lived, was an assisted living facility for Mage-kind with mental illness. Tracey hadn't visited Nana in years because the elderly woman scared her silly.

The memory of the day they took Nana to Tavel House was so clear to Tracey it often haunted her nightmares. Well, before the Shadowman had come along and taken center stage. Nana cried the whole way, yelling every few minutes at Tracey's mom, and accusing the whole family of betrayal. She begged not to be locked up, insisting there was nothing wrong with her. Tracey remembered rain pounding the car's windows and wishing it would drown out the sound of her nana's sobs.

As soon as they climbed from the vehicle, icy wind froze Tracey's ears and sent sharp fingers of cold through the gaps in her clothing. Tavel House towered above them, foreboding and horrible. The building seemed to laugh at them.

When she'd voiced the thought, Charlie said she was imagining things. Simon's eyes were wide — the street light above them exposing his terror. She hadn't been back to Tavel House since that night.

Right now, with her heart pounding in her throat, Tracey pulled open the heavy door and stepped into the silent hall. Her shoes clacked loudly against the laminate floor, announcing her arrival. The corridor was broken every few feet by a solid door. A name tag outside each door identified its inhabitant. Tracey passed an empty communal eating area and a silent television room. Given the late hour the patients must all be asleep. Her skin crawled as goose pimples spread up her arms. The building felt empty.

The nurse at the reception desk gave Tracey an odd look when she asked which room her nana was in.

"My dear, there are official visiting hours during the day. Perhaps you can come back tomorrow?"

"I know. But ... I ... please? Nana called home sounding really upset and my mom wasn't there and ... We live only a few blocks away. I just wanted to see that she's okay."

The nurse frowned. "You should have called first. We could have checked on her for you."

"I know, and I'm sure she's fine. She's probably forgotten she even called, but since I'm here, please can I just pop in and see her? I'll be really quick."

The woman smiled and leaned across the desk. "Well, it's not an official visit, but go on. It'll do her a world of good to see a familiar face. Your nana has been a little quiet over the last few days. Room eighty-four. Follow that yellow line, it'll take you to the right hall."

Tracey looked down. The floor had several different colored lines painted on it. She thanked the nurse and followed the yellow line all the way to her nana's room. As she touched the handle, the door opened. Tracey startled back, biting off a scream.

"Hello Tracey, what are you doing here?" Nana didn't look surprised to see her. Wrinkled hands waved her inside. Tracey couldn't believe how good her nana looked. She was dressed in a long patchwork skirt and a thick knit green jumper. Her hair was brushed neatly; the white curls that clung tightly to her head even looked recently styled. She didn't look crazy or sick at all—she looked perfectly normal. Tracey waited for her nana's magic to embrace her, but the air was still. She frowned and opened the door in her chest. Her skin tingled as her power swelled to fill the room. Nothing. She couldn't find her nana's magic at all.

She pushed harder and imagined her magic wrapping her nana in a

189

big hug. She felt it then. Directionless threads and sparks of misfiring personal energy. Tracey drew her power back, her heart aching. Swiping her hand over her damp eyes, she turned away so the old woman wouldn't see her tears.

Nana's room was small. A single bed pressed up against the window with a television bolted to a shelf on the wall. At the foot of her bed was a round table with an old book, a writing pad and a deck of cards. Tracey sat down in one of the two mismatched chairs.

"Hi, Nana."

"Sweetie, what are you doing here at this time of night?" Nana lowered herself into a padded chair on the other side of the table, shuffling the cards between arthritic hands.

"It's been a long time, Nana. I thought I would visit."

Her nana's milky eyes were almost glowing in the orange lamplight. "Really? It's dark out. You couldn't wait until morning?"

Tracey stifled a groan. *It sounds weird, doesn't it?* "Nana, I want to ask you something, but I don't want to upset you."

"Honey, does your mom know you're here?"

"No."

"Snuck in, huh? Cool."

Tracey tried not to laugh but it was funny to hear an old lady use the word *cool* in a sentence. "Nana, have you ever heard of a story called "'The Stones of Power?'"

The old woman glanced up at the wall above Tracey's head. "Five stones?" she mumbled. "I don't understand."

Springing upright Tracey confirmed, "Five stones? You know the story?" There was no response. "Nana?" Tracey tried again, but her nana seemed to have gone somewhere else. Was this a sign of madness, or simply her dementia? Tracey rubbed her cold hands together to warm them. "Nana?"

"Oh, Tracey. Sweetheart, what are you doing here?" Nana asked when she noticed Tracey sitting at the table.

Tracey closed her eyes. It felt as though there was a gaping hole in her chest. "I came to visit."

"Snuck in, huh? Cool."

"Nana, the story? Have you ever heard of a story about magic stones? They were kept by five Mage-kind who formed a secret club over two hundred years ago." Tracey flinched as her phone vibrated. She slapped her hand over her pocket.

"What was that noise? Did you hear it?" Nana searched for the source.

Tracey pulled the black device from her pocket. "It's just my cell phone, Nana."

The old woman stared at the device but her eyes remained blank. "Cell phone?"

Tracey checked the display. It was a message from her uncle. She'd call him back later. "Nana, the story. Do you remember?"

"Oh honey, it's just a silly story. Don't you worry yourself over it. None of it is true."

"Really?" Relief filled her. Weirdly, tears sprang into her eyes. It was good news. She didn't understand why she was so upset. If the story was just a story, then the necklace was just a necklace. It still didn't explain why everyone was looking for it though. "Nana, what about—" Her voice broke off when the old woman struggled to her feet with a grunt and reached out to hug her. Nana felt so frail. Tracey held on as tight as she dared and then let go, sadness weighing down her heart. Nana grabbed Tracey's arm hard. "Nana?"

"Did you see the shadow?"

Tracey's stomach dropped into her feet. "What?"

"Stay away from the shadow. Don't let it touch you," she hissed, before her eyes lost focus again and widened. "Tracey, what are you doing here?"

"… Nana?"

"Snuck in, huh?" she chuckled quietly. "Scamp. It's good to see you, sweetie. Does your mom know you're here?"

A cold chill ran up Tracey's spine. Her hands shook when she pulled the door open. Glancing back, she found her nana staring blankly at the wall. The cold in Tracey's spine spread out to cover her entire body. She was gasping for air by the time she got outside, wiping tears from her cheeks. *Oh God, what was that?*

"One full of passion,
For learning and love …"

22

Tracey's dreams were filled with nightmares again that night. Nana kept morphing into a shadowy man with a toothy grin. The dreams were disjointed, jumping from Tavel House to the darkened street where she'd first seen the Shadowman, then she was chased through a dismal wood full of trees. Finger-like branches tore at her hair and clutched at her arms to try and stop her. In another dream, she sat on an empty bus and when she looked at the seat beside her, the Shadowman was there grinning madly at her. What startled her awake was when she reappeared back in Nana's little room in Tavel House. Dream-Tracey pulled back the crochet blanket on Nana's bed, and instead of finding her nana she found her own face. A macabre grin split to expel manic laughter.

When her alarm went off, she stared at the flashing clock in disbelief. Her head pounded. She scrubbed at tired eyes and yawned large enough to crack her jaw. Footsteps thudded past her door as one of her siblings ran to reach the bathroom before anyone else.

Grandma gave Tracey an odd look as she shuffled into the kitchen. Clasping a box of cereal to her chest, Tracey slumped down at the table and groaned. She couldn't remember getting ready for school, only blinking back into awareness as she dragged herself into the car. When Simon squashed her against the door she didn't respond as she usually did by pushing him back.

"Are you feeling okay, hun?" Mom asked, glancing at her through the rear-view mirror.

Tracey grunted.

Her mom didn't look happy with that response, and as Tracey climbed from the car, her mom called her back pressing her hand to Tracey's face.

"You're a little warm, sweetie. Do you want to stay home today?"

Oh, how she wanted to, but she needed to talk to Tony. He'd sent her a message this morning about finding something strange on Doctor Chan's website. "I'll be fine, it was only a bad night's sleep."

"All right, but if you start feeling worse, have the school nurse call me — no buts."

"Can I get her to call you anyway?" Tracey said, mustering up a grin.

Her mom pretended to clip her over the back of the head. "Not a chance." She waited until Tracey entered the school grounds before she drove away.

Laura met up with her just inside the gate. "What happened to you?" Naturally, Laura looked perfect, right down to her socks.

"Bad night."

Math was awful. Tracey just couldn't keep track of all the numbers. They swam in her mind as if chasing each other out of her focus. Science wasn't any better as she shared the class with Dave Two. Without control, his magic battered at her mental shields like the racket of a toddler banging on pots and pans.

Lunch came as a relief. Tracey wasn't hungry but grabbed some fruit anyway, figuring she'd feel more comfortable if she ate something. Damian sat at a table on the other side of the cafeteria. He turned his head away from Tracey when she tried to get his attention by waving. Tracey's eye's narrowed. What was wrong with him? He'd been so nice to her on his first day. She slammed her tray down on the table hard enough to bounce her apple right off. It rolled across the surface.

"Trying to lose weight?" The sharp peals of laughter escalating behind Tracey could only come from the evil queens.

Tracey smiled awkwardly but didn't reply. Anything she said would only encourage them. Meena looked disappointed at the lack of response. Tracey didn't relax until the girl sashayed away. Carla followed after her, like the obedient lackey she was. They went and sat down next to Damian. Tracey's mood soured further. Meena looked back as if sensing Tracey's stare. Her grin was poisonous. Tracey dropped her head to the table and didn't move as Tony lowered his tray down beside her.

"Hey," she grunted.

"Hello to you, too. What's wrong?"

"Nightmares." She peered up into Tony's caring brown eyes and felt tears swell in her own. She blinked rapidly.

"Yeah, me too."

"You too? What did you dream about?"

He shook his head and didn't meet her eye. "I think it must have been triggered from the story you told me — the one about running from the Shadowman?"

"You had a dream about the shadow?"

"Yeah, and of a room full of people right out of *Pride and Prejudice*. The Shadowman smashed open the door, filled the room, and killed everyone inside."

"That's awful." She could understand why he wouldn't meet her gaze. It was her fault he was having the dream. She shouldn't have told him about it. She rubbed her eyes. They felt sore and hot, like mini-suns boiling under her eyelids.

"What I have to tell you probably won't help your mood."

"What? What did you find?" she asked.

Tony bit into his apple. Tracey waited impatiently while he chewed. "There was another Easter egg on Doctor Chan's site. It took me to a site of spells I've never seen before."

Tracey sat up straight. Before she could speak, Laura plonked herself down at Tracey's side.

"What's going on?" the beautiful girl asked. Jonny slid into his usual seat against the wall and hiked his chair up onto two legs.

"Hiya all. What's up with Miss Teddy today?"

"Mrs. Beare, Jonny, not Teddy," Laura admonished.

"You should have seen her this morning. Snarling and snapping at any sound. Must be her time of the month right—"

"Finish that sentence, Jonny, and I'll poke your eyes out," Laura snapped.

"You too—? Ow!"

Laura continued hitting him with her book bag until his chair slipped from where it leaned against the wall. He hit the floor with a crunch.

"Ow! Okay, Laura, I'm sorry."

As soon as Laura stopped hitting him, Tracey threw one of her books in his direction. It bounced off his chest. "Idiot."

"Can I continue?" Tony asked rolling his eyes.

"Dude, leaving me to the women? Come on, you should be helping me out, here." Jonny groaned, struggling to his knees. He pressed his glasses back up his nose.

"Are you kidding? You're on your own, man," Tony told him, but did offer a hand up as he continued. "I was just telling Tracey that I found an Easter egg on Doctor Chan's website that took me to a secret site full of spells."

"Cool," Jonny said offering a fist bump.

Tracey's phone buzzed in her pocket. She checked the screen and jerked in surprise. "Fruit tingles."

"What?"

"Uncle Donny. He messaged me last night and I forgot to call him back." She started typing while she said, "I can't believe I forgot," and received a message back almost instantly.

I need to see you

She replied stating she'd meet him at the office after school. His next message widened her eyes.

No, not the office! Meet me at the entrance to the Sachorn Forest film lot at 4:30

"The film lot?" she mumbled. Maybe he'd forgotten that it was Sarah's birthday. She thought about declining for about two seconds. A chance to go to the film lot while they were filming! No way was she missing that. Sarah would understand. Tracey messaged back her confirmation, hoping she wouldn't get home too late and miss the cake. *Fruit tingles, the matches for Sarah's birthday candles!* Tracey swore. Okay, so she'd stop at the store to buy them on her way to meet her uncle.

"What?" Laura was staring at her. "What are you talking about?" Tony and Jonny leaned in to look at her phone.

"Uncle Donny wants me to meet him at the film lot in Sachorn

Forest."

"That's where they're filming *Saving Time*. Oh, can I come?" Laura begged. "Please?"

Each of her friends gazed at her with big puppy dog eyes. Tracey shook her head at their antics. "Sorry, guys." She held out her phone to show them her uncle's next message "Only one guest pass."

Laura grabbed Tracey's arm and pulled her close. "I want to know everything."

Tracey laughed. "Of course, first call I make," she promised as the bell rang.

Meena appeared at Laura's shoulder. "Nice lipstick, Laura." Carla giggled hysterically.

"Go away," Jonny told her.

Meena glared and stepped closer to Jonny. "Who do you think you're talking to?"

Jonny looked very obviously around the room and then at Meena. "Not much."

Oh God, don't antagonize her. Tracey's heart sank as Meena waved to Dave One. He and Dave Two lumbered over instantly. Damian hovered in the background, his face a mask as he stared at Meena. Dave One chuckled, snapping Tracey's gaze back to the more prominent threat. He stopped at Meena's side. "What are you doing talking to the freaks?"

"Get rid of him," she ordered, gesturing to Jonny.

Dave One grinned. "Sure, babe." He grabbed Jonny by the arm. Tony, Laura, and Tracey quickly stepped forward. Tracey's chest tightened as her magic door rattled. She pressed her hand to her heart and willed it to stay closed. Dave One glanced at Tracey then his stare locked on Tony. The Mage-kind boy's hands were fists and he was breathing hard. The trays on the table jittered making a clanging sound. Dave One let Jonny go. Tracey was at once relieved and worried.

Miss Burke stood at the lunch counter. Tracey gestured to her, but the science teacher didn't look up from her cell phone. Laura was bailed up in the corner by Meena who was saying something to her in a low voice. Laura winked over Meena's head, so whatever it was, her friend wasn't letting it bother her. Dave One loomed over Jonny. The smaller boy stepped back, looking wary.

Tracey felt a flame burst to life in her chest. Her fists clenched, mirroring Tony's stance. "Leave him alone," she said.

"Don't do anything," Jonny hissed at both Mage-kind, staring pointedly at Tracey's wrist.

Dave Two was staring at Tracey. He leaned closer to his buddy and whispered a warning.

As Tracey's anger grew, her magic pulsed low in her chest. She knew she couldn't afford to get angry. There were rules about using magic at school, and the angrier she grew, the less control she would have. She breathed in through her nose and out through her mouth, working to relax her hands by spreading her fingers wide.

Carla pointed to Miss Burke. She had turned and was finally looking in their direction.

"Gee, Meena, if you just wanted to know where I got my lipstick, you should have asked. Call your lapdog off," Laura said loudly, drawing everyone's attention back to her. Tracey stifled a laugh as Laura proceeded to tell Meena she'd borrowed the lipstick from Tracey. Meena's face pinched unhappily. She spun on a heel and stormed away, her entourage following along behind, including Damian. Tracey watched him go, sadly.

Laura grabbed Tracey's wrist. "Don't think I've forgotten what we were talking about — I want every detail of what happens at the set tonight."

Tracey laughed, her mood shifting quickly, "I know. I'll call you, promise."

"And pictures, too."

She arrived at the *Saving Time* lot just after four-thirty. Through the imposing gate, the staging area looked like every other film lot she'd ever seen. People ran in all directions, carrying black boxes and tubes, cameras and tracks. Two apron-clad people spread a selection of food along a cloth covered table, and everywhere Tracey looked people wore headsets or spoke into cell phones. Some tapped rapidly into tablets as they walked. It was like watching a futuristic world full of technology and black uniforms, a world Tracey desperately wanted a part of.

Uncle Donny said he'd meet her near the entrance, but all she could see were muscular security men dressed in black, wearing ear pieces and heavy belts. Hopefully they were only carrying Tasers.

Prince Henry might be here today. Her heart pounded at the thought of seeing him actually film a scene. This was spoiler heaven.

A golf cart pulled up to the gate with a loud screech of brakes. Uncle Donny was behind the wheel, dressed in the same outfit as the security guards.

"Hey, kiddo—put this on."

He handed her a yellow lanyard. Tracey pulled it on over her head, tugging her hair out of the way and climbed into the cart. As they drove back through the gate they held their passes up to a guard who barely glanced at them before waving them through. Tracey's excited gaze swung from side to side trying to capture everything at once. Uncle Donny pointed out the actors and crew they passed, racing the little cart further into the labyrinth of trailers, sheds, and tents. Tracey was buzzing, almost vibrating in her seat. She wondered if she'd get into any trouble if she took some pictures on her phone.

"That's the dressing trailer for John Keiler, he's playing Prince Henry's father. That's the makeup trailer, and that's one of the costumers. Her name is Tracy, only without the 'e'." There were no big-name actors in sight, and when she said as much, her uncle laughed.

"They're out on separate location shoots today. Unit B is filming at the base of Mount Hawthy. Prince Henry's out until nine tonight, and that's why I called you. While the cast and crew are filming, I want you to help me search their trailers."

Her mouth dropped open. "What?"

"It's okay—when the director discovered I was a detective, he decided to keep me on as his onsite investigator. I told him I needed my partner's help, so here you are, hence your lanyard."

She hadn't looked at it when he handed it to her, but now she examined the card on the lanyard carefully. Her picture had been copied off the school student page — she recognized her odd one-eyed squint. Beneath it was her name, and beneath that ... *Private Detective — Junior.* "Does this mean I get a raise?" In her head, she squealed. *Yes, finally!* Her grin faded when what he said sunk in. "Wait — we're going through the cast and crew trailers? Why?"

"Props and pieces of costume have disappeared from the cast dressing rooms. The assistant director wants them found." They drove past more trailers. A dog barked somewhere nearby. Sniffing, Tracey thought she smelled sausages.

"You took a new job? So Miss Tearning's case is definitely over?"

"She's dead, Trace. We're not going to get paid," he said, unusually blunt.

She paused while she thought about that. "So you're not going to investigate her murder?" She scratched at the prickles on her neck wondering if there was a plant or a flower here she was allergic to. Her skin was all itchy.

"That's a job for the police." He didn't meet her eye as he spoke.

Sure. "What do we do with the necklace we found? The one hidden in my bedroom?"

"I suppose we should hand it in to the police so they can return it to Miss Tearning's family, but I'd like you to hold onto it for a little longer. I'm thinking this new case might be connected."

"Connected?" Her back crawled like someone was watching her. She looked around and searched over her shoulder. No one was looking in their direction at all. "What do you mean?"

Uncle Donny reached into the back of the cart and removed a small envelope. "Look at the pieces that have gone missing."

Tracey tipped the photos onto her lap and flipped through each one. They were pictures of broaches, necklaces, and bracelets — the center shape of each piece was a butterfly. How was that even possible? Someone on the set must be connected to the story. "They look —"

"— exactly the same as the butterfly on Miss Tearning's necklace.

Yup, I thought so too."

"You think whoever stole them works with the goons who broke into your office?"

"Mighty coincidence if not."

"And that someone might work here?"

"Possibly," he said.

"So where do we start?"

"Left bereft and empty,
Wind burnt and cross …"

23

He pointed to the closest trailer. "You can start there. That trailer belongs to the leading lady, Miss Stella Stanthorpe—the actress scripted to wear the majority of the missing items."

"Aren't the jewelry pieces used by costumers fake?"

"Supposedly," he answered, and headed off to search the costume and wardrobe department. Tracey went to Miss Stanthorpe's trailer. The door was unlocked. Inside the small space was more clothing and furniture than she thought could possibly fit. *It'll take forever to search through it all.* She locked the door and started with the small cupboards located next to the daybed. All she found were a number of multicolored dog-eared scripts. Her fingers itched to flick through them. With an almighty effort, she held back.

Closing the cupboard, she worked her way through the rest of the trailer. Head down searching through a drawer, she jumped when the trailer door rattled. Forgetting she had a completely legitimate reason for being there, her head darted in every direction searching for a place to hide. Before she could find one, a man stepped into the trailer. She looked up at him in surprise. "Officer Jameson?"

"Miss Masters?" The space that had seemed small earlier now felt tiny as the policeman moved further inside. "What are you doing in here?"

She cringed and then remembered her lanyard. "Working," she said holding it up.

"Aha," he nodded. "On what?"

"Missing props."

"That's why I'm here too. The assistant producer reported props had been stolen from the set. She wanted to ensure it wasn't a sign of anything nastier, given the discovery of Miss Tearning's body by the set builders. And besides, I think my captain has a crush on Prince Henry."

"Don't we all?" Tracey muttered.

Officer Jameson glanced around the enclosed space. "Have you found anything?"

She shook her head.

"Do you mind if I have a quick look?" She shook her head again. They knocked elbows several times until they found a rhythm that worked and automatically moved out of each other's way to search the remainder of the trailer. Tracey shuffled through a cabinet jam-packed with silk scarves and chiffon and uncovered a small wooden box with a decorative silver fish on the side. Glancing over her shoulder to ensure the policeman was occupied, she picked up the box. A spark danced over her hand the second her fingers touched it. *Ouch!* Jamming her fingers into her mouth she flicked her gaze at the oblivious man. Officer Jameson wasn't Mage-kind, so he wouldn't have sensed the protection spell. In case he thought the box might be important and took it to his captain, she knocked a large photo album to the floor, squealed and jumped around pretending it had landed on her toe. In the commotion, she slipped the small box into her bag. Her plan to avoid the officer's attention backfired spectacularly when he pushed her onto the daybed to examine her *injured* foot.

"Does that hurt?" he asked, removing her shoe. He twisted her foot away from his chest and bent her toes gently. It didn't hurt, but she flinched dramatically and scrunched her face with pretend pain. Pinching her inner elbow brought genuine tears to her eyes.

"Let's get you out of here. I think there's a first-aid station just up the path toward the crew trucks. Can you make it that far?"

Holding onto her shoe she let him help her stand, but limped heavily. *Don't catch on.* When he held out an arm she grabbed onto it, feeling awful. Now she was lying to a policeman. Pressed close to Officer Jameson's side, she felt the blank space around him that she always felt around Norms. Her brother Simon gave off a similar feeling of blankness, especially when he was trying to hide something from their mom.

She let her footing stumble on the uneven ground outside. Officer

Jameson wrapped his arm around her and helped her hobble into the first-aid station where she dropped into a chair and groaned loudly. *Am I over doing it?* He turned away to rifle through the first-aid kit on the counter, giving Tracey a small window to check the box. She was surprised to find it hot to the touch. Now to get the officer out of here so she could find out what was wrong with it.

"Shouldn't there be a nurse, or a first-aid person here?" she asked.

Jameson turned away from searching through a number of pressure bandages. "Of course, you're right. I'll see if I can find the crew's nurse. Don't go anywhere," he ordered, waving his finger in her face.

"Funny," she told him, pointing to her *injury*.

He passed her a rolled-up gauze bandage. "I'll be right back."

As soon as the door closed, Tracey pulled the box from her pocket and held her hand over the hottest side. The lid resisted her every attempt to pry it off.

Oh, of course. Miss Stanthorpe must be Mage-kind. Objects of power, like this box, could have spells on them to stop them from being opened. Some spells could even attack the person trying to open it. Silk dampened magic, so wrapping a silk scarf around the box would reduce the strength of the spell surrounding it. That must have been what stopped the box burning up in Miss Stanthorpe's trailer.

Looking around the first-aid trailer, she couldn't see anything made of silk. If she returned the box to her bag, it would start to burn again. The gauze bandage in her hand gave her an idea. Seconds later she had the box fully wrapped and tucked away, crossing her fingers it would hold until she got her hands on something silky.

An ancient nurse with a sour expression returned with Officer Jameson and her uncle.

While the nurse examined Tracey's foot, Tracey pulled faces at her uncle until he realized she'd faked her injury. She breathed a sigh of relief when he took charge, quickly assuring Officer Jameson he would handle things from here and sweet-talked the nurse into wrapping Tracey's ankle. He promised Tracey would visit a doctor to get it checked. Officer Jameson left them reluctantly, and after Tracey assured the nurse her uncle would look after her, she was allowed to limp from the trailer.

"What did you find?" Uncle Donny hissed when they were alone. Tracey pulled the wrapped box from her bag. Even with his lower level magic, he would be able to feel the spell surrounding it. His eyes widened. "Shoot!" he said, tossing the box back to her and flapping his hand around blowing on it dramatically. *Seriously, on a film set everyone overacts.*

"Why do I have to keep it?" she asked.

"It's hot, how can even you hold it?"

"That's why I wrapped it."

"It's like touching a flame," he said still blowing on his fingers.

"What?" The box felt warm beneath the bandages, but the wrapping kept most of the heat from her fingers.

"I guess you'll just have to carry it for now, kiddo," he told her. He then gestured to her foot. "Will you be okay?"

"I was pretending, remember?"

He flushed. "Right. Well, keep up the limp in case that young officer returns."

She'd have to remember that. "So how do we get it open?"

He shrugged. "We'll think of something later. We haven't finished here yet. There are more trailers to search." Tracey touched her bag, thinking they might have just found what they were looking for.

"I didn't finish going through Miss Stanthorpe's trailer," she told him.

"Wrap it up there and move to the trailer next door. Try and stay out of Officer Jameson's way from now on, huh?"

Tracey shook her head and moaned. "It's like he's following me."

There was nothing else to be found in Miss Stanthorpe's trailer. Tracey did steal a scarf to wrap around the bandaged jewelry box. The silk would contain its magic — she promised the trailer she'd return the stolen scarf later.

There was no name on the door of the next trailer, but the instant she stepped inside she knew it belonged to a man. Crinkling her nose at the smell of aftershave and sweaty socks she regretted her need to help. *This is too gross!* Left over take out bags and dirty dishes covered every surface. There were clothes everywhere. Shirts, trousers, and jackets lay dumped where they'd been taken off. The trailer was slightly more spacious than the last one, though it looked no bigger on the outside. She checked inside the cupboards. They were bare — not surprising, given the mess around her.

The click of the trailer door opening made her jump. She spun around, expecting Officer Jameson. A cloud of red smoke poured in through the trailer's door. It brought with it a blast of cold air. Tracey gasped and ducked into the closest cupboard. Slamming the door shut she blanked her mind. Dark smoky shadows seeped into the cupboard, drifting over her face and neck. Icy prickles crawled along her skin. She slapped her hands at them as if she'd walked into a spider's web, but they clung to her like cling wrap. That was when she heard it.

Laughter, low and evil, filled the trailer. Tracey threw up a mental shield, imagining an orange bubble around her with her hidden in the middle. The laughter grew as the smoke became thicker, spreading over her shield bubble like paint. *Get off, get off.* Her breathing grew labored. Stars flashed in her eyes. She had to get out, she had to breathe! She burst out of the cupboard in a flurry of movement and fell at the feet of the man in the red mask.

"What's wrong with me?"
"There is nothing wrong with you."

24

Tracey stared at him, her breath stuck in her throat while her ears filled with white noise. She couldn't move. The laughter slowed. Full lips closed over perfectly straight white teeth, but because his mask covered his head like a scarf, she couldn't tell the color of his hair. She couldn't tell anything about him. All she could see were his dark, soulless eyes. He opened his mouth.

"Well, hello there. I was not expecting you."

She gaped, no sound emerged. *What does he want?*

"You know what I want."

Fruit tingles! He can read my thoughts! She tried to stop thinking. Naturally, her mind went straight to everything she shouldn't think about — especially the box wrapped in silk hidden in her pocket. He didn't say anything or look down, so maybe he couldn't exactly read her mind. It felt as though her frozen heart defrosted enough to beat again at the thought. She'd never be able to not think about her secrets. "Want what?"

"The stone."

"What stone?"

"Do not play games with me, little girl," he hissed and grabbed for her arm. She jumped backward, not wanting him to touch her. Her nana's voice shouted in her mind. *"Don't let the shadow touch you!"* Tracey was trapped. Her only escape was through the door behind her captor. If she stayed too long, she risked her uncle coming in to fetch her. Such evil emanated from this man, Uncle Donny wouldn't stand a chance.

And neither would she. "Let me go."

"Why would I do that?" he asked, his voice silky soft. He stepped closer. Tracey backed up until she hit the wall. She felt a strange sucking sensation as his magic pulled close to his body, swirling angrily as it gathered in strength.

Get out. Now! She slammed her hand onto her emergency band. Her personal alarm, bolstered by both of her parents' magic, activated with a screech that nearly blew out her eardrums. The man in red jumped back, slapping his hands over his ears. He snarled angrily and in another moment was gone. The door slammed against the frame at the speed of his exit.

Breathing heavily, Tracey slumped against the nearest surface — a pull-out desk. With a tap of her hand and her spoken password, her alarm fell silent. *Oh God, oh God!* Panting as though she'd just run a race, she pressed a hand to her chest to keep her heart in place if it decided on a quick exit.

The alarm would bring her uncle. Heck, it would bring everyone. *Get out!* She straightened and stared blankly at the sticky note stuck to her palm. She must have put her hand on it when she'd leant on the table. It was a phone number and a name — a name she recognized — Doctor Chan. Why would Doctor Chan's number be here? *Whose trailer is this?* Voices outside told her she'd run out of time. Pulling her shattered confidence around her like a cloak, she left the trailer. Her legs wobbled and she stumbled. Quickly, she sat down on the steps outside.

Several people ran toward her from different angles. Fortunately, Uncle Donny reached her first. "Tracey?"

She knew he could sense the dark power still clinging to her, but wouldn't understand it for what it was.

"Can we get out of here?" she begged. Her voice sounded tiny. Her chest tightened, making it hard to breathe. She wanted to go home and forget about the encounter, but using her alarm would demand an explanation. It was time to tell him everything.

He tugged her to her feet and led her through the crowd of film crew. The black of their outfits freaked her out, and every scrap of red she spied from the corner of her eye startled her. Uncle Donny kept his expression neutral, but she could tell he was worried. *Why am I so cold?*

They sat down at one of the craft tables and Tracey picked at the chocolate muffin her uncle bought for her. She wasn't hungry.

"The chocolate will make you feel better." He blew on a takeaway cup of coffee. The steam curling around his face brought back memories of shadowy fingers. She tore her gaze away before she screamed.

"Talk to me, kiddo," he pleaded when she was silent for too long.

She couldn't meet his eyes. A quick glance around confirmed there was no one close enough to hear their conversation. He watched her through scrunched up eyes before they widened in understanding and he pulled a small device from his pocket. It was his Muffler—she'd helped him to spell it last year. The box, when active, would blur any sound around them for several feet. They'd put it together for him to use during confidential client meetings. She never thought they'd need to use it on themselves.

"Tracey, why did you set off your alarm?"

Hesitantly, she told him about Tony's research into the butterfly necklace and the missing jewelry they thought was connected to Miss Tearning's case. Then she took a deep breath and told him about the trip to the summit of Mount Hawthy, the mysterious empty street they'd found and their confrontation with the man in the red mask.

Uncle Donny's face was pale by the time she finished. Eyes wide, he stared at her for so long she wondered if he'd fallen asleep with his eyes open. He moved at last, taking her hands in his. "You took such a stupid risk, Tracey. You and your friends could have been hurt or even killed. I'm glad you're all okay, but your mom is going to kill me—swear to God, she will kill me when she finds out about this."

"You can't—"

His glare stopped her cold. "I can. I have to. You know I'm not powerful enough to deal with something like this on my own. Even sensing the remnants of this man's magic—half an hour after the attack—it's almost too much for me. I'm going to call in a friend of mine on the Mage-kind Force and pass this on to him. You should never have gotten involved, Tracey. It was foolish of me to ask for your help."

"Uncle Donny, it was a case about a missing necklace. There was no way you could have known it would end up like this. It's not your fault." She clutched his hot hands with her icy fingers, feeling as though she would never feel warm again.

"I'm glad you've finally told me what's been going on, and—"

"We can't give the case to M-Force!" she interrupted. "I'm involved now, Uncle Donny. The man in the red mask knows about me. He's not going to just throw up his hands and back away because I'm no longer working the case."

"Tracey, if you're not involved, he'll leave you alone. I have to protect you and your friends."

She stared into his eyes willing him to hear her. "Uncle Donny, I know you want to keep me safe, but I don't think you can. Only knowing the truth can do that."

"Don't be naïve, Tracey," he snapped. "We can't stay here." He looked over his shoulder at the deserted craft area. "Come on, let's get you home."

When they stepped through the front door, they walked right into the loudest argument Tracey had ever heard between her family.

"It was her birthday present!" Peter shouted. His face was red, as if he'd been shouting for a while.

"She's too young! You'll corrupt her mind." Aunt Gemma snapped back.

Tracey's grandma pointed at Aunt Gemma and snarled, "It is not your place to say what can be done in this house, Gemma!"

Mom and Dad stood near the door, watching them. Their faces scrunched in worry. The room was full of balloons and streamers. *Oh God, Sarah's birthday!* By the looks of it, Tracey had completely missed her sister's party. If Sarah hadn't been angry with her before, she certainly would be now — Tracey didn't even have a present. The shouting grew even louder when her uncle told her parents what had happened at the film lot.

Tracey wasn't allowed to leave the room. She huddled in on herself, pulling her legs up onto the sofa cushion and wrapped her arms around her knees while Mom yelled at Uncle Donny. Tracey's dad remained silent, which was far more disturbing than her mom's screaming. Tracey tried several times to distract everyone by asking about Sarah's birthday dinner and finally noticed Sarah was not even in the room. "Mom, where's Sarah?"

"She's upstairs and she's very upset you weren't here."

"I have the candles," Tracey said, her voice shaky. She pulled them from her pocket along with the matches.

"Too late." The look on her mom's face froze Tracey to the bone.

She shoved the candles and matches back into her pocket, feeling awful. Distraction over, Mom returned to shouting at Uncle Donny. When her words became particularly nasty, Grandma stood up and held out both hands, "Stop this! What's done is done. We can no more undo it than we can stop the tides. We need a plan of attack, and to decide what is to be done from here."

"She's not working for him anymore," Mom snapped. *Ouch, she's beyond angry.* Magic crackled throughout the room. Lines of orange lightning exploded above her mom's head, shooting across the ceiling in long arcs. *Mom's going to blow out a lightbulb.*

"It was just a missing necklace," Tracey muttered, trying to remind them.

"Not helping," Dad told her.

Tracey's mom turned on him in an instant. "That's all you have to say?"

"See what uncontrolled magic can lead to?" Aunt Gemma said from the couch. She smiled, but the smile didn't reach her eyes. They were sharp, pinpoint grey orbs. Her lip curled up in the corner.

"Oh, don't you start," Grandma shouted, setting off another round of arguments.

"You are not investigating this case anymore." Mom pointed a sharp fingernail at Uncle Donny. To Tracey's surprise, he stood up and confronted her.

"I have to."

Everyone stared at him in shock. Uncle Donny was the least confrontational person Tracey knew, and for a detective that was a particularly grating character trait. He'd never stood up to his older sister before, and his behavior silenced everyone. Then Grandma agreed with him.

"There is more going on here than what Tracey is telling us."

Oh fruit tingles. They quickly turned on Tracey. Mom spoke, eyeing her carefully. "She is just a child."

Grandma's face was about as serious as Tracey had ever seen her. "And yet here we are. I warned you, Beth, something was coming. When she was born I told you there was a shadow in her future."

Grandma had a Vision about me? Tracey's blood ran cold. Her stomach pulled inside out and she clutched a hand over it fearing she was going to be sick.

Tracey's dad stepped forward, touching Grandma's arm. "Mom, she doesn't know." The angry family had unconsciously formed a circle in the middle of the living room.

"Know what?" Tracey asked.

Peter threw up his hands, "Someone just tell us what is going on! You're all talking, but no one's actually saying anything."

Aunt Gemma pointed to Peter. "Precisely. Magic is uncertain. The future is unknown for a reason. No one should know what's coming. There's no such thing as fate. Adele is just feeding you all magical nonsense."

"Sit down, all of you. Gemma, if you speak again I will Forbid you from this house!"

Ouch. Magical forbidding was a particularly nasty punishment. Tracey's mom was really upset.

Tracey was just confused.

Aunt Gemma looked at the floor. When she raised her head, her face was a mask. "You're serious aren't you, Beth? I thought you, out of all of them, had some sense. I'll go, but I'm warning you, don't listen to her. Her stories are dangerous. They'll lead Tracey on the same path as Mother, and look at how that ended."

"Get out, Gemma," Tracey's mom commanded, her voice frosty. The front door slammed shut only moments later, rattling all the windows.

Grandma sat down and took both of Tracey's hands. Her fingers were cold, the joints swollen and cramped. "You're getting stronger, honey. You're sensing higher forms of magic, and this investigation is setting you on a dangerous path." Grandma stared directly into Tracey's eyes. Tracey's head swam, her thoughts seemed to slow as her head became too heavy to lift. Her eyes drifted closed as her chin sank to her chest.

"You've been having nightmares, haven't you?"

"Yes," Tracey whispered. Mom gasped softly.

"Of a shadow?"

"Yes."

"Has the shadow become real?"

Tracey nodded, a jagged little movement. "Yes."

"What else?"

She told Grandma about the Vision. Of seeing Miss Tearning at the river and witnessing her murder.

The family remained silent when Tracey finished speaking. "This is why the investigation cannot stop," Grandma said at last. "Tracey is connected to this case. It would be too dangerous for her to be kept out of it now."

"What do you mean?" Tracey forced her head up. Her vision was blurry and her throat felt claggy like she'd swallowed glue.

Mom stood up. "I can't hear any more of this, Adele. We cannot allow Tracey to continue her involvement."

"We must," Grandma argued.

"But the danger ..." Tracey's mom paced the room, the scowl on her face reaching epic proportions.

"I will teach her. She is strong, Beth, very strong. The shadow is coming and we must ensure she is ready."

"She's too young."

"We don't have any choice." Grandma stood up and drew Tracey into the middle of the room to sit her down on the floor. "Close your eyes, Tracey. Picture your shield. I don't want you to hold anything back. Raise your shields around you at full strength."

Tracey let go with a long breath and did as Grandma asked. She flung open the imaginary door in her chest and released her magic, not realizing how many conflicting powers had been swirling around the room until they all disappeared. Her orange bubble snapped in place around her. She let her bubble grow, and then hardened its skin like a shell. She could hear Grandma's voice in her head directing her actions. It was so easy to follow her instructions.

Inside her shell, power began to swell. It swirled around her, growing stronger, pulling her heartbeat outside her body to surround her with the sound. At some point Grandma stopped speaking and in the silence Tracey felt her pulse, a steady rhythm beating against her skin. She drifted.

"Please, I need help."
"Don't hurt them."
"But how?"
"Just stop."

25

Her shield became flexible again, drawing close to her skin like a layer of clothing. She opened her eyes to find she was alone in the living room and the sun was up. When she stood, her legs wobbled. Realizing with a smack of her lips that her mouth was dry, she went in search of a drink.

Her mom and grandma were sitting at the kitchen table cradling steaming cups of tea. Their heads rose in unison as Tracey stepped into the room. Sharp lines around her mom's eyes and mouth betrayed her worry. A spike of sorrow stabbed Tracey's chest at the thought that she'd caused such worry.

"Welcome back," her mom said with a soft smile.

"What?"

"It's Tuesday morning, honey. School started an hour ago. I'll take you in late and we'll tell them you had an appointment."

"Tuesday?" Tracey had sat in the living room for over fourteen hours! Apart from the sore muscles, she felt pretty good, if a little hungry. Actually, very hungry. "Food?"

Mom jumped up and started the microwave. Tracey's mouth watered at the smell of spaghetti sauce. She gulped down the glass of water Grandma placed beside her hand. "What happened?" she asked. Her mom put the reheated dinner down and Tracey ate like she hadn't seen food for days.

"That was a guided meditation, Tracey. You're more gifted than we'd realized," Grandma said. Her whole face moved when she smiled.

Tracey eyed her over her fork. "Don't you only do one of those when you turn eighteen?"

"Normally," Mom said. "I still don't like Donald asking you to help with his case. However little I like it, though, I realize he had no intention of involving you in something dangerous. So, to get ahead of the dangers you're now facing, we're going to help you practice. Work on your shields, and teach you some basic defense spells."

Tracey nodded but kept eating. *I'm starving!* "What about work?" she asked. "And school?"

"School only."

Her head shot up. "But, Mom, I've got a pass to the film set. It's a Prince Henry film. How often does that happen? You *have* to let me go."

Her mom looked at her with *The Face.*

"Please," Tracey begged. Her heart thumped hard — still in tune with it, she practically felt the muscle contract.

There was a long silence while her mom and grandma shared a look. Eventually, Mom nodded. "You stay with Donald at all times. No more splitting up."

Yes!

"Don't get too excited. You have an interview with the agents from M-Force straight after school today, and it depends on what they have to say. They'll be waiting for you at Donald's office."

Tracey gulped. That wasn't going to be fun. Today was probably a day she'd wish school would never end.

"All your friends need to be there, Tracey," her mom reminded. "I've called their parents and they are understandably furious. Tony's parents will bring him in at five-thirty. Mr. and Mrs. O'Shae will stay with Tony during his questioning. Laura's dad will observe Laura's questioning, as will Jonny's mom."

Tracey's stomach, full from eating, twisted sharply. Her friends were going to hate her. "I should get to school," she said quietly, wishing fervently her mom hadn't called them.

Grandma leaned over and tapped Tracey's hand. "Honey, you might be feeling good after your mediation right now, but you're likely to be more open to things. Keep your shields up, okay? Your magic might be a little difficult to control."

Uncontrolled magic? Oh! Tracey fell back into her chair.

Mom looked worried. "Honey?"

"I forgot to tell you something."

"What is it, sweetie?"

She told them about Dave Two and his new powers. "They haven't come through yet—not fully. I don't even think he knows, Mom. No one in his family are Mage-kind. I-I thought ... isn't he too old?"

"Honey, you have to tell him. Your teachers, too. If he doesn't know ..." Mom shook her head. "I'll come with you to talk to your principal. Tracey, are you sure they were coming from him?"

"It was exactly the same feeling as when Sarah triggered," Tracey admitted.

Forty minutes later, Tracey and her mom sat in Principal Shepard's office. The conversation was awkward to say the least. Principal Shepard's round red face began to sweat. Tracey could see it bead in his thinning hair. He tried to convince them Dave's parents should be informed first, but Tracey's mom insisted Dave learn about his abilities before his parents were told. Tracey suppressed a grin. Her mom could be very persistent. They sat in silence, waiting uncomfortably for Dave Two's arrival.

Principal Shepard stood and paced to the wall. He was huffing before he even turned around to sit back down. Tracey glanced at her mom but the older woman shook her head and looked away. Tracey figured the non-magical principal was scared, and he was right to be. She had no idea how Dave Two was going to take the news. *This is going to change his life.* She felt sick to her stomach over it. *Why do I have to be here?*

Dave Two walked in and stopped dead, his gaze darting from Tracey to Principal Shepard and back again. His face changed from curiosity to anger. "I didn't do it."

"Sit down, Mr. Betts," Principal Shepard ordered, pointing a finger to the chair next to Tracey.

"Whatever it is, I didn't do it," Dave said again, not budging from the doorway. His green eyes narrowed at Tracey.

"Mr. Betts," Principal Shepard's hard voice allowed no arguments.

Dave sat down but continued to glare as Tracey's mom spoke. Tracey couldn't maintain eye contact with him and looked away. She didn't want to be here for this. After her mom told Dave he was Mage-kind, he backed toward the door scrubbing his hand over his closely shaven head. "This is bull. You're wrong."

"Mr. Betts, please sit down."

"This is bull. She's lying!" He lunged at Tracey, grabbing her shirt and yanked her to her feet. "Tell them you're lying!"

Tracey kicked out struggling against him but he was too mad. "Mr. Betts!" Principal Shepard and Tracey's mom grabbed Dave's arms to pull him off, but it was like moving an eighteen-wheeler. He didn't give an inch, and his grip on Tracey's shirt only tightened.

It's fine, I don't really need to breathe! "Dave," she gasped, looking him in the eye. "You know I'm telling the truth." He stared at her and she could see the terror in his wide gaze. His nostrils flared as he breathed shallowly. She tried to tell him she was sorry with her eyes. He let her go and collapsed. Tracey fell to her knees with him as he buried his head in her shoulder.

"I don't want to be Mage-kind. My dad is going to kill me."

She patted his sweaty shoulder awkwardly and stared up at her mom. "Help," she mouthed.

"Dave, honey, it's not a bad thing," Tracey's mom said. She waved at Principal Shepard, shooing him back and knelt down beside the distraught boy touching his arm gently. "Sweetheart?"

Dave looked up at her, his eyes red and his nose snotty.

"It will be okay."

"It won't," he said sniffing loudly. "Dad will hate me. He hates all Mage-kind." Dave tugged Tracey's mom's sleeve. "You can't tell him. Please, please don't tell my mom and dad."

For a moment Tracey's mom looked helpless. "Honey—"

Tracey's heart lurched. This was all her fault. She shouldn't have told. "Please, please don't tell them."

"We won't," she promised wanting Dave to stop crying. She didn't remember ever seeing him look this scared before. He was covered in sweat, his face was pale, and she could feel him shaking beneath her hands.

"Tracey—"

"Mom, can't we get him some help? Find someone to teach him the basics until he can tell his parents about his powers? Please?"

"Please, please?" Dave begged.

Principal Shepard shook his head. From his body language, Tracey could see they weren't going to win this battle. She grabbed Dave's arm and shook it until he looked at her.

"We will help you—I promise."

Tears rolled down his face. He looked at Tracey and nodded. It was the barest movement.

"Mrs. Masters, if you would please stay for the arrival of Mr. Betts' parents. Tracey, you need to return to class now."

Tracey helped Dave to stand. His grip on her shirt was so tight she wondered if he was going to tear it. His eyes were glued to hers, begging her to stay, but the principal escorted her from the room. She stood, frozen, outside the closed door. There was no sound from the room she'd just left. A glare from the office secretary forced Tracey to return to class, but she couldn't focus. She didn't pay any attention to her lessons that day, thinking of Dave's face and of the terror in his eyes. She didn't mention it to her friends at lunchtime either, but she couldn't get his face out of her mind.

Dave did not return to class.

When Tracey walked into her uncle's private office later that afternoon, there were two strangers waiting for her. A short man with broad shoulders climbed to his feet at her entrance. He was dressed in an ill-fitting suit—like he'd recently lost a lot of weight and hadn't had time to go shopping yet. His grey-tinged hair was shorn close to his scalp and he had a distinctive long, hooked nose. His watch gleamed, the green bar across the face flashing rhythmically. The woman beside him was taller with long red hair scraped back into a tight ponytail. Her piercing blue eyes looked Tracey over quickly, giving Tracey the feeling she wasn't impressed with what she saw. The female agent's bracelet—a pretty silver chain—had a stone dangling from it that flashed red a few times before it turned green.

Tracey cracked her shield bubble to let her power seep out. *BAM!* They were both at least as strong as her grandma, meaning they rated as Significants. Power swelled and ebbed around them like attack dogs anxious to be let off the leash. Hopefully they'd be strong enough to fight the man in the red mask. A little voice at the back of Tracey's mind started laughing hysterically. She told the voice to shut up.

Uncle Donny sat Tracey down on his little sofa and the M-Force agents stood on either side of the room, forcing her to turn her head to look at them as they spoke. Uncle Donny introduced Tracey, but neither agent stepped forward to shake her hand. She was glad for that. Given their swirling powers, she didn't want them to touch her.

He introduced the man as Agent Malden and the woman as Agent Striker. Agent Striker's voice was croaky like a heavy smoker's when she asked, "Her parents?"

"I'm here as her guardian," Uncle Donny told them.

"And the others?"

"Will be here later," he confirmed.

Uncle Donny sat down beside Tracey and patted her knee. Agent Striker dragged a desk chair around and positioned it right in front of Tracey. "I will touch you now." It wasn't a question.

Tracey jerked her head, her voice soft. "Ah, o-okay."

The woman touched Tracey's wrist with icy fingers and examined her bracelet. The agent nodded at Agent Malden.

Tracey's chest tightened. Could Agent Striker tell her bracelet had been altered?

Agent Malden smiled. "It's okay, Tracey—we know all about your *faulty* bracelet."

Her eyes sprang wide. *They think it's faulty?* She hoped they weren't going to replace it and then realized he was being sarcastic. "How did you know?"

"We've been watching you for some time."

Tracey launched off the sofa and backed away. Their eyes drilled into her skin. She felt naked. The hairs on her arms rose. "Watching me?"

"We have a list of students who use their abilities a little more frequently than we'd like," he told her.

Her voice climbed in pitch. "List? I'm on a list?"

"Nothing to worry about. We know you assist your uncle with his PI practice. It's just an observation. You have done nothing wrong."

She could almost hear Agent Striker add "yet" to Agent Malden's statement. The woman's eyes narrowed. "Sit back down, Tracey," she ordered. "I'll scan you while you give your statement. That way, we will know if you are telling the truth."

Tracey didn't want to sit down. "You think I'm lying?" Heat blossomed across her skin.

"Not at all," Agent Malden interrupted, shooting a dark look his partner's way. "Sometimes we withhold the things we don't think are relevant. Everybody does."

Like I'm going to buy that. Tracey hesitated before she inched back to the sofa. Agent Striker moved so close to Tracey their knees knocked together. Tracey twitched, wanting to move away. This whole situation was horrible. She didn't want to be here. Agent Striker placed her hands on Tracey's knees. The jolt that hit her was so unexpected she almost didn't get her shields up in time. Her bracelet glowed an angry red as she fought her instinctive reaction to push the woman away, both physically and magically. She clenched her teeth and sucked air between them as she waited for the urge to pass.

Agent Striker stared into Tracey's eyes. Power probed at her skin, looking for a way inside. It was eerily similar to the man in the mask's attack and Tracey reacted the same way, pulling everything back and throwing up her protections.

The agent sighed loudly. "You must lower your shields so I can scan you."

Tracey's instincts screamed not to do it, but she didn't have a choice. Closing her eyes and fighting her fear, Tracey bought her shields down.

The woman gasped, immediately lifting her hands and sitting back in her chair. Tracey's eyes sprang open as Agent Malden jumped to his feet. Uncle Donny rushed to stand between the agents and Tracey. Both Agent Striker's bracelet and Agent Malden's watch glowed a fiery red.

"What's going on?" Tracey asked, her eyes darting from her uncle to the agents and back again. *Why are they staring at me like that?* Her whole body was one taut wire.

"How old are you?" Agent Striker demanded.

"One filled with hope,

A fire for the world …"

26

Fifteen, why?" Tracey stood up.

"You have a lot of power. It was unexpected. Please accept our apologies," Agent Malden offered and gestured for everyone to sit back down. When they were calmer, he began by asking about Miss Tearning's death and Tracey's trip up the mountain. His watch remained a steady green throughout the interrogation and Agent Striker's bracelet flashed red periodically.

Tracey told them everything she could remember. Agent Striker's power pressed hard against Tracey's personal boundaries. At one point, as Tracey was explaining how the man in the red mask had probed them, Agent Striker pushed on Tracey's memory center, forcing an image of the man into her mind.

"No!" Tracey cried out, mentally pushing the cruel woman away.

The agent fell off her chair. Jumping to her feet, Tracey backed into the wall. *I don't want to see him again!* Agent Striker stood up, her glare strong enough to melt the plastic coating off her uncle's window sign.

At that moment the door opened and Laura, Tony, and Jonny walked in. They were followed by Tony's parents. Mouths dropped open all around as they took in what was going on. "Hey!" Jonny shouted, racing to Tracey's side.

"Wait in the outer office," the agents shouted in unison.

Tony's parents tugged her worried friends back out through the door. Uncle Donny shot Tracey a quick look to confirm that she was okay and darted after them.

"What's your problem? They were only worried about me," Tracey snapped, chest heaving. An image of the man in the red mask sprang into her mind again. She shook her head wanting to be rid of the memory.

Her stomach whirled and swam. Her hand flew to her mouth as bile rose up into her throat. *Don't be sick!*

The agents shared a look that put her on edge.

"Your uncle rates a Moderate level, doesn't he?" Agent Malden asked.

"Yes."

The agents shared another long look. Agent Malden stepped forward, "Can you picture the man in the red mask? Did you ever see his face?"

She shook her head. "He wore a mask both times."

Agent Malden knelt beside Tracey while Agent Striker moved to the door. Tracey stared at Striker's hands. It looked like she sketched a locking spell around the handle. The door sparked brightly. The pendant dangling from the agent's bracelet flashed red and then stayed that way.

Tracey opened her mouth to demand the woman undo her spell when Agent Malden spoke—inside her head.

Your uncle is in a precarious situation. He should never have taken this case. The man you describe is very dangerous. We believe he is one of the original descendants of the Sect of Five. When Tracey didn't flinch they shared another look. Agent Malden spoke aloud. "If this man gets his hands on the object he is searching for the results could be catastrophic. Tracey, you survived confronting him twice. You should have a good psychic read on him now. We would like to forward this psychic print to our colleagues, and to do that we need you to focus on your memory so we can extract the print. Agent Striker is particularly adept with memory prints. To do the extraction, you will need to let her fully past your barriers. You are more powerful than we realized, which means this will be both easier, and more difficult, for you."

"What do you mean?"

"You are strong enough to produce an excellent quality psychic print of the man in question. However, you are also strong enough, unconsciously, to prevent us taking a copy from your mind. Which means we will need to go a little deeper into your subconscious and you will need to work very hard at letting us inside."

Agent Striker's power pushed and tugged at Tracey's skin in waves. If she didn't do what the agents asked they wouldn't be able to track down the man in the red mask. He could come after Tracey again—he could come after her uncle.

"Okay," she said, dropping back into her seat. As soon as Agent Striker touched her, Tracey closed her eyes and breathed the way Grandma had taught her. When she was almost calm she pictured the scary man. The image came to her quickly, as did the fear and darkness of the shadow. She bit back a scream before remembering it was only in her head. She focused on the red halo of the evil man's power.

A cold feeling rose up over her body like she'd stepped into a pool of water. It flowed over her head and smothered her senses. Her breathing grew faster but she couldn't feel her chest move. Red shadows danced around the edges of her vision until it was all she could see.

She lost track of time. The red smoke coalesced into a line, and the line blurred. Blinking rapidly Tracey found herself staring at a tall staircase, the steps in front of her were red—covered in blood or wet paint. She could see drips and splashes of the deeper red mixed in with a lighter orange. A glance over her shoulder showed the stairs led away from her, down into the darkness below.

Tracey's head swam. She flung both hands out for balance, but there was no railing to grab onto. Everywhere she looked was either staircase or blackness. She couldn't seem to get any air into her lungs. In one blink, she was looking at the empty staircase, in another she stared into the eyes of the man in the red mask. She heard a gasp—one that did not come from her—and then a voice spoke into her ear.

"Focus on this man."

She didn't want to. She fought against the order, but it repeated over and over until she opened her eyes. All she could see was red swirling smoke. It flowed over her the instant she looked at it.

Focus, the word floated in front of her. *What does this power feel like?*

"Cold," she murmured.

The words blurred and rewrote themselves as if someone swirled them with a finger. *What does it sound like?*

She listened carefully. "Like a jazz song. The notes jar, they don't blend."

And the smell?

"Like snow."

Touch? Tracey raised her hand and ran her fingers through the smoke. "Grainy, like sand."

You said it looks red?

"Yes."

There was a loud click beside her ear and Tracey's eyes snapped open.

"Well done," Agent Striker said. Her smile was a little bit creepy, her upper teeth and gums fully exposed.

"What just happened?" Tracey dug her fingers into her temples as pain stabbed into her brain. "Ouch."

Agent Malden sat at her uncle's desk typing rapidly onto a tablet keyboard. He didn't look up. "You just provided us with a magical profile. Is there anything else about the man that you can remember?"

"He's taller than me, his eyes are brown and he has really white, straight teeth."

"Is that all?"

She nodded and winced as the movement sent knives twisting into her eye sockets. "My head hurts. Where's Uncle Donny?"

Agent Striker unlocked the door and called for her uncle. "And bring a couple of aspirin."

Tracey swallowed the tablets as her friends were called into the room. "You're not going to interview them separately?"

Agent Striker rolled her eyes at the question. Tracey flushed. Oh, of course. Her interrogator magic would allow Agent Striker to distinguish between her friends' feelings. Strange, they never showed *that* on TV. Jonny gave the agent a wide berth as he sat down, Tony's parents stood against the wall and Jonny's mom stood next to Tony's mom. The two women looked at each other with worried eyes. Jonny's mom's dreadlocks whipped back and forth as she shook her head. Laura's dad hovered in the doorway, his well-fitted grey pinstriped suit looked rumpled. It was such an unusual sight Tracey couldn't stop staring at him. When everyone had squeezed in, Tracey shared a wobbly grin with her friends.

Striker stared at Tony for ages after he sat down, and for the next two hours, the agents asked question after question about the man in the red mask and what had happened to them in the kitchen of the empty house. Tracey's gaze drifted to Tony's parents. Joelle O'Shae's eyes were fixed on Tony's face. Stefan O'Shae's fingers massaged his temple. Tracey could feel Striker's magic poking around her friend. Tony's pale face was sweaty. He looked sick. Anger curled in Tracey's mind, blocking her nose. She snorted out expecting to see smoke and forced her gaze away. Jonny was staring at her. He tried to smile but the quirk of his lips looked wrong. Tracey had never seen him sit so still before. He was always twitching or pacing. He was like a statue now. Everything about this was wrong. *My fault.*

When the agents finally left, Tracey slumped over on the sofa until her head rested against the arm. Jonny and Tony sprawled out over the floor in front of her feet. Laura remained in her chair, still looking cool and calm as if she'd not been relentlessly questioned for the last two hours.

Jonny's mom and Laura's dad offered to get dinner. Joelle and Stefan wanted to take Tony home but he begged to stay. Reluctantly, they agreed to go with the other parents. "We'll be back soon — don't go anywhere," Joelle said, giving them all a long look over her spectacles.

As soon as they left, Tony sat up. "So now what?"

Tracey lifted her aching head. "You heard them. We're not allowed to continue the case." Her friends looked at her with pleading eyes and puppy dog faces. *When did I become the sensible one?* She sighed loudly — she hadn't told the agents about the box. She'd noticed Uncle Donny neglected to mention it to the agents too. "The box." she whispered to her friends. "Let's try to open it."

Tony grinned. "I think I know how."

"Why didn't you say something before?" Tracey cried as they jumped to their feet.

Holding his finger to his lips, Tony said, "We need to go somewhere else."

She peered around. "We have to be back before Uncle Donny or your parents get back.

"Somewhere close then," Jonny said, bouncing on his toes.

"The alley," Tracey suggested and tugged open the back door. She ran back to grab her bag. Her hands were shaking. "Laura, can you draw a large circle? Big enough for all of us to stand in." She held out a piece of white chalk.

"Me?"

Tracey raised her hands. The tremble was obvious. Laura's lips lifted as she gave Tracey a smile. Tracey unwrapped the silk from the box and found it was still hot to the touch. When the circle was complete, Tracey placed the box in the center.

The four friends stood on the edges of the circle, forming a smaller square within it at Tony's direction. He referred to Doctor Chan's website on his phone and stood opposite Tracey so that the two Mages had a Norm on either side.

Tony eyed Tracey seriously. "When we hold hands I'll be the anchor, so you'll have to direct the spell. Imagine filling the square between us with your power. I'll read it—"

"What about us?" Jonny asked.

"Focus on the box," Tony told him and tucked the paper into his pocket. He held out his hands. "Ready?"

Laura took Tony's hand easily. Jonny glanced at Tony's other hand and said, "Don't get any ideas." He twined his fingers with Tony.

Tony grinned, "Ha! You wish!"

"Ouch—my feelings are hurt," Jonny said with a grin and an over the top wink.

"Guys," Laura shook her head. "We're supposed to be focusing."

Ignoring them, Tracey clasped their hands and stared at the box. *I hope this is a good idea.* Jonny's hand was clammy. Laura squeezed her fingers. When Tracey felt the square between them close, she flung open her closet door and drew out her power.

"Destroyed all that he loved,
Heart black, soul scorched …"

27

The air crackled.

"Whoa." Tracey's eyes sprang open at the sound of Jonny's voice. His foot twitched.

"Don't move," she and Tony snapped at him in unison.

Laura clenched Tracey's fingers tightly. "It's strong," she whispered.

Tracey nodded at Tony to start the spell and focused her attention back on the box. Her mind was humming. The hairs on her arms rose as magic flowed through her. *What a rush!* She felt warm and calm. Her heart thumped steadily. *How can anyone think this is dangerous?* Her eyes drifted closed as power filled her body. It felt … right.

Tony spoke. "Locked and safe, closed and safe, enclosed and safe, circled and safe. Open and stay safe." Tracey cracked her eyes to watch the beauty of the spell. The magic flowing between the four teenagers became a visual mass of tangled orange energy. It looked like chaos, writhing and twisting on itself. All she saw was love and hope. There was a logic to the wild form. She watched the blob move and in her eyes, it was dancing. *Amazing.* She wanted the others to see what she could and focused hard on the pulsating blob. It beat like a heart and grew brighter. Laura and Jonny gasped. Tony kept talking, the spell flying from his lips. Tracey couldn't make out his words. Her body was thrumming. She could hear music; a drum beat that was partly her heart and partly the blob. Tiny threads shot out from the writhing orange ball and stabbed into the box.

Open within this circle, where we will keep you safe. Tracey heard the words, spoken in a British woman's accent, in her mind. She repeated them aloud, and as the last was spoken, the box popped open.

"Can we let go now?" Jonny asked.

Tracey opened her eyes wondering when she'd closed them and stared around at her friends. Laura gasped. "Tracey, your eyes!" She could feel her friends' hands trembling and held on tightly.

"Not yet," Tony blurted out. "Tracey has to absorb the power back in or it'll explode when you break the circle."

She was already pulling back on her power, tugging on the strands that made up the ball of energy, unwinding it gently before drawing it into her chest. When it was nestled back inside her, curled up like a kitten in a bucket, she closed the door. Her skin tingled like she was electrified. Music danced in her mind. She wanted to do it again. Her voice croaked when she said, "Okay, you can let go now."

Her friends collapsed, looking exhausted.

"What a rush," Jonny groaned, clutching his head between his palms.

Laura rubbed her arms, her eyes glowing. "That was amazing."

Wriggling forward, Tony peered into the opened box. "We did it."

Inside the box was a pale oval stone on a bed of dried grass. Painted on the stone was an image of a butterfly. A silver chain attached to the stone with a clasp. "Is that it?" Laura whispered.

It is. Tracey could feel it, warm and peaceful. Still, she held her hand over the stone to check. The air around the stone felt supercharged. "Yes," she confirmed softly.

"Well, pick it up," Jonny pushed.

Her fingers froze mid-reach. *Should I touch it?* The stone was calling to her, begging to be held. She couldn't hear it speak in words but she knew what it wanted. She glanced at her friends' excited faces. An image of Nana appeared in her mind. Quickly, Tracey tapped the lid closed and wrapped the box back up. "We have to hide it. Can't risk anyone finding out that we have it." She clutched the box to her chest. *One little peek couldn't hurt.* She fought the urge. Too dangerous. Her skin still tingled and her fingers itched. She clenched her hands into fists. *Oh, I want to do that again.*

"We can't put it back in Donny's safe. The goons have already broken into it once," Laura reminded her. The four friends gathered everything off the ground and made sure to erase the circle with their feet before heading back into the office.

"Don't tell anyone," Tony told Tracey. "And don't tell us where you hide it."

She nodded, her fingers caressing the now cool sides of the box. A drum still thudded inside her head. She had no intention of telling anybody.

Their parents found them seated in Donny's office in the same poses as when they'd left. Tracey focused on breathing slowly, knowing she'd be under the adults' intense scrutiny. It was the best acting job of her life — pretending everything was normal and that she didn't have a magic infused stone shoved beneath her pullover. Dinner was a quiet affair. The parents must have talked it all over with each other because they seemed a lot calmer. She did worry that when her friends got home they'd be punished. Joelle and Stefan looked especially pale — but of course, they were only ones who fully understood how dangerous the man in the red mask was.

Grandma stood at the door waiting for her when she got home. "How did it go?"

Tracey paused, afraid Grandma would sense the presence of the stone. Her smile was soft, the familiar scent of warm bread, comforting in a way Tracey desperately needed.

Mom walked out of the kitchen. "We're about to dish up dinner. Go clean up. I want to hear everything that happened with the M-Force agents."

"I ate at Uncle Donny's," she said and moved quickly to the stairs. In her mind, she wanted to run. She beat the urge back savagely. *Way to be obvious.*

"You can sit and tell us what happened, though. I want to know what they said. Are they handling — ?"

"Beth, wait until she comes back down," Grandma said. The intensity of her gaze was unsettling.

"Yup, I'll be right back." Tracey climbed the first two steps.

"Oh Tracey, I had a call from Mrs. Betts."

She spun around, her shocked gaze targeting her mom. "Who?"

"David's mother."

Ice traveled down Tracey's spine. "Oh my God, why did she call you?"

"Go clean up. I'll tell you about it when you come back down."

Oh, how she hated it when her mom started a story and then just stopped. The secret stuffed up her pullover sleeve tugged at her mind. She had to hide it away but felt pulled in two directions. The stone, and Grandma's stare, won. As soon as Tracey got upstairs she leaned her shoulder into the dresser to shift it sideways. Both hands and a grunt pulled the corner out far enough for her to slide her hand down the back. She tucked the box next to Miss Tearning's butterfly necklace. As soon as she let go she wanted to snatch it back up again. Her fingers twitched, still feeling the box between them. Noise downstairs increased. Her brothers must be home.

After a quick stop in the bathroom, Tracey returned downstairs. "Hey."

Her family greeted her in their various ways, though Sarah didn't bother to look up.

At the head of the table, Grandma eyed Tracey strangely. Tracey did her best to ignore her. There was one conspicuous absence. "Aunt Gemma?" she asked, looking around.

"Has left," Mom jammed her large knife into the roast. *Right. Sore point.*

Roast chicken was one of Tracey's favorite meals, and she'd missed it by eating with her friends. Still, she grabbed a wing to nibble on as she told her family about the interview with the M-Force agents. Her story was interesting enough that she was the only one talking. Every now and then she glanced over at Sarah. Her sister avoided all eye contact.

"Hey Sarah, what's up?" Tracey tried when her story ended.

The younger girl turned her head slowly. The look in her eyes could have melted glass. She didn't speak.

Tracey's chest tightened. "Look, I'm sorry I missed your birthday. That wasn't the plan, and—"

"Whatever. I don't care."

"Yeah, but I—"

"I don't want to talk to you," she snapped, and scarfed down her dinner so she could leave the table. Tracey watched her sister stomp away. Sarah didn't look back. No longer hungry, Tracey dropped the chicken wing to her empty plate.

"She's still angry," Mom said.

No kidding!

After dinner Mom insisted Tracey help clean up, which wasn't fair because she hadn't eaten anything. She stood at the sink rinsing off the cutlery while her mom told her about the call from Dave's mom.

"She wants me to what?" Tracey lifted her hands from the sink, dripping soapy water onto the floor as she spun around.

"She wants you to teach Dave some basics until camp starts in the summer."

Spend time—private time—with him? No! "Teach? Mom, I can't—"

"Honey." Mom shoved Tracey's hands back into the water. "He's scared, and none of his family have the skills to help him. He chose you."

"What?" Tracey was surprised the glass in her hand didn't shatter with the high pitch of her screech. *No, no way!*

"He told his mother he chose you. Mrs. Betts called to ensure your help."

"She can't make me."

"Honey, you were the one who outed him, and you did promise him you would help."

Tracey stared into the bubbles popping slowly around her hands. She hadn't believed he'd actually take her up on it. "That's not fair."

"Tracey, the Betts are not handling the news well. If Dave wants your help, you should offer it." As she passed over the next dinner plate her hand lingered on Tracey's damp skin. Standing so close, Tracey could feel her mother's magic pulsing brightly, smelling faintly of butter and toast. Dave Two had no one to wrap him in a magical embrace and tell him it would be okay. Her eyes twitched. Blinking, she forced her tears away.

"He doesn't even like me. I don't have time. I have work—"

"No, you don't," Mom countered, her voice firm.

Tracey turned again, dripping water onto the floor. "And ... wait, what? What do you mean?"

"For the time being, you're not working for Donald."

"Mom!"

The lines at the corners of her mom's mouth deepened. "This is the deal. You help young Mr. Betts and then we'll see about you working for Donald again in the summer."

That's so unfair! How could Tracey and her friends keep investigating the stones if she had to work with Dave Two every day after school? All sympathy vanished. *Stupid Dave!*

"Tell you what. I'll pay you the same as Donald if you include Sarah in your after-school club."

How was that an incentive? Sarah hated Tracey and Tracey hated Dave Two. What a miserable deal. At least she'd still get paid, but she was going to have to figure out how to sneak time away. "Fine," she grumped, plunging her hands to the sink water with a splash.

The stone spoke to her in her dreams.

It was one of those times when you know you're asleep, but you can't control the direction of your subconscious. Tracey knew the stone was communicating with her, but she wasn't entirely sure how she knew it.

In her dream, she sat on her bed staring at her mirrored dresser. Instead of locked away in its hiding place, the stone was cupped in her hands. It felt warm and smooth, like a beach stone that had been in the sun all day. It spoke with a calm and somewhat musical voice. She swore she'd heard it before, even though the language was one she didn't recognize. Relaxing back onto her bed she wished she could understand what the stone was saying. Drums beat slowly inside her chest. Her heart pounded in time with it. She heard chanting, felt it in her belly and in her toes. Golden light danced above her head.

Tracey woke in darkness, the dream still clear in her mind, but by the time morning came, the dream was gone.

Two more cards. One was of a pretty lady
and the other was of a giant wheel.
"The past returns ..."

28

Tracey found her grandma and Sarah waiting for her in the living room when she got home from school the following day. Excitement and despair curled low in her belly, twisting into coils like one of those DNA strands from the science posters at school. "Outside," Grandma said, leading them into the backyard. Sarah shot Tracey a dirty look before following. *Gah, this is going to be fun.* Tracey slumped a little before straightening. *I'll make it up to her.*

At the bottom of the garden, trees lined the length of the wire fence where their house backed onto parkland. If Tracey stood on the porch and looked at the fence, all she would be able to see were trees. "This will be interesting, huh?" she tried, looking at Sarah.

Her sister glared. "She's making me do this. I don't wanna be here."

Tracey shrugged. "That's not my fault."

"It's always your fault."

What? "No it's not—"

"Girls!"

Grandma stood in the center of the yard and pointed in opposite directions. Tracey's shoulders were low as she slouched and scuffed her feet in the grass. Sarah, still shooting Tracey feral looks, stomped to her position.

"What are we doing?" Tracey asked.

"Your school friend will be here shortly. I want to teach you a few exercises to strengthen your mental shields before he arrives."

A sudden thought struck her. It was genius. "Grandma, you should lead the training."

The old woman pointed and Tracey felt a spark of magic explode against the front of her shirt. She let out a shriek and flapped her hands at her collar as if putting out a flame. "This role has been tasked to you, Tracey. I understand Mister Betts is concerned with adult intervention."

"But, I have no idea what to do, other than to go over our lessons from camp." That was exactly what she'd been planning to do. Last night she'd even pulled out all her first-year camp workbooks trying to find a lesson for today.

"I suggest you start with creating his mental shields and how to raise them unconsciously. He will need to know how to lock away his burgeoning powers, especially in times of heightened emotion. As a young man I am sure he will have a few of those," Grandma said. It was amazing how she was able to project her voice so that even though she was standing at the bottom of the garden it was like she was right next to Tracey. "The quickest way to work on mental shielding is to defend oneself against attack."

Oh darn. Tracey knew what that meant. A game Grandma had taught them when they were little—Keeping's Off. Rules were that if you didn't get your shield up in time, Grandma would tickle you until you couldn't breathe for laughing. Grandma was super good at this game.

"Can we get on with it!" Sarah shouted.

"Fine, Grandma. Let's do it," Tracey said.

The old woman nodded and got started. The third time Tracey landed on her butt, she decided enough was enough. Everything ached. Especially her belly.

"You are not concentrating," Grandma admonished.

I am. Huffing out a heartfelt sigh, Tracey climbed back to her feet. Sarah was on the grass too. Her hands wrapped around her middle, tears streaming down her face. It was the peals of laughter that ground against Tracey's nerves. "Would you shut up?" Tracey snapped.

More laughter greeted that comment, and just when Tracey thought she was beginning to slow down, she broke out into giggles again.

Oh, for crying out loud! Tracey flicked her fingers in Sarah's direction. "Zap."

Sarah screeched and jumped to her feet. "Stop it!"

Tracey zap-tickled her sister again. *Ah, the perks of having older brothers.*

Grandma stopped their battle just as the doorbell rang. "Well, I had hoped to get through more than that," she said shooing them into the house.

Dave Two stood on the porch, his bike a discarded heap on the grass. He wore trainers and gym clothes like he was expecting a workout. She should probably get used to thinking of him as just Dave outside of school.

"This is all your fault," he said.

Tracey was completely sick of people saying that to her. "Do you want to come in or not?"

Inside the door, he leaned right into Tracey's face. "No one finds out about this, you hear me?" The words were growled softly but she could hear the fury behind them. Unbeknownst to him, his magic whipped around his body like a live wire, as angry at her as he was. She ducked to avoid it. He gave her a weird look.

"Follow me — we're going outside." Her voice was steady but her body was trembling. She shoved her hands deep into her pockets and led the way through the house.

"What the hell?" Dave snapped, his green eyes flashing as he peered outside. He grabbed Tracey's arm tightly. Sarah sat on the grass in the middle of the yard.

"That's my sister."

His face scrunched up as it turned red. "I said no one finds out. She's a kid, and a girl. She'll tell everyone."

"Listen," Tracey said pointing a finger into his chest. He didn't move but his eyes looked suddenly wary. "You came here for help. If you can't deal with it, the door's that way." She hoped he would storm off. It would've made her life so much easier. He held her stare for a moment longer and then glanced outside again.

"Fine, but if anyone finds out …"

She let the threat hang in the air and raised an eyebrow. If he knew she was scared he'd continue to give her crap and if he didn't take her seriously then he wouldn't take what she taught him seriously. At least that was what Grandma told her earlier. Dave had never been to Mage-kind camp. It was the first lesson they were all taught. Magic might seem like a lot of fun, but it could be really dangerous if you didn't know what you were doing. You could hurt yourself and others if you couldn't control your emotions. All Mage-kind learned that lesson pretty early because it was hard not to get emotional when you were a kid. A whisper in the back of Tracey's mind reminded her how wonderful it had felt when she'd opened herself up to all of her magic. How right it felt. How peaceful. It hadn't been chaotic or dangerous at all. Just perfectly normal. She pushed the memory away.

Tracey hoped her sister wouldn't tell Dave about the *warm up* their grandma put them through earlier. Plonking down on the grass beside Sarah, Tracey stretched out her legs. "Quick recap, then we can get started." Sarah copied her, shifting to sit with her legs pointing at Tracey. Tracey looked up at Dave, who had not moved, and raised her eyebrow. "Well?"

"What, you want to sing songs and braid each other's hair?" he grumbled. Eventually, he flopped down onto the grass and refused to look at anyone. From the expression on his face, she knew he wouldn't be open to any touchy-feely exercises.

She looked from Sarah's snotty face to Dave's blank one. *Where to start?* Pressing her hands to her knees she hoped what she said next wasn't going to make her sound silly. "Magic comes in different levels," she started. Sarah rolled her eyes. Tracey did her best to ignore her. "It's not one all-encompassing feeling, or a sense, and most of the time you don't even know it's there. It sits in the background, and you can continue on exactly as you have always done, completely unaware it's there, reacting to your moods."

She remembered what Grandma said earlier. "Uncontrolled magic is very dangerous. To use magic you must have control. That's why we have to be registered and rated."

"I know this."

Tracey huffed out a breath. "Fine, do you know where your magic comes from?"

He shook his head.

"Rating is an exam that scores how sensitive you are to the world around you and how strong your magical core is. The core is a node inside your body that generates your sixth sense. No one really understands how the core works. It can't be surgically removed without dying, nor can it be transplanted into a Norm. Your core is the place where you draw your power from."

"I can't feel it."

"Not yet. It helps to imagine a ball inside your chest, right next to your heart. To work on your controls, imagine a door in front of the ball. When you open it, you let your magic out. When you close it, it locks it away. It's important to be able to lock it up," she said. A weird feeling in her chest cried out at that. *But it feels so good to use.* She told the voice to shush.

As she spoke, her voice dropped to a whisper. It seemed to carry on the air around them. "Your magic is your own. It is the strongest thing inside you. No matter what your strength is—it's the strongest part of you. Look at the grass. It's alive. Life pulses through it. If we stand on it, it will bend, and when we walk away it will bounce back. We can cut it and it will grow. The sun can burn it, rain can drown it and still, it will grow. You are the grass, flexible and strong, alive and growing. Your powers are alive. One single blade amongst a sea of blades. Alone, yet surrounded and protected." Tracey felt warm and at peace. All her worries drifted away as she basked in the knowledge that her magic was there—just waiting for her to open up to it.

"So we're grass?" Dave scoffed. He clambered to his feet.

Tracey opened her eyes. "Where are you going?"

"Home. I came all this way to find out I'm a piece of grass? This is bull. I thought I was going to learn how to use this thing. We don't talk this much at football practice."

She took a deep breath to center herself. "Let me tell you about the first day of camp."

"Oh God, more stories."

She ignored him. "The first thing we're told when we arrive at Camp Mindflower is ..." she trailed off as Dave burst out laughing.

"Camp Mindflower? Seriously?"

"It's the closest camp—you'll probably be sent there," she told him.

That stopped him laughing. His mouth hung open as realization set in that his life really had changed. For half a second she felt sorry for him. He was going to experience firsthand the prejudice and treatment he used to dish out so freely. Karma truly was nasty. Tracey had initially been afraid of camp too, but the first day had proven to be a lot of fun and set her mind at ease about the summer.

She blinked rapidly as the demonstration she'd seen on that first day came back to her. It was what had convinced her she could learn to control her powers. "How about a demonstration?"

Dave took time to think about it. Tracey almost laughed. He'd been trying to get her to use magic ever since she'd first met him, and now he was wary of it?

"Yeah, I'll get what you're talking about if I see it for myself."

"You won't," she grumbled, but stood and gestured to Sarah. Her sister grinned broadly. "Only a little one," Tracey warned.

Sarah's smile slipped. "Fine." She stomped to the end of the backyard.

Tracey threw open her chest closet and let her magic flow into her arms. Hairs rose up all over her body, quivering with the magical charge. Opening her eyes, she basked in the glow of pure magic. *Focus Tracey!* She raised her shield bubble and a moment later felt the vibration near her face as Sarah's zap hit her shield.

"What? What are you doing?" Dave asked.

Of course, he can't see it. Tracey told Sarah to use something tangible. Sarah's grin took over her whole face. *Oh, awesome.*

Her sister picked up one of Simon's baseballs. Tracey glanced at Dave before she sent a spurt of color into her bubble and solidified her shield. It was a bit showy, but he would be able to see what she was doing. She breathed out, widened her stance and checked her balance. Her hair, blown by a nonexistent wind, whipped around her head.

Sarah threw the ball. Tracey, anticipating it, felt the oncoming buzz as air was pushed aside. The ball bounced off her shield, only inches from her chest.

Dave's face lit up. "Cool."

Finally, she had his attention. "That takes a lot of focus and practice—control is really important," she warned.

He bounced on the tips of his toes, anxious to start. *Well, okay then.* "Sarah, why don't you go to the fence and try to make the bell ring."

"Really?" It was an exercise for older kids and required a lot of intense concentration. It would keep Sarah busy and if she did it, it would be a huge achievement. *Maybe she won't be so cross with me if she does it.* Sarah ran down to the bottom of the yard to practice.

Tracey worked for a while on Dave's imagery. After working on visualizing his core, she got him to imagine a bubble and secretly enjoyed throwing energy sparks at him over and over.

The bell on the fence rang. Tracey's head snapped to her sister. Sarah was turned away so Tracey couldn't see her face but she was jumping up and down, pumping her fist in the air.

What felt like only two minutes later, their mom interrupted and called them all inside. The hour was over already.

Sarah scrubbed a hand over the sheen on her face. Sweat beaded on Dave's neck, his shirt clung in damp patches to his chest. Tracey was surprised. She hadn't realized how hard they'd all been working. Sarah's eyes were bright and she couldn't stop smiling. At least she'd had a good time.

"Dinner is nearly ready," Tracey's mom said as they reached the door. Dave followed Tracey to the front door and nearly smiled at her before he grabbed his bike and disappeared in a cloud of dust.

"You do know,
you simply do not trust yourself to know—
you are the only one who can use it, Tracey.
The only one."

29

After dinner, Grandma pulled her aside to talk.

"More training?" Tracey asked. Exhaustion weighed down her arms, making them feel as heavy as concrete blocks. Her eyeballs burned, indicating she had a headache coming on.

"No dear, we're going out for a while."

Sarah appeared in the doorway. "Can I come?"

"No sweetheart, this is just for Tracey." Sarah stared at them for a long moment, her face stony, and then stormed upstairs. All of Tracey's good feelings evaporated. Well, the truce between them hadn't lasted long.

"Grandma, I'm really tired." Her back pocket began to buzz. Oh that's right, she'd promised to call Laura tonight. Grandma waved a hand in front of Tracey's face.

"Yes, you certainly are tired. This won't take long. We're going to see your nana."

Tracey's eyes sprang wide. "What? Why?" Did Grandma know Tracey secretly visited Nana last week? She was afraid to ask. When they walked into the foyer of Tavel House, Tracey stayed quiet and hoped the night nurse wouldn't mention her previous visit.

After Grandma signed them in, Tracey said, "She's worse, you know." Her chest ached as she remembered Nana's blank gaze. She didn't want Grandma to be upset if Nana didn't recognize them.

Grandma just smiled and tapped on Nana's door.

As the door opened, Tracey felt a burst of power explode out from Grandma and when it faded, Nana's eyes were clear. She looked ten years younger. "Adele dear. It's lovely to see you. And you too, Tracey. Come in, come in."

What had Grandma done? Had she fixed Nana? The hope that filled Tracey evaporated when Grandma shook her head, her eyes sad. Tracey bit her lip, determined to enjoy the brief time with her nana of old before it faded. Nana bustled around the room, enjoying her sudden spurt of energy. She cleared things away and seated them both at her little table with a cup of tea. It was wonderful to see Nana so alert, Tracey's jaw was getting sore from all her smiling. Her chest hurt too.

Grandma gestured to Nana's tarot cards. "I was wondering if you could do a reading for us, Mina."

Remembering Nana had played with the same cards the last time, Tracey recalled she'd just shuffled them around in her hands. She didn't know Nana could do a proper reading.

"Of course, Adele."

Nana placed the cards down in front of Tracey. "Can you shuffle these for me, Tracey?"

They were large cards, and Tracey had to concentrate on them carefully as she rotated them, worried they'd fly out of her hands. She missed what her grandmothers were talking about, but as she shuffled, the air around her grew heavy, muffling their voices. It was like listening to music through a giant pillow. Nana's voice came through clearly when she told Tracey to place the cards on the table and cut them into three piles. She did as asked and restacked them when she was told to.

Taking the cards, Nana dealt them face up on the table. Tracey had seen tarot cards before — always artistic, these ones were full of shiny swirling colors, images and numbers. Tracey's nana placed the cards down in the shape of a lopsided cross. Feeling eyes on her face, Tracey looked up to find Nana staring at her. She wasn't looking at the cards at all. Nana's usually dull eyes were deep brown and twinkled in the room's orange lamp light. Grandma sat silently, holding so still Tracey almost forgot she was there. A draft rose up from somewhere tickling the back of Tracey's neck. She shivered in the stuffy room.

There were three cards Tracey didn't like the look of when she examined them. One was a black shadow with dark red eyes. "The Devil," Nana said when she saw Tracey looking at it. She tapped another card. "The

Tower." This card had an image of a large castle turret and a lightning bolt. The tower looked like it was about to be shattered apart.

The last card Nana tapped was a picture of a man hanging upside down in a tree. "The Hanged Man."

The three cards made Tracey uncomfortable. Glancing up to ask Nana to put the cards away, she found the old woman smiling. "Big changes are coming." Her voice was strangely melodic. "It might seem scary, honey, but it is meant to be." Nana pointed to two more cards. One was of a pretty lady and the other was of a giant wheel. "The past returns," she said, brushing her fingers against the cards.

"What?" Tracey's head felt funny. Thick pressure constricted around her forehead like she was wearing a tight headband. She wasn't sure what was going on, but Grandma was leaning forward, her gaze glued to Nana.

"It is coming, my dear," Nana said. She looked bathed in a beautiful bright light. Then her eyes turned cold and dark. "Do not let the shadow touch you."

What? Tracey's chest lurched as her heart gave an almighty thump. *How did she know?*

"You can control it. I see—" Nana's eyes drifted closed and she swayed gently in her seat. When she opened them again her gaze was unfocused and empty.

"Nana, see what?"

But the old woman was gone. Tracey's grandma shook her head and stood. "It's time to go."

The visage of Tracey's nana—alert, vibrant, full of light—blinked at Tracey's grandma, and then startled upright. "Oh, hello Adele, when did you get here? It's been a long time."

"Yes, dear." Grandma said, patting her hand gently. "But it's time for us to go now. Lovely to see you again."

Tracey didn't realize she was trembling until they got back into the car. Grandma took her hands and warmed them with little sparks of heat and light. "What the heck was that?"

Grandma didn't start the engine, but stared at Tracey solemnly. "That was not quite what I expected."

"Grandma, quit talking like Yoda and tell me what was going on in there. What did you do to Nana? What was she talking about?"

"It's time I showed you something," she said instead, staring deeply into Tracey's eyes.

"Show me what?" A dizzy feeling hit Tracey hard. She clamped her eyes shut as everything around her spun. Her stomach lurched like she was on a merry-go-round. When the spinning stopped she opened her eyes to find she wasn't in the car anymore. She stood beside her grandma in what looked like a large wood-paneled room. Books filled every available wall space, and everything was colored black and white, like an old film. A massive, unlit fireplace was in the center of one wall, and a plush sofa sat in front of it. Piles of books were stacked on the floor beside three soft, comfy armchairs. Tracey and her grandma were alone.

"Where are we?" Tracey gasped. She couldn't hear her own voice. Grandma nodded as if she'd heard every word clearly. Without opening her mouth she told Tracey, *We are in a guided memory.* Tracey's eyes opened wide. Voices approached, growing louder through the door to her right. She turned to ask Grandma who was coming, but her grandma had disappeared.

"Grandma?"

She was alone.

A guided memory, Grandma had said. *But whose?*

Three people walked into the room, arguing heatedly. They didn't glance Tracey's way at all. The woman closest to Tracey was … it was the woman from Doctor Chan's photograph. Tracey startled back in surprise. She reached out with her magic to get a sense of the woman, but couldn't feel a thing. Her magic was gone. She clutched at her chest searching for her spark, picturing her closet door wide open — but there was no glimmer, no spark, no power. *What? Where is it? Where?* Her heart raced — she was breathing so hard her chest hurt. Tracey looked up at the three strangers to beg for their help and a thought occurred.

If this was a guided memory, then none of them were really here. She hadn't lost her magic at all — none of this was real. The relief that raced through her made her feel light-headed. She swayed and nearly lost her balance. *Gosh, I hope I'm right.* She tuned into what the three strangers were arguing about, their British accents crisp and formal. If this was Tracey's ancestor, then how did Grandma have access to her memories? Grandma had a lot of explaining to do when Tracey got out of here. The trio sat down on the sofa. It didn't appear as though they could see Tracey at all, which was a relief. She wasn't sure how to explain her presence. She wandered closer.

"It is not a good idea, Charles," Tracey's ancestor said. The lines between her eyes grew deeper as the man she'd called Charles sat down beside her. He attempted to take her hand. The woman snatched it back before he could touch her.

"Stephanie—"

So that's my ancestor's name. Stephanie. Tracey watched as Stephanie lurched off the sofa. Charles and the other woman exchanged glances, conducting a silent conversation with only their eyes. Finally, the woman approached Stephanie and held up a gloved hand. "Stephanie, you must see that we have no choice."

"Not you, too, Millicent?" Stephanie's eyes lowered as her perfect posture slumped.

What on earth is going on? Grandma had chosen to show Tracey this guided memory for a reason, but why? And why did Grandma leave her here alone?

Stephanie stepped forward bringing Tracey's attention back to her. It was so strange to see her face on someone else. "I take it Timothy and Matthew are agreed?"

Millicent nodded. Charles rose from the sofa. He held out a hand, beseeching, "We cannot do this without you. We must be unanimous."

"Then you offer no choice at all."

"Stephanie, please," Millicent said, her voice soft and pleading. Tracey wished she understood what they were talking about. It was like walking in on one of her mom's TV shows—only she had no one to ask and no recap available to catch her up.

Stephanie inhaled sharply, but before she could speak, Charles said, "If you are with us on this venture, you would have the opportunity to control the outcome. Stephanie, my dear, you could end the experiment if you think it is going awry."

"If you believe I will have the strength to stop this once it has begun, Charles, then you are a fool."

Charles lowered his head. Tracey could see a smirk dancing around his lips. He had a sharp face—all lines and angles, and a pointy chin. His eyes were too small. She immediately disliked him. Why was her ancestor even listening to him?

"Very well," Stephanie agreed at last. The instant the words left her lips the room faded and Tracey found herself back in the car with Grandma.

"What was that?" Tracey demanded. It was cold in the car—her fingers creaked. It felt as though her body was a block of ice. Night had fallen and the car was filled with shadows. Her hands flew to her chest. *My magic!* She threw the door open wide and warmth flooded through her. Tingles erupted over her skin as the hair rose along her arms. *Oh thank God!*

Without looking at her, Grandma started the engine and said, "When your nana was first diagnosed with dementia, she'd already lost vital memories. She approached me shortly after her diagnosis and entrusted the memories she had left to my keeping—to be shown to you when the time was right. Unfortunately, by giving those memories to me, her condition rapidly declined."

Tracey gasped. "Will you lose your memory, too, because you shared the memories with me?"

Grandma took one hand off the wheel to clutch at Tracey's arm. "No dear, it's not like that. Dementia is a medical condition, it's not contagious and it was not caused by the guided memory transfer."

"But you said she got worse." Tracey's breath caught in her throat, concerned despite her grandma's reassurances.

"My dear, they were not originally your nana's memories. They were transferred to her from her mother. I believe Stephanie has passed her memories down through the generations so we would know what to do if one of the stones was ever found."

Tracey wondered if these memories were what drove her nana crazy. Could having another person's memories do that? *How could they not?* If they hurt Nana, why would Grandma agree to hold them? Magic *was* dangerous! But the way Tracey felt when she used her magic was so good—joy, pleasure, warmth. Happy. How could that be bad? "But what did the guided memory mean?" she asked. Turning her head she glanced out into the night. *Why is this happening now?* The stone—it all came down to the stone. Her thoughts swirled, but she couldn't focus. All she could see was her nana's blank stare and it made her skin crawl.

"I don't know yet, sweetie." Grandma pulled her hand back to grip the steering wheel and squinted into the darkness.

Tracey was silent for a long time thinking about magic and what was right and wrong. As the car turned onto her street, she asked, "You said there were more memories?"

"Yes, but the time is not right for you to see them."

"How do you know?" Curling her fingers into fists, she stared at her grandma's profile. "If something is going to happen, why can't you just show me? Wouldn't it be better if I knew what was coming?"

"I wish I could show you everything now, but I can only release the memories at the correct time."

When they pulled into the driveway Tracey snapped, "Let me guess ... I can't tell anyone about this." She couldn't look at her grandma anymore. She didn't think the old woman meant to confuse and upset her, but she had.

It wasn't fair. Tracey just wanted to be a normal Mage-kind and assist her uncle to solve minor crimes. She didn't want all these secrets. Now there was too much excitement; hidden memories and ancient magical stones. She didn't want any of it. She just wanted her boring life back.

"The last held desire,
For power and purpose ..."

30

The house was dark when they stepped inside. A light had been left on in the hallway. Another light glowed beneath her sister's bedroom door. Tracey walked straight past, but Sarah's door cracked open. Sleep ruffled and bleary eyed, she poked her head out. "So, what happened? How's Nana?"

"I don't want to talk about it." Tracey felt vaguely sick and just wanted to go to bed.

Sarah sneered. "Of course you don't."

Confused, Tracey turned back. Sarah shut the door in her face. Tracey stared at the wood wondering what that was about. *Gah! Fine.*

As she pushed her bedroom door open, her hand was trembling. She swallowed hard, hot tears welling in her eyes. Tracey scrubbed a hand over them and shut the door behind her. Staring at her dresser, she debated whether or not to take the stone out of its hiding place to examine it. She hadn't seen the stone in the dream-vision, so how did she even know it belonged to Stephanie? Maybe it didn't? In the end, tiredness won and she left it where it was.

Tracey woke covered in sweat and surrounded by dark shadows. It took three trembling slaps to get the bedroom light on. *See— no shadows. There are no shadows.* She collapsed onto her bed, heart pounding painfully. *Why is this happening to me?* She didn't understand why she was still dreaming of the Shadowman. Her chest closet was rattling, her magic as unsettled as her mind.

Flopping back onto her mattress, Tracey flinched as something hard jabbed her in the back. Twisting and wriggling, she poked her hand under the blankets to find what it was.

The stone!

How had it gotten out of her dresser? Shivering, she climbed off her bed to put the stone back, but hesitated. Her fingers closed around the smooth, warm painted face. Her body tingled with magic as music filled her mind. Caressing the butterfly, she could feel the stone calling to her. All she had to do was open the door to her core and — *Whoa!* She blinked several times. *What the heck?* Why was she still holding the stone? She forced herself to let it go, turned out the light and climbed back into bed, but it was hard to fall asleep.

Tracey sleepwalked through most of her classes the next day as her lack of sleep made itself known. She did keep an eye out for Dave Two, but she didn't see him anywhere in the yard. Hopefully he'd turn up for practice tonight. It wasn't fair. She'd barely slept and yet he got to stay home? Thinking of the untrained boy reminded her that she should probably teach him the basic steps of meditation — maybe some calming exercises. She sucked in a deep breath. *Another secret!* There were too many lies and mysteries for her tired brain to deal with. Dave Two, the butterfly necklace, the stone, the guided memory her grandma showed her and her Mage-kind ancestor.

Something landed on the table next to her hand where she was tapping it against her phone. *Ewww, a piece of apple* — post-loved. *Gross.*

She snapped her head around to glare at the lunch table behind her. Dave One sat with Carla. He shot Tracey a dark look and let fly with another piece of chewed fruit. Heat swelled inside her body. She cracked open the door in her chest and squinted at Dave One. He started scratching. She turned away, panicking, and glanced at her phone searching for a distraction. Uncle Donny hadn't replied to any of her texts. She hated it when people didn't respond. It only took a second. What was so hard about that? Mom had blasted him for putting Tracey in danger. He was probably avoiding her. Still, it was rude not to reply.

Jonny put his tray down with such a clang Tracey twitched in her chair. "God, do you mind?"

"Whoa, what got up your shirt?" Jonny's eyes were wide, searching her face.

"What?" she clutched her fork tightly and squinted at him.

"I just got after school detention. So why are you pissy?"

"Me? I'm not. What did you get detention for?" That was unlike him. She pressed her hand against her chest trying to calm down. She was feeling steamed.

"Dave Two went nuts in class this morning. Seriously, I don't know what's wrong with that guy but he needs to chill. I wonder if Meena has any Xanax he can take."

"What happened?" she asked, ignoring the backhander at Meena. "I didn't think Dave was here today." If he got angry and let loose with his magic someone would get hurt. *Should I go find him?*

Jonny gave her an odd look. "Since when do you care if he's here or not?"

"So what happened?" she demanded.

He slumped down onto his chair, the one closest to the wall, and tipped it up slowly. When it was balanced on two legs, he sighed. "Mark grabbed one of his pens and Dave Two freakin' lost it. One minute he was mouthing off behind Mr. Swanston's back and the next minute he had Mark by the shirt and pushed up against the wall."

"Oh my God." That was not good. Poor Dave. Her chest ached thinking about what he was going through. He must be so confused and upset. She remembered the fear in his eyes when he said his dad wouldn't understand. "Wait ... how come *you* have after school detention, then?" She glanced around the lunch room looking for the potentially dangerous Mage-kind. She spied Damian sitting next to Meena again. He sensed Tracey's gaze and looked up. As soon as he caught her eye he looked away. Minutes later, he leaned his head into his hand and twisted his whole body so that he was facing another table. *Ouch — what a total jerk.* She watched as he leaned forward and said something to Dave One. The giant boy was still scratching. Long red marks covered his forearms. He must be allergic to something they served for lunch. Tracey eyed her own barely touched tray and pushed it across the table. Jonny waved his hand in front of her eyes. "What?"

"I said I pulled Dave off of him and the next thing I know, I have detention for fighting."

"Oh, that's not fair," she murmured while removing her jacket. Why was it so hot in here? She felt for Jonny but was impressed her friend had jumped in so quickly to quell the fight. Tracey had the feeling calming techniques were not going to help Dave with his level of anger. Perhaps he needed to see a counselor?

"What's not fair?" Tony asked. He pulled out the chair next to Tracey and dropped his tray to the table. "Are you okay? You look like you had to run somewhere."

She shook her head. Now that she thought about it, her breathing was pretty fast. She felt flushed.

"I heard you got in a fight, Jonny," Laura said, stepping up to Tracey's other side.

Jonny repeated the story while they ate lunch. As he talked, Tracey concentrated on slowing her breathing. Feeling cooler, she interrupted to ask her friends if they were still available the next afternoon to see Doctor Chan again. She wanted a look at that book he'd ordered. If it had anything to do with Stephanie and the stones then Tracey wanted to see it. They confirmed yes and started speculating on what the journal might contain. Raised voices drew Tracey's attention back to Damian's table. He was pinning Dave One's arms to his sides like a wrestler. "Dude, you have to stop. It's bleeding!" Meena ran to the teacher on duty.

Dave One shouldn't scratch at an allergic reaction. It would only make it worse. Tracey hid a smile behind her hand. *Kinda serves him right though.*

Tuning back to the conversation at her table, she realized the boys were now talking about *Demon Hunt*, the latest online game to go viral. She interrupted to blast the low resolution on the fifth battle level, earning her an incredulous look from Laura. "What?"

"You still play those games?" she asked.

"Firestorm the Legendary!" Jonny gushed. "Of course she does."

Tracey flushed a little at Jonny's praise. Actually, it had been ages since she'd played. *I'll jump in tonight.*

"Firestorm?"

"Her gamer tag." Jonny said.

Laura dropped her head into her hands and shook it back and forth sadly. Tracey eyed her and grinned. Laura didn't understand gaming at all.

The bell interrupted any further conversation on gaming. Tracey still hadn't told her friends about last night and had another magic practice session after school tonight so she couldn't do it then. She'd have to try and catch them before school tomorrow. She shot a final look over at Damian. He dropped his gaze straight away. *Was he looking at me?* She shook her head. It didn't matter. He'd chosen to associate with the Evil Queens and Double Ds. She couldn't save him, so it was time to let him go. She had bigger things to worry about anyway.

Dave was late.

"Maybe he's not coming," she grumbled for the fourth time in as many minutes. Grandma looked concerned and her face grew grave when Tracey told her what had happened earlier that day at school.

"He shouldn't be back at school so soon after learning about his talents."

Tracey agreed.

"You might as well get started," Grandma told her, and walked back to the house.

"Do I have to?"

"Hey!" Sarah shouted, her face scrunching up like a troll. Tracey scowled at her. This was the perfect opportunity to get out of the next hour. She figured Sarah would jump at the chance, but instead she looked angry. At their grandma's stern look, Tracey stomped back into position. She worked with Sarah over the next hour reviewing her shielding spells. Sarah practiced raising and lowering them until it became instinctual. It was boring and repetitive, but even Tracey felt energized by the mental exercise. After a little while, she realized it was actually kinda fun practicing with her sister. She'd missed playing with Sarah. *I really need to spend more time with her.* "Ow!" she squealed as a sharp electrical spike hit her backside. "Sarah!" That zap had been stronger than they'd agreed to use. Her skin tingled as though she had a severe case of pins and needles.

Sarah burst out laughing. Tracey grumbled and threw a stronger spark but her sister raised her shield just in time. Pretty good reflexes, not that Tracey was going to tell her that. Rubbing at the ache in her rear end, Tracey's mind returned to the whole reason they were out here.

"Girls, it's time to come in now," Grandma called from the back door. *Finally!*

"If Dave doesn't come anymore, do we get to keep practicing?" Sarah asked, jogging up to Tracey's side.

Tracey shrugged. "I don't know," she said. *I hope not.*

The next afternoon, Tracey told her friends about Nana and the tarot cards. The train carriage they were in was an older model and rattled around them loudly, making it hard to be heard. Still, she barely spoke above a whisper, leaning in so that all their heads were close together.

"You don't believe in those, do you?" Laura asked, looking skeptical.

Tony held up a hand. "Maybe not with the quacks at shopping centers, but with Mage-kind—there's something in it." He tapped Tracey's hand and asked, "How did you feel about what she said?"

Tracey shook her head. "I honestly don't know. My nana is crazy and now that she has dementia, well, you can't trust what she's talking about at the best of times, you know?"

"Do you think The Devil was the man in the red mask?" Tony asked.

"It's gotta be," Jonny said.

Tracey wondered about that herself—but then, what was The Tower supposed to represent? It still gave her the willies thinking about the way Nana had looked at her.

"She said change was coming. But good change or bad change?" Laura asked.

"I don't know." Tracey fell silent. It would be better to act as though she'd not seen the cards at all and focus on what she could control—her research into the stones. She was looking forward to speaking with Doctor

Chan again. Hopefully, he would have the journal. It might give her more insight into the history of the stones, and into Stephanie. Had her ancestor really gone mad? And more importantly, was it hereditary?

"I keep having the same nightmare," Laura said suddenly, leaning forward in her seat.

Tracey looked at her in surprise. "Of the man in the red mask?" She glanced around. The carriage was practically empty, so why did it feel like someone was listening in to their conversation. *Just paranoia, right?*

"Who do you think he is?" Laura asked.

Tony sat back. His body language said he wanted an answer to that as well. Jonny spoke up. "What did you think of those detectives from the Mage squad? I've never seen anything like that before."

Tracey didn't answer. There was too much going on in her head. She felt like she might explode from the information overload. She'd blocked out the interrogation, but now that Jonny had reminded her about it, she began thinking about it again. She tugged her jacket closer around her chest and scrunched lower in her seat.

"Tracey?"

"What?" She looked up. Her friends had continued talking while she'd spaced out.

"What did the agents say to you before we arrived?" Laura repeated. Tracey had the feeling she'd asked the question several times already and was amused at Tracey's lack of attention.

They discussed the interview for the rest of the trip into the city. The walk through the university grounds to Doctor Chan's office seemed to fly by, and suddenly they were standing outside the door to his office. An odd fluttering tickled Tracey's throat. She immediately looked at Tony to see if he'd felt it, too.

"What's wrong?" Laura asked, following Tracey's gaze to Tony. He stood in the middle of the corridor, his face pale and his eyes closed.

Jonny noticed it first. "Hey look, the name plate is missing."

He was right. The plate with Doctor Chan's name, title, and position had been removed from the wall. Tracey couldn't voice what she was feeling but knew something was very wrong. The corridor was chilly and a smell lingered she couldn't quite identify. Like ice or snow, it was cold and sharp.

Jonny bashed on Doctor Chan's office door. There was no answer.

Ignoring her bad feeling, Tracey nodded when Jonny gestured toward the handle. "Try it," she suggested.

He pushed open the unlocked door, and they all gathered in the doorway to stare at the sight beyond.

Doctor Chan's office was empty.

"His soul, but shadow,
Alone in his curse ..."

31

L ike, completely empty.

Tracey pushed into the room and turned a full circle. Even the carpet and the window shades were gone.

"What the ...?" Jonny wondered.

Tracey closed her eyes and pushed out with her power to read the room. *Nothing.* The room was a big empty void. That's what she'd been sensing out in the hall—a void. Not the void a Norm carried around them, like Laura or Jonny. This void felt like someone had gone through the office with a broom and swept it clean of every trace of magical energy.

Tracey passed Laura in the doorway and ran to the first person she could see, a student seated in the hall playing on her phone. "Excuse me, can I ask you something?"

The young woman looked up, peering at Tracey through pink-rimmed spectacles, "I suppose so."

"Doctor Chan's office is empty. Do you know if he's moved to another office in this building?"

The girl snapped her phone case closed. "Who?"

"Doctor Chan? He worked in that room right over there." Tracey pointed toward the empty office.

The girl's eyes widened. "No one uses that office."

"What?" Tracey's body froze at the girl's words. She shook her head, denial springing to her lips as her friends came up behind her.

"No one?" Laura echoed. "Why?"

"I don't know. It's been empty for at least two years. That's how long I've been an advisor here, anyway. It's like it's haunted or something. No one wants it. Look, I have to go."

Tracey let the girl pass and turned to stare at her friends. "Empty? But we saw him."

"You spoke to Doctor Chan, right? That's what you all told me," Jonny said. His brows were drawn so tightly together they appeared to be one long eyebrow.

"Yes, he was right there. The whole office was full of dusty books, files, and paper," Tony confirmed. His face was still pale and his eyes were a bit too wide.

He's scared! He wasn't the only one. Tracey bit at her thumbnail.

Nothing made sense. She remembered Doctor Chan so clearly, from what he'd been wearing — old tweed, to how he smelled — sort of musty. She even remembered the reflection off his glasses.

Could she have imagined all that?

On the train home, all four were confused and tired. They'd spent a good hour walking around the university grounds, questioning various department heads and tutorial guides about the missing Doctor Chan. No one recognized the name. Tony jumped on his phone to search for the teacher's contact details and couldn't find a single reference to a Doctor Steven Chan ever having worked at the university.

"He was real, wasn't he?" Jonny asked. "Someone can't just disappear, can they?"

"Of course not," Tony grumbled.

Tracey was still wondering about Doctor Chan's disappearance later that night. Her grandma was out and Tracey's mom and dad were on their weekly dinner date so she had no one to ask, which meant she was stressing. She paced the living room so many times she figured she was going to wear a track in the carpet. The minute Peter walked in the door, she cornered him and demanded to know if he'd ever heard of someone just up and disappearing. She must have sounded crazy — her words came out all rushed and jumbled together.

Peter stumbled backward. He held out a hand and tilted his head to the side. "You want to know if it's possible to magically disappear a whole person?"

"Well, maybe not disappear. More like block people's memories or delete them so that they don't remember?"

"Why are you asking?"

"My friends and I met someone, and … Oh, never mind." It was too complicated to try and explain.

"So, how's the after-school practice going?" he asked, grabbing a can of pop from the fridge. Tracey followed him as he sat down at the kitchen table. He stared at her strangely, like his eyes were looking right through her. It didn't feel like he was pushing at her magically, so she tried to ignore the crawly feeling his look gave her.

"Oh, you know," she answered. "It's basic stuff. Just good practice."

"How do you feel about what happened the other night—the meditation?"

Why? "I don't really remember it," she said, pulling her cell phone from her pocket. For some odd reason, she didn't want to look at him. Perhaps she could pretend Laura was calling? No, he'd never believe that without hearing her cell ring.

"Have Mom and Dad stopped you from working for Uncle Donny?"

"Yeah." And she was still bummed about it, mainly because Uncle Donny's office was a great place for her and her friends to hang out. They could have used her uncle's numerous online resources and connections to look into Doctor Chan's disappearance.

"Have you heard from him lately?"

"Huh?" She looked up from the phone she wasn't paying attention to at her brother's tone. Peter was trying to sound nonchalant which immediately raised the hairs on the back of her neck. "What?"

"I popped over to Uncle Donny's office and everything was dark. I just wondered if you've spoken to him at all? Was he planning a trip?"

"Not that I know of." That was weird. Uncle Donny tried to keep Fridays free for paperwork—not that he did a lot of that. His electronic card games got more of a workout on a Friday than filing. "Maybe he was meeting a client?" she suggested.

"Yeah, that's probably it. Was he working on a new case?"

She shrugged. Inwardly she feared he was still looking into Miss Tearning's murder. He wouldn't keep investigating after the M-Force agents told him to stop, would he? *Wouldn't he?* She typed a quick text to him and hoped he'd reply.

He didn't.

In fact, he still hadn't replied by the time Tracey went to bed, which was surely why her night was plagued with nightmares. Each one started innocently enough. She was searching for her uncle at his office or at school and every location she tried was empty—like people had just gotten up from their desks and left. Food, hot mugs of coffee and notebooks were left on every available surface. When the Shadowman appeared, Tracey was jarred awake covered in sweat, panting and gasping. By three o'clock, she stopped trying to sleep altogether. She sent another message to her uncle and sat up reading her latest mystery novel until morning.

As soon as it was decent for a Saturday, Tracey called her friends and organized to meet them at Uncle Donny's office. If he wasn't around, then it was the perfect place for a private meeting.

Laura was the only one available. She looked perfectly rested and wide awake when she strolled in at ten o'clock. "How long have you been here?" she asked.

"I've got Uncle Donny's spare keys. I let myself in ages ago."

"Found anything yet?" Laura slurped at her caramel mocha. Tracey practically felt her teeth melting from the smell of sugar. She threw up her hands and collapsed onto the sofa. Laura joined her and they sat staring around the room.

"Where do you think he could be?" Laura asked, shaking her empty takeaway cup. Dropping it into the trash bin she sat back and examined her fingernails for paint chips.

"There's only one place I can think of, but he's not answering his phone or replying to my messages. I don't know for sure. He was working on the set where they're filming *Saving Time*." Something was wrong. Uncle Donny wouldn't up and disappear on her after her encounter with the Shadowman. Not without calling, right? A flicker of a thought pushed its way into her mind. Doctor Chan had disappeared too.

Laura's eyes lit up. She leaned forward to clutch Tracey's arm. "That's right, the film lot! We should go and look for him."

Tracey rolled her eyes. She knew Laura was genuinely concerned about Uncle Donny, but somehow she didn't think it was worry that fueled this desperation. "His phone battery probably just died, that's all." It had happened before.

"No, we should go and check. We should! What if he's hurt?"

Tracey eyed her friend suspiciously. Laura looked so excited she didn't have the heart to tell her no. "I've only got the one pass," she tried. What if Uncle Donny was at work and had dropped his phone in the toilet again?

Laura brushed her off. "Tracey, your uncle is missing. We have to go ask if they've seen him."

She couldn't blame Laura for trying. "Okay."

They spent more time arguing with the security guard at the Sachorn Forest gatehouse than they did getting there in the first place. Tracey had her lanyard, so the guard was happy enough to let her through, but he refused Laura admittance.

"It's life and death," Laura begged. She'd pulled tears from somewhere and now her eyes were red and glassy. She dabbed at her nose with a tissue. Tracey groaned silently. Even crying, Laura looked amazing.

Tracey could see from the guard's set expression that he didn't care. Now that she'd come all the way she didn't want to leave without checking. She pulled Laura back. "I could go in real quick and—"

A ruckus drew their attention to the footpath just inside the gate. A number of people dressed in black raced past in a group. People dressed in outlandish costumes followed along behind, walking much more slowly. A man in a long red jacket glanced up, and, catching sight of Tracey and Laura, headed straight toward them.

It was Prince Henry.

"I'm going to faint," Laura whispered, digging her nails into Tracey's arm.

Tracey barely glanced at her. She was unable to take her eyes off the man walking toward them. *He recognized me?*

"Step back, girls," the guard ordered, holding out his arm.

"Well, hello there," Prince Henry stopped right in front of them. The security guard shot him a confused look.

Prince Henry couldn't have recognized Tracey as the one who'd stolen his necklace because she'd been disguised as Miss Tearning at the time, which meant he recognized her from when she'd met him as herself over a month ago. He must really like his fans. That thought filled her with warmth. She knew he was a great guy.

"Hi," was all she managed, feeling her face flame. Laura didn't say a word.

Prince Henry glanced briefly at Laura and then back to Tracey, "I don't think this is the friend you were telling me about is it? You know you forgot your pictures?"

Oh God, he does recognize me! For a moment she couldn't speak, letting out a barely contained squeak. Laura nudged her by jamming an elbow hard into Tracey's side. "Ah no, this is my other friend, Laura Smith."

"Hello Laura Smith, friend of Tracey."

Prince Henry remembers my NAME? She felt faint.

He gestured to the security guard. "Let them through, they're friends."

Friends! Tracey flicked her eyes to Laura. They both jumped up and down before quickly stopping. Tracey schooled her face, forcing her giant grin into something a little less manic. She wasn't sure she'd succeeded when the guard gave both of them a dark look. "But, sir."

"Let them through. Tracey has a pass, as you can plainly see, and I'm sure she'd be willing to vouch for her friend?" Prince Henry turned the statement into a question as he glanced back. Tracey nodded rapidly. Laura grinned and bounced lightly on her feet, unable to contain her excitement.

"So, I owe you some pictures. Let's head over to my trailer."

Laura waved gleefully as she passed the security guard. Tracey kept her face steady, her eyes lowered and headed straight for the cast trailers. *This is too surreal.*

A woman with a headset and a tablet raced up, but before she could say a word the prince dismissed her with a wave of his hand. Tracey caught a glimpse of the assistant's eyes as she stomped away. She didn't look surprised or offended by the prince's actions, merely exasperated, blowing her fringe away from her red, sweaty face. The poor woman was just trying to do her job. It was a bit mean of him to send her away.

"Did I read that right? Your pass says junior assistant to the on-site detective," he asked.

"Yes, Donald James is my uncle. I work for him sometimes."

"Then you must know where he is."

"What?" Tracey's feet stuttered to a stop as the prince climbed the steps of what was obviously his trailer. *They haven't seen him, that's not good.*

Prince Henry looked back at her in surprise. "The assistant producer has been looking for him for days."

"What?" Tracey parroted again. Cold weaved its way down her spine. She couldn't move.

Poking his head out of the trailer he said, "Well, come on."

Laura practically shoved Tracey off the steps in her haste to get inside. Tracey was too distracted to be upset over her friend's selfish behavior. Her uncle *was* missing. Then she recognized where she was standing. The mess around her was undeniable. This was the trailer where she'd been attacked by the man in the red mask. *The trailer belongs to Prince Henry!* "Did the assistant producer say what my uncle was supposed to be doing?" *This was where I found Doctor Chan's number. How does Prince Henry know him?*

"Investigating some missing jewelry, I think. That's all I really know about it."

"When was he last seen?" she pushed.

"You certainly sound like a detective now, Tracey. What's with all the questions?" He held out a handful of glossy photos but tugged them out of her reach when she tried to take them. "Tracey, what's wrong?"

"I think my uncle is missing." Did Prince Henry know Doctor Chan was missing too?

He handed her the pictures. "You should talk to the assistant producer. I've been out filming for the last six hours. Maybe your uncle arrived after I left and she's seen him already."

She knew something was wrong. *I have to tell Mom.*

"Tracey?"

"Assistant producer. Yes, we'll do that first," she said. She felt weird, spacey all of a sudden. Desperate for some fresh air to clear her head, she stumbled out of the trailer, Laura followed her reluctantly.

"Tracey?" Laura called. "Tracey!"

"What?" Tracey spun around, taking in Laura's reddened face and large eyes. "What, Laura?"

"What's wrong?"

"Uncle Donny is missing. He's not answered any of my calls or texts and he's not shown up at his job—his *paying* job! That's definitely not normal." She kept walking.

Laura raced up to her side. "Look, don't panic just yet. Prince Henry said he didn't know for sure, right? Let's go talk to the assistant producer. Have you met her?"

"No, but Uncle Donny pointed out her office last time I was here. It's over this way, I think." She led Laura to a tiny trailer located behind the director's much larger and far more ostentatious one. She appreciated Laura trying to keep her calm but her head was too busy churning through *what ifs*. They knocked loudly.

No one answered. They waited for over an hour, Tracey paced the entire time. Finally, she scribbled a note and pushed it under the trailer door.

"Hopefully she calls. Maybe she's with him and they're out looking for clues or something," Laura said as they walked away.

Tracey hoped Laura was right, but she had a really bad feeling in her belly that something was definitely wrong.

Three days later Uncle Donny had still not replied to any of her messages. Tracey mentioned his disappearance several times to her family, but they didn't seem as bothered by the news as she was, reminding her that he often disappeared without telling anyone where he was going. Tracey's feeling did not go away. It sat in her gut like a bad egg.

Waiting impatiently in the living room for her once-again late student,

Tracey wondered if maybe she should try contacting the M-Force agents and tell them about her uncle's disappearance. Before she could make a firm decision one way or the other, Dave raced his bike down the street. A large cloud of dust trailed behind him like a cartoonish bad smell.

"You're late."

He dropped his bike onto the driveway. "Whatever."

"Where have you been? You haven't been at school and …" She'd planned a big speech about his attitude and wanted to point out his anger would not help his control when she caught sight of the bruise around his eye.

"Dave—" The glare he shot her froze any further questions. She followed him into the backyard with a heavy heart. They should probably work on calming techniques instead of throwing things at each other. Then again, she suspected today he would prefer to hit something. Maybe physical exercise would help both his focus and his temper. It certainly would help hers. Sarah avoided Tracey's eye altogether. Yeah, maybe start with exercise.

Tracey's grandma taught all of them stretching and holding patterns when they were very little, sort of a cross between Yoga, Pilates, and karate katas. She'd learned a number of them at camp, too.

For a second she flashed back to her first year at Camp Mindflower, and of watching Tony try to hold the Greenleaf pose. She remembered falling out of her own pose because she'd been laughing so hard. Stifling her laughter now so that Dave didn't think she was laughing at him, she started Sarah on the first-year pattern. Tracey worked with Dave to follow Sarah correctly but could feel his frustration bubbling along the surface of the calm she was trying to teach.

"You have to block out those distracting thoughts," she told him, holding the current pose easily—her legs were spread for balance and both hands held out at her sides, one palm pointed to the sky and one pointed to the ground.

Dave's arms shook and sweat beaded near his hairline as he struggled to keep his hands raised. "I'm trying!"

"Hey, it's not a problem," she assured him quietly. He threw up his

289

hands and stomped toward the back fence, staring out into the trees behind Tracey's house. She sighed loudly and called for Sarah to join her in the middle of the garden. Maybe some shield practice would take his mind off his distractions—you had to focus when you were shielding, otherwise you'd get zapped. Dave returned as soon as he saw what she was planning.

She spaced her two students at either end of the backyard, planning to act as a ball machine. The idea was to randomly throw zaps for her students to block. They raised and dropped their shields as she mixed up her throws—alternating light zaps with stronger ones. Usually it was a fun game. Today she was completely serious.

She drew on more power to increase the strength of her next zap. Dave growled and threw up his hands, shouting, "Stop that!"

Forced to suddenly suck her power back into her chest, Tracey zapped herself in the process. "Ow! What?" she cried, rubbing at her sternum. Sarah stared at Dave with wide eyes.

"Stop pushing at me!" he demanded and slumped to his knees. "I can't focus on my shield when you do that."

"What are you talking about?"

"When you're about to throw a stronger zap I can feel your magic pushing at me. I can't focus. I can barely control my own powers. I can't block you out, too, so you have to stop doing it. It's driving me nuts!"

What did he mean "pushing" at him? She wasn't doing that. She stared, feeling a bit stupid, and then spied Sarah nodding out of the corner of her eye. Tracey turned on her quickly. "What?"

"It is hard to concentrate, Tracey," Sarah admitted softly.

"Concentrate on what? I don't know what you guys are talking about." Tracey looked at them both, her skin tingling. Nausea crept up from her stomach. She swallowed hard. "I'm not doing anything."

"... The Devil ..."

32

You are, Trace," Sarah said, breaking the silence.

Tracey squinted at her. *Why is she playing along with this?* A shadow fell over them. Heart in her throat, Tracey's head snapped up but it was only a cloud crossing in front of the sun. Still, a shiver shook her frame. "What are you talking about?"

"You're doing it right now," Dave accused.

Tracey checked her core and was surprised to find she was generating a thin shield bubble. She forced herself to relax, lowered it and checked her power trail. Most of the magic flowed from her chest as usual, but two tendrils snuck beneath her shield. She *was* pushing at Sarah and Dave.

"I didn't know I was doing that. I'm not ... I can't be ..." She closed off the connection immediately. The strands snapped with a tiny ping, bouncing back to her chest. Tracey slumped to the grass, suddenly weak.

"I wasn't sure if you knew you were doing it. You kinda always do it," Sarah said, dropping to her knees beside her sister. "I mean, it's not usually this strong. Still—"

"What do you mean?" Tracey's voice sounded odd, quiet and wobbly. She felt sick. *What am I doing? How could I not know I was doing that?*

"Well, it's usually little pushes or tugs. It's pretty easy to block, but lately, you've been a lot stronger. It kinda hurts a little."

"Why didn't anyone say anything to me?" A cold band tightened around her chest making it hard to breathe. "Why didn't *you* tell me?"

Sarah shook her head. "Mom told us not to."

"What? They knew?" *Why would Mom hide something like this?* Tracey jumped to her feet and backed away from Sarah. She couldn't take the pity on her sister's face. *Pity! Ha.* Sarah must love this, laughing at Tracey's lack of control.

Her thoughts spiraled as her breathing grew faster. She sounded hysterical. Sarah moved into her line of sight, her mouth moving but Tracey couldn't hear her, didn't even want to look at her. She spun away. Questions bounced back and forth finding no purchase in her mind.

Sarah's voice penetrated her panic, "Everyone knows."

Dave, with all the sensitivity of a rhino, flapped his hand in the air. "So, if you're going to stop doing it, can we get back to practice now? Or are we stopping now so you can have a little cry?"

Tracey swiped at her face, scrubbing her tears away. Yes, she wanted to stop. She wanted to find her mom and dad, and demand to know why they'd never said anything. And what about Tony? He'd never said anything to her, either.

She glanced from Sarah to Dave. She couldn't leave him hanging, no matter how badly she wanted to. Checking her watch she found there was only fifteen minutes left of their practice time.

"Sarah, can you work by yourself?"

"Are you okay, Tracey?" Sarah bent her head and tried to catch Tracey's eye.

"Just go practice, please."

"Fine." Her hair flew as she spun around and stomped to the bottom of the garden.

"What about me?" Dave demanded.

"How about you try and zap me," Tracey suggested. That way she could focus on not using her magic at all.

She'd always thought she was helping Uncle Donny when she "boosted" his magic, but then, she thought it had been her choice. *Oh God, what if I'm doing more than just pushing, what if my lack of control ends up ... Sarah said it hurt— she also said it had changed. What's different now?* Tracey pressed a hand against her chest. The only thing that had happened recently was that she'd found the Butterfly Stone. But the stone was locked away in her dresser. It couldn't be affecting her from this distance, could it? Holding a hand up in front of her eyes she watched it tremble. Clenching her fist seemed to halt it. She had so many questions for her mom.

In hindsight, and given Dave's level of frustration, encouraging him to try and hurt her hadn't been her best idea. His anger only grew when he was unable to hit her at all.

"Hold it."

"I can't."

"It's all about focus."

"Yeah well, I can't focus then, can I?" he complained, his face red. There was nothing physical in his hands, but she couldn't help thinking if there was, it would be flying at her head right about now. Dave's chest heaved with his exertions.

"All right, stop for a second."

"Now what?"

How could she word this so he would understand? "What do you …?" she stopped. He wouldn't recognize any of the technical terms because he'd never been to camp. "Try this. When you shield yourself, what do you do? Do you picture an actual shield in your hands like from the movies?"

"How did you know that?"

Tracey thought about the size and shape of the blur she'd seen floating in front of him. "Lucky guess. Do you actually see the shield in your hands?"

"No, it's imaginary," he said slowly as if he thought she was stupid.

She bit back a sigh. "Do you imagine the feel of it? Or a color, maybe? How heavy it is in your hands?"

"I dunno."

This is so painful. "Try imagining a …" What would he be familiar with? "A spitball?"

His face brightened. "Yeah, okay. Now what?"

"Now, imagine aiming the spitball straw."

He raised his hand to his mouth. It was cute. An experienced Mage wouldn't need the physical movement. She didn't draw his attention to it.

"Okay, fire it." She kept her shield down, not wanting to disrupt him by drawing on her magic. At first, she felt nothing. His shoulders slumped. "Try again," she called.

A moment later she felt the barest pin needle against her left arm.

295

"Yes!" she called, "You did it."

Dave's face lit up, "It worked?"

"Yep, I felt that. Great job."

"Again?"

"Sure." Expecting the same pin needle feeling, she was shocked when the next hit landed like a punch to her chest. She startled back several steps. Dave grinned from ear to ear. "Ah, why don't we end this session on a positive note?" she suggested.

"Whatever," he agreed, but he was still smiling. She waved goodbye and remained in the yard needing to think. Sarah hovered in the doorway, watching her silently. Tracey didn't acknowledge her. She sat down on the grass and rubbed at her chest. *I need to talk to Mom.*

Tracey got her parents alone after dinner. She'd wanted Grandma in on the conversation too, but the old woman was still out with her bowling friends and Tracey didn't want to wait.

"What's wrong?" Mom asked, sitting forward on the sofa.

"A lot, actually. Something is wrong with my power."

Her parents shared a look.

"What was that?" Tracey pointed at them. *It's true.* "What's wrong with me?"

"Honey, nothing is wrong with you."

What worried Tracey was that her mom didn't meet her eye when she said that. "Then why …?"

Her mom took her hand. Her touch was warm and made her feel safe. "Honey, your abilities manifested differently than most kids your age."

"Dave said I was *pushing* at him. Mom, he can't even control his —"

"We thought it would be something you grew out of," Dad cut in, standing up. He paced to the wall as if unable to remain still and raked a hand through his greying hair. "We noticed it when you were born. Most kids don't manifest until they reach five or six years old. It trickles in and continues to grow until it reaches full strength at maturity. You were different. You were born with your powers already inside you. We did what we could to contain you as a toddler and assumed that once you started summer camp they'd teach you how to control it."

Tracey had never heard of a baby with magic. A cold tingle started at the base of her neck and crawled all the way down her spine. She shivered in the warm room. "When we realized your control over your abilities was precarious, we taught you all those imagination games to lock it away," her mom added. "You had really good control when you were little."

"But not now?" Tracey questioned.

"You're growing up, honey. Maybe your powers are too?"

"But a level can't change."

"Tracey, magic doesn't settle into a level until you reach eighteen. Perhaps yours is still develop—"

"Am I dangerous?" she whispered.

Her mom immediately pulled her into a hug, "No, honey, no."

Tracey pushed her away. "Sarah said it hurts."

Her parents shared another look. "Then we need to work on your visualizations. Help you regain control." Her mom offered.

Dad held out one hand. "Tracey, I want you to try locking it away completely for now."

Her mouth dropped open. "Completely? Like Aunt Gemma?"

"For now. Let's see if you can manage that first. Then we'll look at training you to use your magic a bit differently."

Her chest ached at the thought of not using her magic. It was all she knew. Ice seemed to settle into the pit of her stomach. "I wish you'd told me." She edged away from her parents and their well-meaning, but strangely pitying faces.

"We're sorry," Mom said softly. Dad moved toward her so that they sat side by side, watching Tracey.

"So I have to lock it away? No magic at all?"

"I'll talk to Grandma. Maybe she'll have some ideas," Dad said.

They were all quiet for a moment. The silence itched at Tracey, but she didn't have anything to say that wouldn't end with her bursting into tears. She wanted to tell them about the Butterfly Stone, but if she did that then she'd have to tell them everything. She couldn't. Knowing about the stone could put her parents' lives in danger.

Her mom made an obvious attempt to change the subject. "Tracey, yesterday you were you saying something about Donald?"

Tracey allowed her the distraction, wanting things to be normal again. "He's missing. He hasn't answered any of my calls or texts and he hasn't been into the office at all from what I can tell. I checked the office camera and his work email, but there was nothing. I even went to the film set with Laura. He hasn't been there either, Mom. It's a paying job!"

"That doesn't sound like Donald," her mom said. She looked to her husband and said, "He was told to stop investigating by the M-Force agents, wasn't he?"

"That's what he told us."

"Okay, I'm going to call them. Tracey, look, I promise we'll talk to Grandma when she comes home. We'll devise a plan to help you retrain your power use, okay? For now, go fetch that agent's card from the fridge. I might need you here when I talk to him."

Tracey did as asked. As she pulled the card from the fridge, she realized her palms were sweaty. She ran a quick check on her inner closet, but the door was firmly locked. If she'd been affecting those around her since birth, she clearly had no real control. But how could she stop using magic? It was a part of her, intrinsic to her nature. Locking it away completely was like losing a limb. She couldn't *feel* her family at all. The emptiness expanded in her mind, sucking at her like quicksand. *It's wrong ... I'm wrong.*

It didn't matter that she'd been leaking magic for years or that her family had just accepted it. She knew it was wrong. It was also dangerous, especially if she was growing stronger. *Oh God, Uncle Donny!* She had to find him, she had to talk to him. *Did he ever notice?* She thought she'd been helping him by boosting his magic, and maybe she had been. His magic was so weak, maybe he didn't know. She was so confused. *Wait ... is that why Mom and Dad let me work for him because it would help him — or me? Oh God, that was the real reason why they altered my bracelet, because of my power?* She vowed to do as her parents suggested and not use her magic at all.

Tracey's mom dialed the number on the card left by Agent Malden and was put through to his office. She spoke to him quietly, then called Tracey to the phone.

"Hello?"

Agent Malden got straight to the point. "Tell me what you've learned about your uncle's disappearance."

Tracey repeated what she'd told her parents.

"I can hear that you're concerned, and your reasoning seems sound. When was the last message you received from him?"

"Last week."

He paused. "Is something else bothering you, Tracey?"

Fruit tingles! "Nothing. I mean, not about my uncle or the case. It's personal."

The agent was silent for another moment and then added, "Is there anything you want to discuss with me anyway?"

"No." It was against the law to use your powers on someone else. Fearing her faulty magic was going to get her into trouble, she felt her heart lurch. Glancing down, she realized her hand was pressed protectively over her chest. "No," she repeated. "I'm just worried about my uncle."

There was another long pause before the agent said, "I'll return to town this afternoon. Let's see if we can pin down your uncle's location. Tracey, if you hear from him at all, contact me immediately."

She jotted down the private cell phone number he read out and hung up. "Agent Malden is coming to look for Uncle Donny," she told her parents. Part of her worried Agent Malden would discover her failing powers. She would have to keep her distance, but she wasn't going to stop looking for Uncle Donny—she'd just have to do it quietly.

Going to school the following morning was a real challenge. Tracey had trouble focusing on her school work with her emotions swirling around so madly inside her head. As soon as she saw Tony, she pushed him into an empty classroom.

"What is it? Have you heard from—?" he began.

"I need to ask you something." She turned away, unsure of where to start. After a deep breath, she forced herself to turn around, wanting to see his face when she asked the next question. "When I use my powers, do you … have you ever noticed anything strange?"

He broke her gaze instantly, and that, more than his silence, told her everything.

He's my friend. I thought he was my friend. "You knew?"

"Tracey, I …"

Her chest felt tight again. She pressed against it as sorrow engulfed her. Tears prickled. She blinked them away and had to force herself to speak quietly when all she wanted to do was scream. "Why didn't you tell me?"

He looked down at his feet. Tracey examined what she could see of his face, searching for pity. She found only sadness. His lips quivered. "You didn't know you were doing it, Trace. You sort of push at people when you—"

"Don't," she cried, spinning away. "How could I stop doing it if I didn't know I was doing it in the first place?" It had always been a conscious effort on her part when she boosted her uncle's magic, hadn't it? *It doesn't feel like I'm pushing out at those around me.*

She jumped when he placed a hand on her shoulder. "I'm sorry."

Tracey shoved his hand away and turned on him, her voice growing louder. "Sorry? I thought you were my friend."

"I am your friend."

She swiped hot tears from her eyes. "A friend would have told me."

"Tracey," he begged, holding up his hands.

"I trusted you!"

"Tracey!" he said more urgently.

"I—what?" The look on his face stopped her cold.

"You want me to tell you? Fine, I'm telling you. You're doing it right now."

It took a full minute for his words to register. When they did she gasped, stumbling back several steps. He watched her with his hands outstretched, as if to ward off an attack.

She couldn't feel her magic at all. She couldn't feel anything other than anger and fear. Wrapping shaking arms around her belly she tried to calm her breathing. When he didn't say anything more, she forced a deep breath, and then another. Closing her eyes, she tentatively felt for her power. The closet door in her chest was wide open. *No! I locked it!* She jolted back in surprise, finding ribbons of power spiraling out of her chest toward Tony. His shield was raised against her. Focusing hard, she felt the pressure from her chest that was pushing strands of power at him. She *was* doing it! "I'm so sorry, Tony," she cried, snapping the door shut to cut off the power transfer.

He stepped forward. His hands still outstretched, this time reaching for her. She backed away. "Don't! Don't come near me."

He froze. "Tracey …"

She ran from the room.

Tracey had no idea what was happening to her. She ran until she was forced to stop, doubling over and gasping for breath.

She needed to be alone, away from prying eyes and the well-meaning glances of her friends. She always *drew* on her power. Her imagination supplied the closet door that she opened to draw her magic out of her chest. How had her mind mixed *draw* with *push*?

The sun was bright and hot on the back of her neck. It dropped to a sudden chill as she walked beneath the bleachers surrounding the football field. Ducking under the closest rail, she walked to a patch of dirty grass.

Sitting with her back to the school, she closed her eyes and focused. It took ages to quiet her mind. She felt her heart rate decrease with each breath until her breathing was slow and gentle. Random thoughts popped into her head — thoughts of her uncle, homework, her nana, Tony, and Dave Two. Dreamy brown eyes filled her mind, giving her a warm, happy feeling. She couldn't decide who the eyes belonged to. Prince Henry and Damian both had brown eyes, and both gave her a warm feeling when she thought of them.

She forced the image away and breathed deeply, in and out, filling her whole body with air. She let her mind drift. The eyes appeared again, only this time they faded to black, and red smoke poured out of them. She bit back a scream as shadowy fingers sprang in her direction.

Scooting back along the ground to escape the shadow's clutches, her eyes snapped open. She was no longer beneath the bleachers—she was somewhere else.

"… The Tower …"

33

Tracey was in a cold white room. There were no walls, no furniture, just white ... everywhere. She tried squinting and then opened her eyes wide, but nothing changed. She was alone.

"Hello?" Her voice echoed through the white void, repeating and fading far longer than it should have.

"Hello, Tracey."

She spun around at the sound of the woman's voice, but there was no one behind her. A red square the size of a television appeared before her eyes. Then a blue outline of a diamond overlapped the square. As the voice spoke, the two shapes undulated and rotated, twisting from parallelograms to diamonds to rectangles and back to squares, dancing in time with the rise and fall of the mysterious voice. "You have called upon my assistance. How may I help you?" The voice did not echo.

"Who are you?" Tracey asked. Her voice filled the air with its repetitions. Clapping hands over her ears did little to muffle the sound. When she slammed her eyes shut, the red and blue lines danced against endless black. Her eyes popped open as the voice spoke again.

"I am who you asked for."

Well, that didn't answer her question at all. She remembered trying to escape the Shadowman under the bleachers—but how did she end up here? "Did you bring me here?"

"Yes." The voice sounded like a woman, old and young at the same time. Tracey couldn't focus on the words as the tones flowed musically around her. The moving shapes twisted and danced before her eyes.

She gave voice to her fear. "What's wrong with me?"

"There is nothing wrong with you."

"Then why is my magic attacking people? How do I stop it?" She stepped forward. Looking down at her feet, she wondered what she was standing on. The room—if it was a room—was the same temperature as her skin. She didn't feel hot or cold. She didn't feel anything at all. It was eerie.

"Your magic is not attacking them."

"Then what is it doing? Why can't I stop it?"

"Why do you want to stop?"

"Because it's wrong," Tracey said—it came out at a higher pitch, almost as if she was asking a question. She spun another circle. The colored shapes were the only things here. She focused on the dance between them, her eyes growing heavy. "That's not the way magic is supposed to work."

"Isn't it?"

"What?"

"Isn't it?" the voice repeated.

"I'm attacking people!"

"What makes you believe that you are? Are they injured?"

"Stop answering my questions with more questions!" Tracey demanded. Her voice echoed, growing louder. The crescendo suddenly stopped, leaving her dizzy from the abrupt silence.

"You know the answers."

Tracey dropped her voice to a whisper. "I *don't* know. Isn't that why I'm here?"

"You do know, you simply do not trust yourself to know—you are the only one who can use it, Tracey. The only one."

"Please, I need help." Her voice sounded raw, as if she ripped the words from her very soul.

"Don't hurt them."

Just like that, huh? This was getting her nowhere. "But how?"

"Just stop," the voice said again. As the musical quality of the words faded, Tracey blinked and found herself back under the bleachers at school. The bright light of day had turned into early evening. She glanced at her wrist and, startled, she realized she was holding the Butterfly Stone in her hands.

306

Tracey stared at it, horror rising in her mind. She'd locked it away in her dresser days ago, hadn't she? She didn't remember bringing it to school. *How did it get here?* The stone pulsed with a warm, internal light. Tracey closed her fist around it and glanced at her watch again. It was four o'clock. Chewing on her lower lip, she realized she'd missed the end of school. She'd never done that before. Her head ached with a heavy thickness that sat behind her eyes.

Dave would be waiting for her. Without thinking, she pulled the thin silver chain over her head and tucked the stone beneath her shirt. She ran home knowing she was going to be late.

Mom appeared in the doorway as she reached the bottom of the driveway. "He's not here yet."

"Oh." Tracey bent over panting. *This is why you don't exercise. It hurts.* The fresh air and warmth in her muscles was a pretty nice feeling though, and for the first time in a long time, her head was quiet.

"Honey, Sarah had to stop at the library on the way home. So she'll be late too."

Tracey nodded. She couldn't help wondering if her sister's homework really was that urgent or if she'd just wanted to avoid practice. *Or avoid me?* Stepping in through the front door Tracey could hear the television playing the theme song of one of her mom's favorite shows.

"Can you send Dave through when he gets here?" she asked heading for the kitchen. She poured herself a glass of juice and drank it down in several long gulps, pulling her shirt away from where it stuck to her sweaty body. *Gross.* As her racing heart slowed, she pulled her cell phone from her pocket. There were ten text messages from Tony. She didn't read them. He was probably checking to make sure she wasn't magically torturing someone. She released a heartfelt sigh and slumped down in the nearest kitchen chair. Her hand brushed against the stone. She needed a distraction. *Where is Dave?*

Tracey woke up with fewer answers than she'd hoped for. Dave hadn't turned up to practice the night before, and there was still no word from Uncle Donny. A feeling of helplessness dragged at her body. Everything was falling apart. Somehow, she muddled through her morning classes. With an anxious feeling twisting like a snake in her belly she dropped her lunch tray onto the table and offered Tony an exhausted greeting. When she'd climbed out of bed this morning she knew she needed to apologize. It wasn't Tony's fault something was wrong with her. She didn't want to lose one of her best friends over this, especially not when she needed a fellow Mage to warn her when she was out of control. "I'm so—"

"Any word on your uncle?" he asked around a mouthful of apple. Dark shadows kissed the skin beneath his eyes. His hair stuck out in all directions. What worried her was that he was wearing a plain dark blue t-shirt. No pictures. She didn't know he owned any. He repeated his question. "Your uncle?"

"No word and I'm seriously worried. Mom even called M-Force the other night." The two friends ate silently before Tracey sucked in a breath to try again. "Look, Tony, I'm really so—"

"I've been looking into Doctor Chan."

"And?" She took the second subject change for what it was—Tony didn't want an apology. She touched his arm in silent thanks. He was too good to her. She didn't deserve his friendship but she'd take it. Always.

His lips quirked in a smile. "I can't find anything on him. I've looked on the internet and the M-Net, and nothing."

"Well that's weird, right?"

Jonny dropped into his chair and pointed at Tracey. "You ditched school? Since when did you get infected with the double-D virus?"

Tracey shot Tony a look and then told Jonny, "It's a long story."

He rolled his eyes. "It would have to be. So, what were you talking about that needs such a serious face?"

Tony repeated the story of his search into the missing Doctor Chan. Laura joined them half-way through but waved at him to continue. She opened up her sandwich and picked out the cheese.

Tracey listened to Tony's story with half an ear, glancing around the lunch room curiously. Damian sat beside Meena. *What a waste.* Still, he was gorgeous. And she had eyes. Thinking about the hot guy was something nice in a brain filled with worry. Meena appeared to hold her entire table spellbound. All except Damian. He kept twisting his head, looking around the room. *Ha! Bored with Meena already?* That hadn't taken long. She smirked to herself and turned back to her own friends. Interlude over, worries exploded in her brain. Foremost was her magic and how dangerous she was. They had to be warned. She felt ill imagining their horrified expressions. Would they run away and leave her sitting alone at the table to be laughed at by the entire school?

I have to tell them. Tony trailed off when he realized she wasn't listening. She stared at each of her friends in turn.

"What is it?" Laura asked in a soft voice.

Tracey blinked and scrubbed at the corners of her eyes angrily. "I have to tell you guys something."

Tony remained silent as she confessed to Laura and Jonny about her faulty magic. They watched her with wide eyes as she told them about the dreams, the meditation and her fear that she was going to end up attacking someone.

When she fell silent Jonny said, "I just pretend to be sick when I want out of school."

Tracey sobbed out a laugh. Laura put an arm around her shoulders and gave her an awkward hug. It brought more tears to the surface. She had the best friends in the world. Tony pitched his voice to a low whisper. "Lots of stuff going on in your head."

"It's okay, Tracey. You know we're here for you. You don't have to keep secrets from us. We may not understand everything, but you know you can tell us anything, right?" Laura said.

She nodded, unable to speak. Her emotions were clogging up her throat, choking the life out of her. When she sniffed, Laura held out a small packet of tissues.

Tracey took three. "I just don't know what to do. Mom and Dad told me to lock it down, for now—until I relearn how to control it." It felt so wrong to lock her magic away. She had an empty hole in her chest where she usually felt at peace. This must be what super heroes felt when they lost their power. She felt sick.

"No magic at all?" Laura asked. Tony looked horrified.

Jonny held out a hand. "I think we should break down the problem. There's four of us and that's heaps of thinking power. Let's just work out a plan to deal with it."

Tracey's mouth fell open. Next to her, Laura and Tony looked just as surprised.

"What?" Jonny snapped. "I can plan stuff. I'm not a total moron."

"We didn't say that," Laura said, laughing. "It's just—you usually don't want to work. We're all wondering if you've been possessed or something."

Tony waved his hand in front of Jonny's face and closed his eyes. "I can't sense anything. Maybe a parasite has taken over his brain? Trace—you're stronger than I am. What do you think?"

Tracey laughed, though the emptiness inside her pulsed and grew larger when she couldn't play along. Their antics did make her feel a little better. A shadow of worry ate at the center of her mind, drawing her back to the problem. "What do I do now? I can't get Tony to follow me around everywhere to warn me if my magic acts up, can I?" It felt as though she was a prisoner, but one who actually wanted a guard to watch over her.

"I told you, we'll plan it all out. Just leave it to us." Jonny told her.

Tony pulled his cell phone from his pocket and opened his notepad app while Laura pulled a pretty purple covered notebook from her bag. "Okay, step one."

All their careful planning went right out the window when Tracey got home. There were two police cars in the street and a dark-colored SUV parked in her driveway. Tracey froze on the footpath. *Uncle Donny?* Her chest remained tight as she ran to the front door. "Mom?"

"Honey, come in, but step carefully."

Tracey jerked to a stop in the doorway. Furniture was strewn everywhere like there'd been a wild party. Picture frames had been pulled from the walls and shattered. Torn paper and broken glass lay all over the floor. Books and DVDs had been thrown from the shelves, and the heavy bookshelves lay toppled over halfway across the room. Everything was a mess. "What happened?" she gasped.

"We were robbed," Mom told her. Mascara stained her cheeks where her tears had run. She sat on the sofa next to Agent Malden. Tracey looked around quickly, but couldn't see Agent Striker anywhere. Her heart ached as she examined all the broken stuff. Someone had been in her house. The Shadowman's goons?

"Did they trash everything? What did they steal?"

"It doesn't look like they took anything," her dad said, walking into the room with two police officers.

"Tracey?" Officer Jameson looked surprised to see her.

"Officer Jameson, hi," she said, waving her fingers awkwardly.

"This is your house?" He gave her a strange look. She figured he must be getting fed up with her appearing at so many crime scenes. Her skin tingled and the back of her neck felt all itchy. She scratched at it and didn't look him in the eye.

"Yes."

"Tracey?" her dad looked from Officer Jameson to Tracey and back again.

She quickly explained that Officer Jameson and his partner were the ones who'd investigated the break in at Uncle Donny's office. Agent Malden watched them talk from the sofa, his expression carefully blank. She wanted to ask him so many questions but didn't want to get too close in case he sensed her failing magic.

Officer Jameson's partner was an older man with short greying hair, a long face, and untrusting green eyes. He spoke to Tracey's dad in a soft voice. She inched closer, wanting to know what he suspected. "At this time, and given that nothing is missing, we believe the break in is nothing more than a prank. A gang initiation, perhaps."

"And not take anything?" Tracey was confused. There were tablets, laptops, and phones all over the house.

Officer Jameson stepped closer to address Tracey's dad directly. She had the impression he didn't want her listening in. No chance of that! "Are you certain there was nothing more valuable kept in the house, sir?"

Tracey's hand flew to her chest. The stone was hidden beneath her shirt. She raised her eyes to Agent Malden. He'd seen her flinch but stayed quiet. Without ready access to her magic, she couldn't tell if he was scanning her. Officer Jameson glanced at Tracey. She could feel his eyes staring a hole right through her. "Perhaps you should check your room, and those of your siblings."

"Okay." She barely waited for her mom to indicate it was okay to leave before running upstairs. A gasp burst from her lips when she saw her room. It was a disaster of clothes, bed sheets and pillows. Books and games lay broken and scattered everywhere she looked. Even her old toys had been pulled from her closet and dumped. On the desk, her laptop was open — the screensaver of Prince Henry rotating slowly. She froze. *I turned that off when I left for school.* She checked her password screen, it was locked. Thank goodness they'd had that cyber-awareness talk at school. Tony, too, was forever lecturing her about having a password that was difficult to guess. She was glad she'd listened and set a long, complicated one.

Stepping quickly, she checked the rest of the top floor, popping her head into each room. Her room looked worse than all the others. To her detective's eye, it looked like someone had systematically searched their house. *The necklace!* Her dresser had been toppled over and emptied, but the hidden door in the back was still sealed. Miss Tearning's necklace was safe and sound inside. When she raised it, the crystal wings and colored stones glinted in the late afternoon sunlight cascading through her bedroom window, turning her walls into a rainbow of color.

Suddenly uncomfortable with the dresser's security, Tracey dropped the chain over her head. The butterfly necklace clinked gently against the stone she already wore.

Officer Jameson appeared in the doorway. He held a notepad in his hand but wasn't writing anything down. "Does it look like anything has been taken?"

She quickly moved away from her dresser. "I don't think so." Voices rose downstairs. It sounded like her brothers were home. "Actually, you should ask my sister to check her room, she doesn't like the rest of us going in there. The boys, too. I can't really tell if anything is missing in their rooms."

The uniformed man stared at her intently. "Are you certain there is nothing missing in here?"

Tracey backed up realizing he was standing awfully close. "Pretty sure."

"I'm glad you weren't here when it happened," he said, and after another glance around the room, walked out.

Staring at her reflection in her sideways dresser mirror, Tracey's hand crept up to her chest. Yes, both the Butterfly Stone and Miss Tearning's necklace were safe, for now.

When she returned downstairs, the police officers had departed. As scary as the break in was she was glad they were gone. Agent Malden sat at the kitchen table with her mom. Both cradled mugs of coffee and spoke softly. When she appeared in the doorway they broke off and turned toward her. Agent Malden was wearing a different suit—dark blue this time and it looked to be a better fit.

Do I go in? She didn't know how close she could get before he could sense her damaged magic. "Agent Malden?"

"Join us, please. I was just updating your mom on the investigation into your missing uncle."

Tracey fell into her chair with a thump. The legs screeched against the wooden floorboards gaining her a glare from her mom. "So what do we do now?"

"I've completed a preliminary search of the town. What I'd like to try now is a familial search."

Tracey's gaze shot to her mom. "Shouldn't we wait for Grandma? She's pretty strong, I'm sure she could help." Tracey wasn't supposed to use her magic and she didn't want Agent Malden to find out. Besides, Mom agreed she shouldn't use her powers. If Mom had changed her mind, she must be really worried about Uncle Donny. Tracey tensed in her seat.

The agent continued, completely unaware of the silent conversation going on between mother and daughter. "Wrong side of the family, Tracey. Strong or not, your grandmother won't be able to effectively assist the search spell. She could even send it astray if we're not careful. I did speak to your mom about involving her mother, but I understand that's not possible."

"Yeah, she's nuts."

"Tracey!" Mom hissed. Tracey immediately felt guilty. What a horrible thing to say about her nana. She bit her bottom lip and grasped the agent's hand. Cracking open the door in her chest the slightest sliver, she took her mom's hand and felt a buzz of power wash over her, the circle between them closing shut with a snap. Tracey's eyes drifted shut as the warmth of her mother's magic enveloped her. Agent Malden's power felt colder in comparison and prickled at her skin.

Her mom shook her hand a little. "Tracey, you need to open up, honey."

"But Mom, I can't," she hissed. Her eyes darted to the agent. He examined her through squinted eyes.

"Tracey?" he asked.

"I-I can't do this. I might hurt you," she gasped backing away from the table. Her mother rose to follow.

"Honey—"

Tracey bolted from the room.

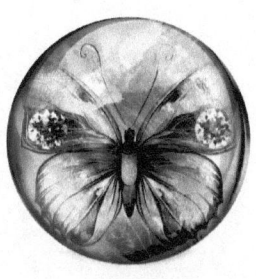

"The Hanged Man …
Big changes are coming."

34

She hid for several hours, unable to face the prospect of returning home to explain why she'd run away. Hunkering down in her special spot by the river, she finally felt safe; alone, where she couldn't hurt anyone. Her gaze drifted around the emerald oasis. Long grass surrounded the trunk of each, thick-barked tree. Giant roots stuck out of the ground making a lopsided circle of odd-shaped seats. When she'd found this place with Laura she'd insisted it was a spot for secret meetings, like the round table out of an old King Arthur story. She and Laura mainly came here to gossip about school and boys.

Tracey sprawled over the root she used as a chair, closest to the large trunk. She leaned back and stared out over the river, not looking at anything in particular as her thoughts swam in circles.

Hopefully Agent Malden and her mom would be able to cast the search spell without her. If anything happened to her uncle now, would it be her fault? Maybe if she'd helped with the spell, they might have found him already.

Her thoughts turned to Aunt Gemma. Her aunt stopped using magic years ago, but what had been the trigger? Did she have the same affliction as Tracey? No one ever spoke about why Aunt Gemma disavowed all magic. Tracey had never thought to ask. She assumed it was like being a vegetarian—just a choice. Pulling her phone from her pocket, she found Aunt Gemma's number. Before she could press "call" it vibrated in her hands. She stared blankly at the message that appeared.

I think I'm in trouble but don't panic—I'm fine for the moment.

Uncle Donny! Tracey hit the call icon and drummed her fingers against the ground as she waited for him to answer. When the line connected she demanded to know where he was and bombarded him with so many questions he wasn't able to speak until she stopped for breath.

"I said don't panic. It's fine, really." His voice sounded calm, but there was something in it that concerned her.

"Boss!" she said using the strongest tone she could. "Where are you?"

He hesitated and then blurted, "Look, I'm sort of trapped."

She sighed loudly. "Explain."

"I need an assist. A spell. One I can cast without any external items ... uh, and without hands."

"Where are you?" she demanded again.

"Wrong question, kiddo. You need to ask what spell I need."

"What spell do you need?" she obediently parroted back.

"A weather one—to stop snow."

"Boss, there is no such thing as a weather spell. Come on, it's the weather. If we could control the weather, wouldn't everyone use it? You need to think smaller."

There was a noise in the background that she couldn't make out. "Tracey, I need you to bring the butterfly necklace. He says he'll trade for it." A blustery roar drowned out the rest. It was like an engine or a fan had turned on right next to him.

Where on earth is Uncle Donny? "He? Who is he?" she shouted. There was so much noise on the other end of the line she didn't know if he could hear her.

"Tracey? Can you hear me?"

"Uncle Donny! I can't bring the necklace. I-I ..." Her hand brushed the hidden necklaces beneath her shirt. She couldn't give the stone to the bad guys. Everything in her screamed not to do it.

"Tracey, you have to." He sounded scared. She'd never heard him sound like that before, and it took her aback.

"All right, tell them all right! Where do I bring it?"

There was so much noise over his end of the phone she missed what he said next. The roar stopped and a deep voice hissed, "The roof of the Central Grand Hotel, ten minutes." Tracey knew that voice. It was the voice from her nightmares, the voice of the Shadowman.

"I can't get there in ten minutes," she told it. "I don't have a car—heck, I don't even have a license."

"Ten minutes. Leave the necklace on the door handle leading to the roof. Go up. You might even get there in time to save your uncle's life." The Shadowman hung up. Tracey ran.

Reaching the hotel with barely a minute to spare, she left the necklace hanging over the roof access door handle and raced up the stairs.

She'd called Tony during her mad dash to catch the bus and luck was with her when the bus appeared almost instantly. Tony answered her call seconds later. He logged onto the M-Net and opened Doctor Chan's secret website. She wouldn't stand a chance if the man in the red mask was there. She told Tony to find her a spell, disregarding them as quickly as he suggested them.

"It's not going to work," she yelled once she reached the roof top. Nothing would work. Bitter wind whipped at her clothing, as if trying to tear it from her body. It was freezing up here. Only an hour ago it was a warm sunny afternoon, now it was snowing.

It wasn't just snow, either. Sleet and rain pummeled her body the instant she stepped out into the open. She could barely see three feet in front of her nose, which didn't matter because she was too afraid to raise her head. The sleet hurt her exposed skin. When she did look up she could only stare in horror. Uncle Donny stood tied to an electricity box in the center of a giant snow pile.

"Uncle Donny!" she screamed, but he didn't respond. His head bobbed against his chest, lips blue from the cold. How could she reach him? The snow was rising fast and it wouldn't be long before he suffocated. She tried to climb the snow pile, slipping and sliding dangerously but it was no use, she couldn't get anywhere near him. *Oh God!* This was all her fault. She had the necklace and the Shadowman had gone after her family to get it.

"Uncle Donny is tied up and snow is piled all around him. I can't reach him."

"Try melting it," Tony suggested.

She could barely hear him through the cell phone's tiny speaker. Something about melting the snow? Dragging her earphones from her pocket to free up her hands she realized with a shudder she had no spell makings with her. The wet slush would wash away any circle she tried to draw.

"Melt it with what?" Who could even create a spell like this? Controlling the weather wasn't possible. A person would have to be incredibly powerful to control a spell that strong. "Tony, is there a spell Uncle Donny can use to untie himself?"

"What's he tied with?"

"I can't see. His hands are buried in the snow." She didn't have time for this. She began emptying her pockets, and when her fingers touched something square, she thought of her sister. "I have matches," she shouted, pulling the small red box from her pocket. She'd completely forgotten she had them. A delayed wave of guilt passed over her again. *I still haven't got a birthday present.* She shook it off, focusing on the task at hand. "I can't build a fire in this weather, Tony, there's nothing up here to burn."

"Hang on, here's a spell. Uh — do you have any rope?" Tony asked.

"Where am I going to find rope up here?" she shouted back. The snow pile now reached her uncle's chest. "Hurry up, we're running out of time."

"What can you see?"

She urgently searched the rooftop. The shape of a mangled box sat in one corner, practically buried in snow. It looked old and water-stained. "A box."

"Have you looked inside?"

It looked filthy. Fighting against the biting wind that tore at her body and whipped her hair around like Medusa's snakes, she pushed her way closer. A quick search brought a shout of glee to her lips.

"Found something?"

"You'll never guess!" she shouted. It was a miracle. Coils of thick white fiber sat inside. "I actually found rope. But what do I do with it?"

"Throw it around Donny."

"It's too windy!" she shouted, "I can't get close to him." Her heart was pounding. The snow pile was growing wider by the second. Uncle Donny was used to her boosts of power. If she errantly pushed too much magic at him it shouldn't hurt—she hoped. Swiping a mixture of rain and tears out of her eyes, she swung the rope over her head.

Wind gusts blew it back into her face. *Fruit tingles!* She cracked open the door in her chest and sent a spark of power into the rope's end. This time the wind caught it at the right angle, and in moments it swung in a wide circle over her head. Releasing it at its highest arch, the rope flew across the roof and hissed as it magically wound around her uncle's giant snow belly.

"Okay, the rope is around him."

"Use the matches to blow a fire along the rope to melt the snow," Tony said.

"What?" *That's not going to work.* "The fire will burn through the rope."

"No, there's a spell on this website—it will keep the rope safe. Repeat exactly what I say when you light the match."

Following Tony's instructions, she repeated the spell and sent her power along the length of rope. Then she lit the match. It went out. She lit another, her shaking hand cupped around it to protect the flame. The second match flickered and died. *Oh, come on!* She tried again. This time the tiny stick ignited properly. Holding her breath, she watched the flames race over the rope surrounding her uncle. Tony was right, the spell kept the flames from destroying the natural fibers of the rope.

The blaze swelled and grew, bursting into a wall of flame that melted the snow in a flash. Tracey withdrew her power at Tony's shouted order and the fire ate through the rope. With nothing to feed off, the fire extinguished itself. Snow continued to fall.

She had no idea how to stop the crazy weather, but at least her uncle was safe. Blinking back tears she rushed to his side and untied his hands. He stirred. When he realized she was there, he pulled her into a giant hug. Just feeling his icy cold skin brought more tears to her eyes. She let them fall and held him tighter trying to warm his frozen body with her own skin.

"Are you okay?" she asked. Tremors wracked his frame. *I have to get him inside.*

"Where did you find that spell?" he questioned, dripping icy water all over her. She rubbed her hands over his arms. "Let's get back. You must be as frozen as I am," he said through chattering teeth.

And that was the strangest thing of all. She wasn't.

Back at the office they dried off and redressed.

"So when you were at the *Saving Time* film lot you heard a scream, and that's the last thing you remember?" Knowing her uncle was safe did great things for Tracey's peace of mind. She felt relaxed for the first time in weeks. Flopping back in her chair she stared, happy to have her eyes on him.

He rubbed the back of his neck. His cheeks were a pinkish color, which was better than the shade of blue they had been. "I woke up on the roof. He made me call you. Thanks for the spell by the way. What did you use?"

"Would you believe Tony found it on the internet?" Tracey couldn't help laughing at her uncle's expression. "So, who took you?"

"I don't know, kiddo."

It had to have been the man in the red mask — he was the only Mage-kind powerful enough to cast that snowstorm spell. It had been limited to that building alone, which was extraordinary magic. "Are you really okay, Uncle Donny?" It was her fault he'd been taken. Guilt sloshed around in her stomach. She rubbed at the ache caused when the muscle spasmed. No, it was the man in the red mask who was truly at fault. Still her belly ached.

"I'm only annoyed you had to give the necklace away."

"Yeah," she agreed softly. Beneath her clothing, the Butterfly Stone nestled warm and safe against her chest. Yeah, she'd given up a necklace. It just wasn't the one the man in the red mask truly wanted and when he found out, he was going to be furious.

"Together, bound to the flame,

Five stones to carry their name …"

35

So Donny has no idea who kidnapped him?" Laura asked. She'd styled her hair differently today, like something out of the fifties and it looked amazing. Tracey felt like a living mess. They all sat at their regular lunch table listening to Tony recount his side of last night's action. The way he told it, it didn't seem anywhere near as frantic as Tracey had experienced it.

"Nothing. All he remembers is standing outside the assistant producer's trailer talking to the costume team. He heard a scream, spun around, and then woke up on the hotel's rooftop. You should have seen how angry Mom was. I think she would have grounded him if she could have."

"Ouch," Jonny winced. He put his feet up on the table. Tracey looked around hoping no teachers were nearby.

"Yeah, and now he's being interrogated by Agent Malden and Agent Striker." The thought of the two agents sent a spike of fear into Tracey's chest. She quickly checked to make sure her magic was safely locked away. It was.

"I thought Agent Striker didn't come back with Agent Malden," Laura said.

"Agent Malden sent for her when Uncle Donny was released." That's what Uncle Donny had told the agents. He said he'd been "released" because neither he nor Tracey wanted them — or her mom — to find out about her involvement.

"They don't think he's in cahoots with the man in the red mask, do they?" Tony asked.

"I don't know." Tracey bit into her apple and chewed slowly. "He was taken from the film set. There's a connection to that location, I'm sure of it. Remember, I found the box in the leading lady's trailer."

"Are we not even going to ask why she had it?" Jonny asked.

It was a good question. Tracey wondered if her uncle had asked.

Laura leaned forward, "You still have the stone, don't you?"

"What?" Tracey eyeballed her friend wondering how she knew. Tracey hadn't told any of them the truth.

Laura hesitated, so Tony spoke up for her. "The stone from the box. You didn't really give it to him, did you?" Tracey looked at him but said nothing. "Well, I guess the good news is that your powers are fine. They worked perfectly last night."

She leaned in as anger mixed with anxiety in her throat. "What are you talking about, Tony? I barely used my magic last night, and that was only because there was no one around I could affect, apart from Uncle Donny."

Tony shook his head. "You've never hurt anyone," he said. "Even when you were *pushing* at me, it felt more like broad pressure — like a wall. I just shield against it until you pull back. Maybe, to even it out, you should try drawing back? I don't know, try to counter-balance it somehow?"

"And if I pull magic out of you instead of out of myself? I told you, Tony, I can't control it." *Why was he going on about this?*

"Tracey, I've never thought you were going to hurt me. I've known you a long time." His eyes looked sad. When she examined the rest of the table she realized they all did.

"Sarah says it's getting stronger." She locked eyes with Tony. "Is she right?"

He seemed reluctant to confirm her suspicions, which confirmed them anyway. Tracey replayed that voice from her nightmares, the one that told her she would hurt everyone she loved. No, she couldn't take the risk. She wouldn't use her magic at all until she knew how to control it.

Jonny leaned forward with a thump of his chair and waved his hand between them. "What about this man in the red mask? We should be worrying about him, not about how you use your power. He broke into your house, Trace! He knows who you are. He kidnapped your uncle to get to you because he knew you had the necklace."

"Jonny, we don't know that for sure," Laura said, pointing her finger at his face.

He leaned back and glared at her, and then his gaze returned to Tracey. "You really think he didn't have a hand in this? Who else could cast a storm spell like that? I heard it's still snowing on Main Street."

"Yeah, M-Force will have to investigate," Tony offered, popping one of his remaining chips into his mouth.

"You have a contact with M-Force. Can't you just ask them what's going on?" Jonny asked.

Tracey widened her eyes, surprised by the question. She didn't have a chance to tell Jonny he was crazy before she was interrupted by a coffee-colored hand tipped with red landing on the table beside her. Tracey followed the arm all the way up to the sneer on Meena's face. Carla, as usual, stood in her shadow.

"What are you all talking about?" Meena inquired. There was a sharp sound to her voice that put Tracey on edge.

"None of your business, Meanie," Jonny said. Meena ignored him, her gaze firmly fixed on Tracey.

Dave One and Dave Two hovered a short distance behind, their eyes alight with anticipation. Damian stood several feet away from them. His face scrunched like he'd tasted something sour. A zap of magic hit Tracey in the thigh. She nearly leapt from her chair. *Fruit tingles!* She should never have taught Dave Two how to do that. Casually she rubbed a hand against the sore spot on her leg. Dave Two started laughing like a hyena. *Jerk!*

Carla stepped up to Laura's side and examined the book beside her elbow. "Ohhh, I love that one," she cooed.

Laura didn't acknowledge her. Jonny rolled his eyes dramatically and said in a high-pitched feminine voice, "Ohhh, I love it because Sean is soooo dreamy."

Tony snorted juice out through his nose, causing Tracey and her friends to burst out laughing.

"It burns!" Tony wailed, clutching at his face.

Tracey laughed even harder. Looking up at Meena, she said, "I needed that. Sorry, did you want something?"

Meena leaned over to hiss into Tracey's ear. "Tell Damian you can't be his workgroup partner."

"Why?" Tracey had been surprised when the lists were read out this morning—happily surprised. The hottest guy in school had been teamed to work with her. Laura's head snapped in her direction. Whoops. She probably should have mentioned that when she first sat down. There'd be an interrogation later, worse than she'd experienced from the M-Force agents.

"Because he's mine, and you're forbidden to talk to him."

At that comment, Laura raised her head, skewering Meena with a dark look. "You can't forbid her. You're not even in the same class."

"Are you refusing to comply?"

"Refusing to comply? What are you? A robot from some futuristic Earth run by spybots and super freaks?" Jonny asked. There were a few chuckles around them, enough for Tracey to realize they'd become the center of attention. Damian watched from a distance. What was disappointing about his behavior was that he just stood there. He didn't say anything to Meena or try to stop what was going on. It was hard to know if he'd put Meena up to this or if he was just a pawn in her game.

Meena ignored the laughter. "Well?"

Tracey wondered if Meena even understood Jonny's comment—maybe she *was* a robot waiting for her next instruction. Another spark hit her arm. *Fruit tingles!* She glared at Dave Two. He grinned back as she felt another one land. Her hand rose to retaliate—she forced it down and flinched as Meena slammed her hand down on the table again. "You don't belong here, freak. Stay away from Damian. He's not a weirdo like you."

Tracey was so tired of people calling her a freak. Heat bubbled in her chest. She stood up, her fists clenching automatically. "What did you say?" Damian looked away. His face red and splotchy. Now would've been a great time for him to be a hero.

Laura grabbed Tracey's arm but she shook her off. Heat flooded Tracey's face as anger continued to build. It felt like it would explode out of her if Meena said just one more word.

Tony grabbed Tracey's hand and whispered, "Now, now, now. Telling you now." She felt his magic wrap around her wrist, zapping at her skin like pins and needles. She sucked in a deep breath, released it noisily and focused on calming her raging temper. *What just happened?* She'd gotten so angry, so fast.

Jonny rolled his apple across the table, knocking it into Tracey's other hand. Her eyes flew to his and he grinned. She clenched her teeth and forced her power to dissipate, slamming the door shut behind it. *How does it keep opening?* Her lack of control was really starting to scare her. "Meena, Mr. Michaels assigned Damian to work with me. I had no say in it. If you're not happy about it, Damian could ask to switch partners." She skewered him with a glare "If *he* wants."

"Or *you* could just switch," Meena hissed.

Tracey smiled sweetly. "Yeah, I guess I could." She wouldn't, though. Focused as she was on the confrontation with the mean girl, in the back of her mind she was terrified over how quickly her magic had risen. It took too much effort to force her power back into her chest. She couldn't let the petty girl get to her — she had bigger things to worry about. Tony tapped her hand to let her know her efforts had succeeded and let her go. She sat down and shoved her apple into her mouth.

With everyone at the table ignoring her, Meena spun on a heel and stormed toward Damian. He refused to take her hand. She growled and stormed off. Before she got far, Tracey's chair wobbled and flew out from beneath her. Tracey landed hard on her butt, crying out from the shock of the fall, partially chewed apple sprayed all over her clothes. Jonny and Tony jumped to their feet as Carla lowered Tracey's gym bag to the floor. The bag's strap was tangled around the leg of Tracey's chair.

"Whoops," Carla said loudly enough to be heard over the laughter filling the hall.

Tracey felt dozens of eyes on her as she struggled to her feet. Her chest burned with renewed anger. Heat warmed her hands. She glanced down to find them glowing. Shocked, she thrust them into her pockets.

"Sorry, Tracey, I was just moving your bag out of the way. I didn't realize it had caught on one of the legs." Carla's grin said she knew exactly what she'd done. Tracey speared her with a dark look, but the girl just laughed it off.

Tony stepped in front of Tracey and pushed her back. "Don't do what you're thinking."

She fought against him, growling softly. "Let me—"

"No, Trace. You have to let it go."

"I just want to teach her not to mess with me."

"Tracey, you have to calm down."

Meena smirked and took Carla's arm proclaiming loudly that she was lucky to have such a thoughtful friend. Carla scratched at her neck as she waltzed away. Another zap slammed into Tracey's shoulder. She was going to kill Dave. Anger bubbled within her—barely contained. Dave shouted in alarm as his pants dropped, exposing his ever-so-colorful cartoon covered boxer shorts. The lunch crowd turned on him quickly, howling with laughter, leaving Tracey alone. Her friends surrounded her.

"God, she is such a b—"

"Jonny, don't stoop to her level." Laura interrupted, grabbing his arm when he went to follow the Evil Queens. She stopped next to Tracey. "Are you okay?"

Breathing deeply, Tracey muttered, "Nothing hurts but my pride. God, I hate him."

"Him?"

"Oh, her. I meant her. Meena."

"Trace …"

"Damian did nothing. I guess he's not the guy I thought he was."

"Yeah, what a dumbass," Laura agreed.

Resolving not to think of Damian or Meena again, Tracey looked around the lunch room.

Kids were still laughing at the sight of Dave Two's underwear. It was rare the bully got his comeuppance and they were enjoying it immensely. Dave Two hiked his pants up around his waist and glared at Tracey. She held his gaze until he saluted her as one soldier to another. She hadn't done anything to his pants, at least she didn't think so, but the timing had been spectacular. She shot Tony a questioning look. He didn't see it.

"Hey, I just had a great idea," Jonny said, grabbing Tracey's gym bag. He handed it to her and stood between her and the rest of the lunch room.

Tracey pressed a hand against her chest and breathed slowly, feeling the heat of the Butterfly Stone warm her palm. "What idea, Jonny?"

"I reckon we set him up, the man in the red mask. I think we should catch him in the act."

"If you believe I will have the strength
to stop this once it has begun, Charles,
then you are a fool."

36

What?"

They all stared at Jonny in surprise. Completely distracted, Tracey's temper disappeared as she searched her friend's face for madness.

"Jonny, we're not playing kid detectives like in the cartoons," Laura said, collecting her things from the table. She packed her book away quickly and shouldered her bag.

"No seriously, hear me out. I think we should set a trap for the man in the red mask. He knows about Donny, so he knows about Tracey. He'll be expecting her to make a play to get the necklace back. If it's not him behind all this—well, then this will tell us one way or the other, won't it? We catch the guy doing something illegal, like using magic against you, and get him arrested."

Laura hissed and slapped at his arm. "That's crazy!"

"No, no it's brilliant," Jonny countered.

"You are crazy," Tracey said. It was an interesting idea, but far too dangerous. The pulsing of the stone against her chest quickly changed her mind. "How?"

"Look. Meet me at ... oh, Tracey, your uncle's back now so we can't use his office anymore, can we?"

"No, and I have practice tonight."

"Practice?"

"Oh ... the ... just something I'm doing with my sister," she said stumbling over the story.

Laura stopped walking. "We'll come to your place, then. We can plan afterwards."

"No planning." Tracey warned them, "And I don't think Dave

would—"

"Dave? Dave who?"

"Shhh." Tracey led her friends out of the lunch room and behind the hall where no one would see them. "Jonny, I'm not supposed to say anything. Look, Dave Two ... he's Mage-kind."

"What?" her friends all shouted at once. Their expressions ranged from horror to surprise. Tony looked pale. "I don't sense anything—"

"Shhhhhh!" Tracey checked over her shoulder as she spoke. "It's only just manifested. He didn't know."

"But he's too old," Tony pointed out, his eyes wide. "And I still don't—"

"I know, I know. That's why—look, I'm helping him, okay? I don't even know if I can continue, given the way my powers are playing up, and—"

Tony swallowed. "What about me? I could help."

Tracey stopped walking. *Is he serious?* As a target of Dave Two's bullying behavior, she was surprised he'd want to help, though it shouldn't surprise her really. Tony was a good person. "You'd do that? That would be great, Tony. Another trained Mage-kind would be a huge help."

"What about us?" Laura asked pointing to Jonny and herself. Jonny bounced up and down on the balls of his feet. Tracey didn't understand why he looked so excited.

"I'll check with Mom. Maybe you can come over later? I'm sure we've got some homework we should be doing."

"Bummer," Jonny said with a groan.

"That sounds like a great idea," Laura pushed Jonny to start walking to their next class.

"Don't say anything to Dave," Tracey warned them all. They looked at her with varying degrees of shock. "I'm serious. Dave could be danger-ous if provoked, and besides, I swore I wouldn't say anything." Her gut clenched. Dave wouldn't be happy when he found out, that was for sure.

"But he's such a—"

"I know, Jonny, but—"

"It's not that easy, Jonny," Tony jumped in. "I think Tracey's doing a good thing."

She felt warmed by Tony's faith. *It's not exactly my choice, though.* She didn't give voice to the complaint as they separated to go to their different classes.

She spent the first few minutes of class fearing Jonny would harass Dave during their shared gym session and spark an outburst. She sent two messages to him, begging him not to say anything to Dave before her phone was confiscated. Time seemed to slow down as the clock inched toward the day's final bell. Retrieving her cell phone from her teacher at the end of the day, Tracey frantically checked her messages only to find Laura had sent several, but Jonny hadn't replied at all. She could have screamed.

Tony waited for her at the school's gate. As they walked toward her home, he talked about the techniques they'd learned at camp and the lesson plans he'd come up with. She ignored him as much as possible, dreading to think how Dave was going to react when he saw Tony. Her fears did not measure up to reality.

"Are you freakin' kidding me? What's that guy doing here?" Dave shouted.

"He's here to help," she said. Dave completely ignored her. He paced back and forth, red-faced and breathing hard. Even with her power locked down, she could feel magic sparks rising off him. If looks could melt bone, Tony would be a steaming pile of goo right now. Tracey, too.

"You lied to me," he hissed. "No one was supposed to know."

"Well, I do. So get over it," Tony snapped. "I'm here to help. If you don't want it, just leave."

"Tony!" Tracey complained. "You're not helping."

Sarah watched silently, standing by the fence where she'd retreated as soon as she'd seen the horrified look on Dave's face.

"Look, Dave. You're the one who wanted me to stop *pushing* at you. Until I get a handle on my magic, I can't help you. Tony is here to assist, okay? Just settle down. He won't tell anyone."

"Won't I?" her friend muttered, and this time Tracey did glare at him.

"Seriously, you are not helping."

"Fine!" Tony backed up several steps. "Do you want me to leave?"

337

Dave continued to pace in the distance. Tracey shook her head. Tony's presence was the only thing stopping her from completely losing it. She asked him to start with Sarah. Her sister shot her a dark look in response. Tracey felt like throwing up her hands and telling them all to leave if they didn't like the decisions she made. As she faced Dave, she saw Tony sit down with Sarah in the center of the yard and wondered what he was telling her. She wished she was over there instead of standing here placating the known bully.

The stone against her chest began to pulse. "You know what, Dave? Tony's right. Just leave if you don't want to join in. Getting angry all the time is not going to get you anywhere. You're just a big bully and I'm over it. You wanted secrecy, well fine. If you don't want me to tell anyone your secret, you'll stop zapping me at school and stop picking on Tony. Now shut up and sit down next to Sarah, or go." A wind whipped up around her as she spoke. Her voice was cold and clear and she could feel Tony and Sarah watching in the distance. "I have way too much to worry about right now and I don't need to worry about you, too."

She stomped away and the wind settled. *Oh God, it happened again, didn't it?* She felt like she was falling apart. And there was nobody around to put her back together again. Blinking back her tears she realized it was time to invoke another one of her mom's life lessons. Fake the appearance of control until she really achieved it.

Tracey didn't look back to see if Dave was following. She sat down next to Tony. He looked at her with wide eyes. "What?" she snapped at him.

"We were just talking about the power of dreams, and Sarah told me about a really interesting one she's been having lately." He gestured to Sarah. "You should tell her."

Tearing her eyes from Tony's scared expression, Tracey looked at her sister. Sarah shrugged. "It's just a stupid dream."

"So? Tell me about it anyway," she urged.

Dave slumped down onto the grass next to Sarah. "Are we just going to talk? Cause if we are, I'm gonna leave."

"Shut up, Dave," Tracey snapped. She pressed her hand to her chest. God, this was getting out of hand. "Sorry," she muttered.

Sarah looked away from them all and stared down at the back fence. "It's just a dumb dream. I keep hearing a woman's voice. I think she's British—she sounds like that lady from that show you like. Five people are dressed like in the olden days, you know, with long dresses and gloves and hats? And they're all standing in a large room, arguing, and then a shadow appears at the door. It fills the whole room and smothers everyone. That's when I wake up."

Tracey was shocked. Her sister was describing the same dream Tracey kept having. Tony nodded, having realized the similarity. She glanced at the house. If Grandma was home, she would have run in to fetch her.

"That's weird," Dave said, leaning forward.

Tracey was pleased to see him engaged in the conversation, but the look on his face freaked her out. "Dave?"

"Yeah, I've had it, too."

They all stared at each other. That couldn't be a coincidence.

Tony nodded. "Should we tell them?"

"Tell us what?" Sarah stared at Tracey and repeated, "Tell us what?"

Jonny and Laura showed up when they were all shouting.

"I want to help," Sarah said, practically stomping her feet.

Tracey's arms were crossed. Dave hovered off to the side, trying to avoid the argument while simultaneously interjecting and making it worse. He caught sight of Laura and Jonny. "Christ, is everyone from school coming here today?"

"Shut up," Tracey said, but her words held no malice. She turned back to her sister. "Sarah, no."

"You're planning something. It's the only reason your friends are here. You can't leave me out of it," she whined.

"No," Tracey said. Her tone indicated her words were final.

"You never include me in anything," Sarah shouted. "You leave me out all the time! You forget about me and don't want me around. It's not fair! Why do you hate me?"

"What? I don't hate you," Tracey was so shocked by the accusation she actually stumbled back a few steps.

"You do! I know it. You didn't even bother coming home for my party. You're always whispering and hiding things from me. And when I want to help, you tell me to go away. Grandma takes you out on secret missions. Uncle Donny even let you go to the film set! I don't get to do anything."

"Sarah, I'm—"

"Whatever, I don't care," she shouted, her face red. She stormed away. The door slammed shut behind her after she entered the house.

"Tracey, what is going on here? What were you fighting about?" Laura stood on the garden path, watching them.

Tracey sighed, "Sit down." She quickly brought her friends up to speed about the dream.

"The *exact* same dream?" Laura asked.

"I know. It's weird, right?" It wasn't only weird, it was worrying. The man in the red mask was seriously scary, and she didn't want her sister involved. What would Mom say if Sarah got hurt?

Tony grabbed onto Tracey's arm. "Maybe your sister *can* help us."

"Tony, *WE* shouldn't be doing anything. I'll call Agent Malden and he can handle it. We're not confronting the man in the red mask ourselves." Movement out of the corner of her eye reminded her that Dave was still listening. "Dave—"

"Well, well … if it isn't Nancy Drew and her friends, plotting and scheming. I know all about it now, so if you don't want me to tell everyone, you're going to tell me everything."

After she finished explaining, Dave demanded, "So what's the grand plan Jonny keeps talking about?" He didn't call Tracey crazy or tell her it was stupid. He actually looked interested in what they were going to do.

"I never thought I would say this, but finally someone is listening to me," Jonny announced grandly.

Dave held out a fist for Jonny to bump. Jonny looked surprised but awkwardly bumped it in return. "I'm sick of all of this talking. Let's get on with the action. Now, what's the plan?" Dave asked again.

Tracey shook her head. "No plan. We're not doing anything. I'm going to call Agent Malden and—"

"Just listen to my idea, Tracey," Jonny's eyes begged her to give him a chance.

She relented. "Okay. What's your plan?"

He pushed his glasses back up his nose. "We know the man in the red mask wants the stone, right? So let's leak the news that we've found it."

"That will never—"

"How did we find it?" Laura asked, leaning forward.

Tracey's head snapped to her friend. Laura approved of this plan? Had the world spun off its axis? Laura could always be relied upon to be the sensible one out of their strange little group.

"Whoever kidnapped your uncle knows about you," Laura said, her voice suddenly serious. "The goons have obviously been watching him since they broke into his office. They blackmailed you into giving them the necklace to save his life so we know he suspects you have it. They even broke into your house looking for it. Whether you want M-Force or the police to handle it, it's already too late. The goons know about you, and they must know by now Miss Tearning's necklace isn't the one they want. Miss Tearning was murdered for that necklace. They're serious. You can't put your head in the sand about this. I think, and I can't believe I'm saying this, but I think we should act first."

Is she right? The man in the red mask had to know the butterfly necklace was not the real stone. It was only a matter of time before he realized Tracey still had it, which would put her and her family at risk of another attack.

Laura was right. Tracey had to do something now, before the man in the mask attacked again.

Taking a deep breath, she eyed each of her friends in turn. They met her gaze without flinching. So, they were determined to do this. She nodded, accepting it.

"Okay, so what's the plan?"

"But as with magic,
Truth begets truth …"

37

The thing was they had no real idea how to get the message out. Tracey couldn't just walk around town shouting to the population that she had the Butterfly Stone and hope the man in the red mask heard about it.

"Do we assume they're watching you as well as Donny?" Laura asked.

Tracey shrugged. "I don't want to think about it." When she did, nausea swirled in her stomach, making her want to hurl.

"If they're watching Donny, they might have hacked his email account and his phone," Tony suggested.

"Do you think they have?" she asked. Oh God, was someone reporting her every move to the man in the red mask? Her skin crawled. *Who?* She hadn't seen anyone watching her strangely. *Who would do that?*

"I think if you send an email from your work account, they'll see it," he said.

"What if they're magically tracking Uncle Donny?" Tracey asked.

"Well, magical tracking searches like electronic tracking does — by keywords. If they're magically watching you then the same keywords should register."

"Email and phones are electrical. Doesn't magic work a bit like that?" Jonny asked. "Traveling through the air like WiFi?"

Tracey raised a brow at Tony. She'd never thought about it that way. "So we send an email? To whom?"

"What about to Doctor Chan's website?" Laura asked.

Tony began snapping his fingers. "Yeah, if we use all the keywords we think the man in the red mask is searching for and send it to a magic site, theoretically it should activate both magic and electronic … listening, for lack of a better word. Especially if we send it from your work email,

Trace. I think we'll get his attention."

Even though she felt like it was a long shot, she agreed. They headed straight to her uncle's office.

Tony immediately jumped on Tracey's computer, opening the M-Net and her email. He sent a simple message to say he had a lead on the stone, and then they waited.

Two days passed, and nothing happened.

After another silly argument dissolved into a shouting match, Sarah stopped talking to Tracey all together and refused to come out for magic practice. Dave still came after school, though, and with Tony's help, Tracey soon had him raising his shield and throwing zaps easily. As his control strengthened, his anger seemed to lessen. He even backed off on his harassment at school, avoiding all confrontations, likely wary of Tracey's temper. She was glad for it, as her control was growing more precarious. They were all waiting for something to happen, and when it did, the form it took was completely unexpected.

They met at Uncle Donny's office after Tracey assured them he was at the film lot working. The five teenagers sat scattered over the furniture. It was roasting inside the small building. Tracey quickly checked the thermostat and found it set too high. She dropped it back and threw open the window as they stripped off their pullovers. Poor Uncle Donny, he must still be feeling the effects of his frozen adventure.

Tony called for their attention. "I received an email from Doctor Chan last night."

"You don't think Doctor Chan is the man in the red mask, do you?" Laura asked, sipping from a takeaway coffee cup.

"Well, okay, no. The email wasn't signed. I hadn't thought of it but I guess I don't have any proof that Doctor Chan actually sent the email. Just that it came from his email address." Tony's face twisted in thought.

Tracey shook her head, knowing instinctively he wasn't. "Doctor Chan might be being followed by the man in the red mask. We know he's investigating the stones."

"Is this plan going to put Doctor Chan in danger?" Laura asked. She put down her empty coffee cup and picked up a piece of printer paper.

"For our plan to work, we just need the man in the red mask to show up," Jonny said, stretching out full length over the sofa. His feet dangled over the arm.

"I knew this wasn't going to work," Tracey said. She was sitting behind her desk. When they glared at her, she raised her hands. "What did the email say?"

"Whoever sent it wants you to meet him at the *Saving Time* lot in Sachorn Forest."

"Why would he want to meet you there?" Laura asked. She was seated in Uncle Donny's comfortable office chair, which she'd dragged into the main room. She rolled it over to Tracey's desk waving the fan she created by folding up the paper.

Tracey could see the sense in the location. The film set was a public place, with tons of people coming and going twenty-four hours day. It would be easy to hide in the confusion, if you had an access pass. The problem was she wouldn't be able to sneak her friends in. There was an outcry when she explained that to them.

"Well, you can't go in there alone," Laura said. "We'll have to find another place to meet."

"We don't have time," Tracey told her.

Tony held up a hand. "It sounds like a trap." Both he and Dave sat on the floor in front of the sofa Jonny lay on.

Tracey didn't want to remind her friends that she'd warned them. Her words hovered over them anyway. "What else did the email say, Tony?"

"That they — he — urgh, yeah let's go with he. He wrote that he had something to trade for information on the butterfly necklace."

"What butterfly?" Dave asked.

Tracey quickly explained about Miss Tearning's necklace.

"So, the stone the man in the red mask wants is called the Butterfly Stone?" Dave asked when she finished. "So what are the other four called? Dragonfly, March fly, Firefly and Fruit fly?" He laughed out loud. Tracey was impressed he could list so many flies off the top of his head. He caught her look and explained. "Junior school assignment, I had to list over twenty of the damned things — I hate flies." He huffed out a breath, sweat beaded at his temples. "Don't you have AC?"

A worrying thought kept bouncing around Tracey's head. Before she could give voice to it, Jonny jumped in.

"Well, no matter what the stone is called, it can't help us avoid this trap, can it?" He waved a hand around to emphasize his point.

"What if we give him a thumb drive with the information on the Butterfly Stone that we have, and I add a virus? A tracker that we can give to M-Force?" Tony said.

"Tony, that's … a good idea. Did he say what time I'm supposed to meet him?" The more they spoke about the plan the more real it became. She was going to be out there—in the forest—alone. And she couldn't rely on her magic. She felt sick.

"Tomorrow night."

This didn't seem like such a fantastic plan anymore. What if the man in the red mask attacked? She'd be all alone and helpless.

"Give me some time to set up the thumb drive," Tony begged.

"Tony, we don't have time for you to create a computer virus," Laura said, her face glistened with sweat. She looked radiant. Tracey probably looked like a tomato with wilting hair. "If we're going to sneak onto the set, then we have to go early tomorrow afternoon. We need to get there before whoever it is arrives so we can see if the man in the red mask is following him." The worrying thought bouncing around Tracey's head finally exploded out of her mouth. "What if it *is* the man in the red mask? What if he's the one who sent the message?"

No one replied. After a moment Tony leaned in. "I don't need to create a virus from scratch, just load one onto the thumb drive. I'll get it ready."

Though Tracey didn't want to admit it, she was scared. Why was she going along with this? Because she wanted to protect Uncle Donny.

Her biggest fear was that the man in the red mask would go after him again. And next time it might end very differently. She fumbled around in the top drawer of her desk. "I have my pass, but we still have to figure out how to sneak the others in. Any ideas?"

"Can you talk to your uncle? Maybe he can get us more passes?"

"If we tell him anything, he'll know we're up to something more than trying to sneak onto a film set."

"Tracey, you know Prince Henry. Could you talk to him?" Laura suggested.

"You know Prince Henry?" Dave asked, staring at Tracey in surprise.

She flushed. "Uh, yeah," and slapped at Laura's hand.

"How? Whatever. Why can't we just use magic?" he asked.

Tony and Tracey immediately shook their heads. "You know there are strict controls on the use of magic outside the summer camp program. Dave, you've bullied us enough over them. Consistent use will be caught, and then we'll be monitored forever. My grandma only got us a pass for practice after school because it was to be held at my house." Tracey lifted her arm, waving her Mage-kind identification bracelet around.

Dave waved his empty wrists in reply. "Haven't got mine yet." He cocked his head to the side. "But you use magic all the time, I've seen you."

"Actually, no she doesn't. She only uses it when she's working for her uncle, and he has a license to practice magic," Laura told him.

Dave narrowed his eyes.

Yeah okay, so that wasn't entirely true, given her faulty magic. Tracey wasn't going to explain that her parents hacked her bracelet, or that she was already on M-Force's underage users list. "The point is, I can't magic up an entry pass or sneak us in."

"I have an idea," Jonny said, jumping to his feet.

"Death, loss, and madness marked,
Their lives now accursed ..."

38

Tracey decided to remove the Butterfly Stone from around her neck. If it was affecting her magic, it would be better to take it off before the secret meeting. The problem was, she *couldn't* take it off. Every time she raised her hands to the chain, her chest tightened and there was a roaring in her ears like a waterfall. With clenched teeth, she forced her trembling hands to the chain and closed her fingers over the clasp. *I can do this. I will do this.* As soon as it came undone the stone dropped to the floor. Everything inside Tracey cried out at its loss. With trembling fingers, she scooped the necklace up and fumbled it back on. When the stone's familiar weight touched her skin, her whole body relaxed.

Okay, so she wouldn't try that again anytime soon. She'd have to tell Tony. Maybe he could help her remove it.

Jonny's plan called for Tracey to sneak out of the house just after her family had dinner. She was foiled when Grandma stopped her at the front door. Caught, she resigned herself to a grounding or worse, wondering how she could let Tony know she wasn't going to make it.

"Tracey, before you leave, I have something for you."

She paused at the tone in Grandma's voice before spinning around. "Another guided memory?"

"It's time."

"Do we need to visit Nana again?" She hoped not. The plan was to meet her friends at the entrance to the *Saving Time* lot in under an hour.

"No, come on through to my room." Behind them, she heard her parents planning to pick Sarah up from the library. It looked like sneaking out was going to be a lot easier than she'd thought it was going to be. She followed Grandma into the guest room and sat down on the end of the bed. The old woman closed the door securely and moved to sit beside her. "Take my hands."

It seemed quicker this time. Closing her eyes on Grandma's bedroom and opening them in the black and white guided memory room was almost instantaneous. Tracey made her way to the fireplace as Stephanie entered. The woman appeared unsettled, pacing in front of the sofa, wringing her lace-gloved hands together in agitation.

Tracey's ancestor huffed out a breath and stared into the mirror above the fireplace, coming to stand right beside Tracey. "You cannot do this."

For a second Tracey thought Stephanie was talking to her. The pale woman pressed her hands to her chest and closed her eyes, breathing deeply. Tracey was startled to recognize the familiar pose.

At the sound of approaching footsteps, they both spun around.

The man who entered was vaguely familiar. Tracey identified him as one of the men she'd seen in Doctor Chan's picture. Handsome, with dark hair, he had a longish nose and mesmerizing eyes. He gazed at the woman beside Tracey hungrily. "Stephanie," he said, striding toward her. "You are having second thoughts."

"I confess I am," she replied, taking his hands in her own.

Tracey watched the man kiss her ancestor's lips. Was this her great-great-great-great-great-grandfather? She didn't think she'd ever heard his name. Stephanie turned her head as he tried to kiss her again. Her eyes were cast down, not meeting his gaze.

"Stephanie?"

She stepped away, and his hands fell helplessly to his sides.

"What are your concerns? Perhaps if you talk them through you will realize they are not insurmountable."

"I am afraid they are, Timothy. People will be hurt by this turn of events. Of that, you cannot convince me otherwise."

"I would not attempt to convince you of that, my love."

Stephanie paled, peering around furtively. "Hush, Timothy. The others may—"

"The others are not here." His voice grew soft. "Even now, at the conclusion of our work, will you not acknowledge us?"

"Timothy, I—please, do not ask this of me. I am promised to Matthew."

"As I am well aware." He turned away from her. This time Stephanie followed, placing her hand on his arm to halt his retreat. Unbeknownst to Stephanie, the expression that crossed his face was dark and bitter.

Tracey couldn't believe what she was seeing. Her ancestor appeared to be caught in a Mage-kind love triangle. If the Five were planning to cast a dangerous spell, Stephanie and Timothy's heightened emotions could affect it. The Five could lose control of the magic, which could end in catastrophe. *Is that what Stephanie's worried about?*

Again, as with the first dream-like guided memory, Tracey could see no wrist monitors on either of their arms. It was such a strange sight to see a Mage-kind adult without one.

Thinking that the love triangle was what she was supposed to see, Tracey was surprised when the guided memory did not end. Enthralled and fearful, she watched as Timothy embraced Stephanie. "Tell me of your concerns," he murmured against Stephanie's neck.

"Transferring our magic is a dangerous undertaking. If our powers are unable to be contained—if we were to fail, we could destroy the world."

"Nothing will go wrong, my darling. We are focused, our intention is pure—"

"Is it?" Stephanie dropped his hands and stepped back. Again, she didn't look him in the eyes.

"What are you suggesting?"

The young woman's face flushed. "I am aware of the private assignations between you and Charles over the last few days. What are you planning?"

His lips curled. "Planning? You make our conversations sound positively scandalous. They are nothing to concern yourself with. Purely discussions of business and politics, nothing more."

"Political discussions?" Her eyes were wide, her lips parted on a gasp.

"Stephanie—"

"So you *do* want to announce our presence to the world? Do not lie to me. Charles has admitted as much. You *cannot* be serious—"

His gaze narrowed as his jaw clenched. "He has told you this? When?"

"Timothy, this way lies madness. The world cannot learn of what we are. Mage-kind communities have remained secret for hundreds of years. You cannot make such decisions without the consent of the entire council of clans."

His expression blanked. "Perhaps it is time."

She followed him, imploring, "Timothy, listen to yourself. The world is on the brink of terrifying industrial progress. Machines are being built by the day; giant industrial machines that will replace the need to work. At last, people will have time to study and create, they will have time to think and produce! Imagine it — art, music, and theatre will flourish, and with more time —"

"— people will die, Stephanie. You cannot be so foolish as to believe machines replacing humans will lead to anything more than war and death! Your understanding is as simple as a child's —"

"Timothy!"

"We must be prepared. Now is the time for our people to come out of the shadows. To take our rightful place."

"Our rightful place?"

"As the leaders of this new world," he announced, throwing his hands into the air.

Stephanie stepped back, Tracey could see her shock all too clearly. "You are mad."

"We all are. We remain hidden, our powers contained, never experiencing the true magnificence of what we are. You have felt it during our experiments. I know you have." His voice dropped low during his impassioned speech. He stared intently into Stephanie's eyes, his voice taking on a melodious cadence. Tracey wanted to reach forward and snatch Stephanie away from him. His look terrified her. "You have felt the pure joy that comes in embracing your full abilities."

Tracey's mind swam back to her own experiences with the stone. Using magic was beautiful. Stephanie forced her eyes away and shook her head. "This is madness."

He gripped her arms tightly, shaking her until she met his gaze. "You must speak the truth, Stephanie. You have felt those moments of pure power." His pupils began to glow, a reddish hue that grew brighter the longer he stared at her. "Speak true."

"I-I have felt it," she admitted.

"Now must be the time we act. We cannot hesitate for long. I know you feel as I do."

"I-I do but—"

"Perhaps we do need to talk more, yes? We will gather the group and discuss our plans further to ensure we are well prepared for any eventuality."

"I—yes, that sounds—yes, very well." Stephanie relaxed into Timothy's arms.

Tracey gasped as magenta tendrils reached out from Timothy's body to twirl around Stephanie. With her acceptance of his will, his power seemed to flow into her very skin and she began to glow. He clasped his hands around her waist to draw her close and whispered into her ear. The reddish glint in his eyes flared brighter. The magic threads around them tightened.

Tracey blinked and found herself back on the bed beside her grandma.

"Stephanie didn't know what he was doing, Grandma. She was tricked," Tracey shouted.

"By whom, dear?" Grandma's eyes looked darker than usual, her face slack. She blinked several times. "Tracey? How did it go?"

"You didn't see it?"

"No dear, as I said the memories are for you alone. I cannot see them, I am only the conduit."

Tracey blinked back sudden tears. Her stomach felt cramped. She clutched at it as her emotions spiraled. From her history classes, she knew the Mage-kind community announced their presence to the world in 1820, immediately after the failed Mage-kind revolution. Many on both sides had died during that single week of terror. Had Stephanie been involved in the revolution? *Had she been the one to start it?* Tracey didn't know what to think. She caught sight of her watch. Nearly seven. She was late.

"Grandma, I have to go." Her grandma didn't raise her head. Tracey hovered for a moment, wondering if she should call someone. "Grandma?"

The old woman glanced up at last. "Go. You have work to do. Stay safe, honey."

Outside, Tracey found her brother peering beneath the hood of his car. "Peter, I'm really late — can you drop me off?"

He looked up at her face, shrugged and lowered the hood. "Sure." Wiping his hand on a filthy rag, he gestured toward the car door. "Where are we going?"

"You are, Trace ..."

Why is she playing along with this?

"What are you talking about?"

"You're doing it right now."

39

Is Uncle Donny meeting you here?" Peter asked when they pulled up to the darkened gate. A few floodlights were positioned a short distance past the gatehouse. They pointed away, leaving most of the gate in shadow. Weak lamp light shone inside the small building.

"Yup," Tracey confirmed, tying her hair into a ponytail. She jumped out of the car and walked briskly toward the gate, hoping her brother wouldn't follow.

When she heard his car wheels crunch over the pebbled road, she released the breath she held and peered at the silent surrounding shadows. Suddenly she didn't want to be out here. She hesitated, her foot hovering above the ground. *Go home!*

"Where have you been?" Laura hissed, emerging from the darkness. "We were supposed to get here early." The rest of her friends appeared behind her. Laura pocketed the nail file she held. "We've been waiting for ages," she said by way of an explanation.

"I know, I know. Grandma had another guided memory for me."

Laura shook her head, her plait whipping around her head with the movement. "No time to tell us what it was about now. Come on, we have to go in." She hovered next to Tracey, just as she had last time, and they were in luck when they discovered the guard at the gate was the same man they'd spoken to before.

"You again?" he asked, shining his flashlight into Tracey's face and then at Laura.

The two girls crowded close to the window and begged to be let in, blocking the guard's view of the gatehouse entrance. Tracey felt the moment Tony sent a mild zap into the scanner. When she waved her fingers, willing the guard not to see them, the stone against her chest pulsed. She slapped a hand against it hoping the guard didn't notice. The three boys crouched low and snuck past.

"Go ahead, girls — I remember the prince speaking for you both." He gave Tracey's pass a cursory check and ushered them through the gate. They met up with the boys behind the cast trailers.

"Now what?" Laura whispered.

"Tracey — your magic? Are you going to — ?"

Her chest tightened at Tony's words. "I can't. You're here. I don't want to hurt you."

He took her by the shoulders, turning her so he could stare into her eyes. "Tracey, if you need to use it, use it. Don't worry about me. Promise?"

Cold air brushed against the nape of her neck like icy fingers. She shivered at the intensity of his gaze. He wouldn't let her go until she nodded.

"Say it," he ordered.

"Yes, I promise," she said.

Jonny interrupted, "Tracey, the message said to wait at the camera storage locker. Do you know where that is?"

"Yes." She pointed to a well-worn path through the woods that led away into the darkness. "We have to separate here if you want to approach the storage locker from the other side. One Mage-kind each. Tony, you go with Laura. Jonny, stay with Dave."

The two groups activated the flashlight setting on their cell phones and disappeared into the night. Tracey clutched her own phone tightly, her finger hovering over the button to call M-911, and headed down the dark path alone.

The camera storage locker was a shed the size of a minivan. Fully enclosed, it was made of a strong sheet metal, secured by half a dozen locks. There were two small lights attached to the locker door, but they didn't do much to brighten the ground around the shed. Tracey's head snapped from side to side at every sound. Sure, a secret meeting was supposed to be secret, but did it have to be so dark and creepy as well?

"Ah, Miss Masters, lovely to see you again." Doctor Chan's voice floated up out of the woods, and in moments she could see the pin-needle

362

light of his flashlight as he approached.

Her mouth fell open. *Doctor Chan sent the email?*

"Are you alone?" His face, lit from below by the residual light from the flashlight, looked like her brothers' faces when they told campfire ghost stories.

"Yes." She was desperate to ask the teacher dozens of questions. What was he doing here? Was he being hunted by the man in the red mask? Did he know about the masked man? The look on Doctor Chan's face made the crawly sensation against the back of her neck spread over her entire body—right down to her toes. She stayed quiet, glancing casually at the woods behind Chan, wondering where her friends were hiding.

"I have a lot to tell you. Thank you for meeting with me. I suppose you have a few questions?" His voice was an odd, husky whisper.

That was her way in. "We came back to the university to see you, but you'd disappeared."

"Yes, I could no longer stay. It had grown too dangerous for me." He lowered the hand holding the flashlight. It lit the ground beneath his feet and threw his face into even deeper shadow. She couldn't make out his eyes anymore.

"Dangerous? How?"

"My investigation into the story of the stones drew unwanted attention."

So he did know about the man in the red mask? He must have gone into hiding, but why, then, come out to speak to Tracey? Hopefully she hadn't exposed Doctor Chan's presence to the man in the red mask. She raised her phone, but her flashlight app didn't reach him. "Attention from whom?" *He stopped so far away.* She couldn't be sure, but she didn't think the microphone on her cell phone would pick up his voice clearly from this distance. She held her finger over the little red LED light that indicated the phone was recording and shuffled a little bit closer.

"M-Force agents—I believe you recently made their acquaintance?"

"Why would that bother you? M-Force are the good guys," she said, glancing around again.

"Are they?"

What does that mean? Inching closer she asked, "Doctor Chan, why were you investigating the story of the stones?" She was really proud that her voice barely quivered.

"My benefactor has need of the stones. You said in your email you have a lead on the Butterfly Stone?"

Benefactor? Oh no. She reversed her steps, suddenly afraid. "Who-who is your benefactor? I want to know who's looking for the stones."

Doctor Chan smiled. It was not a nice smile. "Don't you want to know what I have to trade for it?"

The bad feeling in Tracey's stomach exploded into frantic loop-de-loops. *He's working with the man in the mask.* "What do you have to trade?"

"Information on someone close to you."

"Who?"

Tracey's phone buzzed in her hand. Startled, she nearly dropped it. A glance at the screen showed a message from her mom.

Have you seen Sarah? She wasn't waiting for Dad when he went to pick her up. Did she call you?

Tracey looked at Doctor Chan, uncertain. *Did he mean ...?* "My sister?"

"For the information."

"Where is my sister?" Fire burst to life inside Tracey. The stone was a hot pressure against her chest and her wrist burned. She glanced down, shocked to find her bracelet pulsing with red light. "Where is my sister?" she demanded. Stepping forward she hit an invisible wall and pounded against it with her fists, her fury mounting.

"Miss Masters, we are not children, and this is not a game. Give me the information you have on the Butterfly Stone."

She stepped back, "Now!" Four cell phone flashlights snapped on, surrounding Doctor Chan as her friends stepped out of concealment.

"You lied," he said.

"You kidnapped my sister! Tell me where she is!"

Doctor Chan's lips quirked into a sinister smile. He raised his hand. Large floodlights burst to life, covering the entire area in a bright white glow. Four masked men appeared, one behind each of her friends. Two of them Tracey recognized as the men who had broken into her uncle's office. Tracey's friends were forced to turn off their phones and raise their hands.

"You're working for the man in the red mask!" she accused. Her fury banked as fear slid to the forefront of her mind. Her chest thumped with her increased heartbeat. Sweat slicked her palms.

"As I was saying, Miss Masters, this is not a game. My benefactor requires your information on the Butterfly Stone."

Tracey eyed Tony. She knew he wanted her to open up her magic. Not yet. She had to get Doctor Chan to talk, to admit to what he'd done. There were too many bad guys here. If Doctor Chan sensed her sudden increase in magic, he could hurt her friends in retaliation. She had to wait, though urgency to find her sister beat heavily in her mind. Tony's nod was almost imperceptible. She fought down her anger and fear until it simmered low in her chest, and very slowly reached into her pocket. She withdrew the thumb drive they'd loaded with fake data. It wouldn't withstand much scrutiny, but hopefully it would get him to release her sister before he used it and loaded Tony's virus onto his computer.

The horrible man waved a hand to lower the invisible wall he'd spelled and took the thumb drive from her. "Miss Masters, I would like you to now come with me."

What? "Where?" She backed away from him. The look in his intense gaze was scary.

"To meet my benefactor. He would like a word with you."

"No."

Doctor Chan moved like lightning and grabbed her arm. Before she could call on her magic, a ball of energy hit the ground at their feet, throwing Tracey and Doctor Chan to the ground. Tracey flew one way, Doctor Chan flew the other. The thumb drive hit the ground between them.

Standing on the edge of the lit circle was a man wearing a long grey cloak. He blazed with energy, the tails of his cloak flapping from a non-existent wind.

The goons grabbed her friends and pointed their weapons at the mysterious hidden figure.

Tracey climbed to her feet, eyeing the fallen thumb drive. The information on it was completely fake, but she needed Doctor Chan to think it held valuable data. She had to make a show of trying to get it back.

Doctor Chan rose, his broken glasses dangling from one ear. He took them off with one hand, and with his other he threw a ball of energy the size of a baseball at the cloaked man. The man blocked the attack with a wave of his hand and drew back his hood, demanding, "Release the children."

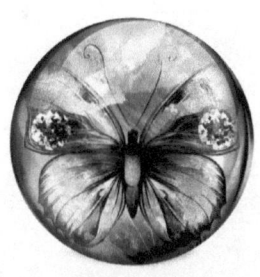

Wait … is that why …?
Because it would help him—or me?
Oh God, that was the real reason
why they altered my bracelet …?

40

Everyone froze. The cloaked man was Prince Henry! Relief flooded through Tracey along with a lot of confusion. She'd never sensed magic in him, yet now he blazed with it. *How is that even possible?*

Doctor Chan swung his hands at Tracey. They flared brightly. "Stand down."

She raised her hands in return, prepared to open her closet and call on her shield bubble if he attacked. Out of the corner of her eye, she saw Tony and Dave do the same. *Oh my God, oh my God!* This was really happening.

With a quick glance, she checked her non-magical friends. Jonny looked angry and struggled against the grip of the goon holding him. Laura stood frozen, watching Tracey with wide eyes. When she realized Tracey was looking in her direction, she winked. There was something shiny clasped in her hand. Her nail file! It appeared she was waiting for Tracey's signal.

Prince Henry stepped forward. Tracey couldn't believe he was here. Doctor Chan focused on him completely, recognizing him to be the greater threat. Prince Henry caught Tracey's eye. She glanced down at where the thumb drive lay in the dirt. He nodded. The light powering his hands faded as he lowered them. "Let the children go."

The prince and Doctor Chan exchanged a few barbed comments, moving slowly in a circle to keep the other in sight. They paid no attention to Tracey. She focused on a tree just behind the goon holding Tony, cracked the door in her chest open and fired a zap at the trunk.

The goon turned his head at the impact. Tony stomped on the man's foot. The goon let go with a howl and clutched at the injury, hopping angrily and cursing loudly.

Everyone turned in his direction, and in that moment Tracey's friends made their move. As Tracey dove to the ground to scoop up the thumb drive, Laura slammed her nail file into her masked goon's leg, pulling away as his grasp loosened. Jonny thrashed harder and then stopped, letting his body fall limp. He slipped out of his jacket—and the clutches of the goon holding it—taking off toward the woods. The bad guy chased after him.

Dave used his weight and football training to push his goon into the nearest tree, slamming the man into it, over and over again. With her heart pounding, Tracey slipped the thumb drive into her pocket and shouted for her friends to run.

She could barely be heard above the fighting. Prince Henry deflected Doctor Chan's blasts into the woods, unable or unwilling to fire back because Tracey stood too close. She saw his dilemma and raised a hand to zap at the fake Doctor. She hesitated, afraid to draw on her magic, and that proved her undoing. Doctor Chan threw an uncontrolled blast her way.

Instinctively she got her shield raised just in time and the orange blast glanced off it, slamming against the storage locker. The loud bong it made reverberated through Tracey's stomach. The distraction provided a window and Prince Henry took it, blasting Doctor Chan off his feet. The rush of magic was like a strong wind. Tracey's ponytail whipped against her face as cold air pressed against her skin.

"Get your friends out of here!" Prince Henry shouted, turning to fire at the goon chasing Jonny.

"He's got my sister!" Tracey screamed. She wasn't going anywhere. Laura and Tony ran to her side. "Get out of here."

"Not without you," Laura told her. Tony stood beside the non-magical girl and raised his shield to cover her as an errant blast from Doctor Chan reflected their way. Tracey didn't get her shield up in time and was flung backward as it exploded.

She landed with a groan. Her hearing fuzzy, her head spun like the time she and Tony snuck out of camp with the bottle he'd borrowed from his mom's cabinet. She could hear someone shouting but couldn't make out the words. Staggering to her feet, Tracey watched two goons rush in to attack Prince Henry. He appeared more than capable of holding his own, diverting his magic back to catch them full force. She turned toward the last member of their group. Dave was still fighting, grinning madly as his punches landed. *Trust him to be enjoying himself!*

"Tracey, what do we do?" Tony shouted.

"Zap the goons!" To Laura, she said, "Find Jonny." They nodded and disappeared into the shadows beyond the reach of the floodlights. Still afraid to open herself fully, she aimed at the black-clad man attacking Dave. The strength of her tentative zap barely fazed him.

Doctor Chan targeted Prince Henry's exposed back, but when he saw Tracey he changed priorities. A powerful ball of orange magic flew toward her. She got her shield up and somehow reflected it back at him. Doctor Chan dove out of the way, avoiding the prince's next strike in the process. *Whoops.* The air crackled with expended magic. She could smell burning wood.

"We need to get out of here," Dave shouted. He took a nasty hit to the face and stumbled. The goon pressed his advantage, punching Dave over and over again.

"He has my sister!" she shouted.

"Are you crazy?" Dave twisted, taking the next hit to his body. He lashed out as his attacker over-extended. The goon slumped ungainly to the ground.

"Go and shield Jonny!" she ordered.

Doctor Chan flew backward as Prince Henry's next shot connected. Tracey ran to the fallen man and shouted, "Tell me where my sister is?" Prince Henry appeared at her side, raising his hands in case the doctor tried to attack her. She grabbed a fist full of the doctor's shirt and threw her closet door wide open. Magic flared in her chest.

The mad doctor's eyes widened and he started to laugh. "So it *is* you." His body seemed to become liquid as he twisted out of her grasp. He threw one hand out along the ground and fired an orange ball of magic the size of a ping pong ball toward the nearest floodlight. It exploded, sending an electrified ripple to the next floodlight. One after the other, the lights snapped off.

Darkness enveloped them. The sound of fighting stopped as everyone realized they could no longer see friend or foe. Tracey swallowed back a scream. Beside her, the prince breathed heavily. "Stay still," he said.

The ground began to shake.

"What's that?" Tracey asked.

"Earthquake!" someone shouted.

Tracey was too busy trying to keep her footing to panic. Fearing the earth was going to split apart and swallow them whole, she froze. Laughter filled the air. It swelled around them and then cut off abruptly. Tracey gasped.

"That doesn't sound good," Prince Henry muttered.

The floodlights snapped back on—without the electricity that powered them. They glowed with a magical reddish hue. A man stood in the center of the blood-colored light. He wore a red mask and in one hand grasped the neck of a small girl. Tracey cried out at the sight of her sister. Under the man's grip, Sarah looked terrified. Tracey was desperate to run to her or let loose a fiery bolt fueled from her fear and anger. She barely held back. Fear for her sister was the only thing that stopped her.

"Enough of this," he said quietly.

Prince Henry didn't lower his hands, though the light faded from his fingers. Doctor Chan climbed to his feet and ran to the masked man's side.

"Let her go!" Tracey shouted.

The masked man shook Sarah violently. She squealed. Tracey bit back a scream knowing he was watching her reaction. His eyes flicked over her friends and widened in surprise as he recognized who stood beside her. "So, you are Malden's secret spy? Lower your hands, Your Highness."

Prince Henry sighed loudly but did as ordered. "Be careful," he whispered to Tracey.

"What are you even doing here?"

"Agent Malden is a friend."

"May I continue?" the masked man snapped, his patience obviously wearing thin.

Tracey stopped herself from an automatic apology by gritting her teeth. "What do you want?" she demanded. She couldn't tear her eyes away from Sarah. Her sister was trembling, tears poured down her cheeks.

"The information on the Butterfly Stone. I am prepared to trade your sister for it. I will let her go if you come with me."

Tracey sensed more, then saw Prince Henry shake his head.

"No, you can't!" Laura called out. Jonny, Tony, and Dave all mumbled something similar. Tracey looked at her terrified sister. Sarah's eyes were clenched shut. The man holding her tightened his grip, making her cry out in pain.

"Bad trade," Prince Henry muttered under his breath. "Stall."

Tracey barely glanced at him. Of course it was a bad trade, but it was her sister. She didn't have a choice. "Doctor Chan already agreed to trade the information for Sarah."

"I'm offering you a different deal," he said.

"What do you want with me?"

He smiled. "Come with me and find out."

Sweat dripped down Tracey's spine. The smoky air was saturated with the smell of sulfur. The expended magic coated her skin like gritty oil. Sarah was her little sister. It was Tracey's job to keep her safe, even after all their fights and arguments, she couldn't let her sister get hurt.

The moment she made the decision, the world around her grew still. She straightened her back and lowered her hands. "All right."

Her friends objected vehemently.

"No," Prince Henry said, grabbing for her arm. She flung off his hand and stepped forward. The man in the mask grinned at her, his eyes glittering as she drew close. His lips quirked in pleasure.

"Let them go," she ordered, gesturing to his captives. To her surprise, he did.

Sarah backed up quickly but then froze. "Go!" Tracey shouted at her. The frightened girl sprinted toward the woods. As Sarah reached the edge of the light she paused again, her voice shook as she asked, "Trace?"

"Go!"

Laura clasped Sarah's hand and pulled her away. Tracey glanced at the rest of her friends. "Go with her." Unhappy with her order, they backed away from the goons and followed the two girls into the woods. Prince

Henry didn't move.

"If you wish Tracey to remain unharmed, you will leave as well, Your Highness," Timothy ordered.

With what appeared to be great reluctance, Prince Henry looked to Tracey for guidance.

"Keep them safe," she told him. He nodded once and disappeared into the darkness. Left alone with the madman, Tracey trembled. Her breath caught in her throat.

The masked man strode toward her. "Hello, Tracey. It is a pleasure to properly make your acquaintance at last." His voice flowed over her like chocolate sauce over ice cream. The air became thick, making her dizzy. Everything she looked at blurred. He loomed over her, growing closer until he filled her vision. She blinked, but the nightmare did not change. Her head rolled heavily toward the woods to where her friends had disappeared. She thought she imagined them standing in the shadows watching her, her sister safely surrounded. "Get out of here," Tracey called, but her voice sounded wrong.

Through her hazy vision, her friends disappeared.

Tracey was alone with the masked man.

And she was terrified.

"Power lusted,
Magic will betray …"

41

What do you want with me?" she asked, her voice cracking from the emotion clogging her throat.

"You are an important piece of this puzzle and I would like your assistance to solve it." He spoke softly, drawing her to him with only his voice. His dark eyes were large beneath the mask, his gaze focused only on her. She sensed the goons move in to surround them only to stop a few feet away, allowing their boss to speak undisturbed. She didn't see Doctor Chan anywhere. *The coward ran away.* Tracey found herself drawn to the masked man's eyes. She hadn't realized he'd moved so close until he took her hand in a firm grasp.

With her free hand, she fumbled for the thumb drive. "Take it, then," she said, thrusting it toward him.

"The information means nothing to me. I know more of the stones than you can possibly imagine. I require *you*, Tracey. I require your help. Only your power can unlock the magic stored within the Butterfly Stone."

"Unlock?"

"It was spelled to prevent my access."

She didn't understand. She didn't want to. Tracey tugged on her hand, but he refused to let her go. "Who are you?"

Raising his free hand he pulled away the mask.

Tracey gasped. "You!"

Officer Jameson stood before her. Or, it was *almost* Officer Jameson—there was something wrong with his face. The shadow of another man hovered over it. He wasn't Officer Jameson now. "Who are you really?" she asked again.

"I was once named Timothy," he said. His voice deeper than the officer's. The image of the face hovering over Officer Jameson's features solidified, and Tracey recognized him instantly as Stephanie's secret boyfriend.

"Unlock the stone," he ordered. His hand rose to her neck. He pulled on the silver chain she wore and the Butterfly Stone came into view.

Tracey could feel its vibration beating against her chest as if the butterfly's painted wings were alive. It called on her to use the power stored within. She fought it with every breath she took.

Timothy held the stone level with Tracey's eyes. "Unlock it, Tracey. You are the only one who can do so." He dropped the chain so that the stone thudded against her chest. She clasped it instinctively. As soon as her hand closed around the stone, she was pulled out of the woods and thrown into another memory.

This time it was different. Stephanie stood in a white room. She looked exactly as she'd looked in Grandma's guided memory. "You must fight him, Tracey. Timothy cannot be allowed to possess the stone. I can boost your strength to aid you in your battle, for without your help, he cannot locate the remaining stones—if you do not stop him, he will destroy everything."

"I can't fight him. He's too strong!" Tracey cried, feeling hot tears roll down her cheeks.

"Your magic is as powerful as his, Tracey. You must have faith in yourself. You have what he does not—friends and family who love you. You must have faith."

"But my magic isn't working. I can't trust it." She scrubbed a hand over her eyes hoping Stephanie would disappear and that she'd find herself waking up from yet another nightmare wrapped safely in her bed.

"That is your core awakening. The Ice Stone—the true name of what you call the Butterfly Stone—can aid you. It can focus your magic. Open yourself to it fully."

"But I can't control it."

Stephanie smiled. "You don't have to. Open yourself to the chaos of your true power. Control has no place here."

"I've never—"

"Tracey, you have always helped your uncle and your family. You have used your magic instinctively for years." The white figure faded and then her image reappeared. Her eyes glowed.

"But, I'm hurting people!" Tracey cried, gasping as more tears fell. She couldn't get enough oxygen. Her chest was tight. She pressed her hands to it to find it was as hard as stone.

"Tracey—"

"I don't know what I'm doing."

"—Tracey—"

"Stephanie, how is Timothy even here? What is he?"

"His spirit was captured within the Fire Stone when our circle was destroyed. If he embodies flesh now, then the Fire Stone has been discovered. That poor vessel has no knowledge of what he is being made to do. Timothy is powerful, Tracey, but I know that you can do this. Let go of your control. Open yourself to your full power. Draw from the stone, use its magic."

"How do I—" she was torn from the memory and hit the ground hard, gasping in shock.

Timothy stared down at her, anger lighting his eyes on fire. They burned brightly in the reddish glow of the floodlights around them.

"I won't help you," she told him and raised her hands to throw her magic at him. Nothing happened. She tried again.

He laughed. "I know your secrets, Tracey. I know your fears. You cannot fight me without hurting those whom you love. I will spare them. I will even release poor Officer Jameson, if you consent to come with me."

"No!" she gasped, her strength crumbling as she scooted backward. She didn't want him to go with him. He'd use her power to unlock the stone and become even more powerful … but … he had promised to let her friends live. She hesitated.

He reached for her.

A ball of golden light shot between them. Timothy jumped away, his furious gaze turning to where the magical blast originated.

Agent Malden and Agent Striker stood with Sarah and Laura. Agent Malden's hands pointed at Timothy. Agent Striker held a large gun. The gun flickered and disappeared only to reappear again. *A magic-powered gun!* A shout drew Tracey's attention to the opposite side of the clearing. Prince Henry stood flanked by Dave, Tony, and Jonny.

Tears stung Tracey's eyes as she realized her friends had come back.

"Take them!" Timothy ordered. He grabbed Tracey and hauled her to her feet. "It appears we must go. Unlock the stone, Tracey."

She thought of Stephanie, who she somehow knew died fighting this man. She thought of Sarah, who had been hurt by him, and of her nana, who had gone mad holding onto Stephanie's memories. Tracey closed the fingers of her free hand around the stone and yanked her captured hand back. "No."

His eyes burned — she saw the flames rise. "The stone —"

"No!" she shouted and threw out her hands.

Nothing happened. Her mouth dropped open. "What — ?"

He raised one hand, his fist closed. He laughed. "Did you honestly think you could attack me? Give me the stone, Tracey."

She stumbled back. "I won't."

Agent Malden ran toward them, his hands alight with golden fire.

"Then I will take it!" Timothy shouted. He flung back his head and red smoke spewed from his mouth. The smoke hissed as it grew into a giant Shadowman, rearing up into the darkness above her.

The Shadowman began to laugh.

Tracey screamed.

"In the end, we learn,
What we already know ..."

42

The Shadowman's screech drowned out Tracey's scream as it flew toward the two agents. Tracey struggled against Timothy's imprisoning grip. He lowered his head to stare into her eyes. When he vomited out the Shadowman, she'd hoped Officer Jameson would be released from Timothy's control, but his eyes still burned with red flames.

She fought in earnest. Her fear increased her strength, but it was not enough. Timothy dragged her toward the woods. Tracey heard her friends shout out behind her, felt their young magic fill the air alongside the deeper vibrational blasts of the agents and Prince Henry, but it did no good.

Unable to focus her thoughts properly, her power could find no purchase in her mind. Timothy dragged her into the woods and away from the fighting.

Tracey stumbled in the dark, unable to see even a hint of her hand in front of her face. The cold fingers clasping her neck refused to budge. Timothy turned her around and backhanded her across the face. She fell to her knees, her face stinging. "You are trying my patience, Tracey."

"Let me go!" she begged, sobbing as she scooted backward. Her fingernails dug into the solid, unforgiving ground. She didn't see the next slap coming but heard the air move. Her head snapped hard to the side as sparks flared behind her eyes. She fell.

With her thoughts spinning, she flung her hands up reflexively, crying out in her mind for help to protect against his next strike. Timothy was thrown back, tree branches snapping loudly in the distance as he crashed through them. Tracey was suddenly alone in the dark. Holy crap—her magic worked! Her face burned. She quickly scrubbed her tears away.

Run, Tracey!

In the distance, Tracey heard a loud bellow.

Scrambling to her feet she ran — only to hit the ground again, stumbling over invisible bushes and tree roots. Forcing herself back up, she held her hands out in front of her body and kept running. Branches clutched at her. Boney, finger-like twigs tore at her face and arms, tugging and snatching at her hair and clothing. Her breath burst from her mouth. She couldn't stop crying.

The Shadowman was back in that clearing fighting her friends, and after it killed them it would come for her. She couldn't think, couldn't breathe. Silence surrounded her. She had the sudden sensation of being underwater, where no sound carried to her ears over the pounding of her own heart.

Spinning around, she found the darkness was absolute. Gulping, she sniffed and scrubbed at her tears. *Which way?* The Shadowman might be here, watching her, standing right over her and she'd never know until it was too late. She needed a light.

My cell phone. She scrabbled at her pockets. The hard plastic dug into her leg. If she turned it on, she might find the Shadowman, or Timothy himself, *was* right in front of her. If they weren't near, the light could draw them to her by exposing her position. She panted, indecision tearing at her mind.

Her hesitation saved her.

A blast of fire burst through the wood and exploded against the tree trunk right in front of her.

Tracey spun around. In the distance, Timothy readied another ball of fire. The tree in front of Tracey crackled and hissed as it burned, but the flames provided enough light for her to see a dirt path. She took it and ended up back in the clearing where she'd started.

Prince Henry lay on the ground, unmoving. Dave knelt beside him, clutching his head and moaning softly. Tony stood over them, his shield up but faltering under the barrage of blasts from the remaining goons. Sarah huddled close to Laura, shielding them both. Agent Striker's twisted figure laid on the ground, her skin blackened and dry like a mummy. The agent was almost unrecognizable, except for the pistol shaped burn on the ground beside her wizened, claw-like fingers. Tracey slapped a hand over her mouth at the sight. *Oh God!*

Agent Malden was still fighting. The Shadowman hissed and gurgled above him, throwing its insubstantial weight back and forth like a snake, trying to strike where the agent was weakest. A tendril slapped out at Sarah's shield. Tracey's appearance distracted it. It swung toward her, hissing loudly. As soon as the Shadowman turned away, Agent Malden pulled a fist-sized pouch from his pocket and poured glittering emerald powder into the palm of his hand.

Tracey darted back. The Shadowman dove toward her, but she got her shield up in time to repel its attack. Behind the Shadowman, Agent Malden cast his spell.

Strings of magic flew through the air, lighting a circle Malden must have drawn during the fighting. The circle, lit with magical energy, closed with an electrical crackle of sound, trapping the Shadowman inside. Walls rose up from the circle and a lid closed over the top with a snap. The monster railed against the magical containment, but there was no escape.

Tony fell to the ground, exhausted. Agent Malden lowered his arms. He wavered unsteadily on his feet. The Shadowman fought its imprisonment. They could hear it lashing back and forth as it threw itself against the rounded wall. A roar behind Tracey made her spin around. Timothy shouted her name again. *He's coming back!*

Sarah lay curled up on the ground, her arms wrapped around her knees. "We have to go," Tracey screamed and ran to her sister's side. Sarah didn't move.

Tracey tried to pull her up. Sarah slid from her arms and slumped back to the ground.

Tears ran down Sarah's face, her jaw was red where she'd been hit. "Use your magic, Trace."

"But I'll hurt you! I can't control it."

"I trust you. Use it like you've always used it."

"She's right," Dave said, stumbling. "You're stronger than all of us. You're stronger than this guy. Take my power. Draw on us."

"Take mine too," Tony called.

Tracey's gaze snapped over at the sound of his voice. He blurred as tears filled her eyes. Could she do it? Open her core to the chaos as Stephanie instructed? "I'll hurt you!" she cried. *I can't, I won't!*

"I'm offering," Tony said, staring at her.

Sarah nodded. "Kick his ass, Trace."

They'd been fighting for her, they were here to rescue her and they'd gotten hurt because of her. She had to fix this. "I'll save you," she promised. Raising her hands, she opened herself to the stone's power, and instead of pushing out with her magic, she drew it in. Her magic crackled and fizzled as it exploded to life inside her. She clutched the Butterfly Stone tightly in her hand.

And then she called for more.

Her power swelled as it pulled in thick tendrils of orange light that poured from her friends. The hairs on the back of Tracey's neck and along her arms rose. Her ponytail whipped around her head by a wind only she could feel.

Timothy burst into the clearing and froze at the sight before him. The last standing goon stumbled toward Sarah. Tracey threw her hands wide. The gathered power roared out of her. The goon flew backward into the woods, followed by a scream and loud crunches of bone echoing in his wake.

Timothy waved a hand and the cage trapping the Shadowman shattered. The Shadowman wailed as it rose up into the air, free at last.

"Get the girl!" Timothy ordered.

At his command, the Shadowman hurtled toward Tracey. She didn't budge, calling for all of the light she could from the stone, her friends, her sister, Agent Malden and the still unconscious Prince Henry. Long lines of orange light wound around Tracey, circling her body. The Shadowman reared back, suddenly uncertain. Tracey let her light pool in her chest, growing in strength until she could barely stand it.

She opened her eyes and screamed, throwing her hands forward to unleash the tempest straight at the Shadowman.

Power poured from her body, flaring white hot like a supernova.

The Shadowman emitted a horrific, tortured sound. It twisted and spun, trying to escape the glowing ropes that tightened around it. Its screams grew louder and higher, and then it exploded.

The world fell silent.

Timothy pulsed with anger. He spun and aimed his hands at Laura and Jonny.

"No!" Tracey cried, reveling in the power flooding through her. No longer afraid, she knew she could end this here and now. With one great push, she could destroy Timothy and free herself. She threw up an orange barrier in front of Laura and Jonny to protect them.

Howling, Timothy fired blast after blast at Tracey. She laughed them all off, reflecting them with ease. Drawing in more power, she failed to notice Dave fall, sprawling in the dirt behind her, completely spent. Tony dropped to his knees. Agent Malden worriedly glanced at them. Tracey blocked their emotional distress until the only thing she could feel was rage. Rage that this man would dare to attack her. Rage that he would set the nightmare Shadowman upon her friends. Rage that he would dare to kidnap her sister.

She threw out her hands again and again — lines of light flashing like knives hurled toward Timothy. At the first sign of his shield faltering, she increased her attack. She drew on more power, firing rapidly, not giving him a chance to recover. More ribbons of fire wound around him, sparking and exploding over his shield, until at last the shield dropped. The next blast took him off his feet.

Agent Malden collapsed. Tracey didn't turn at the sound.

"Tracey!" Sarah screamed. "Stop! You have to stop!"

Drawing in even more energy, Tracey sent wave after wave of fire down upon the fallen man's body. She would end this now.

"Tracey! Stop! You're hurting us!" Sarah begged.

Her sister's terrified voice bought Tracey back. She blinked and looked down. Sarah's face was shriveled and paper-thin. Pale as the moon, her eyes poked out like those on a doll. Tracey's worst fear realized — instead of saving her friends from attack, she was killing them.

"Please!" Sarah begged. Tears streaked down her face.

Tracey glanced at her own glowing hands. Ribbons of white hot energy flowed from her chest toward her friends. No, not toward them, pulled from them. Sarah's power had been sucked from her so fast she was almost mummified, appearing ancient under the eerie reddish light of the clearing.

Just like Agent Striker.

Light extinguished from her hands as Tracey mentally slammed her closet door shut. "Sarah?"

Her sister screamed.

Tracey spun, raising her hands, but Timothy's blast hit her side on. She flew through the air and landed hard, gasping as sharp stabbing sparks spread throughout her body. Sarah pulled herself toward Tracey and grabbed her hand. Through pain-filled eyes, Tracey watched Timothy gather his power.

He's going to kill me.

Sarah caught Tracey's eye. "It's okay."

"I'm so sorry, Sarah," she whispered, knowing this would be the last thing she ever said. Tracey's chest hurt, her whole body hurt. She struggled to breathe. A palm-sized ball of light burst to life in her sister's hand. Stephanie's voice blasted into Tracey's mind. Tracey's mouth moved, shouting out Stephanie's instructions. "Into the air." Without pause Sarah threw her ball of light into the center of the clearing. Timothy began to laugh. His laugh cut off abruptly when Sarah's light was hit by two more.

Tracey's gaze darted to Dave and Tony as they fell back, expending the last of their energy on the final throw. With each impact the ball grew in size becoming a giant ball of flame. Tracey opened herself fully to her magic, reaching out to Sarah, not to take but to share. She joined her power with Sarah's. The world began to hum as their magic entwined. Feeling the safety of Sarah's magic around her, Tracey let go and Stephanie took over. Her hands rose twisting and twirling as she chanted. The ball pulsed and grew larger. With a sharp movement she propelled the ball at Timothy.

He threw up a shield but the ball burst through as if it wasn't there, exploding as it hit him. Timothy writhed, his screams growing louder and louder. The tortured sounds cut off as red smoke poured from his mouth.

Officer Jameson's body collapsed.

The red haze surrounding the area went out at once. A loud thump signaled the return of electricity and the floodlights snapped back on, pouring a bright, clean white light across them all.

"Is it over?" someone asked.

Stephanie released her hold on Tracey's body and let her fall back to lie next to her sister. Sarah weakly wrapped her arms around Tracey's neck. "You saved us," she whispered.

"No," Tracey said. "We saved each other."

"Control, focus, faith,

Reap what you sew."

43

Agent Malden knelt next to the body of his partner. Whispering softly he covered her withered face with his jacket. Tracey turned away to give him privacy. With Sarah's help, she limped over to her friends. They gathered together near the storage locker. Prince Henry walked toward the fallen body of Officer Jameson. The body twitched.

"So he's alive, then," Dave grunted.

Tracey was glad. The thought of another death, one that she'd caused, made her stomach twist. For a second she thought she was going to be sick. Covering her mouth, she breathed slowly and looked away.

"The next time you decide to *set up* the bad guys, count me out," Dave said.

Tracey just looked at him. "Are you okay?" she asked. At his nod, she ran her gaze over the rest of her friends. Laura looked like she'd been dragged backward through a blackberry bush. She was covered in scratches and strands of her hair had pulled out of her perfect plait hanging around her face in a teased halo. Jonny looked much the same. Dave was pale, and fighting to hide the tremors still racking his body. Tony looked exhausted, dark shadows blackened the skin under his eyes.

Now that Tracey was no longer draining her sister of energy, her skin had regained some of its color and youthful life. Tracey pushed a little magic in her direction, hoping to replace what she'd stolen and was shocked by how quickly Sarah's skin returned to normal. Sarah still had a hand-shaped bruise on the back of her neck. Tracey hugged her tightly. "I'm so glad you're okay."

"You, too."

"Miss Masters?"

Tracey looked up at the sound of Officer Jameson's voice. "Yes?" She straightened. Sarah clung to her for a moment longer. Tracey hugged her again. "It's okay," she said before pulling away.

Prince Henry helped Officer Jameson to his feet, steadying him when he stumbled. She was glad to see the prince up and moving again. He'd been unconscious for most of the battle. "I'm okay," he confirmed when she asked, though he looked a little green. Sarah whispered he'd taken a massive hit to the chest protecting her from the Shadowman. Tracey didn't know how to thank him.

"Miss Masters?" Officer Jameson's voice was shaky and thin. "What's going on? What are you doing? Do you know these people? Where are we?"

Tracey laughed.

She couldn't help it. His questions sounded so innocent. After everything she and her friends had been through she couldn't stop herself. In moments her friends were laughing with her.

The officer only looked more confused. He glanced at the man helping him, and then looked again. "Prince Henry?" he asked, his face betraying his shock.

The look sent Tracey into hysterics. The prince just nodded.

"Are you okay, Officer Jameson?" Laura called.

"Why is Prince Henry helping me? And what's so funny?"

"Officer Jameson, do you remember anything from the past few days?" Tracey asked as her laughter subsided.

"Anything?" he repeated. His eyes didn't focus when he looked at her and his footing remained unsteady. Prince Henry tightened his grip.

Tracey shook her head. "Do you remember finding a stone with a picture painted on it?"

"Oh, yes," the dazed man said, patting at his pockets. "Huh, it's gone."

"I'll take him to the first-aid station," Prince Henry told her. "Good work, Tracey." He winked, and to her complete amazement, she felt herself blush.

"We are SO talking about you being Mage-kind later!" she called out after him. He waved a hand in her direction but kept walking. Something

394

vibrated against Tracey's leg. It took longer than it should have for her to realize it was her phone. A feeling of dread washed over her at the name on the screen. Her mouth fell open. *Mom!*

`Have you heard from Sarah?`
`Tracey answer me!`
`Where are you?`
`Do you know where Sarah is?`

With shaking fingers Tracey typed out a short message.

`Found her, she's with me. We're fine. Sorry I`
`didn't see your messages. Love you.`

Would that be enough? Her phone trilled its upbeat song and danced in her hand. *Of course not.* Biting her bottom lip, she hit accept. "Hi Mom."

"Where are you? What happened? Where's Sarah? Why wasn't she at the library waiting for Dad?" The questions peppered Tracey's ears like getting caught in a hailstorm—fast, hard and unavoidable.

"Mom, I—"

"Something's wrong? What's going on? Tracey, are you okay?"

Tears filled Tracey's eyes. Through the anger she could feel her mother's love and her genuine fear. "Mom, we're fine now." She wanted to blurt out everything; wanted her mom to tell her she was going to be okay. The stone pulsed against Tracey chest with pent up energy, begging to be used. Slapping her free hand over the stone, Tracey willed it to be quiet.

"Do you need us to come get you? Dad's picking up the car keys right now."

The word "yes" hovered over Tracey's lips. Her eyes drifted to her friends. They stood in a loose circle, looking like they'd run a marathon. Laura saw Tracey watching and waggled her fingers in a little wave. "We're with Laura, Tony and Jonny. I'm sorry, Mom."

"Tracey, I know something happened. Tell me you are okay." Tracey swiped hot tears from her eyes.

Her voice wobbled a little as she said, "Yes, Mom. Everything is fine. I'll bring Sarah home soon."

"You take care of her," Mom ordered.

"Always," Tracey vowed. She shoved the disconnected phone back into her pocket and breathed out a slow breath. How had she ever thought she could hide this from her mom?

Agent Malden approached slowly, moving as though he was a hundred years old. The battle had taken a toll on all of them, but none more so than him. His hair was now streaked with white, his cheeks drawn inward like he'd had all the fat sucked out of him.

"I'm so sorry, Agent Malden," Tracey told him as she caught sight of his fallen partner again. She ached for his loss. It was her fault Agent Striker had been killed. Their stupid plan to catch the man in the red mask seemed so childish now. She and her friends were lucky the agents and Prince Henry had shown up when they did. The thought of what Timothy might have done sent a shiver through her body.

"Tracey, are you and your friends okay?"

"Yes," she said, answering for all of them. At least she hoped they were.

"Do you still have the stone?"

"Yes." Pressing her hand against her chest, she felt relief at its solid presence. "Is he gone?"

"The spirit? I believe so, for now at least. Did he tell you who he was?"

"Timothy. He was one of the original owners of the stones." Tracey heard Tony and Laura question how Timothy could be alive after two hundred years. She thought she understood. Timothy wasn't really alive. He existed only because of the power stored within the Fire Stone. The same way Stephanie existed inside the Butterfly Stone.

"Tracey, the stone you are wearing is very dangerous."

"I know," she said, and reluctantly reached for the chain to pull it over her head. He stopped her with a gentle hand on her arm.

"You will have to take great care of it," he said. "We're going to need your help to find the other four stones."

His words sucked the air from her lungs. Drawing in a deep breath, she demanded, "Why do we have to find them? Why can't we just let them vanish into history?"

Stephanie's voice whispered into her ear. *Timothy is not dead, Tracey. He will return. He must possess all five stones to restore his physical self.*

Agent Malden kept talking, cutting over the ghostly voice of Tracey's ancestor. "We didn't destroy his spirit, Tracey. I believe he will keep searching for the stones, and we must find them before he does."

"What about Doctor Chan? He knows a lot about the stones, and he's working for Timothy." Oh, that reminded her. Tracey reached into her pocket searching for the thumb-drive. Her pocket was empty.

The agent eyed her carefully. "Our investigation into the stones led us to Doctor Chan. When we discovered he was working at the university, so close to you and your friends —"

"You said you were watching me?"

"We watch a lot of people," he said. She just looked at him. He continued, "When Doctor Chan disappeared, along with all of his research into the stones, we knew the timetable had moved up. Prince Henry discovered Doctor Chan's presence here tonight and called for backup, suspecting the doctor was going to make his move. Imagine our surprise to find your friends running for the gate. They were very brave. They refused to leave you here when they had the chance to escape and insisted on coming back for you."

"They could have been hurt," Tracey complained. "You should have kept them away. As an adult, shouldn't you be the one telling us this is too dangerous, and that we shouldn't be involved? We could have been killed."

"Yes, this is dangerous, and yes you could have been killed. But no, I am not going to tell you to stop." He halted and said, "I'm going to need your help."

My help? He couldn't be serious. "I can't control the magic from the stone — I might be as dangerous as Timothy," she said. The words sent a spark of fear through her body like a lightning strike and she knew it was true. She was dangerous. Now, more so than ever.

"Open yourself to the chaos."

"We will help you to keep control," Malden said.

"We?"

"Prince Henry and myself."

"Timothy accused him of being your spy. I didn't even know he was Mage-kind."

The agent stepped closer. Lowering his voice, he said, "Prince Henry has worked for me for several years. He and I will train you and your friends to help us hunt down the remaining stones."

Tracey threw up her hands. "Timothy almost won," she said, pacing away from him.

"But he didn't."

Spinning around, she pointed a finger into Agent Malden's chest. He didn't react, not even to glance down at it. "I just want to be normal. I don't want any of this."

"You are not normal, Tracey."

I know. She cast her eye over the damaged ground. "This is crazy."

"The stone only works for you," he reminded her gently.

She knew that. Stephanie had told her that. Timothy had too. But she'd been incapable of clear thought when using the stone's magic. It had given her rage the strength to hurt anyone she wanted, anyone at all. With the added magic of the stone, she had access to a dangerous amount of power. If Sarah hadn't stopped her, she would have killed Officer Jameson just to get at Timothy. And she'd loved the feeling. Even now, she could feel it in the back of her mind, whispering to her, wanting her to use it again. She had no idea if it was Stephanie's residual power or her own, but she desperately wanted more.

Pressing her hand to the stone, she reminded herself there were only five stones. Timothy, wherever he had gone, must have the one Officer Jameson had held. Or he knew where it was. That left three. She would have to find them before he did.

Looking over at her friends now laughing and smiling, recovering from the horror of the last few hours, she realized she had to accept this mission. If she didn't, they would be lost—the whole world would be lost. Tracey had seen Timothy's madness and felt it in his power, so dark and terrible. If that power was ever released, it would destroy everything.

Agent Malden joined Laura and Jonny, asking how they were feeling.

Tracey would have to do this for all the non-magical people in the world, too. They would have no idea what was coming. They possessed no way to stop it.

Tony and Dave moved to Tracey's side, followed by Sarah. Tracey smiled at her sister and hugged her again. She knew it would be up to her—to them—to stop the Shadowman from rising again.

Five spirited Mages,
Five stones of power.
Spelled to hold, will and wish,
Binding soul to life, forever.

To contain or conceal,
Enslave or ensnare?
Bewitch or betray,
Deceive or repay?

Dealers of death,
Absorbing magic through dreams.
Strength growing, unknown proportions.
Their end will reveal,
The mistakes they've made.

The one who leads,
Who dreamed of more,
Lost her mind in the fire,
Her charge now her curse.

Another in love,
Betrayed by fear.
Trapped, bitter, and frozen;
Vision lost.

One full of passion,
For learning and love.
Left bereft and empty,
Wind burnt and cross.

One filled with hope,
A fire for the world.
Destroyed all that he loved,
Heart black, soul scorched.

The last held desire,
For power and purpose.
His soul, but shadow,
Alone in his curse.

Together, bound to the flame,
Five stones to carry their name.
But as with magic,
Truth begets truth.
Death, loss, and madness marked,
Their lives now accursed.

THE STONES OF POWER WILL CONTINUE . . .

ABOUT THE AUTHOR

Laurie Bell is a former teacher who has worked with children of all ages in the literary sphere. She is a science fiction aficionado who is regularly featured by publications such as the Antipodean Science Fiction E-Magazine.

Laurie maintains an active blog of science fiction, fantasy, and flash fiction pieces, and serves as a volunteer in her local theatre company.

The Butterfly Stone is Laurie's first novel.

Discover more about Laurie Bell at:

www.solothefirst.wordpress.com

A THANK YOU FROM THE AUTHOR

I'd like to thank the following people who helped *The Butterfly Stone* become what it is — so much fun.

Linh, Margo and Carolyn for reading it over and over, and for your CP & Beta-ery goodness! Every time I received an email from you, my writing became better. You are just fabulous. Keep on keeping on. I can't wait to read your words soon.

Mum and Dad, who read it time and again, and didn't sigh too much when I said I had another version.

Marissa Fuller — you made my words sing! Thank you for everything.

Kate Foster, Kit Carstairs, and Stuart MacDonald — your guidance and assistance with one, help with all.

Helen, for believing.

For all the kids I taught in the few short years I was a teacher — you inspire me.

Hayley and Stefanie. (You are my Laura!)

Lauren Lynne, *THANK YOU*.

D.C. McGannon, Michael McGannon, and Holly McGannon — for everything!

Gerry, for loving me and for listening to my doubts, changes, thoughts, edits, and for being made to read it! (And for the printer! Oh, how I love thee.)

I love you all so much. Thank you!

For this and other exciting titles, visit:

www.WyvernsPeak.com

www.twitter.com/WyvernsPeak
www.facebook.com/WyvernsPeak

Sign up for our newsletter, get free stuff, and be the first to know when new books from your favorite Wyvern's Peak authors are released.

Follow Laurie Bell on Twitter

@LaurienotLori

Like Laurie on Facebook

www.facebook.com/WriterLaurieBell

Visit her website at

www.solothefirst.wordpress.com

www.ingramcontent.com/pod-product-compliance
Lightning Source LLC
Chambersburg PA
CBHW051210120726
47905CB00004B/1056